INFERNO

JULIAN STOCKWIN

INFERNO

HODDER

First published in Great Britain in 2016 by Hodder & Stoughton
An Hachette UK company

1

First published in paperback in 2017

A CIP catalogue record for this title is available from the British Library

ISBN 978 1 444 78546 3

Typeset in Garamond MT Std by Palimpsest Book Production Limited,
Falkirk, Stirlingshire

Printed and bound by Clays Ltd, St Ives plc

Hodder & Stoughton policy is to use papers that are natural,
renewable and recyclable products and made from wood grown in sustainable
forests. The logging and manufacturing processes are expected to conform to the
environmental regulations of the country of origin.

Hodder & Stoughton Ltd
Carmelite House
50 Victoria Embankment
London EC4Y 0DZ

www.hodder.co.uk

In Memoriam

Orlogskaptajn Tonny Larsen
Royal Danish Navy

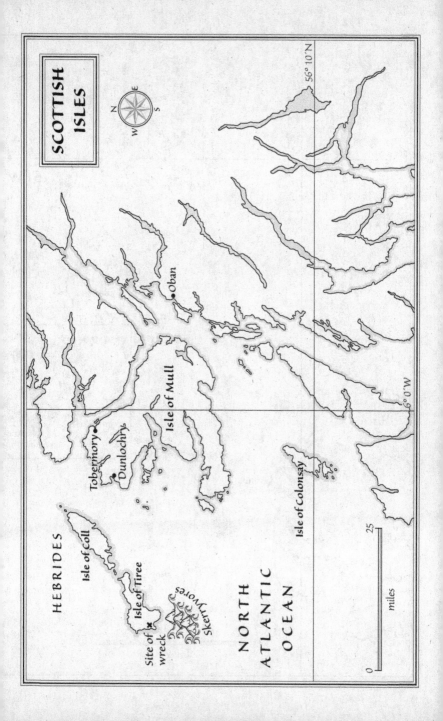

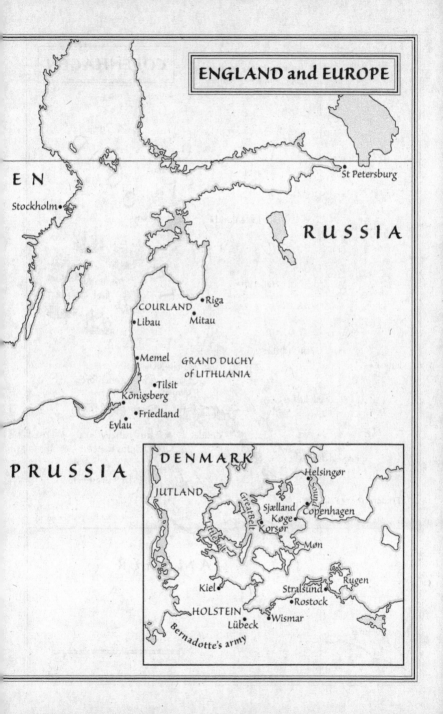

ENGLAND and EUROPE

Stockholm

St Petersburg

E N

RUSSIA

Riga
COURLAND
Libau
Mitau

Memel
GRAND DUCHY
of LITHUANIA

Tilsit
Königsberg
Friedland
Eylau

PRUSSIA
DENMARK

JUTLAND
Helsingør

Sjælland
Copenhagen
Køge
Korsør
Møn

Kiel
Rügen

Stralsund
Rostock

HOLSTEIN
Wismar
Lübeck

Bernadotte's army

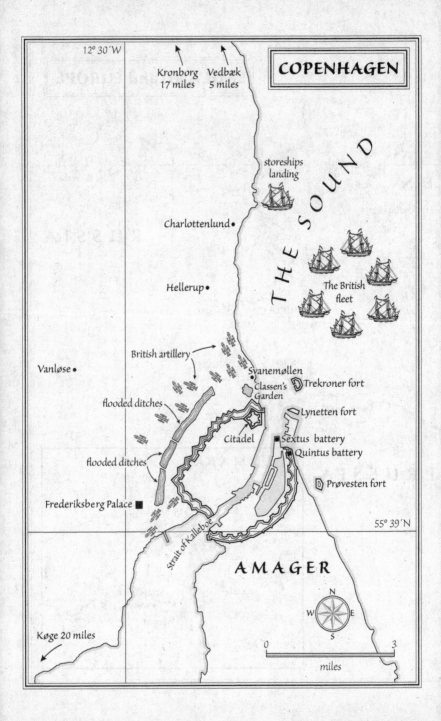

Dramatis Personae

(*indicates fictitious character)

*Sir Thomas Kydd, captain of HMS *Tyger*
*Nicholas Renzi, Earl of Farndon, friend and former confidential secretary

Tyger, ship's company

*Bowden, second lieutenant
*Bray, first lieutenant
*Brice, third lieutenant
*Dillon, Kydd's confidential secretary
*Doud, quartermaster's mate
*Halgren, coxswain
*Joyce, ship's master
*Maynard, master's mate
*Stirk, gunner's mate

Others

*Adams, lieutenant, 52nd Regiment of Foot
Alexander I, Russian tsar
Antoine, Duc d'Angoulême, husband of Marie-Thérèse of France
Baird, lieutenant general
Bennigsen, German general in service with the Russian Empire
Bernadotte, Maréchal de France
Bernstorff, Christian, foreign minister, Kiel
Bernstorff, Joachim, minister in Copenhagen
Bielefeldt, *generalløjtnant*, in command Danish land forces
Bille, *kommandør*, sea defences
Bloomfield, major general, artillery
Bonaparte, French emperor
Bruun, Danish gunboat captain
Canning, British foreign secretary
Castenschiold, general, artillery
Castlereagh, British secretary of war
Cathcart, general, commander-in-chief British land forces
*Cecilia, Countess of Farndon, née Kydd
Christian VII, Danish king
Colville, captain, Gambier's fleet
Congreve, colonel, in charge of rockets
d'Antraigues, French royalist, spy
d'Artois, count, brother of French king, Louis XVIII
Danican, French spy
*Devenant, colonel, Whitehall functionary
Duke of Portland, prime minister
Essington, retired admiral recalled; as a captain gave Kydd his step to the quarterdeck

Mulgrave, first lord of the admiralty
Murray, deputy quartermaster general
*Överste Taksa, colonel, Swedish patriots
Oxholm, general major
Perceval, chancellor of the exchequer
Peymann, *generalmajor*, commander defences of Copenhagen
Popham, captain of the fleet
*Reid, corporal
Rist, Danish chargé d'affaires, London
Russell, admiral
Stewart, brigadier, 43rd Monmouth Regiment
Swenson, Danish gunboat captain
Tucker, British envoy
Wellesley, major general, later the Duke of Wellington
Westmorland, lord privy seal
Wilhelm Friedrich, Prussian king
Wulff, gunboat captain
Zeuthen, gunboat captain

Chapter 1

Eskdale Hall, Wiltshire, England. Summer 1807

The night had turned unseasonally chilly. Captain Sir Thomas Kydd sat before the fire with his particular friend, the Earl of Farndon, and his wife, who also happened to be Sir Thomas's sister. The evening's reception and stately ball had been accounted the most splendid held for many years, and he'd been introduced to a dizzying quantity of the county's highest society, who'd been particularly attentive to the acclaimed sea hero. But now he gazed vacantly into the flames.

'Are you not enjoying your Armagnac, Thomas?' Cecilia asked in concern. 'Nicholas keeps back his 'seventy-nine for your visits alone, my dear.'

'Pray take no notice of me, sis. I'm in a complicated mood.'

'Oh? What can this mean?' she teased.

'To tell it straight, Cec, my intellects are in a whirl for all the fanfaronade since we made port, and I've a mort of things to think on. I confess what I crave most is nothing more than to sit and stare at a wall for above a day.'

'Well, I'll allow the lot of a public hero is an active one.'

Lord Farndon – or Nicholas Renzi as he would always be known to his bosom friend – set down his glass and smiled indulgently. 'Now, my dear fellow, you cannot persuade me that it was all of it a burden beyond bearing. I do recollect your distinct pleasure in telling me of the subscription dinner by members of the Exchange and the presentation of silver at its conclusion.'

'Yes, that was handsomely done. Baltic traders at the Virginia and Baltick in Threadneedle Street in appreciation of my contribution to the safeguarding of their interests, even if I'm at a loss to fathom why an action in support of the Prussians counts as that.'

'But that nasty fuss in the newspapers!' Cecilia added, her face stormy. 'Such words about your—'

'Those scurvy villains are a contemptible crew and I'll thank you to pay no mind to 'em, sis.'

Recalling the bitter turmoil that had followed a *True Briton* report of Kydd's opinions after the notorious Popham trial, Renzi chuckled. 'Well, that's certainly no longer of any consequence to your sea prospects. Have you not received an intimation of the Admiralty's entire satisfaction at your conduct?'

'I did that,' Kydd agreed. 'A private letter from the first lord wishing to assure me of his continued interest in my naval career.'

'Just so.'

'And this is a rum one, Nicholas. Lord Camden, somebody big in government, wants me to be a Member of Parliament in the Tory interest.'

'Why not, Thomas?' Cecilia squealed. 'You'd make a splendid figure standing up in the House with a speech as will make the scoundrels sit up and listen.'

2

'No, sis. I've no hankering after arguments all the day long. Besides, when will I have time to take *Tyger* to sea?'

Renzi looked fondly at his friend. 'So, Kydd of the *Tyger* it is, to be sure. Long may he sail the high seas against the King's enemies!'

There was a trace of wistful envy in his voice, which Kydd knew came not from any wish to be a celebrated hero like himself but the knowledge that he could no longer taste the freedom of the sea in all its lure and mystery.

'On another matter entirely,' Renzi added quickly. 'You said Toby Stirk – or is that Gunner's Mate Stirk – did survive his injury?' Renzi and Stirk had been with Kydd since his first days as a pressed man, and Renzi had seen him learn much from the leathery old seaman.

'He did, Nicholas. Hard as nails but he was sadly knocked about and dead to the world for near two days. Came round after we arrived at Sheerness. We had the devil's own job getting the beggar to agree to go ashore to the hospital for observing, and only my personal vow he wouldn't be removed for another in *Tyger* had him off.'

Renzi gave a half-smile. 'Dear fellow, I own I'm at the loftiest rank of society but there are moments I'd give it all away to possess the true-hearted devotion of the ship's company of a fighting frigate like *Tyger* . . .'

Chapter 2

The next day Kydd took coach in neat but anonymous gentleman's dress.

After the near hopeless battle against three frigates and the following desperate days nursing a wounded *Tyger* to her refuge, he craved space to find himself again, to get away somewhere blessedly remote, where the ferocious wars of Napoleon Bonaparte were another world, and to feel something of the old times when the only concerns were the success of the harvests and the jollities of market day.

Tyger was under repair but had been given precedence by an Admiralty keen to show its intention of setting one of its most famous frigate captains at sea again as soon as may be. It had been classed a 'small repair', even though she'd suffered untold injuries, for, apart from a docking to replace the damaged strake between wind and water, there was nothing that would require taking down her hull. Nevertheless, an unknown number of weeks would pass until he could claim her.

Before he could let the benison of rest do its healing,

Kydd needed to journey to Sheerness to visit the hospital where so many Tygers were paying the price for his triumph.

The last mile across the marshes from Queenborough brought back memories of the dark year of the great Nore mutiny where his destiny had changed irrevocably: from the prospect of a noose at the yard-arm to the felicity of treading the quarterdeck as a king's officer.

It was humbling to be received joyfully by men with shattered limbs who would never again work a long splice or race aloft in the teeth of a gale for the honour of their ship. They would be turned ashore, the lucky ones to a berth in Greenwich Hospital, others to a sailor's sad exile on land.

'The gunner's mate on your books,' Kydd asked an orderly. 'Tobias Stirk. Is he still here, by chance?'

'Don't rightly know. Gets these moods, like. Drifts off an' no one knows where till he returns. Odd sort – and claims he won't be bound by no long-shore coves tellin' him what to do. I'll see if'n he's about.'

He wasn't, and Kydd felt the stir of unease for the hard and fearless seaman of old, now taken with phantoms of doubt and mortality and wandering abroad in a futile effort to lay them to rest. He couldn't leave without at least wishing his old shipmate a good recovery.

There was a drawing room for the families of visitors and Kydd settled in a chair to wait. On the table were newspapers and old issues of the *Gentleman's Magazine*. He flicked through one but when he saw his name in it he turned it face down, embarrassed, and picked up another.

From time to time, curious staff offered refreshments, with well-meant platitudes. Dusk drew in and a lamp was brought. He knew he should think about leaving: his continued presence would be causing awkwardness for the hospital. Should he write Stirk a note, perhaps a light touch about the time when they were both foremast hands in the old *Duke William*? Or not: he had remembered the man's sense of pride and—

A figure appeared in the doorway, difficult to make out by the light of the single lamp.

'Mr Stirk?'

'Aye. They said y' wanted t' see me.' The husky voice was defensive and Stirk removed his shapeless hat awkwardly.

'Do come in and sit, Mr Stirk,' Kydd said, wondering whether it had been such a mercy to seek the man out after all.

Stirk came forward into the light but remained standing. He was not in his usual comfortable seaman's rig, instead wearing a shabby dark coat and a muffler. His eyes glittered in deep-sunken pits.

'I – I came to see how you were, Mr Stirk,' Kydd ventured. It sounded affected before the reality of the fine old seaman who stood before him.

'Sir. Nothin' that can't be put right by a spell o' canvas-backing.' This was a sailor's term for taking refuge in his hammock.

'They're saying you're out and about a lot. Are you—'

'Got no right t' tell you that,' Stirk grated. 'Poxy bastards! Sir.'

It was ridiculous, Kydd thought, for him to be sitting at his ease in an armchair while a man he admired more than most stood before him like a felon. Kydd got to his feet. 'Are you in want of anything, Mr Stirk? Prize money is a long time coming and—'

'I'm right 'n' tight, Mr Kydd,' he replied flatly.

'Well, then—'

'An' I thanks ye for the askin' of it.'

Was that a glimmering of feeling in his voice? 'So you'll be off soon to see your folk, I'd guess,' Kydd chanced.

'I might.'

'How are they all? Romney Marsh, isn't it? A fine place this time of year.'

'Cap'n. It was right dimber of ye to see me, an' I'll not keep ye any longer.' His voice had dropped so low Kydd struggled to hear.

He wanted to reach out to Stirk but there seemed an unbridgeable gulf between them. The tough, indomitable figure was bearing the strain of something beyond his mastering but was trapped in the husk of his own iron-hard character.

'Well, yes, time to leave,' Kydd said. Then he paused as if contemplating a sudden idea. 'To tell the truth, I'm off to seek a mort of quiet to settle my thoughts. I'm looking for a place to stay as is peaceful and out of the way. What do you say to Hythe by the Marsh?'

There was no response, merely a steady gaze from unblinking black eyes.

'Stage to Maidstone, another to the coast, as I remember. Oh, and I'd be gratified should we travel together,' he added casually. If he could just get Stirk to his family . . .

'No.'

'May I know why not?' Was the distance between them too much?

'"Cos we don't live there any more.'

'Where . . .?'

There was the slightest hesitation, then: 'Scotland. Dunlochry.'

'I'm not certain I've heard of it.'

'Had to skin out o' the Marsh. Revenoo took against m' young bro. Had t' quick find somewhere quiet, like.'

Kydd held silent for a moment. 'Quiet? This Dunlochry sounds just the place to lay up for a while and hoist in some peace.'

'You'd be going all the ways up there?' Stirk said slowly, the sunken eyes never leaving his.

'The barky's in for some weeks. I've got the time.'

The moment hung.

'It's a wee place. They'll realise you're—'

'I'll go as plain Mr Thomas Paine, heading north with my old friend Tobias Stirk. No one to know else. Right?'

Chapter 3

It was days on the road by the Glasgow mail, but there was little opportunity to talk because Stirk had taken it upon himself to ride outside. They ate together at the stops but Stirk was still held in some sort of inner thrall that did not admit others: he answered only in monosyllables.

Then it was two days in a cramped, fast packet to the new whisky-distillery town of Oban on the Firth of Lorne in the Hebrides.

Kydd stood on the little quay in the tentative sunshine. The wild beauty of the Western Isles reached out to him, ramparts of blue hills, islets beyond counting and an unutterable sense of remoteness. If he was going to lay the ghosts of the recent past it would be here.

Stirk had left him with the baggage and returned a little later.

'Thought I'd turn up the little scroat in the Three Bushels,' he rasped. With him was a wild-eyed youth, who regarded Kydd with suspicion. 'Mr Paine – this'n is Jeb, m' younger brother. An' Jeb, Mr Paine's a gent who's come here for a

9

spell o' resting. Now, you minds y'r manners – he's an old matey o' mine and I'll not have him vexed b' your rowdy ways.'

Stirk humped their baggage to the end of the quay and dropped it into a half-deck ketch strewn with fishing gear. Without a word he swarmed down a mooring line and landed lightly on the after end. Not hesitating, Kydd did the same.

Jeb looked on with respect. 'As ye've been a sailor, then, Mr Paine,' he said, as he alighted and went forward to see to the lines.

Before he threw off the tiller beckets, Stirk lifted up a corner of the untidy mass of nets to reveal three small casks. He spluttered an oath. 'Ye just can't leave it alone, can ye, y' clinking fool?' He let the nets drop and spat pointedly over the side. 'I see any more an' you're out o' here, cully!'

A black mood descended, and Stirk set sullenly about the hoisting of sails and casting off. Kydd took the main-sheet and they leaned to the wind and out into the choppy waters of the firth.

The scenery was dramatic. Caught by the sun the bare Hebridean islands lay with spreading pale beaches and black rocks stretching seaward, throwing up surf in vivid white against the deep green of the sea, the more distant islands scattered in a romantic misty blue-grey. Despite its beauty, the seaman in Kydd knew it could all change within minutes: the dark skerries at the edge of the islets would turn to cruel fangs to tear out the bowels of any vessel lost in the murk.

They made good speed, the red sails board-taut, and the breeding of the plain but stout Scottish fishing boat shone through.

Kydd slid along to Stirk at the tiller. 'What's her name?'

He thought the big man hadn't heard but then came a gruff, '*Maid o' Lorne*. As belongs t' my sister's husband.'

'Sister?'

'It's what I said, didn't I?' Stirk caught himself and turned to him, stricken. 'Sorry, Mr K— Paine. Didn't mean t' go ye. Ain't m'self lately.' His hand fidgeted on the tiller. 'Jeb's to take her out wi' some island younkers as crew, like. Herring, and long-lining for haddock and whiting, mebbe some cod.'

At the fore Jeb looked obstinately away. He'd given up the helm and authority of the boat without question to Stirk, and Kydd sensed there was much not being said.

'How far's your Dunlochry?' Kydd asked Stirk.

'This'n is the Sound o' Mull.' He gestured at the long sea passage ahead. 'We's on the outer coast t' larb'd.'

They emerged into the open waters and the power of the Atlantic's vast reaches: a massive swell, wind-driven to surging white-tipped waves. As though born to it, *Maid* conformed in an easy long lift and fall, effortless in her economic movements.

This was a different realm from the close lochs and firths of the inner isles – more remote, a wildness Kydd had never seen before. He suppressed a smile at the thought of how Renzi would react to them: the sublimity would, without a doubt, have brought on a paean or two, even if his friend was as aware as he himself was of their deadly character to the unwary mariner.

Chapter 4

Dunlochry, Isle of Mull, Scotland

By the time they had reached the sharp foreland pointed out as the entrance to Dunlochry, Kydd had prised most of the story out of Stirk.

His sister, Constance, had married a Scot who held a valuable position as gamekeeper to the laird of the Isle of Mull. They lived in an estate cottage. When Jeb's difficulties with the Revenue had cropped up, he had thought to come here and lie low with his sister, the understanding being that he would make his way by working the *Maid*. It had not been a complete success, Stirk's younger brother being so headstrong and unreliable.

'And your folks?' Kydd asked politely.

'A year or so back, in Kent. Ain't no more.'

'And so . . .'

'These 'ere are all the kin I got.'

Around the point a deeply indented bay opened up, snugly sheltered between weathered dark cliffs by a twist of topography. Steep tree-stippled slopes converged on a small village with a tiny jetty and a gaggle of boats at moorings in the barely ruffled inlet.

They dropped the mainsail and glided in, the smell of pines, heather and the stink of fish mingled with the smoke of peat-fires coming out to enfold them in a fragrant welcome.

Curious eyes watched them disembark. As Stirk straightened, there was a hail, and a short, stout individual lumbered across. 'Wha' hae, m' fine friend!' he puffed, clapping Stirk familiarly on the shoulder. 'Away wi' ye, but it's bin a hoora long time.' Shrewd eyes swept over Kydd. 'Then who's this'n?' The Scottish burr had fallen away to a more understandable English at Kydd's appearance.

'It's . . . an old navy shipmate. Name o' Paine.'

'Aye. Well, pleased t' take the hand of owt who knows Toby, Mr Paine.'

Stirk introduced him to Kydd. 'This is Brian McFadden. We calls 'im Laddie. Hails from the south, like we. Owns the fishing boat, *Aileen G*,' he added.

Kydd shook hands, taking in the hard, calloused grip. The life of a fisherman would be far from easy in these waters.

'Mr Paine, I'd be obliged should ye go wi' Laddie to the White Lion in town while I sees m' sister, like. Pony an' trap will be along for ye after.'

Stirk lifted his sea-bag and swung it over his shoulder, then stumped off up the hill out of Dunlochry.

'I'll be takin' your bags an' all, Mr Paine,' McFadden said, rapidly sizing Kydd up. 'Nowt to worry on.'

The diminutive village consisted of a short main street – a church at the higher end and two taphouses by the waterfront, with several shops between in an uneven row of houses. The late-afternoon sun had tempted several patrons to take their beer at the tables outside and they looked up with guarded curiosity.

Inside the White Lion a comfortable stink of sawdust and beer toppings lay thickly on the air, and there was an animated hum of conversation from the men at the tables. A fiddler played to himself in a corner and a tapster idly cleaned the counter.

As they found a table, talk tailed off and faces turned: creased, work-worn features, characterful and wary.

'What can I get you, Mr McFadden?' Kydd asked. It fell into a stony silence. The man stared back at him, unblinking. 'A beer – or is it a whisky you Scots prefer?' Feeling every eye on him, Kydd started to ask again but then eased into a smile. 'I'm sorry, Laddie, I didn't ask properly, did I?'

McFadden's weathered face split into a grin. 'Aye, ye dinnae.' He swivelled around and called loudly to the tapster, 'A shant o' gatter, twice, Angus lad.'

The conversations about them resumed.

The beer was dark and strong. Kydd relished it, after so long with fine wines, and eased back in his chair. He allowed McFadden to make the running. It turned out that Stirk had come to his rescue in a street brawl in his youth. Stirk's family was liked in Dunlochry, even if they kept to themselves most of the time. And if it wasn't too personal, could he know how Mr Paine, with the cut of the gent about him, had got to know the likes of Toby Stirk?

It was easy enough recounted. In perfect truth he told of his press-ganging into *Duke William* and Stirk's inspiration to him as a young seaman. Their ways had parted but they'd met again, and Kydd, being of a mind to seek a spell of peace, had come up here with him.

'So ye've done well out o' Boney's war, then, Mr Paine?'

'Better than some,' was all Kydd would say, giving a saintly smile.

True to his word, Stirk soon arrived with the pony and trap.

'Ah, Connie's fine an' all, but 'ud be much obliged if you asks accommodation here, seein' as the cottage ain't in proper shape t' have ye stay.'

'Of course.'

'An' begs you'll sup wi' us tonight.'

It was a long drive up a rutted road not much better than a sheep run, through glens and around the bare crests of hills to the edge of a wood. The stone cottage was snug and well-kept; a vegetable garden laid out in orderly rows among a bright profusion of foxgloves. A whitewashed kitchen was hung with hams and spotless copper utensils. The neat and colourfully ornamented rooms spoke of tranquillity and contentment.

They sat down at a scrubbed-pine table as an awed maid bustled at the dishes. Kydd was given the place of honour opposite the host, Stirk at his right hand.

Conscious of the quality of Stirk's gentleman friend they were stiff with reserve, but soon melted at Kydd's earnest praise of the game pie. Mr McGillie was a dignified, upright Scot, with curiously neat manners. When he spoke, all listened respectfully to his slow-voiced and precise opinions. His two boys sat in awed quiet, fixing Kydd with wide eyes, and Old Widow McGillie pursed her lips in vague disapproval.

The rosy-cheeked Connie McGillie was transparently proud of her brother and insisted that he tell of his adventures on the seven seas, tales that she was sure her guest would not credit in a thousand years. At Stirk's red-faced hesitation, an amused Kydd was assured that her brother was not one for many words but after the whisky came out there might be more.

Chapter 5

The evening had been a sovereign remedy for his hurry of spirits – and the next morning Kydd borrowed a gnarled stick and set off for the cliff-tops to take his fill of the fine views.

It was a steep climb out of the village but he soon found his stride.

Four or five miles ahead in the glittering sea a pair of islands stretched across his vision. They were effectively the guardians of Dunlochry, a rampart against the open Atlantic beyond, that would throw a lee to all but a south-westerly.

Kydd breathed deeply. The Outer Isles – no more distant and lonely place could be conceived.

In winter, with howling gales and lashed by storms, it would be a very different place but now it reached out to him. There was not a thing of man in sight – and he was utterly on his own with his thoughts, which returned to what he had so recently gone through aboard *Tyger*.

He stopped walking. A lump grew in his throat and he sat on a flat rock to look out on the limitless sea through fast misting eyes as emotion took hold. His head dropped and he surrendered to the feeling invading his soul, a long, racking and consuming passion born of that experience of carnage and heroism, peril and desperation – what might so easily have been and what triumphantly was. It swept over him like a torrent, cleansing and scouring, leaving him shuddering and weak with the unstoppable force of it all.

Then as if in a dream of long ago he heard a voice. Infinitely kind and gentle, one that his reason had clung to in the gulf of years that separated the famous frigate captain of now from a young seaman in his first skirmish against the enemy, a voice that had then seen him through to the other side. 'How's this, Tom, m' old shipmate? Somethin' has ye by the tail, then?'

Low and concerned, just as it had been so long ago.

But the hand on his shoulder was real enough. He rubbed his eyes, looked up and saw Stirk's seamed face drawn in care. It brought on another bout of uncontrollable feeling and he reached for control.

'I – I'm s-sorry, Toby, j-just came over me.'

It sounded foolish but he couldn't help it.

'Don't be sorry, cuffin. Things in life, well, they's natural an' we has t' see 'em through ourselves and be buggered to any who says else.'

The same patient, practical good sense.

'Why . . . why did you come here?'

'Someone said as how you're heading up these 'ere cliffs an' I came to warn ye off 'em. So easy t' slide over the edge – it gets a sousing from th' rain.'

'Thanks, Toby. It's right . . . oragious in you, cully.' The words he had used in a past existence.

The hand patted his shoulder awkwardly. 'Look, mate.

How's about we two duck down to the kiddleywink and sink a jar or three? Right handsome lot they is in the Lion.'

With rising feeling Kydd realised Stirk had seen him in difficulties and reacted as he would with a messmate. Kind, understanding words and the extending of the rugged mateship of the foremast jack.

There was no need for pretence: he was being treated as any other shipmate – in a man-o'-war that was home to half the races of the world, quirks of character and origin were passed over.

Kydd pulled himself together. 'Toby. Can I talk straight with you?'

'Tom, mate, it's a sad thing if'n ye thought ye couldn't.'

'We're . . . we're talking here as if . . . all those years . . . well, as if nothing happened.'

'Aye. An' I figured as that's how it should be, youse bein' set hard a-weather, like.'

'It is. Toby, I'd take it very kindly should you stay that way for me for a space. I've had a – a grievous lot to take in lately as a whole parcel o' gentlefolk could never understand. Could you?'

'In course, matey. Could be we c'n bear a hand f'r each other,' he murmured. Then, in a stronger voice, 'Right then, cully. We's for the Lion?'

'I'll be with you presently, Toby. Just want to be on my own for a while.'

Chapter 6

Stirk set off down the path with a fixed expression. Seeing his old messmate in such straits had disturbed him more than he cared to admit. Kydd had reached out to him. Was it to do with the stiff fight they'd all been through? He himself had taken a knock and since then had been plagued by nightmares of hours at the guns, going at it like a madman. Then whispers of fear stealing in. Was he was getting old, no longer carefree, not so spry on his feet when it came to the absolutes of combat to a lethal conclusion?

There were others coming on ready to take his place. War at sea, these days, was a young man's game: the harsh conditions, constant threat, endless sea duty. However, in his very being Stirk was a deep-sea mariner and wanted no other life. The prospect of leaving it was impossible to contemplate.

His thoughts returned to Kydd. He could only dimly perceive that the lot of a captain was different. He'd known Kydd as a callow young sailor and even then had seen he was cut from broader cloth. In a way Stirk had secretly gloried in his advancement, first past himself and then across the near unbridgeable divide between fo'c'sle and quarterdeck.

He bore no resentment or jealousy because he took Kydd for what he was – a born seaman and leader of men – and had actively sought out his ships to join; he trusted him completely. Even in *Tyger*, which he'd known was in mutiny, he'd taken it for granted that Kydd would sort things out.

To be a captain, that was a rum thing to think on. True, they had all the honour and comforts going but he, as a gunner's mate, would have no hesitation in passing a knotty problem up the tree to an officer – that was what they were paid for, wasn't it?

He suspected that officers didn't have the same close-knit intimacy born of danger and interdependence that seamen took for granted and could call upon at any time without shame. And a captain – he had no one. Kydd had taken *Tyger* into battle with not a soul to talk freely with, to offer suggestions, to argue with, or after the event to say he'd done the right thing – or not. Yes, before there was Mr Renzi, of course, but now he was a noble lord, tending his grand estate.

Tom Kydd would find his old messmate Stirk there when he needed him, and be buggered to what any cove made of that.

With that thought, he felt better.

Chapter 7

The first dark ale at the White Lion went down with relish, and Stirk was about to put in for a threepenny ordinary when he felt his sleeve twitched. 'Laddie! Ye gave me such a start—'

'Toby, I needs t' talk wi' ye,' McFadden whispered, looking about nervously.

'I'm listenin', mate.'

'Not 'ere! I cannae— what I wants t' say is private, you 'n' me, like.'

At this hour in the afternoon the snug was free and Stirk settled next to him by the inglenook of an unlit fire. 'Well, what's it about, then, Laddie?'

The man looked away, as if wrestling with a decision, then leaned closer. 'It's a sad puzzle I has, Toby, an' no one to tell it to for near a twelve-month.'

'An' now ye're going to split wi' me.'

'You're the only one I trusts, Toby, ye know that.'

'I don't peach on m' friends, if that's y'r meaning.'

'No, mate, it's more'n that.'

Furtively checking that no one was watching, he felt about in his breeks. His calloused hand slowly uncurled and in his palm was a single golden coin. 'Toby, I knows ye've seen near everythin' on y'r voyaging about on the high seas. I want ye to tell me what this is. Go on, take it, an' have a good look.'

Stirk inspected the coin. All of an inch across, it was of substantial thickness, ornately stamped with a large, equal-sided cross on one side and filigree work. 'It's Spanish, Laddie, I'll give ye that. But it ain't one I know, mate. Pieces-of-eight, why they's silver only, an' I dare t' say are made better'n this.'

That only made McFadden more excited. 'Yair, as I reckon too. Now I has m' ideas about this'n and I'd give anything t' know for sure.'

'Ye've found treasure, is th' size of it. Am I right, cuffin?'

McFadden's eyes glittered. Then he sat back with a sigh. 'Aye, lad. I think I have, but it's not in m' hands. An' that's the rub – this gets out, an' every man on the island'll be down firkling about like demons an' I'll lose it.'

'Ye can't get at it y'self, and are a-feared t' go asking as y'r secret'll get shared.'

'Like y' say.'

'Well, now, an' you're at a stand. Either ye tells someone and loses y'r secret or you don't, an' ye never gets to lay hands on y'r treasure.'

McFadden winced. 'True enough.'

Stirk raised an eyebrow. 'Ye'd better lay it before me, cully. Y' knows I'd give ye a right steer.'

'An' promise not t' tell?'

'On m' honour, Laddie – as can be sealed wi' a muzzler of ale.'

Stirk's price duly met, McFadden lowered his voice. 'It's like this. When I fishes an' it comes on to blow I generally makes f'r the lee of one o' they outer islands, Coll, Tiree or similar, and short-line for plaice an' eel. One time, last autumn it was, I was in with one of 'em – never mind which – and I'm in close, sees one o' them sea caverns, not s' big, and decides to bait up for conger just off it.

'While I'm laying out m' lines I notices there's a wreck bung up in the cavern. An old 'un, ye can always tell. We've more'n our share o' shipwrecks in these waters so I doesn't notice. There's a good bite an' we fights until I hauls him in, a right knaggy conger. I tells the skinker t' settle him an', it gettin' on for dusk, heads back an' I send him home. While there's still light I guts the catch, an' when I get t' the eel . . . out pops this'n!'

'Ye're sayin' he ate the coin?' Stirk chuckled.

'Fish go for bright 'n' shiny things, y' fool, everyone knows that.' McFadden snorted.

'So what's it mean?'

'Right, well, a conger don't stray much. He finds a hole in th' rocks an' stays there, comin' out to take any fish or such as passes.'

'So?'

'Can't ye see it? If he took the coin it's because it was right there, an' couldn't be anywhere else 'cos he don't go a-cruisin' like other fish.'

'And—'

'Yeah! The coins – they're spillin' out o' the wreck. We got to go there an' get diggin' quick. But if I goes an' they see me worritin' away at th' wreck all day, why, it's all over begob!'

'You think . . .'

'That there shipwreck is from y'r Spanish Armada as was, them years ago. A fortune o' gold aboard and, like them

24

others, piles ashore in a storm. Could be a treasure s' high a man can't jump over it. Think on it, Toby – if we can get our fists on it we'd live like lords for th' rest of our days!'

Stirk's eyes gleamed. 'We, y' said?'

'I can't do it on m' own, Toby. Come in wi' me and it'll just be we two . . .'

'We gotta plan well, then, matey. Has ye any ideas?'

'Yeah. I takes ye there and y' slips over the side and gets in the cavern. I forgot t' mention, there's no way y' can get down into it from above, and it's out o' sight anyways. That's why no one's touched it, see.'

'So I digs an' sweats while you're a-catchin' y'r fish.'

'Y' knows I can't be seen at it, Toby,' McFadden said reproachfully.

'Don't take on so, cuffin. I'll do it f'r such a prize, never fear. Now, first thing is t' be sure this is what y' say, out of an Armada barky. If not, there ain't goin' to be more gold – stands to reason. No other ship has treasure chests.'

'And how are we goin' t' do that? Can't ask about – the laird hears of it an' he'll not rest until he's got it all, the bastard.'

'Well, now, and I might 'ave an idea on that, Laddie . . .'

Kydd would be coming in for his bracer soon, and who better? He could be trusted and he had a head-piece. He would know what it was or how to find out.

But he was an officer and they had a different slant on things. What if he took it into his noggin to tell the Revenue or such? Kydd was a true north sort of cove right enough and if he . . . No, he wouldn't. He knew the way of a Jack Tar and right now didn't he want to be a part of it? He'd not turn them in.

Chapter 8

When Kydd entered Stirk gave a cheery hail. 'What ho, Tom, mate! Bring y'r arse to anchor wi' us.' Whatever had passed up there on the heights seemed to have done him a power of good. 'What'll ye have?'

Kydd gave a wry smile. 'The usual, Toby.'

Stirk turned and bellowed, 'A jorum of y'r finest ale – with th' splicin's!'

After it had arrived, Stirk beckoned him closer. 'I've a favour t' beg of ye, Tom. See, Laddie here's found somethin' and he's vexed t' know what it is.'

'Oh?'

'He wants it to be like, confidential, no bugger t' know he has it or they'll be after him. So ye'll keep it to y'rself?'

'If that's what he's asking.' Kydd glanced at McFadden curiously.

'Right. Here it is.' Stirk pushed out a fist, leaving the coin gleaming on the rough table.

Kydd shielded his hand as he palmed it up, looked at it closely, then passed it back.

'Well?' Stirk demanded, with a frown.

'Laddie, where did you get this?'

'Never mind. What is it, f'r God's sake?'

'No question. This is a gold doubloon, dates back a ways, time of Good Queen Bess, I shouldn't wonder.'

'Spanish Armada, like.'

'You could say that, yes.'

Stirk and McFadden exchanged triumphant glances. 'Well, that's right good in ye t' tip us the wink. We's obliged.'

Kydd's face tightened in suspicion. 'You've found this, haven't you? Came up in your fishing gear. A wreck or similar.'

'Told ye he was a sharp 'un,' Stirk muttered.

'Your duty's clear – it's to report to the Receiver of Wreck directly, no delay. Else you'll have every kind of juggins up to hookum snivey to plunder it.'

'I never said it come from a piggin' wreck, did I?' McFadden retorted hotly. ''S mine, an' that's the truth!'

'Stow it, Laddie. It came from y'r poor ole aunt as died, didn't it? No need t' trouble that Receiver gullion then.'

Chapter 9

Next morning the inaugural meeting of the Dunlochry Treasure Company took place, Tobias Stirk in the chair and secretary Brian McFadden recording. There being no others present they came quickly to the business before the meeting.

'Equal shares – equal rhino,' Stirk stated. 'All them in favour?'

'If it means if a cove puts in more pewter an' he gets back more'n the other's share o' the cobbs, I'm agin it!'

'No, mate. Chair says as we all puts in the same. Them as hangs back loses their share.'

'How much—'

'I've a bit put by, if'n you's short. Now we votes. All in favour?'

'Aye.'

'Carried. So y'r boat comes in wi' *Maid o' Lorne*. Rest of it is—'

'Hold, y' scallywag. If your boat's in that means Jeb Stirk has t' be in on it too. Can't sail her else. Does he get shares?'

'Does yourn Wee Laurie get shares? No, cully. Boat 'n' crew all the same – one share.'

Chair then called an intermission. After pots had been duly refreshed the meeting came to order.

'So what's next up?'

'We go get the treasure!'

'Not s' fast, Toby! If we goes and—'

'It's Mr Chair.'

'Bugger Mr Chair! I'm sayin' as how I stand t' lose every-thing once ye sees where it is. What's to stop ye crackin' on one night an' liftin' it all for y'r self?'

'Ye're a chuckle-headed ninny, Laddie, but you've a fine heart. If'n that was m' lay I could've asked y'r little skinker where ye went that had a wreck in a cave, right? We got to be in it as muckers or we'll get nothin', savvy?'

Chapter 10

Early the following day two fishing boats hoisted their red sails and left Dunlochry, heading south-west past the holy island of Iona as if making for the rising shoals of mackerel in the open sea.

Aboard *Aileen G* and *Maid*, however, there was unrestrained glee, for in a few hours they could be as rich as barons. Both Jeb and Wee Laurie had been told their mission only once they were out, their silence secured by the strictest oaths and the certain promise that if any blathered a word they would end up with nothing.

When they were well out to sea and the horizon innocent of land, they bore up for Tiree, to its remote south-west tip, passing inside the long, menacing black reefs of the Skerryvore to reach the end of the island. Even in the glory of the early-morning sun there was an unsettling, sinister air about the place. On this side the light of day could not touch the gloom of the craggy fastness. The sea heaved and struck in sullen white explosions against the dark coast, and as they neared the tortured tumble of rocks, it seemed impossible that they could reach through to the glittering prize that lay inside.

Aileen G sailed by a long grey-sand beach and low pass leading down it to the precipitous pinnacles of the next point. Following on closely, *Maid* doused her main at the same time and the two eased on their sheets to come to, just beyond the highest headland and close to an inward twist in the tall crags.

It was as Laddie had said: a narrow inlet flanked by two majestic buttresses and there, on a stony slope leading to the impenetrable dark of a sea cave, the blackened remains of a considerably sized wreck.

All about were seaweed-covered rocks, even in this good weather seething and soughing – some unknown captain had achieved a miracle to con his ship through into this last haven in dark and storm to what he must have thought was blessed safety.

The cave, however, had been a deadly trap for there was no way out: the vertical outside rock-face was a hopeless barrier, and no soul could have survived the swim of a mile or more through the currents while being hurled against razor-sharp barnacled reefs.

Anchors were cast – two, this close.

The malefic aura reached out and quietened both boats as Stirk prepared. He looked down into the opaque green depths and shuddered. No sailor cast himself into the sea without good reason but there was nothing else for it.

In loose tunic and trousers he eased himself over the side.

The cruel cold bit into him but he wasn't going to let it deter him. He struck out for the slope, feeling the great surge and pull of the swell as he made for his goal, now looking so far away.

A clumsy swimmer, Stirk progressed slowly across the thirty yards to shore. He'd taken it on partly to be sure there was fair play but also to see for himself what lay in wait for them. Puffing like a walrus, he finally felt the pebble seabed under him and emerged on all fours next to the wreck timbers.

He had a light cord tied to his trouser belt at the back, which he used to pull in an oilskin bundle floating on a pig's bladder. It contained a warm jacket, a short spade and a pick.

Throwing a quick reassuring wave, he crunched forward, sizing up the task.

The ship lay sagging and spiritless, the ribs gaunt and jagged, weed slimed and decayed. The decks had long since collapsed and the timbers been driven clear; the outline of the frames was now stark and unrelieved. Stirk moved past the beached hull towards the bow and entered the cave proper. It was dim and stank richly of seaweed and brine. Every step on the shards and pebbles echoed sharply.

He shivered: up this far he might be coming on the bones of long-dead sailors – or, worse, trespassing on the haunt of mermaids and sirens. Every nerve on edge, Stirk fought down his fears and entered the wreck through the skeletal ribs. It was almost unrecognisable, a jumble of anonymous weathered timbers and decay above the tide-line and below it more of the same, green-slimed.

He stumbled about inside, looking for anything that could bring life to the remains, but it was quite bare. The ship's bottom timbers curved away and he made out foot-waling above it; the decks overhead were completely gone. The wreck had been scoured clean.

It was a bitter blow. Here and there were shapeless, encrusted masses but a few exploratory blows with the edge of the spade showed them to be mast stumps, the iron of fittings, a tangle of heavy cable nearly eaten away – nothing resembling a treasure chest.

Shuddering with the bite of the wind he stumped about, trying to think. It was no good hacking at the wreck – these were the last vestiges, the hold and bottom timbers. Nothing more was below it.

If anything had fallen out, could it be on the tiny beach next to the remains? He clambered out and at random attacked the hard-packed silty sand and rock fragments.

Half an hour's solid work revealed nothing more than sand fleas, a pair of energetic little crabs and a rapidly filling hole.

He straightened, glancing out into the brightness of the sea. *Maid* was there, dutifully 'fishing', while *Aileen* would be out of sight around the point expecting a signal. All aboard were waiting for his sudden cry of discovery.

Wearily he went further down, nearer the water and began again. After twenty minutes he knew he was beaten. Neither in the wreck nor outside it was there the slightest sign of treasure. If there was any, it would take an army of diggers and even then . . .

He paused to think. It was odd. Wrecks he'd seen, even old ones, had in them at least a few sad and poignant reminders of those who had lived and died in them. A barnacled pewter tankard, galley pots, a trinket, masses of rigging and blocks from the boatswain's stores, fittings, bottles.

Why had this ship been picked clean as a whistle?

His brow furrowed as he pondered the mystery. Then the answer burst in with a finality that put paid to the whole venture. The conger eel!

They were all nothing but a crowd o' loobies. If the eel

had swallowed the coin, by definition it must have been under water! He smacked his forehead in realisation.

Stepping back a pace or two from the wreck he sighted down it. Sure enough there was a slight but definite incline. Over the years the seas had surged into the cave and, bit by bit, washed all that was movable down into the ocean. In despair he went to the water's edge and stared bitterly at the innocent waves. In the depths, within yards of where he stood, was their treasure – but as far out of reach as though it were on the moon.

Chapter 11

'Chair says brother Laurie shuts his trap an' gets the ale. Meetin' has a mort o' thinking t' do.'

'Aye! A right settler for them as don't deserve it!' spluttered Jeb. 'Why, if we'd have—'

'For Chrissakes!' roared Stirk. 'Put a reef in y'r jawin' tackle! 'Less anyone has somethin' t' offer, keep y'r gob shut!'

It wasn't meant to be like that, and the frustration was keenly felt by all of them. To know a fabulous treasure lay almost within arm's reach was too much to bear.

'We throws out a grapnel an' drags it up?' McFadden offered.

'Don't be a ninny, Laddie! They're not in the chest any more – that's how y'r conger got one. They's scattered about over the bottom o' the sea.'

Jeb sullenly interjected. 'Y' told us once how in the Caribbee there's natives as dive f'r coins you throw in the sea. What's wrong wi' us—'

''Cos we ain't divers! Born to it, they is, like fish. And in them seas it's as clear as glass an' they can see what they're a-doing.'

The shareholders of Dunlochry Treasure Company slumped back.

Laurie came back with the ale. 'Has ye done wi' your havering?'

Too depressed for words, Stirk only growled at the lad.

'Then why don't ye ask Mr Paine? He's a knowin' gent, won't mind helpin' us out.'

'We can't. 'Twould mean a-tellin' him what we're doin', an' he's down on it.' But as he spoke Stirk realised that Kydd wouldn't turn them in: the worst that could happen would be a refusal to help.

'He's at the hall, suppin' whisky while the young lasses dance,' confided Laurie.

'Go an' ask him t' step this way, it's important. Mind ye say it politely, like.'

Kydd soon arrived, a look of concern on his features. 'Laurie said you'd a serious problem, Toby. I hope I can help.'

Stirk cleared his throat. The others crowded forward, silent and watchful. 'It's like this'n, Tom.' He swallowed and avoided his gaze. 'When I asks ye for a steer wi' the coin, I didn't tell it all, an' it's gettin' to me as I wasn't square with ye.'

'Oh?' Kydd said carefully, drawing up a chair.

'Well, ye're right an' all, we've found treasure.'

'Ah! And you want to know where to hand it in.'

'Not as we should say, Mr K——, that is, Mr Paine. See, we've found it but can't get at it an' was hopin' ye'd see y'r way free to givin' us some advice.'

Kydd frowned. 'Let's be clear on this, Toby. You say—'

'Tom, mate. We found a wreck right 'nough, Spanish

Armada an' all. Nobody knows of it. Ye can't get at it from the shore-side, so everything's still there. So we gets together a little venture an' goes out to dig it up. Trouble is . . .'

He tailed off at Kydd's look. 'Toby. You're asking me to compound a felony by assisting you to—'

'No, no, mate! Whatever we does, that's our own business. All we're askin' is a course t' steer. Nothin' to clap t' your tally a-tall!'

'Oh?'

'Well, could be there's not one piddlin' syebuck there, but we has a notion t' try, is all.'

'Go on.' The liberal measures of highland whisky he'd enjoyed at the hall were doing nothing for his concentration but he heard Stirk out. The least he could do was to give his opinion to an old shipmate.

Chapter 12

Maid bobbed to her anchor off the cave, and Kydd strained to see what he could of the wreck. It was on a small pebble beach within a terrifying twist of rock and had the sombre dignity of centuries about it.

He surveyed the area carefully, squinting as the pain behind his eyes became intrusive – generosity in the matter of libation at his offer of counsel had not been stinted. The incline was certainly enough over time to account for the wreck washed clean, but had the contents been scattered on the seabed below?

The first thing was to make soundings.

They had brought a coracle with them and Stirk set out in it. Under Kydd's direction he paddled it on a straight course and lowered a lead-line at regular intervals.

Kydd soon had a picture: the beach incline led into the sea and quickly levelled to a flattish firm silt undersea plain, at this state of tide, of the order of three fathoms deep over a respectable area. There must have been high-water springs when the ship struck for it would never have cleared it otherwise. There was every possibility that whatever had been brought down had settled and gone no further.

On its own, however, this was not enough. The area was within two buttresses of rock, which would have protected it from the worst of the seas, but the most insidious foe would have been tide scour, currents regularly swirling back and forth about the craggy points as the water ebbed and flowed. It would not have been long before loose objects had tumbled into deeper water.

Kydd took in the situation carefully. Tides were always local and could take any number of courses, even down to individual outcrops of rock. Here, with the tide on the make, he could see from the pattern of ripples that, while it passed offshore, the little bay itself was not disturbed.

Almost certainly the relics were strewn within twenty or thirty yards of the end of the wreck – in but three fathoms of water.

Chapter 13

As the Dunlochry Treasure Company reconvened, the chair recognised Mr Paine as counsellor.

'We's awaiting y'r report, Mr Paine,' Stirk stated respectfully.

'Well, Toby, it's not—'

'It's Mr Chair,' McFadden said importantly. 'If'n I has to, he must.'

'But of course! Mr Chair, this is not good news for your little endeavour. It's my judgement that whatever the wreck held is indeed on the seabed – and is, therefore, sadly, quite out of reach. My advice is that the venture be now wound up.' He felt a stab of sympathy for them and a small twinge of disappointment. If they'd been luckier it would have been an interesting diversion.

'Hey, now – that's not what we want to hear.'

'I'm sorry, Laddie.'

'We want t' know how to get up our treasure, not how's about it's so difficult.'

'You're talking about salvage. Like *Royal George* where they recovered so much.'

'Aye, that's it!'

'Sadly, this is not within your means. They used one of Dr Halley's diving bells, which I'd be sanguine are not readily available to the ordinary folk.'

'If we need 'un we'll find 'un, never fear on that.'

'They're tons' weight of bronze, or is it copper? Never mind, your *Aileen* could never lift one.'

'So we rafts the *Maid* to her! Look, Mr Paine, we thanks ye for your advice, right kindly in you, an' we'll get it on ourselves.'

'I really think—'

'Thank ye again, Mr Paine, and if we needs your services further, we'd be obliged if we c'n call upon ye.'

Kydd took his leave and the meeting turned to the matter before them.

'I heard o' them diving bells,' Jeb enthused. 'Marvellous things, they. Ye sit inside, lowers down and next thing you're in among all the fishes but dry as a bone. Goes right down to the bottom o' the sea and all ye does is pick up what you wants!'

'Sounds like what we needs. Where we goin' t' find 'un?'

'Hold hard, y' bugger. Think on this – it's goin' to take a hill o' chinks to hire. Where's *that* comin' from?'

'We puts in equal dibs.'

'And if *Maid* an' *Aileen* both can't swing it between 'em we has to find a bigger barky. This is gettin' a mort ticklish f'r me, Laddie.'

'Ye're givin' up afore we starts?' McFadden said scornfully. 'A day's work an' we'll be rich as Croesus and all I hear is groanin' about a few guineas.'

'Well, tell me this – where's one o' your divin' bells t' be found, then? They'll all be in the south, Portsmouth, London, never in these pawky islands.'

'Ah! That's where ye're dead wrong, mate. Five year back, when *Fox* sloop piled up on Colonsay they had in a bell at the trot, and all her guns up in a week.'

'You're sayin' as they has a diving bell at the ready, like?'

'Well, nearest navy is t'other side o' Scotland, Leith. That's only about five hundred sea miles to bring it, what do y' think?'

'Well? Where is it, then?'

'Can only be Tobermory. There you has the whole o' the Western Isles before ye, anything runs ashore.'

The meeting came to order and it was resolved that an expedition to Tobermory be mounted without delay to locate a diving bell.

Chapter 14

⁂

The little coastal track meandered interminably along the west shore of the isle but it was what Kydd craved – deep rural silence and solitude, with a sublime view of the sea and islands. In a wafting fragrance of peat and heather, it was working its magic on his soul.

A flock of sheep across his path scattered in alarm and he spotted a figure in highland smock standing against the skyline, watching him.

He rounded yet another foreland and saw, far out on the glittering sea, a fishing boat with patched ochre sails on its way round to Dunlochry. He watched as it went about, each action economically one after the other, not all together, smart navy fashion. She would have only a tiny crew.

He looked more closely: was it *Maid* back from a fruitless search for a diving bell?

He felt a stab of remorse. Toby Stirk had been a true friend and shipmate, bringing him without question into the warmth of his family, but now the old salt was way out of soundings.

Kydd's paltry advice was little return for what he'd given.

There was no way he could be involved in the venture, of course. As a king's officer it would be a scandal if it were ever known. However, he could still give counsel and that right willingly, although he doubted he would be asked again.

He began to walk back.

By the time he reached the village *Maid* had moored and her crew were sitting on the jetty.

When they saw him they got up and hurried across.

'Mr Paine. Sir. We has t' talk wi' ye.' Stirk's battered hat was in his hands.

'Aye, an' urgent, like, if y' please,' added Jeb.

'Very well. At the Lion?'

'No! This'n is serious. Don't want no prattin' gabblers hearin' what we've to say to ye.'

It seemed that only on *Maid* at her buoy could they talk freely.

Kydd sat in the place of honour on the fore windlass.

'Shut y'r geggy, Jeb, an' let me tell 'im,' Stirk demanded, then laid it out for Kydd.

Tobermory was a rising and important maritime town with a small dockyard to care for the little fleet of storm-tossed naval sloops guarding the northern approaches to the kingdom. This had been their first port of call, and he'd been right in his hunch that there was a diving bell in town. His informant, a blacksmith taking a wet before an afternoon at the anchor shop, was positive: he'd forged a grappling hook for the beast.

The second part was more delicate. Stirk's story had been ingenious: he had with him a Dutch philosophical gentleman who prayed he might set eyes on such a wonder, if it were at all possible.

The master attendant's clerk had been most sympathetic, nodding bemused at the heavily disguised Laddie but regretted that for the last two years the thing had been on the books over at Leith, called on only when needed. And he knew of no other bell in the Western Isles – that is, no king's bell.

Picking up on the last, Stirk prowled the few slips and only shipyard and even asked about in ships' chandlers, sailors' flophouses and the like. On his way back to *Maid* he had been stopped by a ragged messenger, who took him back to one of the chandlers.

The man had quickly disposed of Stirk's tale and put it to them that they had a treasure map or similar, which had given them certain knowledge of the whereabouts of a rich sunken wreck. Why else would they be looking for a diving bell?

Brushing aside their protests, he put a proposition to them: they were never going to secure a diving bell in all of Scotland, and in any case it would provoke intolerable curiosity if they did. But he had a solution. For a consideration he would provide the means to recover the hoard.

Years ago, a Mr Lethbridge of Newton Abbot, the legendary Wrackman, had invented a diving engine quite different from Dr Halley's bell. In it he had successfully brought up much wealth from a Dutch East Indiaman in Madeira, more from wrecks at Cape Town and other parts, and had retired a rich man. His son had followed him and they'd even come to Scotland with the diving engine and, among other feats, had lifted thirty-five elephant teeth, worth a fortune, from a sunken East India Company merchantman off the Isle of May.

The son had got into difficulties and eventually gone bankrupt, but had left a complete diving engine with this very chandlery establishment as pledge against his debts. It had been kept safe against its redeeming but the son had died without claiming it – and it lay locked away on the premises ready to do its duty once more.

So what was it to be? To walk away from a fortune, or allow the respectable Jacob Meares to join the venture with a proven apparatus for the salving of treasure?

'Ye said as how ye'd not be spare wi' your advice, so now we's askin', Mr Paine,' declared Stirk.

'Ah. I'm not sure how far I can help, as I've no knowledge of these, er, engines and such.'

'Ye can't help, and wi' all your sea service?' Stirk burst out. 'Who we goin' to ask, then?'

'Steady on, Toby. Your Mr Paine's only bin a lubbardly foremast hand, mate,' Jeb said.

'Look, Mr Paine. You bein' a gent an' all, this Meares cove'll steer small wi' you. All we're askin' is that you comes t' see the bastard and let 'im make his play, an' keep an eye t' weather and see if he's flammin' us, that's all,' Stirk begged.

The others looked at him with imploring eyes and Kydd knew he couldn't refuse. It was advice only that he would be giving, he told himself. 'It'll cost you a stout Tobermory whisky but I believe I'll bear you a hand.'

He pretended not to notice the chase of emotions on Stirk's face.

Lines were cast off and *Maid of Lorne* took up on the brisk south-westerly with an eagerness that pleased all hands.

On the way they discussed strategy.

'Gentlemen. This will only work for you if Mr Meares can produce the apparatus. And for that, what assurance do we have that it's the authentic article?' Kydd pursed his lips. 'For that matter, has anyone heard of this Wrackman? I haven't.'

'He's not askin' for coin in hand, Mr Paine. Only a share.'

If there was any sharp practice it was difficult to see what could be gained. 'If he's on shares then we've grounds to go forward.'

'*We?*

'In the larger sense, Laddie,' Kydd admonished, with a grin.

Chapter 15

Jacob Meares greeted them warmly, as though he'd been expecting a return of his visitors.

After their counsellor had been introduced, he ushered the party into a back room, which was not large but private.

'You'll understand, Mr Meares, my principals are anxious to establish the . . . practicality of what is being proposed.'

'Certainly, Mr Paine. May I enquire, have they acquaintance with the salvor's art? No? Then it's as well they're in good hands. I myself—'

'They are most desirous at this stage to take sight of the diving engine, if this is at all possible.'

'By all means! I should state that it has been quite some years since the device saw salt water and it may be a little dusty, but do take it from me, it was the actual article that was used to—'

'Mr Meares. Have you any authority that can stand by your words?'

He beamed. 'But of course. I can appreciate your very understandable circumspection. Therefore I have for your viewing newspaper cuttings of its successful use at the Isle of May – this very machine, sir!'

'We shall wish to inspect it closely.'

'Quite. Now, there are a number of matters that it would be meet to dispose of before we get to considerations of a more weighty nature. Shall I be candid? It goes without saying that your presence reveals your search for a diving bell has been in vain, so it crosses my mind that my diving engine is your only recourse. It is within my power to drive an infernal bargain that would embarrass your means, but I will not. All I wish is fair recompense. A fifty per centum of the proceeds. A not unjust claim, for without my engine you will have nothing. This, I venture, is a small request, but without its granting I say with all sorrow that my further interest will cease.'

Kydd tried to detect the feeling of the Dunlochry Treasure Company but saw only set, worried looks. 'Short of a fifty per centum interest in the venture you will not move.'

'That is so.'

Stirk gave Kydd an almost imperceptible nod.

'Very well. Shall we now see the apparatus?'

'Certainly. This way, if you please.'

The diving engine was in a substantial outhouse, with piles of junk, rope and fittings. It was enormous and encrusted with the dust of ages.

Kydd moved across to take a closer look. Propped up against the wall, like a long straight-tapered barrel, with strange elephant trunk appendages, forged iron bands and two opaque glass eyes, it was mainly of wooden construction, like a ship's cask, but inspection revealed the timber had shrunk and twisted, with gaping fissures everywhere. The trunks appeared to be arm extensions and were made of leather, but they were withered and hard. If this device had ever seen sunken treasure, it would never do so again. 'I'm sorry, Mr Meares, but this contrivance is too far decayed for us to risk using it. It will not meet our purpose.'

The man smiled indulgently. 'Of course it is, considering its age. Yet you will have no doubt noticed its construction is intended to be maintained by those unskilled in the diving arts. Even your ordinary cooper might be relied upon to restore it – after all, he labours to make a cask hold water in without seepage, who better placed to achieve the converse?'

'And you will be saying a glover or some such artisan can be trusted with this leather?'

Meares contented himself with another smile.

'Then is this apparatus complete? That is, are all the requisites for its operation in place, sir?'

'You may satisfy yourself, Mr Paine.' Meares went to a chest, opened it and gestured that Kydd inspect the contents.

There was a mass of equipment: pincers, claw dogs, sieves, bellows – and a small canvas packet.

'Take it – look inside.'

Kydd flicked through a collection of dog-eared papers; lists, diagrams, numbered instructions, accounts slips.

'There you will find guidance and directions for Wrackman's crew.'

The chest also yielded muster lists of equipment and a check-list of operations.

'I see. Then it would appear we have a possible means to go forward. Now you—'

'Mr Paine. You've now satisfied yourself of the apparatus. I would think it fair, sir, for you to satisfy me with your prospects.'

'Laddie,' Kydd ordered.

McFadden fumbled in his pocket for the coin.

'An Armada gold doubloon,' Kydd said. 'An earnest of what will follow.'

Meares took it with reverence, holding it up to the light as if to catch its full refulgence. 'And this—'

'Yes. We've located the wreck and are ready to recover same. Do we have an arrangement, sir?'

The man's eyes were agleam. 'Ah, there's much to discuss. Perhaps you and I . . .?'

McFadden began to protest but Stirk intervened, deftly retrieved the gold coin, then said, 'Go wi' him, Mr Paine. Settle it.'

They sat together in a small office, the elderly clerk instructed to take himself elsewhere.

Kydd opened: 'My principals will be happy to allow me to represent their interests but I have no function or shares in this venture beyond that of advising.'

'I quite understand. Then shall we to business?'

It didn't take long. The diving engine would be provided by Meares, the boats and wreck location by the other shareholders. Undoubtedly there would be costs, these to be borne equally in proportion to claims on the treasure.

'Shall we review our outgoings?' Kydd suggested. He was not going to leave his friends to continue alone.

The list grew. First there was outlay for refurbishing the engine. A cooper for five days – at double rates to buy his silence. A glover for three on the same conditions. A black-smith to contribute skills as needed at a goodly fee. An allowance for materials, the extent of which to be determined.

It was further agreed that proceedings be kept in the

strictest confidence and operations would be in the presence of all parties.

It was usual to seek Grant of Wreck to gain sole licence to raise valuables from a particular site. This was to keep rival speculators at a distance but would have the effect of alerting the authorities to their activity, not entirely desirable. Meares fell in with Kydd's suggestion that it was quite within reason that such formalities be kept until there was tangible return from the wreck, at which point the whole matter could be reviewed. After all, why trouble the Receiver if nothing was there?

They joined the others.

'So, gentlemen, I give you Mr Jacob Meares, desirous to be a shareholder in the Dunlochry Treasure Company.'

Agreement was reached within a very short time.

Following receipt by Mr Meares of the subscribed capital of the others he would add his own, undertaking then to bring the diving engine to a state of full readiness.

On his announcement, the device, with the said gentleman, would be taken aboard *Maid of Lorne* and the location would then be revealed.

With every expression of hope for a fortunate outcome, hands were shaken and the little band returned to Dunlochry.

Chapter 16

Stirk waited until they were alone in the kitchen. 'Connie, m' dear.'

'Aye? If it's more o' them bannocks ye're wanting—'

'No, lass. It's a-ways deeper'n that. I want t' talk wi' ye.'

She picked up on his tense mood and sat beside him at the table. 'Tell me, Toby, what's on your mind, then?'

'It's like this . . .'

He told her. The gold doubloon, the visit to the wreck, their distinguished guest's opinion of its lying about the seabed with the fishes. 'And t' think under me as I swam was a pile o' gold ready f'r the picking – it was enough t' choke me, I swear!'

Her eyes widened and she clasped her hands in sudden realisation. 'Toby – d'ye know what I think it is? You've gone an' found the Tobermory galleon, that's what! They's been searchin' for it these hundreds o' years, the Duke o' Argyll an' all – it's filled wi' gold an' silver beyond all counting. Toby, if you . . .' She tailed off at the enormity of it all. 'What'll you do now, love?'

He laid it out for her: a miraculous diving engine that had been used to raise treasure before. A partner wanting a half-share but making it all possible. Their big chance! 'So, sis, if we c'n raise a purse that'll see 'em satisfied they has their expenses, why, we c'n start diggin' it out an' no waitin'.'

'How much does they want?'

It seemed so very reasonable when Kydd had neatly listed the outgoings, but spelled out in pounds, shillings and pennies it was a formidable sum.

'That's more'n McGillie earns in a year – two,' she said faintly.

'I knows it,' Stirk said soberly. 'I've some prize-money comin' but I'll never see 'un for a dog's age yet. Laddie's got nothin' without he sells his boat.'

'Your nice Mr Paine. Will he . . .?'

Stirk shook his head. 'He can't be seen gettin' involved, more'n it's worth f'r him.'

She sighed, then said, with female practicality, 'I'll speak t' McGillie when he comes home. He'll know the right of it.'

As the summer dusk settled, the figure of the gamekeeper appeared at the door. 'I'm home, lass,' he boomed.

She hurried up and fussed at his coat. 'Toby's got something he has t' discuss wi' you,' she said firmly.

'Oh, aye? I'll tie up yon dogs an' be with him directly.'

Stirk exchanged significant glances with his sister, nodding to where Widow McGillie sat in her rocking chair, sewing, her beady eyes missing nothing.

'Would ye excuse us, Ma? The men have some talkin' to do.'

It was tough going. The hard-bitten man of the land was

having no truck with tales of buried treasure and declared surprise at one of Stirk's years being taken in by such old sailors' yarns.

Only after it was explained that a respectable Tobermory merchant was putting his own money into it and, should the McGillies not be found wanting, he would be enabled to take a significant share did he see his way clear to discussing it further.

The door burst open. 'Be damned to ye for a puckle-headed loon, lad!' his old mother threw at him in shrill fury. 'Ye has a chance t' fill y'r boots wi' Spanish gold from the Tobermory galleon. Are ye a-feart to open y'r purse for that?'

It was eventually settled that he would go to Auld Mackie, tell him all and, if the canny village elder himself put down hard coin, so would he.

Chapter 17

❧

Kydd wasted no time in setting to work on the packets from the chest, eager to find out just how the contrivance worked. The writing was strong but unlettered, and had the curlicues and phrasing of his father's day. However, it was well diagrammed, intended for humble workmen. It detailed the parts, then listed assembly and checking routines. There was a section for attendants in the boat, another for the intrepid diver, and one more for the master of supporting vessels.

Kydd sorted the instructions into their sections.

The essence of the engine was clear. It was in effect a closed watertight barrel with two thick windows and sealed leather sleeves that allowed the diver's naked arms to protrude. The whole apparatus was suspended by ropes under one or two substantially sized boats or ships anchored over a wreck.

He skipped the detailed preparations and went straight to the diver's instructions, curious as to what it would be like to go into the sea and be at one with the fishes in their own kingdom, but they concentrated on procedures and were disappointingly short on vivid descriptions. It seemed that the diver would be lying full length, angled down, and peering through the portholes as the engine was gently lowered.

He had an external cord buoyed by corks that was his only communication with the surface and, using it, he could signal that he wanted to be moved forward, that he had artefacts in his netting sack to be hauled up – or that he was desirous of more air.

Time on the seabed would be limited by depth; ten minutes working on a wreck could be expected in ten fathoms if the man were not called upon for strenuous activity. Stirk's careful soundings had shown no more than five fathoms, which presumably would translate to a whole twenty minutes. The implements a diver had to work with were simple but effective. Short picks, crow-bars, rakes, the netting bag for small and precious articles and a range of claw hooks lowered down for affixing to larger objects for hauling up.

Kydd found it impossible not to be stirred by these bald statements, written for men who had actually gone on to bring up treasure trove. He leaned back, picturing the scene. Down and down to the ocean's depths and the sea-bottom with all its mysteries, no doubt thronged with curious fish. Then poring over the scattered relics of the wreck – and over there, a half-open chest with glittering contents, an octopus gliding over it, other creatures looming . . .

Damn, but he envied Stirk his undersea adventure!

Chapter 18

The wait for Wrackman's diving engine was hard to bear. Excitement had seized everyone in the know, and there was eager speculation about the outcome. The two McGillie boys, sworn to secrecy, were open-mouthed in awe at the adventure to come, and even their father allowed there might be interesting times ahead.

Kydd knew that his role in the affair was at an end but was drawn nevertheless into the ferment of expectation. There was no way he wanted to miss the proceedings. Perhaps he could find himself a quiet corner in the boat and take it all in.

A week went by.

One evening, the McGillies were quietly finishing their supper when there was a knock at the door. The room fell quiet: visitors at that hour invariably spelled trouble.

The gamekeeper got to his feet, glancing at the blunderbuss above the mantelpiece.

'Why, Mrs Finlay!' he said, in astonishment. 'Come in.'

A sharp-eyed woman in a shawl against the cold entered quickly. A young girl followed her, eyes wide.

'Is there something amiss, m' dear?' McGillie asked, with concern.

'Aye, well. We came t' see if there's owt we can do for you, Mr McGillie.'

'Do – for me?'

'Aye. We just heard o' how youse are a-goin' to dig up the Tobermory galleon an' we thought—'

'Where d'ye hear this?'

'In course, y'r Jeb. He's down at the Lion a-sayin' as how he's t' be rich as a prince in a brace o' weeks. My, he's right blootered an' b' now it's all around the village, I ken.'

Stirk shot to his feet, his fists working. 'That poxy shicer! He's blabbed, an' we're done for when the laird hears o' this!' He snatched up a coat and flung himself out.

'Just that I thought yez goin' a-rovin' after treasure, someone should stay wi' Connie an' the bantlings an' all,' Mrs Finlay added smoothly. 'Ain't that the case, love?'

More brazen was the blacksmith, who turned up demanding a job with the engine whatever the task. He was sat down with a mug of beer while Connie dealt with the others flocking up.

Soon the little cottage was a-buzz – the secret was out.

At the Lion Stirk found Jeb out cold from drink. The entire tavern was alive with red-faced folk avid to hear more of the fabulous tale. He looked about in despair and spotted Kydd in the corner, quietly reading a book over a whisky.

'Mr Paine!' he called urgently. 'A word wi' ye.'

Kydd came over. 'Yes, Toby?'

'An' we're dished, ain't we?'

'Not as I'd noticed.'

'All th' world knows now! The laird'll be down on us like lightnin', an' you . . .'

'I don't think so.'

'This'n is a small village, I knows it. Some wicked dog beds a wench an' every bastard hears on it afore the sun's above the yard the next mornin',' he spluttered bitterly. 'We's scuppered!'

'No.'

Stirk peered at Kydd suspiciously.

'It's a small village, that I'll grant – but that's why your secret's safe. They all know your family, Toby. What do you think'll happen to any who run to the laird with a tale? No, cuffin, they're all afire for your big adventure.'

Chapter 19

❧

Word finally came. *Maid*, followed by *Aileen*, slipped to sea and made Tobermory under all sail. They found a discreet mooring and waited for the cloak of night.

Meares was nervous and fidgeted as the boats were brought up to the quay. 'I'm saying as how this is a load of coffins bound for Iona,' he confided. The engine was well concealed under a canvas shroud but there was no hiding its great weight as the dockside crane took the strain. 'That one will need the other boat,' he muttered, indicating the remaining cargo. It was a small but extraordinarily heavy item, which caused *Aileen* to sink nearly a foot and McFadden to swear in alarm.

Meares turned to Kydd. 'I'd be obliged if we could be gone, Mr Paine.'

'Directly. But you are addressing the wrong man. It's Mr Stirk who's in charge of this enterprise.'

In the safety of the open sea the principals of the company crowded into *Maid*'s little cuddy for a conference. It was brief and led to a unanimous conclusion: there was nothing to be gained by procrastination. The good weather was likely to hold for a day or two more, but in these waters it could easily take a turn for the worse.

Nowhere was free from prying eyes for trials of the equipment that anyone could think of – except the Armada wreck itself.

During the remaining hours of darkness they kept to the open sea to the south, and when dawn finally came they set course for Tiree.

The dark cave and the patch of sea before it had a repellent, cold feel. Kydd wondered if they were being given warning that trespass on the subsea kingdom would not be forgiven.

There were grave expressions and Kydd saw he wasn't the only one with qualms.

'Um, sir, how should we . . .?' muttered Stirk, drawing him aside.

'I'm a bystander only, Toby,' Kydd answered quietly. 'I can have no part in this.'

'I – I read th' writings, but . . . but what do we first?'

'I'm sorry, but you're in charge. You'll have to—'

'Bugger it, Tom! Don't top it the gent wi' me now – I'm askin', mate!'

Kydd grimaced. By insisting on keeping his distance he was pushing his old friend into public humiliation or worse. There was no lack of courage in Stirk's stout-hearted character, but Kydd as an officer was trained in the cool analysis of a situation to its elements and the devising of a course of action to meet it.

He gave a friendly pat on Stirk's shoulder. 'You're in charge,

Toby, sure enough – but if I were you, I'd set a kedge and stream killicks out to each side, then rig a stayed traveller and purchase between, so . . .'

In an hour they were ready. The two boats lay thirty feet apart with shared hoisting gear and were held in place by anchors spread to the four quarters.

The huge bulk of the barrel lay along the deck of *Maid* ready for swaying out into the cold green depths. Its copper staying bands and glass eyes flashed in the sun and the varnish of the new timbering shone gaily. To its underside was now clamped the massive black-painted long lead weight that had been the other load.

'We'll dip th' beast in, see if it leaks,' Stirk decided.

All hatches and stopcocks were closed, according to the list. Then, with curt seamanlike orders, he had it suspended at the right angle and began lowering.

'I make no warranty, Mr Paine. None at all,' Meares said, his hands wringing. 'We filled it with water overnight to test it, but in the sea, well, it might be different, is all.'

The barrel touched the sea but as it was lowered deeper it twisted and writhed, refusing to go further, heaving and bobbing half submerged.

In despair Stirk turned to Kydd in appeal. 'It don't want to,' he croaked.

'And neither should it, Toby. There's nobody aboard. Should you weigh it down heavier with something?'

A body's weight of anything that could be found was stuffed inside and it was lowered again – this time to sink obediently below the waves. Every eye followed it until the diminished shape faded from view in the depths with nothing left to tell of its existence but the taut ropes plunging straight down.

In silence it was raised again, the squeal of the block sheaves startling in the quiet, until its glistening bulk broke surface.

Meares pressed forward gingerly and worked the stopcock. A runnel of water dribbled out, then ceased. It had not leaked. Hatches were opened and the barrel was cleared. There was now every reason for the first dive to take place. All turned to Stirk.

He paused, then threw back his shoulders and marched to the main hatch as if to his execution. At the opening he hesitated, glancing back over his shoulder, then to the heaving water. For a long moment he stared out, his face working.

'Can't do it!' he burst out, in a hoarse cry, looking round with a face of blind horror. 'Not in there, f'r Chrissakes. I can't!'

Shocked, the waiting crew drew back, confused.

Kydd felt for the man but tried to encourage him. 'Toby, you have to. It's your duty.'

Stirk stared at him wildly.

Kydd realised he must have a horror of confined spaces – and there would be nothing more calculated to bring him to the edge of madness than to be hammered shut into an underwater coffin. 'Don't worry, Toby. It's really your job to be in charge, not go diving. We'll ask Laddie to go down and get the gold. Right?'

'S-sorry, Mr Paine. It's m' arm, like. Been gripin' me an' it wouldn't be right if'n I couldn't haul in the cobbs, leaving 'em all lying there, like.'

'Jeb?' The younger man shook his head mutely, his face chalky white.

Kydd turned finally to Meares. 'So it looks as if—'

'Not me! On my life, not me!'

'But if it's not you, then—'

'It's your share.' He gulped. 'Supply the boats – and that means crew as well! One o' *you* goes down!'

Chapter 20

It was the end of the adventure. So close and . . .

Kydd shared their terror of the unknown, but this was a unique chance to enter an underwater world, the other dimension of the sea.

What lay below? Reason led one way, myth and fantasy another, but if he went down in the diving engine he would find out. 'So it appears it shall be myself,' he found himself saying.

Stirk came over, his face set. He took Kydd's hand and shook it, looking deep into his eyes. 'I won't forget this of ye, Tom. Never!'

Twice they went through routines, including communications, then Kydd challenged them to repeat every one back. When he was satisfied he indicated he was ready.

Laddie had the checklist up. 'Oil!'

Kydd stripped to shirt and trousers and was well soused in train oil before he was helped up to the main hatch. With mixed dread and excitement he let himself be fed into the contrivance, moving down into the dark recesses with only the bright discs of the windows ahead to relieve it. He reached them, just remembering to ease his arms one at a time into the leather ports before he felt his legs held, then secured with straps as he manoeuvred to get the windows each side of his chin directly in his line of sight.

Within the engine it was cool and damp, yet his arms outside were feeling the morning sun – it was a disturbing sensation, but there were things to do. He felt the side of the barrel to the right for the cord that was his communication to the surface.

A double thump on the barrel was a question. He was as comfortable as he was going to be so he slapped the side twice in return.

There was a rattling and heavy *thunk*s as the main hatch was closed, then the cocks. He was sealed in.

The lurch as the engine was raised caught him by surprise. Suspended full-length and tilted down he saw through the windows the deck under him move away to be replaced with a view of green waves dancing in sunlight. The transit stopped with a swing and, with wildly beating heart, he watched the surface close with his gaze until suddenly the glass eyes met it. In an instant his world changed to a dull blue-green immensity.

He was conscious that his arms were submerged and impulsively he waved them across his vision. They seemed pale and feeble in the eerie light, not his own, and at the neatsleather seals he felt an uncomfortable constriction. Once again he felt for the cord that was his only connection to the world he had left. Vague particles flitted upwards as the engine sank further, and fearfully his eyes searched for meaning in the vastness all around. The cold was rapidly clamping in – no doubt why he was smeared with oil.

A dim shape flicked in and out of existence at the corner of his vision and his heart began a manic bumping, made worse when a sudden deafening crack and prolonged creaking sounded as the timbers took up under the pressure. Then, without warning, he became aware of a rumpled grey plain under him, stretching away into a blurred nothingness in every direction.

The bottom of the sea! He was living and breathing in the kingdom of the fishes . . . and, dare he admit, mermaids and all of Neptune's creatures? Kydd held his breath at the stark wonder of it, and knew he would never forget the moment as long as he lived.

Descending slowly he saw it take form and colour – a drab silty undersea moorland with the bulk of rocks protruding from the side, covered with the green and brown of sea-growths and in the central plain suggestive hummocks and rises as far as the eye could see.

Almost in a panic as the seabed rose quickly in the last few feet he remembered to tug the cord to indicate lowering was to stop.

The barrel ceased its descent abruptly and he was left suspended and swaying gently just a foot or two clear of the ground. He saw his hands reach out – and touch the bottom. He could feel it: soft silt that rose up in clouds and within it a hard object – but it was only a small shellfish that promptly clamped shut in his fingers.

A crab scuttled indignantly away and Kydd's fears fled in the enchantment. He reached for another lump to one side and felt the whole diving engine obediently rotate to conform to his desires. He found it possible to pull himself along a yard or two, giving increasing manoeuvrability. In rising excitement he oriented himself – over there dimly was the darker bulk of the nearer buttress of the cave rearing up. Scrabbling around, he saw the suggestion of another: he must be exactly where they had planned, in the slight gradient down from the wreck.

If the contents had been washed out of the ship over the centuries they had to be here. Any one of the many bumps and irregularities in the muddy silt could be . . .

Kydd clamped a hold on himself: he was there to do a job. He would begin at this spot, work over to the left then up a yard or two and return across, making his way up to the wreck.

A subliminal movement – a flash in the strange half-light. Primeval fears slammed in until he spotted a small shoal of fish flitting past the rocks. Spellbound, he watched their synchronised swooping and darting.

Back to work, damn it!

He addressed himself to the first likely lump, feeling its hardness, an irregular length. He fumbled in the tool net slung under him for the pick. The concretion yielded and he caught the dull brown of what could only be man-made iron. It had no value but he stuffed it into his finds net. It would be his souvenir of a lifetime. Another, close by. It was rounder and set slightly deeper in a cranny. It wouldn't come away and he teased all around it with the pick, panting at the effort.

It was worth it: waving aside the turbid cloud he saw a dull gleam and attached to it a dark rod of some kind – and then its form yielded itself. In a delirium of joy he touched the remains of a rapier of the Spanish kind of centuries past.

The encrusted blade bent and lost its concretions as he worried it clear of a crevice and then he held it before him

69

in reverence. Barely recognisable, but for all that a stunning confirmation of their purpose. Feverishly he stuffed it into the finds net and moved on, sweating with excitement.

An unmistakable semi-circle protruded up, and more work in the cloudy water revealed a pewter plate, battered and worn, with crude engraving that he couldn't make out.

Panting deeply, he rested for a moment, ears ringing. The inside of the barrel was running with condensation, puddling not far from his chin and it was getting difficult to breathe.

It was time to surface.

Three quick tugs on the cord and he was smartly yanked away from the magical scene.

The barrel broke surface into blinding sunlight and swung about dizzily as the crew hastened to bring him up with the boat. By now he was panting in shallow gasps, desperate for air, his whole being in need. If they forgot the procedures he was done for.

Kydd felt panic build as the stuffy air gave up its last vitality and he saw the deck of *Maid* slide past as at a distance. There was activity: knocks, thumps, scrapes. Then the round port under his chin fell away, the water gurgled past, and into his prison came cool, fresh life. Thrusting his mouth crudely over the opening he drew in huge gulps of air, hanging there in a delirium of relief.

The larger port above his head was next and the nozzle of a bellows was thrust in and applied, forcing more of the precious coolness inside. He pulled back from the opening and lay exhausted as the last of the water trickled away.

There were faint shouts outside. They'd found the articles in the net and were joyously celebrating. And so they should, Kydd thought weakly. It was working: not only had they entered the magic realm but had found what they were looking for.

After a few minutes he became aware that Stirk was bending under to see into the glass eyes. He caught sight of Kydd, who winked at him. In huge relief the big sailor spoke into the port. 'We saw what ye found, cully!' he hailed, in humble admiration. 'How do y' feel?'

Kydd was suffering nausea brought on by the rapid change in air conditions and replied in a voice he hardly recognised as his own, 'Leave me to rest for a few minutes, Toby, there's a good fellow.'

'Tom, does ye want t' get out?'

One half of him was desperate to escape his confinement but the other yearned to slip back to his newly discovered undersea world. 'No, I'll be down again shortly.' This time he'd make damn sure he watched for the signs of his air giving out.

Kydd managed two more dives, staying in the engine as it was refreshed on the surface.

When he was below he had no idea of the weather conditions above but knew that Stirk would never risk anything. Then he realised that the gentle up-and-down motion on the seabed was the boat's rising and falling with the waves; it was slight, which indicated continued balmy summer weather.

Punctiliously, he worked his way crossways up the slope. His little haul grew, and with it the likelihood that, sooner or later, he would make the big find. It was astonishing how many relics of familiar life at sea were scattered around: combs, buckles, common oil lamps, spoons, trinkets, carpenter's tools. He didn't bother putting these in the net and went after the larger, more suggestive lumps.

By the end of the afternoon he was exhausted, his nose

bled and he had a ferocious headache. But undoubtedly they were closing in.

The prize find came unexpectedly. While he was extricating what was probably a navigational instrument an irregular lump instantly caught his eye: a glint of gold! It was heavy and he quickly recognised it: two doubloons welded into an encrusted mass of silver coins.

At dusk, it was time to return home for the day. As *Maid of Lorne*, followed by *Aileen G*, entered the bay they saw that the little waterfront was crowded with people. More were coming down the steep road from the village. Faintly the skirl of bagpipes could be heard on the air, and lights gleamed in every house. This was a welcome!

News was quickly shouted across as willing hands took their lines, and then it was off to the White Lion in a ferment of elation to hear the details. Mr Paine was cheered as the hero of the hour, and in the bedlam his fatigue and headache fled.

An embarrassment of ladies clustered around him with wide eyes as he tried to tell of the magic allure of an undersea world, and the moment he had held gold that had last known a Spanish nobleman's hands. He spoke guardedly of his hopes for the treasure chest itself – after all, if the little baubles he'd found had survived it couldn't be that far off.

A glowering fisherman had to be reassured that the diving engine was not about to put him out of business – he couldn't see how Kydd, right there in the middle of the fish, wouldn't simply reach out and snatch them one by one as they passed.

Eventually a great weariness descended on Kydd and he had to make his excuses – even the merriment in the taphouse below failed to prevent a fathoms-deep sleep.

Chapter 21

To foil any crafty attempt to follow them, it was given out that they would sail with the tide at ten. Instead *Aileen* and *Maid* set off while it was still dark. With the same feint to the south-west, they raised the Skerryvore at daybreak and were comfortably moored by the wreck at an early hour.

The barrel was readied and Kydd was impatient to start again. He knew exactly what to expect and where he would resume the search. At the seabed he quickly found his place. The early daylight entered at an angle, and eerie patterns of light shafted down, leaving the underwater reaches to the cavern in a baleful gloom. But, caught up in treasure-hunting, he had no time for gawking – he had to make every minute count.

The diving engine was well designed for the work. Unlike a diving bell, where men sat about its edge with long-handled tools hoping to fish things up, he was actually on the sea-bottom feeling and manipulating with his hands.

He turned up more finds: a scatter of bullets, a small bucket and an object of intricate contriving that was so corroded as to be impossible to make out. The cannon would be too heavy to be washed down the slope and were probably buried where they had fallen, beside the wreck.

After refreshing for air and giving the usual instruction for a move of a further six feet he descended again and, almost immediately, spotted the outline of a crucifix and many small personal items of a quality that Kydd felt could only have come from the captain's cabin. He probed carefully, waving aside clouds of silt and wielding his pick on anything likely-looking. There was an oval framed miniature portrait, much corroded silverware – and an attractive marble statuette, only a foot or more long but barely affected by centuries under the sea.

A little further on a small triangular protrusion took his eye. He hauled himself over and prodded around it, an easy task as it was immersed in a depression of silt. It grew bigger – and Kydd breathed deeply in a wash of shock as he stared at the corner of what any captain could identify instantly, then chipped away to expose its iron straps and antique bronze locks.

It was the ship's strongbox – and of substantial size. Kept in the captain's quarters, it would contain all the official valuables the ship possessed.

Kydd dug away feverishly until it lay exposed in all its muddy glory.

They had done it!

He forced a calm to his thudding heart.

Noting exactly where it was located he signalled a refresh.

On the surface he told Stirk to prepare a double strop to go down with him. Back at the box he eased a rope over either end and bowsed them tight, with turns for a doubly secure hoisting tackle. Then he signalled another refresh: he wasn't going to miss the great event.

Stirk's face broke into a broad grin when Kydd demanded to be released and helped out.

With a squeal of protesting sheaves the load was hauled in – and for the first time in centuries the coffer was kissed by daylight.

'B' Jesus, ye've done it!' yelled McFadden, snatching at the line to bring it inboard.

'We're rich!' squealed Jeb, flailing his arms like a madman.

Stirk swayed it in, to land with a satisfying thump on *Maid*'s fore-deck.

Then they heard the voice of Meares – loud, strident and demanding. 'Open it! Get it open – *now*!'

'No, wait—'

'*Stand clear, y' bastards!* Jeb yelled, wildly swinging an axe. They fell back as it struck the old fastenings with savage, smashing hits.

'That's enough!' roared Stirk, as the lock disintegrated and skittered over the deck. He bent over the chest and heaved at the lid, without result.

'Give it some more – at th' hinges, bugger it!'

Nothing could stand the fury of the attack for long. Suddenly a black line appeared all along the line of the crusted lid. It was free.

Meares pushed past and reverently knelt to open it.

Chapter 22

Eskdale Hall, Wiltshire

'Go on, Thomas! What was in it – do tell!' the Countess of Farndon urged, proffering another dainty sweetmeat to her brother.

'You really want to know?' Kydd teased.

'*Tell us!*'

'Do please, old chap,' Renzi added.

'Well . . .'

'*Pleeease!*'

'Then I'll reveal all. It was the captain's strongbox right enough. But inside was naught but some seals, a small bag of silver coins and a couple of gold ones. No treasure.'

'*Oh, no!* None?' Cecilia exclaimed.

'Not worth the name. You see, it was truly an Armada bark but not like your Tobermory galleon, only one of the lesser sort as didn't carry a pay-chest or other.'

'Ah. So nothing for your efforts, then.'

'No, not really. Saving the adventure, of course.'

'Oh dear,' Cecilia said. 'Then your friends are sadly inconvenienced in the article of investment, poor souls.'

'Yes, it was a wry crew returning to their welcome at Dunlochry. Jacob Meares insisted they first take him and his diving engine back to Tobermory and disappeared without so much as a thank-you.'

'And the village would be much cast down.'

'They were. I couldn't help but conceive it my fault for giving them false hope in the matter, to put up their hard-won means in the enterprise and lose it all.'

'I'm desolated to remark it, brother, but it does rather seem you did.'

Kydd nodded gravely, then rose, saying he must go to his room. He returned shortly with an object in his hand. 'This is what we found earlier.'

It was the marble statuette. He passed it across to Renzi. 'I was able to tell them that while we may not have raised treasure, this find is valuable enough to recompense each and every one to his full amount.'

'But—'

'I assured them with extravagant enthusiasm that I recognised it and knew a gentleman of an insatiable habit of collecting who would pay much for it. I promised them they would get a good price and I would remit the proceeds back promptly.'

'But, dear fellow, this is only your common santos as may be seen in any Papist shrine.'

'Nicholas, I know. I fancy my fur-salvage money will be a trifle lighter for the experience.'

Chapter 23

No. 10 Downing Street, London

His Grace the Duke of Portland paused between the two Corinthian pillars at the entrance to the Cabinet Room. His waiting ministers rose in a massed scraping of chairs. Supported by a footman, the prime minister of Great Britain made his way to his place at the centre of the long table. Although old and in failing health, he was arrayed in state robes and a full-bottomed wig.

'I trust Your Grace is taking well of his Ward's drops,' murmured a tall, nearly bald man. The remaining hair at the sides of his head was ridiculously dressed, but no one in the room would say as much to George Canning, the imperious foreign secretary.

'I thank you, sir, but it does not answer, I'm grieved to say,' Portland replied, in a thin voice.

Canning allowed a shadow of concern to appear. 'Your Grace, I'm persuaded I speak for all present in wishing you speedy relief from your bodily trials.'

'That is kind in you,' the prime minister answered, with a civil nod.

Further down the table an intense-featured man, handsome in a distant, patrician manner, muttered, 'As we have been here assembled to do business of the realm, let us not waste time in flatteries.'

'My lord Castlereagh,' Portland said, to the secretary of state for war, 'be assured, we've come to discuss the gravest of matters. Do set aside your differences, I beg of you, in the face of this peril.' He looked around the room, then paused to collect his thoughts.

Spencer Perceval, a pale individual, the able and principled chancellor of the exchequer, prompted, 'Meaning Bonaparte's Continental System, Your Grace?'

Perceval had performed heroics to fund Britain's lonely stand against Bonaparte without ruinous taxation imposts and stood outside the poisonous feuding between the power-hungry Canning and the gifted Castlereagh.

'Quite, quite. Gentlemen, it doesn't need me to remind you that this has been a truly momentous development. When Bonaparte issued his Berlin decree, prohibiting any from trade with this country, we were not to know that within months almost the entire continent would be closed to us. His master-stroke has been to hurt us grievously without ever a shot fired in battle.'

His cabinet stirred restlessly. It was the fate of the most talented government for a generation to be led by a frail figure of the past – the previous administration, following Pitt's inspired leadership and then premature death, had been called the Ministry of All the Talents but had collapsed in ignominy. The Tories had returned to power, but under this enfeebled figurehead leadership.

'For the sake of clarity in our deliberations I would call upon you severally to state your opinion as to our position from your perspective as a minister of state. Foreign Secretary, would you outline to us how you believe we stand in these parlous times?'

Canning pursed his lips. 'Easily laid out, Your Grace. Napoleon Bonaparte has devoured most of the civilised world. This leaves us with precious few friends. To the east of France, Austria is tottering and Prussia is being overrun as we speak. At the present time, sir, the only nations in the whole of the continent not under the tyrant's boot are Denmark, which as ever remains strictly neutral, Sweden, with its eccentric king, Gustavus, and Russia. As this last is ruled by the ambitious but dim-witted Tsar Alexander, we can be sure of nothing. To the west of France there is only Portugal, our last and most loyal friend. And a pitifully vulnerable liability.

'In sum, Boney and his puppets hold a vast empire stretching from the Russian border to the shores of the Atlantic. There is nothing left, I'm grieved to say, and it must be faced that the entire European seaboard, save Denmark and Sweden, now girdles his private fiefdom.'

'Hmmph. Secretary of State for War?'

Castlereagh wasted no time outlining his views. 'In fine, we have a stalemate. At sea we are peerless and unconquerable. On land Bonaparte stands invincible. Only if he puts to sea to try conclusions with us, which I very much doubt he will do, or on the other hand we make landing with an army to match his millions, which I equally doubt, will there be any chance of resolution. This is the essence of the situation – a stalemate.

'Yet with this Continental System he seeks to break the impasse and take the war to a different dimension. It's now a species of trade war, of economical contention, and I fear one we are sore pressed to counter. Europe is near cut off to our exporting, bar some contemptible smuggling, but should things turn even more against us we lose, in addition, our vital imports of materials for industry. Frankly, I confess I cannot see any way in the military line out of this situation.'

His words hung in an uncomfortable silence until Perceval said heavily, 'In course this is not to be accepted.'

Canning's response was immediate. 'Not to be? My dear sir, it *has* to be accepted, for this is where we are, and no amount of—'

'Sir!' Perceval retorted. 'Tolerating a state of impotence is not to be countenanced. And why? Let me detail it for you. The raw materials market now closed to us has consequences that set us on a downward spiral to oblivion as a nation. There is—'

'We all know this, Perceval. When—'

'Let me finish! We were lately in prodigious growth, our industries propelled by steam power and machines producing goods in quantities that the world marvels at. Without markets it's as nothing to us. In my tour of the north there were howls of anguish from the merchantry. I saw ironmasters ruined, manufactories silent, the working masses turned away at the gates to penury, a sight may I say to wring the hardest of hearts, sir.

'And I appeal to you, where is now the revenue to continue the war? At ruinous expense we maintain our far-flung navy and its dockyards, the army must prepare for any assault on these islands and—'

'Hold, sir!' Canning interrupted. 'Are you saying you'll have us put down our arms? Cravenly yield to the tyrant?'

Perceval breathed deeply. 'His Grace wishes a summation of my views. I shall continue. And it is to say that there is an even worse prospect that looms larger as we procrastinate. I point to the situation where France within the Continental

System has complete and unfettered control of the markets. What, then, of us? Europe, sir, is turning by degrees into a captive marketplace for French goods alone.'

He paused significantly. 'Then later, at any peace, we will see all our customers lost to the French. Without exports to pay for our imports we will face ruination, sir. It will then be far too late for idle discussion.'

Portland harrumphed, then said weakly, 'It does seem that time is not on our side. I put it to all of you that we must decide on a course of action that can break this stranglehold. I beg I might hear of some suggestions.'

Castlereagh sighed. 'A hardening of our orders-in-council against neutral shipping and the like in reply to Boney's decree risks upsetting any remaining uncommitted nations, the United States in particular. It would be a blow indeed to see them ally with the French as they did back in the American war, do you not agree?'

'What other instruments have we to hand in a trade war?' Canning rapped. 'Only the navy is active in this matter, and to tie its hands . . .'

'Gentlemen, gentlemen, do remember your dignity. What is needed now are answers, not difficulties. Now, is there among you any constructive line of thought that can be brought to bear?'

As the room erupted into an ill-tempered babble, Canning gave a twisted smile. 'Well, there is one thing that is on our side. With the Whigs in such disarray we've little to be feared from the floor of the House. We've some small space to arrive at a decisive solution . . .'

Portland ignored the barely concealed contempt at his handling of the parliamentary opposition, and declared loftily, 'Well, it can hardly be worse for us, now, can it?'

Chapter 24

Tilsit, Duchy of Lithuania

The maître d'hôtel of the Hotel Tilžê primped his moustache and looked out over the packed dining room with swelling satisfaction. The little town of the Teutonic Knights, now a modest spa resort on the southern Baltic, had been thrust into an astonishing prominence by the workings of Fate, sudden shifts of destiny in the world of war reaching even as far as there, and who was he to question it?

What was incredible was one simple fact: they had been spared.

Prussia, aided by young Alexander, Tsar of Russia, had dared to defy Napoleon Bonaparte but had been halted at the blood-soaked battlefield of Eylau earlier in the year. From there Emperor Bonaparte had thrust his army, like a sword, through the vitals of Prussia and even into the ancient lands of east Prussia, an unstoppable juggernaut.

They'd trembled for their safety as news and rumours of the approaching French host had flooded in – but had bravely cheered Count von Bennigsen as he marched across the border to confront them with some ninety thousand men and hundreds of guns.

It had not been enough. Even with King Friedrich falling back to his last redoubt, Königsberg, at the extremity of Prussian territory, the French had pressed hard against his desperate resistance.

And only three weeks ago, no more than fifty miles away at Friedland, the two armies had come together in a titanic clash, which had finally ended after twenty hours of desperate hacking. The chaotic rout and slaughter of the Russian Army had left nearly fifty thousand bodies carpeting the battlefield. Terrified, the townsfolk had prepared for the inevitable, but it was not to be. Bonaparte, in his wisdom and mercy, had halted the advance and granted a general armistice.

Then the rumours started: it was for a reason, a world-changing purpose that had as its objective the forging of a continent-sized empire. This was nothing less than a meeting of emperors to determine the fate of the civilised world. Tsar Alexander of Russia would stand face to face with Emperor Bonaparte of France as equals to cease the useless bloodshed and decide the destiny of nations for centuries to come.

And all this was to take place in Tilsit, beside the Neman River between Prussia and the quaint old medieval Duchy of Lithuania, under Russian dominance since the dismembering of Poland in 1795.

It was a stupefying change of fortune for the town.

The Tsar was processing from Russia with his nobles and court. Coming from the opposite direction the newly victorious Emperor Bonaparte would arrive to stand at the banks of the Neman in recognition of the limit of his conquered territories, with his staff and generals, and who knew how many followers?

That meant a gratifying number of nobles and ladies, statesmen and grandees, all needing accommodation and entertainment at what better establishment than the Hotel Tilžê?

His ransack of the champagne and fine wines, caviar and *foie gras* from far and wide was paying off handsomely as notables gathered for the greatest spectacle of the age. In the dining salon before him were the cream of the nobility of central Europe, generals and ambassadors. If he could maintain standards, there was a fortune to be made.

The maître d'hôtel surveyed the busy scene again. In yet another stroke of luck, he'd been able to procure the services of a first-class head waiter, Meyen, a Polish Jew recently fled from Königsberg. He was a born professional, working the tables with attention and poise that was neither intrusive nor fawning. When this affair was over, he would most certainly see to it that Meyen found a secure position at the hotel.

'Do you recommend the duck at all, my dear Meyen?'

'If your ladyship craves adventure,' the head waiter answered, with a roguish smile. This was the flirtatious Helga, Countess of Hesse-Darmstadt. He happened to know she was in an affair with General Gülstorff, sitting opposite, who had managed with desperate heroism to extricate himself and his cavalry from the field after Friedland.

Meyen leaned past her to align the silver cutlery to perfection and heard them resume their conversation in German.

'When can we get away, Hans? It's been so long.'

'Not now. There's a dispatch due, telling us whether we give ground on Hanover or not.'

He looked up suddenly at Meyen who returned a glassy smile of incomprehension and went on with his rearranging.

'This whole thing is a catastrophe from start to finish. I swear that if Bonaparte asks for the crown we'll have to give it him.'

Interesting.

Meyen withdrew with every expression of politeness and threaded through the room, ignoring other diners with practised ease to arrive at the table of Marshal Kuril, the Russian soldier who had arrived too late to make any difference to the crushing of the remnants of Tsar Alexander's imperial ambitions. The occupants were sunk in the deepest gloom, and Kuril's wife sat rigidly, letting her husband mutter on at his loyal adjutant.

Meyen carefully took position behind the marshal, order pad and polite smile at the ready. In their dejection he wasn't noticed and his expatriate Russian was quite adequate to catch the drift of what was being said: it was the considered opinion of Kuril that if Alexander failed in his confrontation with Napoleon he would most certainly suffer assassination, like his father, Tsar Paul.

It was a rich haul he was getting from this concentration of the highest as they feverishly discussed the fateful meeting to come. His paymaster would no doubt be accordingly grateful.

Chapter 25

The muffled sound of a military band ceased. French soldiers with gleaming sabres lined the main street as jingling cavalry with glittering breast-plates passed down it, a brave and shocking sight. On the other bank, stolid lines of Russian soldiers spread out and a column of Cossack cavalry, resplendent in red with fierce black moustaches, took up their positions.

There was no doubt now that this day would be touched by history. In the precise centre of the river was a pavilion on a broad raft, gorgeously emblazoned with pennons and every detail of chivalry, signifying that this meeting of emperors would take place on impeccably neutral territory.

The stage was set: let the drama begin.

Meyen, careful to hang back a little, joined the throng that jostled at the windows of the hotel, trying to get a glimpse from the high balcony of the epochal meeting.

On the French side there was a swirl in the crowd – a carriage! It could only be . . .

The man who had set the world ablaze, who had wrested

for himself an emperor's crown and who now stood astride the continent, like a colossus, was handed down, bowing this way and that to the gathered nobles of a dozen countries. In white breeches and waistcoat, a dark coat with the splash of gold epaulettes, a single light-blue sash and knee-length black military boots, there was no mistaking Emperor Napoleon Bonaparte.

Opposite, a train of brilliantly clad figures began to form up and the procession slowly wound down to the riverside.

'The Tsar!' gasped a lady behind her fan.

It was indeed the Emperor and Autocrat of all the Russias, of Moscow, Kiev, Vladimir, Lord and Grand Duke of Nizhny Novgorod, Sovereign of Chernigov, the Tsar Alexander I, and until three weeks ago an implacable enemy.

Boats arrived at each bank and the principals were rowed out to the pavilion. Simultaneously they stepped into it by opposite portals. The hangings were drawn firmly across and all functionaries retreated in their respective boats, leaving the two leaders in solitary splendour.

It had happened. Behind the rich drapery the world was in the process of being dismantled.

After an hour the entertainment palled, then someone noticed a lone figure in glittering court dress pacing up and down on the bank, lost and forlorn.

'Who's that?' Meyen asked innocently, although he knew full well.

'You'd never credit the sight!' the Duchess Izvolsky gushed. 'It's Friedrich Wilhelm himself, poor man!'

The King of Prussia, excluded from the meeting that would decide if his country could continue to exist after this day, or perhaps should be shared out among the great powers as so recently Poland had been, now a forgotten relic of past ages.

Late in the afternoon the principals emerged. They were seen to embrace before they took boat and urgent speculation began.

That evening was one of gaiety and tension, pomp and formality as everyone flocked to the greatest and most glittering ball ever seen – but not a whisper emerged of what had transpired on the raft.

It was an extraordinary night. Conquerors and the conquered mixed with the utmost refinement; nobles of ancient houses fearing for their very existence received the most elegant of bows; and at the banquet Napoleon Bonaparte sat next to Tsar Alexander while exchanging platitudes with the King of Prussia.

Meyen had been engaged to attend at the banquet and he wasted no time in adding to his store of rumour, opinion and fact. He slipped in and out of the breathtaking mêlée, imperturbable, unctuous, attentive – and invisible.

Mere archdukes were spurned for princes, generals for marshals, while all eyes were continually turning to the high table where Napoleon Bonaparte himself was on show to all the world at his greatest and most glittering triumph.

The next day Bonaparte went riding with the Tsar before resuming deliberations on the raft.

There seemed little doubt that the two emperors had reached an understanding, and that the Tsar had not been confronted with impossible demands as a prelude to a catastrophic resuming of the war. The presumption was that a dividing process must be under way. What would be the result?

It was said that the beautiful Queen Louise of Prussia had

come to intercede personally with Emperor Bonaparte, but had been coldly scorned. It was further rumoured that the cynical and ambiguous Talleyrand, foreign minister of the French Empire, had been refused attendance by his master after objecting to the scale of his demands.

Three more days passed. Then, quite abruptly, the proceedings concluded. Each emperor retired to his side of the river and all Tilsit waited in unbearable tension.

A little after midnight all was resolved.

Ink still wet from the printers, a bill was distributed, the treaties and expressions of resolve made public.

Meyen snatched one and scanned it.

What he saw made him act immediately. With gold coin, he secured a private carriage and headed urgently for the north.

Chapter 26

Memel, East Prussia

The British ambassador to Russia, Lord Granville Leveson Gower, had not been invited and, even as representative of a principal ally, hadn't expected to be. He'd heard of the theatrical meeting on the raft and knew that events beside the Neman were rushing to a climax that threatened Britain as nothing else had done, but he was helpless to do anything about it.

Alone in his study that night, there were dispatches to write up. They could contain little of substance for he was not a spectator but a helpless pawn, holding a travesty of a diplomatic presence there, going through the motions of one disinterested in anything the French were doing.

Then Meyen arrived.

'Good heavens, man! You're looking dreadful – come in, come in. A restorative?' Gower fetched a glass and the brandy decanter from the sideboard. Drawn and pale, the man was restless, driven, not the controlled and smooth cosmopolitan he had last seen. 'You've news?'

'Of course. I came as soon as I could. Sir, what do you know of the meeting of emperors?'

'I've heard nothing beyond that they met in a pavilion on a raft. There've been rumours but—'

'Then prepare yourself. There is an agreement. Europe is to be divided between the two. Alexander has been duped by the tyrant and is in his power. Sir, we are lost!'

The news was devastating. The two emperors had achieved their agreement, a treaty of friendship that was stark and clear in its implications. Russia was out of the war and now in a state of amity and concord with France. The alliance with Britain was dead, leaving her quite alone, with not a single friend of consequence on the continent.

Prussia was spared – but at a cost. Half of its territories would go to the newly created Kingdom of Westphalia to be ruled by Bonaparte's brother Jérôme. Its lands from the partition of Poland would be handed over to the equally new Duchy of Warsaw. And the two emperors would assist each other to bring peace to the world: France would proffer its best offices in treating with the Ottomans, and Russia would offer to mediate in a peace treaty with Great Britain.

The ambassador slumped back, appalled. Meyen was right: it could not possibly be worse.

Since the beginning of the wars British strategy had been to deploy the wealth from its industrial might in subsidies and arms to any nation that stood against Bonaparte. It had been remarkably successful so far – but it had relied on two factors that now no longer existed.

No nations of consequence continued to resist. And with the entire continent in Bonaparte's power, the industrial products that generated Britain's wealth could not be sold into a continental market that the Emperor controlled absolutely.

Meyen's overheard information was priceless and revealing – yet it did not change the essence of what had happened on the raft. But Gower now had an idea of the cynical scrabbling and manoeuvring among the lesser powers to readjust to the reality of the situation. He knew that they no longer saw Britain as a player in the big game.

The man was paid and Gower left to his thoughts. They were bitter and helpless. It was not Britain's fault, she had lost no battle – but Bonaparte had won the war.

He got out pen and paper and set about preparing his dispatch, which he knew would shock his countrymen to the core. He had barely started when an expressionless under-secretary handed him a note. It was in bad French but to the point. A friend of England had secret and powerful information for his ears alone. Well placed in the Tsar's court, he was privy to secrets that would bear grievously on his conscience should he fail to disclose them. If Gower wished to hear them, he must allow himself to be conducted, unattended, to a private room where the writer, not wishing to be identified, would speak to him through a curtain.

'The one who brought this, is he . . .?'

'He waits below, my lord.'

The private room was not far away, evidently chosen hastily for the occasion. Inside there was a dividing makeshift chintz screen and Gower was ushered to a solitary chair next to it.

'You have information for me, I believe.'

'I haf, lord.' The voice on the other side was muffled but Gower thought he knew who it was. It didn't matter: he could establish authentication in other ways.

'Then in order for me to assess your standing, you will tell me the appearance in court of the lady of Count Speransky.'

93

'Ha! He is a vidow.'

'Very good. In the Tsar's throne room, do you enter from right or left?'

'None. From ze centre, bowing much.'

'Yes, that is so. May I then hear your information, sir?'

What he heard sent him into a chill of despair for it multiplied the danger England faced to a near intolerable pitch.

It seemed the Treaty of Tilsit had two faces, public and secret, both equally binding. The public one he knew of, but there had been agreed secret covenants far too dangerous in their implications to be let known, even to the respective governments. The canny Bonaparte had dangled the promise of 'common cause' before the callow Alexander. In the matter of the Ottomans, Russia would at last achieve the cherished dream of Catherine the Great: the conquest of Constantinople and its reverting to Orthodox Christianity. In the event of difficulties, France would show common cause with Russia in the contest. On the other hand Alexander would mediate in the imposing of severe peace terms on England, which, if refused, would result in his showing common cause with France.

To Gower it was a nightmare. In one stroke a land route for the invasion of India had been created, and by the same, Russia would be free to enter the Mediterranean as a great power. Yet the greater significance was that Russia was not only out of the war but had changed sides. From now, with all its millions, it would be an active enemy.

While he tried to grapple with the reality, the Russian behind the curtain spluttered with helpless indignation at how Alexander had been taken in. The Tsar had held out for the preservation of Prussia, true, thinking it to be a buffer between him and the French, but he'd been outsmarted by Bonaparte, who had delayed the evacuation of his troops from the rump of Prussia until reparations had been paid. He had demanded an impossible sum and therefore the country would remain under French occupation.

There was now little doubt as to the shape of this new world. The only question left: where would Napoleon turn next?

With a heavy heart Gower returned to his study and his dispatch. It was essential to get it to London as fast as possible, but with as much material evidence at this crucial time as he could muster. It was hard going, his phrases coming across even to him as plaintive and defensive.

Starting with his exclusion from the fateful stage he went on to detail how, as ambassador to Russia, he saw developments:

'Bonaparte has obtained complete possession of the mind of the Emperor Alexander . . . who has become a dupe of his insidious flattery . . .' He pictured the ambitious and impatient Canning reading his words and stiffened them. 'I see nothing other than that unless you make peace England will be engaged in war with the whole of Europe at intolerable cost . . . The most deadly blows are aiming at the very existence of the country: for be assured that the dangers which threaten England at this moment infinitely exceed what we ever before apprehended . . .'

There was nothing more he could do.

Chapter 27

No. 10 Downing Street, London

'Prime Minister, I must protest!' the secretary of state for war said, as the Duke of Portland entered the Cabinet Room. 'This news is of monumental importance and you've granted us but an hour to prepare for this meeting.'

'As you say, Lord Castlereagh, the matter is of dire significance to the realm and therefore an early and sufficient response is required, I believe.'

'All the same, sir, we cannot simply—'

'Shall we move on, do you think?' Canning's sarcasm was not lost on Castlereagh, who shot the man a look of venom.

'We shall leave aside our differences for now, gentlemen, and see if there's something we might do.' As Portland cautiously gathered his thoughts, his frail, aged figure was in stark contrast to the youth and vigour of those sitting around the table. 'My own position is settled, I feel sorry to say,' he said uncertainly.

He stared down at the table for so long that Canning interrupted heavily, 'And pray what is that, my lord?'

Portland looked up, confused, then collected himself. 'That

is to say, there seems no other alternative before this govern-ment. Gentlemen, I desire your views on this: that we move to seek peace terms of the French.'

'A surrender?' blurted Canning. 'Sir, you cannot be—'

'Not a capitulation,' the prime minister huffed. 'Recognition of our powerlessness in this new order, to treat for the best terms we can. As we did in Amiens in the year two.'

'A surrender!' Canning breathed.

'Not so, Foreign Secretary,' Portland hissed. 'We found peace before. We do so again!'

'My lord,' Canning ground out, 'we're now dealing with an emperor of limitless cupidity and ambition. Let loose from the continental prison we confined him to, he's free to seize anything he fancies in this world, to—'

'Thank you for your views, sir. Chancellor?'

Perceval looked up with a twisted smile. 'Prime Minister, if you insist we go by the precedent of the Amiens Treaty, of a certainty in return for peace we must give up our conquests and probably our colonies into the bargain. Given that Bonaparte controls the entire continent, where are our markets? I fear this course will see us decay into a contempt-ible third-rate power with quite indecent haste.'

Canning burst out, 'Enough of this craven talk! Our response is to strike a blow, hard and defiant, that shows Boney and the world that we're not beat. We've still got the navy, for God's sake!'

Portland looked imploringly at the first lord of the Admiralty. 'Ah, it's true, we're lords of the sea. Unhappily, our Mr Bonaparte has learned the lesson of Trafalgar only too well and keeps his fleets in port. Without they come out, how is our great victory possible?'

'Damn it all, there must be something!'

'Secretary for War?'

Castlereagh responded instantly: 'No one doubts that a gesture at this time is to be much applauded, but as we've heard, if the French fleet cannot be drawn, this implies we must go to them. Is anyone at this table seriously suggesting we should land our contemptible little army on the coasts of France to try conclusions with Napoleon's crack divisions?'

That brought on a heated exchange, which Portland tried in vain to control, but the implication was becoming all too plain.

His Majesty's Government had no answer to Napoleon Bonaparte's master stroke.

Chapter 28

The residence of the Earl Grey, London

His book was not holding his attention. With a sigh he put it down and stared out of the window. The Earl Grey, Whig, consort of Sheridan and Fox, had lost his office as secretary of state for foreign affairs when the Ministry of All the Talents had fallen. In opposition, he was now forced to watch the odious and ambitious Canning make the running in his stead.

He missed the play of diplomacy and threat, the secrecy and stealth in matters that would never be revealed. Now all he could look forward to was the next visit by the shady and venal French royalist the Count d'Antraigues, no doubt to peddle some scheme or other that would cost guineas, but with dubious return to the government.

The man was half charlatan – but which half? His services in writing salacious articles about the Emperor Bonaparte for the *Courier d'Angleterre*, a propaganda newspaper clandestinely distributed on the continent, were undoubted, but his other contributions as a political analyst and alleged middle man for the passing of agents into French territory were less clear.

And why did he insist on visiting now that Grey was out of office and out of power?

His visitor arrived suspiciously early, looking more furtive than usual.

'M'sieur le Comte,' Grey greeted him languidly.

'Milord,' he answered, an edge of excitement to his voice. 'I've something for you, ver' interesting!'

'Oh?' Grey said politely. 'And what can this be?'

'From my man in Tilsit.'

'Ah. You'll not be telling me that Emperor Napoleon had eggs for breakfast, will you?'

'He get the Russian Bennigsen drunk, hears something he know you fear.'

Grey gave a small smile. 'Very well. The usual terms, then.'

'Bonaparte, he now setting up a maritime league against England. All of zem – Russia, Denmark, Sweden with Spain, Portugal, Dutch – all their fleets! They sail together, you cannot win!'

Grey stiffened, then went cold. At Trafalgar there had been the French and the Spanish only. What if all these nations combined under French command and sailed simultaneously from their ports? In sum, at least a hundred or more ships-of-the-line converging on the half-dozen Collingwood had off Cádiz, the eight in Plymouth . . .

He looked intently at Count d'Antraigues. 'Why are you coming to me with this?'

'Canning, he not listen to me any more after—'

'This is too grave a matter for that. Sit down – here. Now put down on paper all you know. I'll see it gets to him immediately.'

Chapter 29

Rouen, France

Danican froze: outside there were shots. Distant, then many more, closer. This city had always been a dangerous place for a royalist spy and provocateur, and in these fevered days it was even more so. The musket fire hammered into a crescendo and he mopped his brow in relief. This was only the coarse Poznań soldiery using the excuse of Napoleon's Tilsit triumph to make riot again.

In the shadows of the garret a single candle flickered as he bent to his work, the ciphering of a desperately urgent intelligence. It was from a double renegade Irishman in Paris who had stumbled on a plot so threatening it had to be in the hands of his spymaster on the coast this very night.

It was nothing less than the invasion of Ireland and subsequently Britain. Intricately contrived, its deadly progress would start on the Elbe. Marshal Bernadotte at the head of his fifty thousand would get orders that would see him strike north across the frontier, up the Danish peninsula of Jutland, then on to occupy its main island of Sjælland. There, he would demand the surrender of the Danish Navy, which would be employed immediately in the conveying of troops on a daring voyage around Scotland to descend out of the mists on the unprotected north of Ireland.

The genius of the plan was that this was not the true objective. While the distracted British scrambled to bring their troops north to oppose them, a force consisting of all French soldiers between Brest and Bordeaux would embark with a full regiment of United Irishmen to come to the aid of a long yearned-for rising in the south.

This stab in the back would give Bonaparte what he'd always craved: a major conflict face to face with the British – on land.

The last code groups were cast. Danican carefully burned the plaintext at the candle and folded the lethal message many times into a tiny square that he hid in a shoe.

Then he crept out into the night.

Chapter 30

No. 10 Downing Street, London

They came quickly, the summons to Cabinet brusque to the point of impoliteness. Portland was already there, appearing more than usually frail, with a hunted look.

'Sit, sit,' he commanded, in a weak voice, between coughing fits. 'There's no time to be lost. I'm unwell so I've asked Canning to speak to you.'

The foreign secretary got to his feet and leaned forward over the table, a tigerish smile in place. 'Gentlemen,' he began silkily, 'events have moved forward at a pace that will allow no further delay and procrastination. The meeting will not disperse until a joint plan of action has been decided. This is at the express wish of the prime minister. Is that clear?'

There were no objections and he resumed his seat, shuffling his papers into order.

'There have come to my notice developments in the situation – intelligence that is of extreme gravity to the security of this kingdom. I shall detail them to you . . .'

By the time he had finished there was an appalled silence.

'All of Europe under Bonaparte,' the home secretary murmured, shocked. 'It doesn't bear thinking of.'

'Not the least of it, sir. Conceive of above a hundred battleships launched at our shores. With a dozen Nelsons we could never withstand it.'

'And the threat to Ireland, a land war,' quavered Portland. 'In all my days, I cannot recollect—'

'So my previous comment stands proud. That a supine submission to the will of Napoleon will not answer, only a savage thrust at his vitals as will—'

'This we've discussed *ad nauseam*, Canning. There's nothing within our power that can go against the tyrant.'

With a look of savage triumph, Canning wheeled on Castlereagh. 'But there is. And one calculated to solve our other problems in a bold stroke.'

'Oh? I'd no doubt be entertained to hear it.'

'You shall, I promise. Now, all our present troubles stem from one thing – that by subverting Russia, Boney is seeking to clap Europe behind a ring of iron that excludes us both from all trade with the continent and our vital – no, crucial – naval stores out of the Baltic. End to end, we face an unbroken and hostile shore that will ensure we must capitulate for want of essentials.

'At the same time he will concentrate the fleets of the continent into one colossal force that even our entire navy combined is powerless to resist. The writing is on the wall – in one month, at most two, having completed his conquests and forced a peace, he will be ready to turn on us with all the power and resources of a conquered continent.

'Gentlemen. Time has finally run out for us all. What I propose is the only sanction.'

'We're still listening,' Castlereagh drawled, fiddling with a pencil.

Canning winced but ignored him. 'We break the ring of iron and at the same time secure this crucial Baltic trade.' All attention now on him, he continued more quietly: 'I have explicit intelligence that I've no reason to reject. It reveals that pressure will be put on Denmark to deny us the Baltic by closing the Sound, failing which Bernadotte on the Elbe is poised to invade and seize their fleet. I've information that suggests the Danish will conform. First Lord of the Admiralty?'

Mulgrave nodded. 'Oh, yes. A trustworthy captain by name of Pembroke swears that he witnessed the Danish fleet in Copenhagen preparing for sea. Stores, equipment on the wharves, all signs of—'

'Thank you. I'm as well in possession of a dispatch from our head of mission in Denmark, Benjamin Garlike. He points out with understandable unease that the fortress of Kronborg, commanding the entrance to the Sound, has been considerably reinforced with artillery. To cap it all, the Danish chargé d'affaires in London, Rist, is unable to account for any of these developments or to lay before me the true position of the kingdom of Denmark in respect of the treaties of Tilsit.

'With the loss of the Russians to our cause it can mean only one thing. That Denmark sees its best interest in siding with Bonaparte.'

'Foreign Secretary, I mislike where you are leading us,' Portland's querulous voice interrupted. 'Are you suggesting—'

'Your Grace, I beg you will allow me to finish. If the Russians were to join with the Danish, at the very least, sir, they have made the Baltic a French lake, which is a dolorous prospect indeed. Therefore what I put forward to you is this. In the time left to us we pre-empt this catastrophe. In one swift move we strike to drive a cleft into the centre of Bonaparte's continent, isolating the Russians in the east and at the same time preserving our Baltic interests. Gentlemen, I propose that we should demand of the Danish that they surrender into our keeping their entire fleet. Without it they are powerless to block the Sound to our Baltic trade and at the same time it not only sunders Bonaparte's ring of iron but ensures he can never later use that fleet against us. In fine, we will have broken his domination of the continent.'

'A valiant plan,' Castlereagh said acidly, 'with but one flaw. Denmark is strictly neutral and this . . .?'

'Quite,' Portland fussed. 'There's no question that England can demand such of a neutral. Supposing they do not comply? We shall then be obliged to step down from our demand with grievous loss of countenance.'

'We do not back away. If necessary we bring force to bear that—'

'Sir, do not quibble! That would be nothing more or less than a calculated and deliberate attack on a neutral country in clear violation of every tenet of civilised conduct. This administration will not be a party to such—'

'Then, sir, you are putting your name to this government's abject submission to the Emperor Napoleon's will!'

'Ah, this is a hard matter. It beseems we should think on it long and hard before—' Portland tried.

'There's no time!' rapped Canning. 'If we're to move at all, it has to be before Bonaparte has consolidated his seizure of Prussia, before he can then turn and himself take the Danish fleet. And above all before the Baltic ices over when it'll be too late to do anything.'

'If the Danes resist and we assault them, Russia will declare war against us immediately,' Castlereagh said quietly. 'Are you prepared for that?'

'They're Bonaparte's creature. They'll do so anyway.'

Perceval leaned forward. 'Has anyone considered what the cost of alienating Denmark would be? No? Then I'll remind you all that eighty per centum of our current exports to the continent are brought in by us and transhipped through Danish ports. We stand to lose all of this, in the sum of uncountable millions, should we offend them.'

'It might not come to that. The Danes are a practical race. They'll see where their best interests lie.'

'And if they do not?' Castlereagh drawled. 'I for one am not forgetting our late lamented Lord Nelson before Copenhagen in as hot a battle as any he fought. Since then there's little doubt but that they've taken steps to increase their defences. I rather think they'll be confident enough behind them to defy our entire fleet, with or without a Nelson, and then where will be your threats?'

Canning raised an eyebrow. 'I do concur. Copenhagen is probably impregnable from the sea – but not from the land.'

'Are you . . . are you seriously considering a landing and siege?'

'The appearance of a force of unanswerable might in the Sound. A great fleet equipped with the means to do so. The Danes will see that while Bonaparte is a threat we are a promise. They will give up their fleet into our safe custody and we will withdraw, our breaking of the iron ring complete.'

'A show of force!' mocked Castlereagh, his contempt plain. 'Since when—'

'Swiftly done, no warning – do recollect, they'll know we've successfully made landing before at the Cape and again at Buenos

Aires, no matter how it turned out later. In any case, our object here is not to take territory, only to bring pressure to bear sufficient for them to think to release their fleet. That's all.'

'And if your mighty fleet fails to move them?'

'Then our hand is forced,' Canning said evenly. 'A landing is made in overwhelming numbers as will oblige them to accede to our request.'

'Our demand!' snapped Castlereagh. 'And the world will see that England has attacked and assaulted a neutral country in furtherance of its own—'

'Prime Minister!' rapped Canning, leaning forward in his intensity, his face pale. 'This is too much. I require that you demand of the secretary of state for war that he reveals his own design to preserve England from ruin.'

'Why, er . . .'

'Failing which,' he ground out, 'he's desired to hold his tongue.'

Portland held his head in his hands, rocking to and fro as if in pain. 'My lord Castlereagh, Foreign Secretary, I do *beg* you to reconcile in the face of what confronts us. We must move forward, and unless there is an alternative put before us, I fear we must accept this plan, however painful it is to our honour.'

There was a hiss of indrawn breath and every eye went to Castlereagh. But then he gave a lop-sided smile and said lightly, 'Very well. If we are of like mind then, in course, I shall give my support, and in full, Prime Minister.'

Visibly relieved, Portland made much of obtaining opinion and there being no counter-proposal, declared that in principle an expedition of such a nature be maturely considered.

'A fleet of size,' Canning opened, steepling his fingers. 'Is this possible at such notice, my lord?'

The first lord of the Admiralty, Mulgrave, considered for a moment and replied quietly, 'We're sore stretched at the present time as you will know, sir. Yet . . . I can say you will have one.'

Castlereagh leaned back and twirled his pencil. 'Should we not look first to the scale of task? I would think that, besides a substantial naval squadron of not less than ten or fifteen sail-of-the-line, there'll be need for a substantial showing of troops if they land – say, ten or twenty thousand.'

'What? So many?'

'You require the Danish to yield to a paltry number when Bonaparte has sixty thousand to their south? If this is to appear as formidable and unanswerable as our foreign secretary desires, we have no choice, sir.'

'Very well.'

'And pursuing the same theme, our plan to affright the Danes will all be undone unless we display our resolution and capability. If the troops land, they'll be seen with guns, field pieces and mortars in numbers to convince them that we can level the city if we choose.'

Portland intervened hesitantly, 'This does seem a frightful thing to contemplate. Can we not achieve our ends by other means?'

'Not possible,' Canning said flatly. 'All avenues have been explored diplomatically. The Danes are obdurate and unmoving, saying they will not be seen to align with any power.'

'And your intelligence would seem to indicate they are, and with Bonaparte.'

'I'd conceive they fear Boney more than they respect us, Prime Minister.'

'I see. Well . . .'

Castlereagh continued briskly, 'Then we have the question of command. Is it to be a naval affair, as last time with Nelson, or . . .?'

'There are more recent precedents,' Mulgrave said. 'The taking of the Cape, Buenos Aires. If the matter is settled without assault, the navy will remain in command. Should there be a landing, the general once ashore assumes direction over his troops and the two are in a state of co-operation. I see no difficulty.'

'On a point of practicality . . .' the red-faced lord privy seal, Westmorland, intervened fussily. 'Where the devil are all these soldiers to come from?'

Castlereagh was ready. 'Sir, we have the lamentable situation whereby Sweden, our only ally, has been obliged to call on our assistance in what amounts to an evacuation of its last continental territory in Pomerania, not so very far from where they'll be needed. In addition, therefore, to those of the Stralsund garrison, we may call upon quantities of the most loyal King's German Legion all in good order, and with our military in readiness in the kingdom, we shall be tolerably well served, I believe.'

Portland coughed pitiably into a handkerchief, but then spoke firmly. 'Ah, yes. Then it seems, gentlemen, we have a measure of agreement. A more positive attitude in you, it must be said, which I'm glad to see. In essence, therefore, we are seeking to request the Danes to cede custody of their fleet to us for the duration of the war, nothing more. No territorial demands, forced alliances or any other form of coercion. They shall then be left in peace to conduct their trade and relations as they see fit. A firm and decisive move that, I have no doubt, will give heart to all those who groan under the tyrant's yoke. Upon this point therefore I would ask the secretary of state for war to produce plans for an expedition such as we've been discussing with a view to their implementation in the very near future.'

A dignified robed figure at the end of the table stirred. 'Prime Minister, there is a compelling matter to dispose of before we embark on a course of action in this tenor.'

'Yes, Lord Eldon?' Portland said warily.

This was the lord high chancellor of England, senior law lord and one who could make things very difficult for a government bent on rapid but contentious measures.

'I'm obliged to point out that any operation of a military nature by His Majesty's arms must necessarily be undertaken in his name. What this meeting is here contemplating is an act of force, of compulsion if you will, against a legally blameless neutral. I insist, sir,' he declared, with ponderous deliberation, 'that the wishes of His Majesty be known in this before anything further is committed.'

'An astute and, may I say, prudent course, Lord Chancellor. I shall seek audience with the King at the earliest possible time.'

Chapter 31

Canning stood warily in the doorway. 'You wanted to see me, Prime Minister.'

'Yes. Please come in, sir.' Portland gestured absently to a seat opposite in the empty Cabinet Room. 'We have a little, ah, difficulty to face.' He looked up with a frown. 'His Majesty has scruples concerning this action that are wholly to his credit. He conceives that a descent on Denmark without warning will bring down odium on Great Britain from friend and foe alike.'

'You impressed upon His Majesty the doleful necessity of so doing, of course.'

'I rehearsed the reasons both strategical and political and was graciously accorded a fair hearing. While acceding to the grave imperatives of our circumstances, he nevertheless wishes that every avenue for a diplomatic settlement be made before we—'

'In course you told him that we've deployed every argument, persuasion and threat in our possession but the damned Danish are mesmerised by Bonaparte and will not yield an inch.'

'Nevertheless he insists that, before any display of aggressive intent, we take positive steps to ensure that the Danish court is made fully aware of the consequences.'

Canning's face tightened. 'Prime Minister! He must be made to see that any delay – even of days – can result in our surprise being set aside, resulting in Bonaparte making a pre-emptive attack. I implore you, sir, if—'

'Foreign Secretary! I beg you will remember whom you are talking of. His Majesty is well aware of the cost of delay but is suggesting a different mode from the diplomatic, more a personal approach.'

'Personal?' Canning choked.

'Quite. May I bring you to remembrance that the King of Denmark, Christian VII, married his sister? King George has every desire and cause to preserve amity between our two crowns. He proposes the immediate dispatch of an emissary charged with laying the facts before His Danish Majesty, one untainted by motives of politics or statecraft in any form. In short, a noble of impeccable ancestry who will speak plainly and discreetly and in courtly form.'

'Where will you find such a paragon, sir? I demand to know!'

'Leave that to me, sir,' Portland said smoothly. 'To achieve his object I would have thought it most necessary that he not be seen to be associated with your office in any way.'

'Be damned to it! How will I know what he's up to if he's not reporting to me?'

'The answer is simple. You may mount your expedition, sail the armada to the Sound and lie in dreadful array, but His Majesty will not countenance any motions against the kingdom of Denmark until the emissary specifically reports that he has failed.'

Chapter 32

Sheerness, Isle of Sheppey, England

It seemed he was not to be suffered to rejoin his ship without the most punctilious ceremony. Watched by a gathering crowd, and accompanied by the martial thump and clash of a military band, Captain Sir Thomas Kydd boarded his barge at the steps of the harbour.

The boat was new varnished, picked out in scarlet and green; even the oars were delicately tipped in white and the tiller worked with decorative knots. The boat's crew were kitted in smart black and yellow striped jerseys, blank expressions on each sea-weathered face. His coxswain Halgren's usual characterful sea headwear was now a smart low-crowned black hat, with an elaborate *Tyger* to the fore, picked out in gold thread.

Kydd stood for a moment to acknowledge the crowd's adulation, then gave the order to put off for the stirring vision of the powerful frigate at anchor by the point.

Tyger was in such different shape from what she'd been those weeks ago when she'd faced three of her kind in a battle to the finish. Given priority by a gratified Admiralty, her hurts had quickly been made good and no expense spared to bring her to a distinguished splendour – bright-sided, gun-port lids in scarlet, new bunting, and her figurehead a dazzling white and gold.

Such a contrast with the mutiny-ship he had first come aboard. Now there was no row-guard slowly circling, no boarding nettings rigged to deter desperate men from deserting, no dowdy neglect or decrepit makeshift: she was the picture of a prime frigate in the first line of securing freedom of the seas for Great Britain's widening empire.

When Halgren's answering bellow, '*Tyger!*' had formally advised the frigate of her commander's approach, there was an instant response. To the urgent rattle of drums men swarmed up the shrouds in a disciplined rush. Reaching the fighting tops, they extended out along each yard-arm and, clasping hands, stood motionless.

Coming aboard, from the corner of his eye Kydd took in the figure of Stirk, standing with the side party. There was a tiny flicker of conspiratorial recognition on the hard face, then a return of the blank countenance. They'd had rare times ashore in Scotland but it was clear that this would never be touched on. Kydd was the captain, back in *his* rightful domain; Toby Stirk, gunner's mate, just where *he* wanted to be.

There was a moment's stillness. Then the figure at the mainmast head, the highest point of all, raised his cap and whirled it about with a cry. From two hundred throats came an answer: the full-hearted roar of a cheer – and another, and another.

Kydd stood bare-headed, his mind charged with emotion as the noise volleyed and echoed in the anchorage. This was his ship, and he and her company were now indisputably one with her.

As he entered his cabin Tysoe, with impeccable bearing, took his boat-cloak and gold-laced bicorne. Kydd settled with a sigh into his favourite armchair at the stern windows. As if by magic a plate of delicate caraway biscuits had appeared on the occasional table at his side, with a single glass of Manzanilla Pasada.

The great cabin was transformed. The stored furniture from *L'Aurore*, his previous command, had been sent for, the Argand lamps, miniatures, ornaments – even the ornate multi-compartmented escritoire. Silver gleamed on the sideboard and the central table shone in a deep lustrous mahogany. His bedplace now held a proper cot, and the washstand was equipped with all of the conveniences that a gentleman of fashion could possibly desire.

Another sigh escaped. In the short time that had passed since *L'Aurore* had been in the Caribbean, Fortune had both smiled and frowned on him.

Chapter 33

That evening Kydd dined his officers in his great cabin. He entered in full dress uniform, resplendent in sash and star. Without a word all rose in respect until he had taken his chair.

Kydd sat in affable humour, but there was no getting away from it: he was being held in a reverence bordering on hero-worship. He didn't know whether to be irritated or touched but one thing was clear: it had put a distance between himself and them. Would Dillon, his confidential secretary, who had not yet arrived back on board, be in the same thrall to one whom history had singled out for notice?

After the murmured toasts a deferential silence descended once again. Kydd tried small-talk with his first lieutenant, Bray. The man rumbled a polite reply in monosyllables while the table waited: it was tradition that no officer might address the captain unless spoken to first, but this didn't mean they couldn't talk among themselves.

The first dishes were brought in and wine poured. Still

the stiff formality. The dinner progressed, an elegant repast. The cloth was drawn and a stoppered decanter of port was placed before the mess president. An awestruck Mr Vice intoned the loyal toast and glasses were raised.

Everyone sat rigid.

Something had to be done. Excusing himself to the president Kydd left the great cabin. He returned shortly with a smug expression. Out of sight beyond the polished bulkhead there was movement and into the respectful quiet came the sound of a violin, experimentally drawing long chords before launching into a lively tune. Then, a fine voice broke into song. It was Ned Doud, quartermaster's mate and long ago shipmate of Tom Kydd. His once-youthful timbre was now broad and full and he sang powerfully, with feeling, the old forebitter favourite, 'The Saucy *Arethusa*':

> '*Come all ye jolly sailors bold,*
> *Whose hearts are cast in honour's mould,*
> *While English glory I unfold,*
> *Huzzah for the* Arethusa!'

The officers looked about, bemused. Kydd watched, waiting for reaction. Then he slapped his glass down and sang lustily, in a fine baritone:

> '*Let each fill a glass*
> *To his fav'rite lass;*
> *A health to the Capt'n and officers true,*
> *And all that belong to the jovial crew*
> *On board of the* Arethusa!'

Brice, the boatswain, and the gunner took up the refrain, waving their glasses in time with the music but the others hesitated.

Kydd roared out, 'Mermaid!'

The capstan fiddler launched the sprightly tune and the hidden Doud lifted up his voice:

> '*One Friday morn, when we set sail,*
> *And our ship not far from land;*
> *We there did espy a fair pretty maid*
> *With a comb and a glass in her hand, her hand, her hand –*
> *With a comb and a glass in her hand.*

> '*While the raging seas did roar,*
> *And the stormy winds did blow . . .*'

This time there was no hanging back in the calamitous tale of the ship that dared sail on a Friday – producing, in the confined space of the cabin, a deafening roar of good humour.

It was not until much later in the evening that the gathering broke up.

Chapter 34

Yarmouth Roads, Norfolk

It was a bare day's sail to Yarmouth, through blue seas and a quartering breeze. In accordance with her resumed commission, *Tyger* was to rejoin the North Sea squadron directly after making her number with the naval base.

To Kydd's surprise, not only the squadron but Admiral Russell's flagship and a surprising number of battleships and other vessels were crowded into Yarmouth Roads. Coming to a smart moor in the wreathing smoke of their salute, Kydd wasted no time in reporting his ship to the admiral.

'Do sit, m' boy. So glad t' see you. Sherry?'

Russell was brief and to the point. The squadron was recalled from station off the Dutch coast for a particular service of grave importance, which would be revealed in due course. They would be part of a larger force to be sent on a mission into the Baltic under the command of a senior admiral. Beyond that he was not at liberty to say.

'Baltic? Surely they don't think to—'

'Don't tease the brain so, Kydd. It'll out in the end, and then I promise it will confound everyone. Be so good as to victual and store for a month or two, and we sail to join the main fleet in a few days.'

'Main fleet! Then this—'

'All will be made clear when we rendezvous at Gothenburg. I beg you will leave me to my work – I'm sore over-pressed you must believe.'

That afternoon Dillon arrived on board. He was met by a buzz of excitement and speculation; every member of *Tyger*'s crew had an opinion on what the future held.

Whatever was in the offing was of great moment: ships were joining by the hour, both great and small, summoned for an event that promised to be noticed by the world.

Kydd welcomed him warmly. 'Good to see you, Edward.' He motioned him to a seat. 'You had a fair liberty, I trust?'

'Well enough, Sir Thomas,' he said, taking the other comfortable chair in Kydd's cabin. 'I had a mind to look up a friend, take refuge in his books. Can't understand the fellow, not to be abroad and hoisting in life at the first hand.'

Kydd grinned. 'Some will have it that way, I've no idea why.'

'Sir, there's quantities of rumours afloat as to our destiny. I don't suppose . . .'

'We're at three days' notice for sea, and now you know as much as I, your captain.'

Chapter 35

Captain Kydd's officers' invitation to join them for dinner had not been unexpected, and as he took his seat at the head of the table in the gunroom, he was not unaware of the silent presence of seamen and marine servants, agog for every word.

After the customary pleasantries he launched straight in: 'I'm desolated to tell you that their lordships have not seen fit to inform me of their intentions. That is a fact. And so your views on what will be are as well to the point as any I might conjure.'

Surprisingly it was the sailing master, Joyce, who first spoke. 'We're not for Europe, that's lost t' us. No, gennelmen, there's only one design worthy o' this cloud o' battleships an' similar.'

A suspicious gunroom waited for him to continue.

'Why, not islands in the Caribbee but the whole sea! It's Spanish Florida, that's where! You take Florida, you're gate-keeper to the sugar islands as can't be beat. I've a friend there, tells me them Indians and settlers can't wait t' be set free and would welcome we British and—'

'I respectfully disagree,' Dillon came in. The cabin turned to him in interest. 'There's only one thing of consequence that's happened which warrants such a show of naval muscle.'

'Tilsit?'

'Just so. The treaty is a master-stroke of Bonaparte that sets Tsar Alexander's face against his old ally. What we're seeing is an assembly of might that's to sail into the Baltic to check Russia's ambitions and demonstrate that we're still a force to be reckoned with.'

It was received with a murmur of respect, until a quiet but insistent voice intervened: 'I'm not one to dispute strategics with a scholar, as we must say, but there's a difficulty.'

'Say on, Mr Brice,' Kydd called encouragingly.

'If we take a look from the deck, we don't see a naval squadron as can fight a Ruskie fleet. There's transports, bombs, frigates and sloops. And of 'em all, I say the transports are the tell-tale. They've soldiers aboard, and this can't be but a landing. It has to be Hanover, the Austrian Netherlands, who knows? Anything to distract Mr Bonaparte.'

The following morning brought still more ships and a rare sight for Yarmouth: several columns of marching redcoats, the faint sounds of martial bands carrying out to the watching sailors, the heady thump of the drums suddenly ceasing when they reached the open spaces to the north.

Within a short time tent cities had been erected and the wisps of cooking fires arose. These soldiers would not board the gathering transports until the last minute to preserve victuals and water. Another column arrived from a different direction, this time led by a headquarters staff all a-glitter and mounted on black horses. Later, even more soldiers marched in, but by that time the novelty had worn off and *Tyger* continued with her routines.

Kydd saw no reason to go ashore and took the time to read his passage orders once again – really, a direct voyage to Gothenburg, and *Tyger* knew the way.

A knock at the door broke into his thoughts. It was the young master's mate whom he'd seen mature so quickly in the striving and destruction of *Tyger*'s recent action.

'Mr Maynard?'

'Sir. I've been passed a note and, well, sir, it seems my brother is with the 52nd in camp ashore. He's to sail with the expedition and desires he might see me before we leave. Sir, it would—'

'Certainly you shall,' Kydd replied. 'Back aboard by gunfire, mind.'

Chapter 36

The shore boat had waited and Master's Mate David Maynard lost no time in boarding it, conscious of a lifting warmth at the prospect of seeing his younger brother – and in army uniform. It was hard to imagine the sensitive, fine-featured Francis in the red coat of a soldier.

He'd heard of it from his parents, who'd despaired of keeping the boy in the family business with news of such dire peril for England in the newspapers every day. They had found a vacancy for an ensign in a regiment of light infantry and purchased a commission for him.

David had a spasm of guilt at the thought that Francis had probably been swept up in the tales of heroism and victory with which he'd regaled his brother on leave and didn't want the elder to bear all the glory. Now he would find out the other face of war.

Yarmouth was heaving with soldiery. Some glanced at him curiously but a sentry amiably pointed out the encampment where the 52nd might be found.

It wasn't long before he saw striding towards him a proud

and resplendent junior officer, who snatched off his tall, plumed shako and swept down in a low bow. 'David!' he cried. 'I'm so glad you could come.'

The sailor eyed his younger brother in a mix of envy and pride. The lobsterbacks certainly knew how to cut a figure: red coat ornamented with silver, buff breeches and long black gaiters; a high collar with silver gorget, and crossbelt, the gilt belt plate embossed with a bugle-horn and the number '52'; a scarlet sash around the waist. A fearsome curved regimental sabre nestled on his left hip.

Catching his glance, Francis made a wry grimace. 'Better part of four guineas, brother, the damn villains.'

Despite his seven years' sea service David was not yet entitled to bear a sword but kept his views to himself. In his plain blue frock coat with its single row of polished brass buttons, relieved only by discreet white piping, and his perfectly plain round black hat, he was no match for this vision.

'Shall we lift a jar together, bro? The chaps of the mess rather favour the Star and Mermaid.'

They walked off together to town. Salutes were thrown to the young military officer, who acknowledged them airily.

'Have you been told our destination at all?' Francis asked.

'As I hoped you would know. All the fleet's in a taking.'

'It must be an occasion – why, with your Kydd o' *Tyger* and our Major General Wellesley it's set fair to be as entertaining as any venture I've heard of.'

The touching hint of bravado brought out a surge of protectiveness. 'Shall we leave aside the supposing, Francis? I'd like to hear more how you're faring as a redcoat.'

The taphouse was overflowing and they were content to sit in the sun on the outside benches.

A foam-topped jug and tankards arrived and they toasted each other, David covertly sizing up his brother. So young and innocent, taken with writing and poetry, those big brown eyes the same, childlike and artless. He hoped the junior officers' mess, or whatever a cockpit was in the army, was less barbarous to the untainted than in his own experience.

'So you took the King's shilling. What did you then?'

'The 52nd is a light infantry regiment.' Francis waited for understanding, then, not seeing it, explained, 'We're different from your regular line regiment. They stand in mass against the enemy with volleys of musketry. We go out on our own in groups to harass the enemy and . . . other things.'

David grinned. 'No doubt a mort to take on board.'

'A quantity of field commands you'll believe. All passed by bugle-horn and drums. And drills – my God, every day we drill, rain or shine. Two things – musket and manoeuvre. Firelock exercise by number until we can do it blindfold, then still more. Marching – forming fours, column to line, line to square and such all day long. At Shorncliffe – that's our home – Colonel Moore will not have it other than every officer new to the regiment does fall in with the men and drill with them until he's satisfied. A good notion, I'm persuaded, as will bring respect. Then it's to be advanced exercise. For the light bobs, it's things like advancing in extended order while firing so each may cover his fellow.'

'So now you're a regular-borne officer.'

'To be clear, I'm to take a body of men with the adjutant through any or all field evolution by word of command until he's happy to let me loose on the enemy. And, as you see,

I'm with my regiment now on active service. Ensign Francis Maynard,' he added, tasting the words. 'Of the second battalion, the 52nd Regiment of Foot.' There was pride and immense satisfaction in his voice.

'Aye. Francis – I'm proud of you.' David leaned across and gripped his brother's hand.

For some moments they did not speak. Then Francis said, in a low voice, 'David. We'll be on our way very soon. We . . . we may not have a chance to see each other again. You'll tell Mama that—'

'Of course, dear fellow.'

'It's just that . . .' He paused. 'Well, to tell it straight, David, you've seen the enemy, you've taken fire and had men fall by your side. Not once, but many times.'

'Not so many, old chap.'

'What I'm trying to say is that I've never even had a Frenchman make a face in my direction, let alone look down his musket at me with death in his heart. I – I'm an officer, but how can I know I'll behave well when it, er, happens? Dear brother, is there anything you hold to that . . . takes you through . . . to the other side?'

David was at a loss for words. They were only a brace of years apart in age but an aeon in what they'd lived through. Should he reply with words of glory and honour or tell it as it really was – stark terror conquered only by the burning need not to let his shipmates down?

'Really, dear fellow, it's not so bad. Once you get into the battle, you've too much to worry on to get a fit of the frighteners.' This was at least half right. 'And all there's left to remember is what you're taught and go at it like a good 'un,' he finished lamely.

What was a tender, innocent soul like Francis doing in the

midst of the hellish cauldron of mortal combat? He managed a small smile. 'We'll meet afterwards and have a rollicking good time, won't we at all!'

'Right, David. I won't let you down, I promise . . .'

Chapter 37

Three days later *Tyger* sailed with the tide. Flank escort for a war convoy of more than eighty ships, she found herself to starboard of a sea crowded with sail, set and drawing for Sweden where they were to rendezvous and come under the orders of the commander-in-chief, Admiral Lord Gambier.

In warm summer sun and calm seas it was a bare three days before the distinctive hexagonal white lighthouse of the Skaw was raised, the northernmost tip of Denmark. It was a seamark of legend. Around the point, roils of discoloured water showed where the mouth of the Baltic met the open ocean.

The convoy did not delay, heading directly across the forty-mile entrance to the opposite shore until the Vinga beacon was raised. Ahead lay Sweden and Gothenburg.

There they were met with a sight that took the breath away. Anchored in those outer roads to Gothenburg was a huge fleet, an uncountable number of ships of all kinds, hundreds in warships alone, comparable to Nelson's Trafalgar fleet, but with store-ships and transports amounting to far more.

In the centre was the largest. This was the expedition they were to join and the ship was the stately 98-gun *Prince of Wales*, flying the flag of Admiral Gambier.

While they waited for the busy aviso cutters to bring orders out to the newcomers, there was time to take in more of the spectacle.

'There's *Agamemnon* as I'm not a Dutchman,' Joyce said, and gleefully began his yarn about the time he had seen Nelson in the admiral's favourite ship.

Second Lieutenant Bowden had been a midshipman in *Victory* at Nelson's final battle and had lived through much. 'That seventy-four beyond *Prince*,' he said quietly, '*Mars*, as I last saw taking fire from five battleships around her. She didn't strike but lost her captain.'

'She's always been forward in any kind of action,' Brice said, with feeling. 'We were too late to assist when she took on *Hercule* seventy-four near the Pointe du Raz in a wicked state o' tide.'

Knowing looks were exchanged: the frightful reefs and rocks on the Brest blockade were well feared.

'Fought her to the finish – the Frenchy sees more'n three hundred drop and had to douse her flag. Pity of it is that Captain Hood didn't live to see it.'

Bowden came in again: 'Some other fine acquaintances I spy. Isn't that *Vanguard*? As will stay with me for all my days on this earth, as a new-breeched midshipman I saw her, masts by the board, being carried on to the rocks in Sardinia, Horatio Nelson being sent to his doom. Captain Ball in *Alexander* tries to pass a tow but he's sent away to save himself. He ignores Our Nel's orders and, in a right welter of seas, tries again and again. Only when the water's shoaling fast does he get a line across and hauls her clear.'

'And shortly goes on in her to immortality at the Nile,' Kydd said, behind him.

'Oh, hello, sir. Didn't see you standing there.'

The others fell back respectfully.

'Well, finish the count.'

'Sir?'

'Isn't that *Goliath* I see two astern of her? As signal luff in *Tenacious*, I do remember well her going in first at the Nile. She it was under Foley who thought to pass inshore of the line to take 'em on both sides and win the battle.'

'Aye, but over there's a lady beats 'em all f'r the smelling o' powder,' Joyce said, pointing.

'*Orion*?'

'Sir. Was wi' ye at the Nile, but as well at y'r Glorious First o' June, at St Vincent – even Trafalgar she made sure she were there.'

Such a roll-call of history. Were they to go on to further glory, conceivably against the Russians to free the Baltic?

A cutter interrupted from alongside with instructions for mooring and the spell was broken.

Chapter 38

At anchor, Gothenburg Roads

The expected signal, 'All captains', was hung out promptly, the Yarmouth accession to strength being the last contingent to join.

Piped aboard through the entry-port to the middle gun-deck of *Prince of Wales*, Kydd could see the flagship was in an advanced state of readiness. Were they expecting trouble this early?

There was a welcome on the crowded quarterdeck: Gambier and no less than four other flag officers.

Kydd paid his respects to the unsmiling, formal commander-in-chief, aware that this was a careful-to-the-point-of-cautious admiral whose devotion to the Good Book had earned him the nickname 'Dismal Jimmy' from irreverent sailors.

There was one other rear admiral he recognised instantly.

'Why, well met, sir!' Kydd said warmly, crossing to the figure. This man had been captain of *Triumph* in which Kydd had served before the mast as master's mate. After the bloody battle of Camperdown it was he who'd given Kydd the acting lieutenancy that had set him on the path to where he was

133

today. The two had last met shortly before the politically charged court-martial of Commodore Popham.

Essington beamed. 'Why, how singularly gratifying to be noticed by the hero of the hour. And now returned to the scene of his apotheosis?'

'As I will be in the finest company,' Kydd replied stoutly. 'And you, sir, untimely recalled from retirement? Shame on their lordships.'

He knew another: Commodore Keats, whose name would be for ever linked with that of his famous ship *Superb*. In a single action he had taken on not one but two monstrous 112-gun Spanish four-deckers. In the gathering darkness he'd left them firing into each other and sailed on to take a third.

As a junior frigate captain Kydd had been with Keats as part of the fabled race across the Atlantic by Nelson, missing the French fleet by hours until the fateful meeting off Spain weeks later. To his mortification Keats and *Superb* had not been at the battle but had nevertheless gone on to further distinction.

'Sir Thomas,' Keats greeted him coolly. 'An honour to have you with us.' His hard expression belied his words.

Kydd picked up on the stiffness. Surely this great seaman was not to be numbered with the envious. He considered bringing out shared remembrance of the immortal commander but thought better of it and murmured a polite reply.

The admiral's day cabin in the flagship was barely furnished with a vast table stretching right athwart. At it sat the senior captains, those of the line-of-battle ships. Lesser mortals took chairs provided behind.

When all had found their places Gambier entered and sat at the head. At the opposite end, oddly, there was an empty chair. With peculiarly precise movements he ordered his papers in front of him, then looked up. 'Gentlemen. I will not keep you long.' He glanced at the crush of resplendent uniforms. 'This will be the first and last time we shall meet together as a whole. The purpose of my calling you here is to establish at the outset the objectives and methods of this expedition. After today you shall be severally in receipt of my orders and those of my subordinate commanders and will have no need to attend on me.'

He gave a thin smile. 'This is not to say that we shall not meet hospitably as from time to time the needs of the service allow but it must be understood that we are on a mission of the utmost significance to the safety of the kingdom.'

Polite expressions of attention were all he was going to get from such seasoned warriors and he wasted no time in moving on. 'The sole objective of this expedition, gentlemen, is to secure the delivering of the fleet of the kingdom of Denmark into our custody.'

Now the faces about the table showed astonishment, puzzlement and blank incomprehension.

'I don't have to tell you that the result of Tilsit is to leave us alone and isolated in Europe but, worse than that, we have intelligence that Bonaparte now intends to combine the fleets he has at his disposal as a consequence of his conquests into an irresistible armada to throw at our islands.'

Gambier continued, 'And, further, he is casting a ring of iron around the entire continent, closing it to our trade. The key to his plans is Denmark. If he can coerce it into closing the entrance into the Baltic to us, we are placed in acute difficulties. Should we, however, be successful in removing the Danish fleet, then the means to close off the Sound is denied them. Not only that, but Denmark's fleet will no longer be available to Bonaparte. Therefore I will leave you in no doubt that this mission must succeed. There has never been such peril under which England now lies. It cannot fail.'

In the charged atmosphere Kydd found himself saying, 'Sir. Denmark is most certainly neutral. How can we ask this of them?'

Gambier's gaze was troubled. 'Your qualms do you credit, Sir Thomas, but these are harrowing times. In the first I'm persuaded that if the situation was reversed it's without question that Napoleon Bonaparte would not scruple in any wise to take measures against a neutral – he has done so before. And to the second, be advised that the government has considered the matter and takes the position that the greater hazard is to do nothing. The King shares your view but agrees on the imperative of action. This expedition is in his name.'

'But—' Captain Graves began.

'We are all, every one of us, in the King's service, sir. We do not question his orders.'

Gambier waited then went on, 'To which end, as you can see, I've been granted the best resources in ships and men the navy has at hand. As you may notice, we boast Keats of *Superb* and Kydd of *Tyger* . . .'

'Then you expect the Danes to contest the loss of their fleet?'

'They are an old and proud race, and will not yield lightly. We are therefore here arrayed in such force as will allow them to accede gracefully.'

'And if they do not, sir?'

'Then we make demonstration of our earnestness in the matter.'

'A sailing past of their capital?'

'No, sir, since they will feel safe behind their defences, which are now too great to be threatened from the sea. It will be achieved by a landing in strength on the island of Sjælland whereon it lies and a passive encirclement.'

'This is hard, sir. Monstrous hard!' Captain Colville came in. 'And on a blameless neutral – it were nothing less than an invasion.'

'Sir, I'll thank you to keep your feelings to yourself. I will hear no further discussion on this point. Our duty is clear and that is to secure their fleet by whatever means.'

'Then in terms of operations,' Graves insisted, 'if an encircling does not persuade?'

'The landings will be made with all impedimenta as if for a siege, with guns and materiel of investment. Nothing will be hidden and all will see the dread implements of beleaguerment poised on their inner flank. I rather fancy that terms will be accepted with some rapidity.'

'I've heard that Boney has thirty thousand under Bernadotte lying in readiness at the southern border. If it's heard . . .'

'He has, and that is why this expedition proceeds with the least possible delay. I'll now ask the captain of the fleet to outline the plans that concern you, gentlemen. Before he arrives I will point out that there is no other in the service as experienced in conjunct operations as he, and I beg you will attend his words with the utmost seriousness.'

Gambier muttered an aside to his flag lieutenant, who left to call the man who was at the centre of planning and execution of the entire expedition.

Kydd wondered why he'd felt it necessary to introduce him at length . . . then saw standing in the doorway, a light smile playing as he surveyed the assembled officers, Captain Home Riggs Popham.

There were gasps of astonishment and muttering, which Popham ignored as he took the empty chair. He turned from one to another, nodding and smiling for all the world as if renewing acquaintances. Kydd tensed but when his gaze came to him it was as if Popham had looked right through him. It bordered on the incredible, but it seemed that he had levered himself back to a position of trust and responsibility in the few months since he had been found guilty of quitting his station without leave at court-martial.

How had he achieved it?

Gambier broke in on Kydd's thoughts: 'Captain Popham, be so good as to outline the dispositions of the fleet in this enterprise.'

'Certainly, sir,' Popham said, with crisp efficiency. 'Your orders will tell you so, but in summary we have this. The main force, *Prince of Wales* flag under Lord Gambier, and myself first captain, remains offshore by way of deterrent should our business be disputed by the Russians or indeed the Danes. A squadron under the flag of Rear Admiral Essington, *Minotaur*, will be closer inshore and a roaming reserve will be held under Vice Admiral Stanhope in *Pompée*.

'Bombs and lesser craft will be ordered by Commodore Hood in *Centaur* but the most important task of all is left to Commodore Keats.' He looked up to give him a winning smile.

To Kydd's puzzlement, he saw that Keats had reddened.

'This distinguished officer is given the singular duty of sealing off the island of Sjælland while our little enterprise is under way to prevent undesirable interference from the outside – the French and similar. I need hardly say how inconvenient it would be should our land forces be set upon from behind.'

There was more: signal codes, squadron liaison, watering, stores, order of battle. All dealt with ably and decisively.

Gambier nodded. 'Thank you, Captain Popham. Do please return to your work. We won't detain you further.'

With another genial smile, Popham picked up his lists and left.

In seconds the cabin was in bedlam with one voice raised above the rest. 'Sir, this is insupportable!' Keats exploded, slamming his hand on the table and glaring at Gambier, who winced. 'We are to be made inferiors to – to such? It's not to be borne, sir!'

So Keats was one of Popham's inveterate enemies. It explained his coolness to Kydd, who'd been quoted in print in his defence.

Hood came in with unsettling intensity: 'He has a point, sir. There are at least three distinguished captains about this table with many years' more seniority who have been overborne by his elevation.'

'And I'm reminded that this officer has never commanded a ship in action,' Stopford, an elderly battleship captain, spluttered. 'Added to which I'm exercised as to how an officer lately condemned by a court-martial is suffered to rise to prominence so. Sir, I do protest – if he persists in command, you shall have this in writing.'

'And mine,' echoed several others.

Gambier's expression tightened. 'I will not tolerate any further discussion in this vein. The appointment of Sir Home Popham follows my application to their lordships for the most suitable officer experienced in combined operations. The name of this officer was put forward with other recommendations – the Duke of York was mentioned in this regard.'

Kydd smiled cynically. So that was how it had been done:

Popham had gone over the heads of the Admiralty to curry favour with the head of the army directly. Ironically, he *was* the leading contender for the post, with more experience and practical understanding of the difficulties of amphibious warfare than any other present.

'Therefore I'll make it abundantly clear. The orders of Captain Popham are to have the same force as if issued by myself. If any of you cannot accept this, you shall be removed and another put in your place.'

As a threat it had no meaning: these senior captains knew their duty and would conform. The protests in writing would no doubt come but would not affect the present situation, leaving only rancour and animosity to bedevil the expedition.

Gambier pointedly pulled out his fob watch and frowned. 'We shall pass on to other matters. The army of twenty-four thousand is currently embarked in readiness to land, should the Danes prove obdurate. They are commanded by General Lord Cathcart, who I'd hoped would be in a position to apprise you of their role. He is indisposed at present and begs to allow his second in command to perform that duty.'

He nodded to the flag lieutenant, who left quickly.

'This will be Major General Sir Arthur Wellesley, a soldier of distinction, who I'll allow is well connected with the government. Hard service in the Netherlands and remarkable successes in India, he's much talked of by Horse Guards.'

A tall, lean figure in a red tunic, with restrained frogging, and white pantaloons tucked into hessian boots, appeared at the door.

'Sir Arthur, you're welcome indeed. Do take your seat.'

As he passed by, Kydd was struck by his air of patrician disdain and the intensity of his bearing. He would not be a man to cross.

He found his chair but remained standing, austere and reserved. 'General Cathcart desires I should lay before you his dispositions, should the Danes not acquiesce to our demands.'

Without referring to notes, he rapped, 'Three divisions will be landed, the first under Lieutenant General Sir George Ludlow, with a brigade of the Coldstream Guards and one of the 79th to the left of the siege lines, the second under Lieutenant General Sir David Baird, with three brigades, to the right.'

That had Kydd's special notice. Baird had been governor of Cape Colony after leading the army of conquest against the Dutch and was eminently qualified for the kind of service to be expected here. But he'd been removed from his post and never again employed at that level, following his support for the seizing of Buenos Aires – talked into it by Popham . . .

'The third division will be led by myself, with elements of the 95th and others, and will be responsible for outer defence. Cavalry in the amount of three squadrons of dragoons will be under Major General Linsing, and four brigades of the King's German Legion will be available to us for general deployment.'

He paused, as though choosing his words. 'To establish to the Danes our resolve in the matter, we are landing artillery and engineers in numbers conformable to an investment of significance. Major General Bloomfield will field eighty-four guns and a further hundred and one siege pieces, including mortars and similar. These will be deployed in open array should negotiations prove unfruitful.'

Cold, professional and precise. If the Danish command chose to defy the British it would be a desperate affair for them, Kydd reflected, with a shiver.

'Thank you, General. I rather think it will not come to that, but you never know.'

Wellesley took his leave, and Gambier let the rumble of comment die. 'So there you have it, gentlemen. You may believe I'd rather the sight of our grand fleet will be sufficient to persuade, but if not, these are the steps we will take. You should be comforted to know that my own authority to proceed in any action is suspended indefinitely, until I receive positive advice from an emissary of the King that a settlement is impossible.'

The trigger that would send this great armada into an unknown conclusion with the Danes.

'We sail tomorrow morn, by which time you will have your orders. It leaves me only with the prayer that our Lord in Heaven will see fit to order our future to the greater good of our cause.'

Chapter 39

Eskdale Hall, Wiltshire

Renzi looked up from his desk. 'Yes?'

The footman stepped into the library, bearing a silver tray. The card that lay upon it was plain and discreet: a Colonel Devenant, the address, Whitehall, London.

Commoners simply did not call on the aristocracy when it suited them – but the address gave Renzi pause. It was not outside the bounds of possibility that . . . 'I will see him.'

Dressed quietly in town clothes, the jolly-looking man came up from his bow with a flourish. 'Lord Farndon, I do apologise for my intrusion, which Mr Congalton assured me you would forgive.'

Renzi knew Congalton was a highly placed official at the Foreign Office, dealing with clandestine affairs. Controlling his mounting feeling, he enquired evenly, 'You've travelled far? Perhaps some refreshment.'

'Thank you, my lord. A dish of tea would answer admirably.'

The footman left quietly.

'You've come for a reason.'

'I have, my lord, and one that presses. Are we at liberty to talk privily?'

'This is my library. We will not be disturbed. Please sit.'

'Your lordship will have heard of the affair at Tilsit.'

'Indeed.'

'There have since been developments of a grave nature that have caused the government to contemplate action of a . . . most serious character that they would wish it were in their power to forgo.'

'Go on, sir.'

'My lord, Mr Congalton desires me to enquire most sincerely after your constitution.'

It *was* a call – they wanted him.

With Cecilia's loving ministrations, Renzi had recovered from the harrowing experiences of his mission in Turkey to dislodge the French and he assured Devenant that he was in perfect health.

'Then I'm to say that there has arisen a service that you are peculiarly fitted to perform. Of a most weighty description and one that would be of the highest value to the Crown.'

'Pray, when shall this be?'

'It is of the most urgent nature. I'm not to quit your presence this day until I have an understanding – in the one or the other tenor.'

Renzi gave a half-smile: if he refused they would have time to find another.

But then the events in Constantinople returned in a rush – the loneliness, dread and fearful decisions that had ended in blood and turmoil. Could he face it again?

Congalton would not have asked it of him unless he thought he could do it, and would not have made an approach unless it was for a particularly compelling reason.

There was really only one answer.

'Very well. May I know the essence of the affair?'

'Your understanding, my lord, is greatly appreciated,' Devenant replied, with evident relief in his voice. 'The details will be laid before you by Mr Congalton himself.'

'So, a visit to London?'

'The matter is of the first importance, my lord. At the risk of importunity it were not too soon . . . this hour?'

'If such is the urgency.'

'My lord, you should not think to return for a little time. You may therefore find it convenient to arrange for your own and her ladyship's baggage to follow on.'

Renzi stiffened. 'The countess?'

'Her absence would be most unfortunate.'

'This is another matter entirely, sir! I will not have—'

'Dealing as it does with affairs at a royal level at which her absence would be remarked.'

'Royal?'

'My lord, I'm not in a position to be specific, but it were necessary you convey full court regalia with you, for yourself and her ladyship. And I can certainly say that, in the palace of the sovereign concerned, you may apprehend no danger to yourself or the countess, let me assure you.'

Chapter 40

'Cecilia, my dear.'

'Nicholas – I thought you were at your words again.' Cecilia rose from her household accounts and kissed him lightly.

'I was, and untimely interrupted.'

'That Jago again!' Cecilia frowned. She'd never taken to Eskdale's under-steward. 'You must get rid of the man, he's—'

'Not at all. My dearest, we have to talk. Time presses.'

'Oh?' she said, with unease.

'I . . . I've had a visitor. From London. I'm needed again.'

Her hand flew to her lips. 'You didn't say yes – did you? Please tell me you didn't!' Her eyes filled.

'This is of vital importance, and I'm told your husband is the one most suited for the mission.'

She blinked back the tears. 'Dear Nicholas! There are times when I feel you're too honourable for this world. Of course you must go.' She stiffened. 'And take me with you this time!'

Renzi shook his head sorrowfully. 'Darling, this affair is

at the highest level there can be. My wishes are not to be consulted in this, you see.'

'Oh. When will you go at all?' she said, in a small voice.

'The carriage is waiting.'

'No!' she gasped.

'For myself alone.'

'Nicholas!'

'You will follow later in the barouche.'

'Wha—?'

'I said, it is out of my hands, Cecilia. Your presence has been specifically desired and I could not refuse them.'

'You're a perfectly horrid man, Farndon!'

'Probably, dearest. But this time you'll be at my side in an occasion that I can say is of royal moment and of no hazard to be noticed.'

'Where—'

He put his finger to her lips. 'Later. Do direct our baggage be prepared for a court reception and audience in a land . . . said to be like our own climate. For only three weeks or so, shall we say? Oh, and your Hetty will no doubt be grateful for the airing. I must go now.'

Chapter 41

The Foreign Office, London

As he mounted the steps in Whitehall, Renzi pondered where the assignment had to be. Sweden, Denmark and Portugal were the only nations not at war with England. With Portugal being of a warmer clime and Sweden an open ally, this left neutral Denmark.

'My lord, so very kind in you to visit,' Congalton said, catching the eye of his clerk, who left, discreetly closing the door behind him.

'So, Copenhagen,' Renzi said crisply. 'To make a showing at King Christian's court as will convince him to turn his face against the blandishments of the Corsican.'

Congalton raised his eyebrows. 'Quite. Yet a little more than that, was our thinking. First, a customary appraisal of the situation that faces you.'

It was delivered in the same dry, elegant tone as before. The critical juncture of events that, if left to ripen, would end with Bonaparte sealing the Baltic and therefore the continent as a whole. The frightful prospect of above a hundred sail-of-the-line moving on England.

'There is then really no alternative to some form of action to break the building menace, save our treating for peace terms, which the prime minister has quite set his face against.'

'An action against the kingdom of Denmark, which is steadfast in its neutrality? Surely not, sir.'

'If we're not realists, my lord, we should not be in the business of meddling, but we are. Thus we recognise that, whatever the Danish might wish, their coercion into a league against us is not impossible. Recollect, they've done it before and, but for Admiral Nelson, we would be suffering now.'

'Then what kind of action is contemplated, pray?'

Congalton gave a thin smile. 'We require the Danes to make irrevocable pledge of the security of the Sound and therefore the Baltic.'

'By an alliance or alignment of interests? I cannot think that likely, sir.'

'Nevertheless, this is the only and final requirement of His Majesty's government. To this end a large fleet is assembled and will appear off Kronborg Castle to add weight to our request.'

'A species of threat.'

'Of persuasion.'

'Sir, you well know that my previous appearing was at Constantinople where Admiral Duckworth's grand fleet promising a bombardment was singularly unsuccessful in its object of cajolery.'

'The lesson was learned, my lord, do not doubt it. Therefore the fleet is equipped and stored for an expeditionary force of not less than twenty-five thousand troops, to be landed in siege of Copenhagen if all else fails.'

'Good God! Against a neutral country? The consequences

to our standing and reputation in every chancellery in Europe will be incalculable.'

'By this, you will now understand the extremity in which the government feels it has been placed. The gravity of the matter cannot be overestimated, sir.'

Renzi went cold. On the one hand it smacked of the kind of political gesture that had led to the dispatch of a fleet that had comprehensively ruined his mission to Constantinople. On the other it was difficult to see what alternative act could bring the necessary pressure to bear. 'Diplomacy is futile?'

'There has been nothing but prevarication. My lord, this is the last sanction and I cannot very well see how it may be avoided.'

'And if the Danes resist?'

'We fervently pray that they will see it in their best interest to comply with our request and enter pledge against our security.'

With growing unease, Renzi said carefully, 'Then what is my mission, pray?'

'This action has been suspended as of this date,' Congalton said, in an odd voice, 'at the peculiar desire of the King. It is his wish that we attempt a final rapprochement but on an entirely different plane. A personal emissary under the seals of His Majesty is to go to the Danish court to seek audience and beg, as king to king, that a way must be found to avoid a confrontation.'

'How can it work when—'

'The emissary will get an honest hearing, I'd believe.'

'I shall have the honour?'

Congalton nodded wordlessly.

'And how long is it supposed that I have to extract a pledge?'

'My lord, you will be the best judge of that. Shall we say that it will probably be to the point at which you consider further discussion meaningless?'

'At which?'

'You will have done your part and may withdraw.'

'And then?'

'Presumably a military posture will be suffered to go forward.'

His mission of personal emissary was a long shot, but worth taking if it in any way prevented a disastrous armed conclusion – and it would keep faith with the ageing King George, whom Renzi well respected. 'I'd be obliged, sir, if you would be good enough to summarise the points upon which I might base my arguments.'

'By all means, my lord.'

They were potent and several, but unspoken was the central dilemma: that the Danes were being intolerably torn between the two most powerful nations on the planet warring against each other and therefore would not dare to favour one above the other.

'Then the entire affair reduces to just one objective: that Denmark is induced to offer an earnest of security that will satisfy.'

'Quite.'

'I cannot well see how this can be achieved.'

'There is one alone that has sufficient merit, which can satisfy us in the particulars to allow our fleet to withdraw.'

'An aligning? But that will—'

'That the naval fleet of the kingdom of Denmark be temporarily placed in our custody for the period of this emergency.'

'They will never allow it.'

'There are several advantages, the chief of which is that Britain will be conciliated and will no longer threaten, and the other that without a fleet Denmark cannot enforce Bonaparte's will even if it wished, and therefore will no longer be of interest to him.'

'So our fleet in the Sound is a *force majeure* to which Denmark may honourably yield.'

'Indeed.'

It made sense, but depended on the Danes recognising their own best interests – and the manner in which it was offered.

'I see. Then I am to go to Copenhagen to play the courtier.'

'There are complications.'

Renzi sighed, then allowed a reluctant grin to show. 'Say on, dear fellow. There always are in these affairs.'

'Our own king's sister, the Danish king's consort, was caught in an illicit liaison with the court physician, one Struensee. He was barbarously executed while she was banished. You will not wish to make reference to her while you are there.'

'Oh.'

'And after you've paid your courtly duty to King Christian the Seventh you'll then be taking your leave and seeking out the true autocratic head of state who possesses all the powers you will need.'

'Not the King?'

'As to His Majesty, the King of Denmark and Norway, for some time he has been declared for all intents and purposes insane. You will not be desiring to discuss high strategy in his presence.'

Renzi waited.

'Instead you will be seeking out Crown Prince Frederik who is de facto regent, possessing all kingly powers.'

'Ah.'

'He will not be in Copenhagen, rather in Kiel, well to the south, where he broods over his army, which faces the French multitudes across the border.'

'Then their government – prime minister and cabinet or similar. If—'

'You are not a representative of the British government in any capacity and will have no dealings with politicians or diplomats. You are an emissary of King George the Third and are above such creatures.'

'Quite.'

'Besides which there are none of that ilk. Denmark is autocratically governed from the King's own hand and does not trouble with parliaments.'

'Um, yes.'

'You may, however, be approached by one of the Bernstorff brothers.'

'Who are?'

'Joachim is a minister in Copenhagen, Christian the foreign minister, with the Crown Prince in Kiel. Both are of long standing and implacably loyal.'

'Our own representation?'

'One Benjamin Garlike, whom the Foreign Office suspects of weakness and is in the process of replacing.'

'The French?'

'Théodore Gobineau, Comte de Mirabeau – a tawdry Bonaparte confection only, for venal services rendered. Chargé d'affaires and irredeemably corrupt but beware – for some reason he has the ready ear of Bonaparte.'

'Staff?'

'Not so very many. The Danes won't allow it.'

'Their position?'

'Pressing strongly for Denmark to join the Continental Blockade, which is equally firmly resisted. I fancy, however, you will have no difficulties with them while Bonaparte still has business to conclude in east Prussia. Then it will be another matter – do observe that the window of opportunity is rapidly closing, sir.'

Chapter 42

The Sound, entrance to the Baltic

After the grey bluster of the North Sea, the calm and glitter of the Kattegat was a welcome change. The ship loosed more sail for the quick run south between Sweden to the left and Denmark to the right, heading for where the entrance to the Baltic became the strategic narrows known as the Sound.

For centuries Denmark had levied toll on the flood of shipping that passed through the sea highway to Estonia, Prussia, Stockholm, the medieval Hanseatic states, St Petersburg and the realms of the Tsar of All the Russias.

At the most confined passage a great fortress ringed with guns dominated the waters – Kronborg, massive and brooding.

Scores of ships were undertaking the transit but all made due obeisance, their barque being no exception, striking topsails in salute and anchoring while the formalities of the Sound toll were set in train.

'This, my dear, is your Denmark,' Renzi said, as the sights spread out before him.

On his arm, Cecilia looked up at him tenderly. 'Darling, the very first time we've been together on – on an adventure!' she breathed.

Wide-eyed, Hetty stood respectfully at a distance and tried to take it all in. 'I've never ventured out of England,' she cried. 'I'm so excited.'

The master came up and removed his hat. 'M' lord, I'm to step ashore and pay m' dues.'

'So this is . . .?'

'Helsingør, so please you, m' lord.' He added that they were still some twenty-five miles from Copenhagen.

Renzi touched Cecilia's hand. 'Do look across and see what you will, my dear.'

She shaded her eyes. 'Why, it's a little town, just tucked behind the point and in front there's a remarkable big square building with spires . . .'

'Indeed. You're now looking into Elsinore – Shakespeare's *Hamlet, Prince of Denmark* comes to mind. And your edifice is none other than the mighty castle and grim battlements of Kronborg, where it all took place.'

'Oh, Nicholas – it's only just there across the water, so near. Can we not visit?'

Renzi allowed that it would be of value to observe these iconic fortifications at the first hand.

He turned to the master, 'Sir, it would oblige me should we stretch our legs on the land for a short time. Would this be at all possible?'

'Why, yes. We'll be here some hours, I wouldn't wonder.'

On the way in, Renzi was told something of the lore of the Sound: if any ship passed an imaginary line connecting the Trumpeter's Tower with the King's Tower they would be brought to with a blank warning shot. If this was ignored a live ball would follow and the guardship, a frigate, would be sent to detain the offender. Naturally the cost of powder and ball would be added to the subsequent Sound due exacted.

The toll proceedings was a convenient time for masters in the Baltic trade to meet in the old Skibsklarerergården while awaiting assessment, there to exchange gossip of commercial possibilities. With an obliging ship's chandler acting as clearing agent, and an opportunity to store local fresh produce and water piped down from the lake, it was a congenial waypoint.

The town of Elsinore – or was it to be Helsingør? – was no sleepy medieval relic but a working town, devoted to the servicing of the endless stream of shipping in transit of the Sound. Busy shipbuilding and repair slips lay about the small harbour, and the many chandlers and shipping offices lined neat streets.

And overtopping all – Kronborg.

They took a shay and, at the towering gate, found that it was by no means unknown for English visitors to come to gaze upon Hamlet's castle. An English-speaking guide could be had for a small sum, and a delighted Mr and Mrs Laughton were greeted at the Dark Gate Ravelin entrance through the towering Crownwork ramparts, and led into Kronborg.

The louring towers and casemates, frowning apartments and lofty trumpeter's spire had an air that was at once menacing and deeply mysterious. It was pointed out that Hamlet's battlements were part of the original Castle Krogen belonging to Eric of Pomerania, now dwarfed and built over as Kronborg at the very time Shakespeare was penning his masterpiece.

Banqueting halls with fading tapestries, rooms of ancient armour and regalia all added to the atmosphere. Renzi and

Cecilia admired a brooding statue of the legendary Holger Danske, lost to the mists of history but sleeping in the bowels of Kronborg, ready in time of peril to rise up to save Denmark from her evil assailants.

That brought Renzi up short, a reminder of why he was there, and cut through the warm cocoon of his romantic tryst with Cecilia.

Damn it all! There had to be a resolution to the insanity before the gathering storm broke over this calm and ordered land. He'd do all that was possible to spare its inhabitants.

Chapter 43

Copenhagen, Sjælland, Denmark

When they arrived in Copenhagen it was grey and raining softly, increasing Renzi's mood of melancholy. They rounded to and, after exchanging hails with a harbour craft, passed by the low-bastioned ramparts of a vast citadel into the heart of the city.

Waiting for the English noble and envoy on the quay was a small party of well-dressed officials, who stood patiently in the wet until their barque had been warped alongside and the brow put in place. One detached from the group and boarded, throwing back the hood of his cloak in a spray of droplets. He had pale, sensitive features and a natural dignity but shrewd eyes.

The man swept down in a courtly bow. 'My lord, I extend welcome from His Majesty the King of Denmark to you, emissary of His Britannic Majesty. I am Count Joachim Bernstorff, minister in foreign affairs, and I have been instructed to render such services as shall be convenient to you.'

'Your welcome is most appreciated, sir, coming as it does

on this day of inclement weather. May I present the Countess of Farndon, who has expressed to me an earnest desire to know more of your ancient kingdom?'

They descended to the stone landing and were introduced to lesser dignitaries, then conveyed to a state carriage, the accoutrements and footmen almost quaint, of another age.

Bernstorff climbed in with them, explaining that, as honoured visitors to his king, they would be his guests at the palace.

The carriage clattered on to a broad plaza, with an imposing equestrian statue gleaming in the rain. Across its corners stood four stately buildings. An honour guard waited stolidly in the drizzle, and as they descended from the coach, a small military band broke into a thin tune that Renzi did not recognise. Bernstorff ushered them up the stairs to a waiting official.

'The residence of His Majesty, King Christian the Seventh. This is the Lord High Chamberlain Herre Møller, who will conduct you to your apartments. My lord, I will bid you farewell and will see you at the reception tonight.'

The palace was sumptuous and stately, and Cecilia took Renzi's arm as they mounted the steps to the upper floors to enter their regal suite. A haughty lady-in-waiting at the head of a troupe of footmen and maids greeted them and, in passable English, explained that she would ensure smooth household functioning as Lord Farndon's entourage settled in. The reception would be at seven and court dress would be expected but if the countess wished to refresh herself after her journey . . .

Renzi occupied himself in a book-lined state-room. He took down a volume and blew the dust from it, a venerable work in German on architectural terms. The one next to it was another dealing in great detail with the origins of a minor noble house of sixty years before. He smiled wryly. Libraries in palaces were always the same, an earnest collection of works presented over the centuries and never once put in order for a scholar's perusal.

The doors squeaked open and he turned about.

'Lord Farndon?'

'It is.'

'My lord, Benjamin Garlike, head of His Britannic Majesty's mission in Copenhagen.'

They exchanged polite bows but Renzi was instantly on the alert. 'So good of you to call, Mr Garlike.'

He recalled Congalton's warning – that it was crucial to keep the secret of the dispatch of a British fleet from hostile ears, for fear that the French would see it in their best interest to intervene immediately and head it off. It was probable therefore that Garlike had not yet been informed of the move.

'Sir, I was made aware of your intended visit only in these last two days, leaving small time to prepare, I fear.' There was a peevish undercurrent.

'You've been told the purpose of my visit, sir?'

'Only that an audience is sought. That is not so readily attained, my lord.'

'Then for your ears only, I will divulge the true object of my being here, the better to acquaint you of its importance.' He allowed a note of pomposity to take hold. 'His Majesty is sore exercised by the parlous state of relations between Dane and Englishman and notes the singular lack of success of politics to effect a reconciliation.'

'My lord, for some time we've been endeavouring to no purpose to extract a pledge of security, which—'

'He believes that a crisis is fast approaching that must be met by every effort to conciliate. My presence here is by his express desire to convey to the King of the Danes both his distress at the situation and to offer such understandings and advice that only one sovereign privately upon another might achieve.'

'Do pardon the direct speaking, my lord, but this is hardly work for those not perfectly versant in the diplomatic arts.'

'His Majesty wishes it, and it is therefore not to be questioned, Mr Garlike. I shall require audience and that, I believe, is within your competence to arrange, sir.'

'Very well, my lord. You should be aware that King Christian is taken by a malady of the reason and, while audience may well be secured, all executive powers are held by the Crown Prince.'

'So I understand. Nevertheless, the King specifically charges me with the expression of his fraternal regard and that I shall right willingly do.'

'Then I honour you for it, my lord. Shall you also be seeking a meeting with Crown Prince Frederik at all?'

'At Kiel? Yes, I think it were proper in me to do so.'

Chapter 44

The evening's reception was glittering and noble. With the Lord Farndon in splendid attire of silk breeches under a strikingly cut black velvet dress coat with gold buttons and his countess in dove-grey satin lavishly embellished with seed pearls and a long train, they caught every eye.

Renzi had no qualms about the display – it was expected and, born to it, he found no difficulty in sustaining the figure. He was immensely proud to see Cecilia as serene in the person of Lady Farndon as though she, too, had been raised in the peerage. Shrugging off his gloom and sense of foreboding, he progressed through the crowd.

He knew the Frenchman Gobineau even from across the room: the pretence at conversation with a lady while a speculative stare took in Renzi's every move, the faultless Paris fashion of high-collared quasi-military full dress, the superfluity of ornamentation. Before long the man appeared in front of him, made an exaggerated bow and, ignoring the elderly Dane Renzi was with, said smoothly,

'My lord Farndon! Since no one seems inclined to introduce me I will do so myself. Théodore Gobineau, Comte de Mirabeau and chargé d'affaires to the French Empire in Copenhagen.'

Renzi returned a slight bow and regarded him with lordly disdain. A saturnine, worldly-wise individual, whose every movement and gesture seemed calculated. 'Since you seem to know my name and style, sir, I will refrain from returning the compliment.'

'In these uncertain times you visit this fair city for a holiday with the countess, *n'est-ce pas?*' His innocent puzzlement was a trifle overdone.

'I come on a mission of some importance I'll have you know, sir,' Renzi said scornfully.

'At such an eminence, I've every expectation it is,' replied Gobineau. 'Now do let me guess. You are a personal emissary from King George.'

Renzi took a glass from a passing footman. 'Do go on, M'sieur le Comte.'

'To make intervention at a kingly level in the decisions that must face the Danish court at this time.'

Encouraged by Renzi's wordless acceptance he continued silkily, 'The essence of which can only be that you are in this palace to begin negotiations in the delicate matter of seeking union between the Houses of Oldenburg and Hanover, namely the marriage of the Princess Caroline of Denmark to Prince Adolphus, Duke of Cambridge, son of the King of Great Britain.'

His breath taken away by the claim, Renzi could only stare. Then he spluttered, 'Sir, how dare you pry into the affairs of our royal houses? This is a private matter of the highest degree and does not concern the French government in any wise.'

164

The man's barely concealed look of triumph was all that he needed, and Renzi finished irritably, 'I find this conversation both tasteless and odious. Good night to you, sir.'

Gobineau bowed and backed away with a faint smile.

Chapter 45

'The minister Count Bernstorff,' intoned the newly arrived Jago next morning after breakfast. Renzi's retinue had followed on behind.

'Ah. I will see him in the withdrawing room.'

Cecilia gave an enquiring look, but Renzi shook his head. 'We'll see what he wants first, my love.'

She knew his mission, for he'd given the matter much thought on the passage to Denmark and had come to the conclusion that it was more risky to have her in ignorance of his objectives and an unwitting hindrance than to break secrecy and divulge his goals.

His predecessor, Lord Stanhope, had rarely travelled on his own missions without his wife. Without a doubt they must have come to a similar conclusion, but the good lady had never once given indication that she was privy to deadly secrets. Cecilia would be following in the same tradition.

Bernstorff rose and bowed. 'Lord Farndon, I'm here to inform you that an audience with the King has been arranged for four this afternoon. Would that be convenient?'

'Perfectly,' Renzi said, relieved. The sooner the preliminaries were out of the way the quicker he could get to the real work.

'Then it would give me great pleasure, my lord, to show you and the countess something of Copenhagen. As you may see, the weather is looking more kindly on us this day.'

'That is most generous in you, sir,' Renzi answered politely. There had to be something behind it, a busy minister taking the time to conduct a tour with an idle aristocrat.

'Then might we say carriages at ten?'

Copenhagen gave an impression of both hardihood and calm: neat and clean, frowning Lutheran churches, and houses in bright Scandinavian colours, charming shop-lined canals and imposing public squares.

Their first stop was at the Dyrehavsbakken park to enjoy its deer and amusements. With Cecilia and Hetty exclaiming happily ahead, and two attendants behind, the men fell into step beside one another.

'A very proud and ancient country,' Bernstorff offered. 'Gorm the Old dated from before your own Alfred, which renders Denmark yet more venerable than England, I believe. And with Harald Bluetooth, Sweyn Forkbeard and, of course, the peerless Cnut, we have modest claim to a history much entangled with yours, sir.'

'Vikings descending on the northern monasteries have been mentioned in some accounts,' Renzi agreed.

'We are a small, hardy race and have found ourselves so many times caught between the fires of nations far larger than ours.'

Renzi murmured in sympathy.

'Yet we have found a sturdy refuge in neutrality that has served us well. Do you blame us for this, my lord?'

'Sir, I am not a political and cannot possibly speak to that.'

At coffee in the medieval Nørregade, which Bernstorff introduced as the Latin Quarter, Renzi was startled to hear conversations that sounded different from the jagged sibilances of Danish. 'Latin! The students practising?'

'Just so. Lord Farndon, do forgive my raising the subject but it is imperative, I know. My position at court demands it.' He leaned forward intently. 'Tell me, are you here in contemplation of opening negotiations towards the marriage of Princess Caroline to the—'

'Minister Bernstorff, I can solemnly declare to you that our sovereign king has no intentions whatsoever in this regard.'

'Oh. I had it on good authority, you'll understand.'

'I see.'

'Well, if Lady Farndon feels she is able to bear it, we shall go to a most colourful and curious part of Old Copenhagen.'

It turned out to be Nyhavn, the busy waterfront facing the Sound. Dark, smoky taverns with enticing signs of mermaids or crude model ships lined the place where the canals of Copenhagen met the sea. Tall warehouses, in dashes of colour that would never be seen at Wapping, stood along cobbled lanes, some with ornate escutcheons of merchant houses on their elaborate doors, others with votive statues high on their walls. Everywhere there was bustle and noise, with carts and stevedores.

'My lord, this is what I brought you here to see,' Bernstoff said, escorting Renzi to the end of the wharf. 'Be so good as to look to seaward.'

On the left the channel led to the open sea and, in the distance, a long island with a peculiar rectangular appearance, while immediately ahead was what could only be the entrance to the harbour proper.

'You are privileged, Lord Farndon. This is a sight denied to your fleet under Nelson when they came to teach us a lesson in 1801. That island is the Trekroner Fortress, which you are seeing, from the inside. The naval dockyard and base is to your right. It was a hard fight, in truth.'

Out there, not so very long before, the British fleet had been locked in mortal conflict with the Danes, a battle dearly won in which Admiral Nelson had famously made play with his telescope and blind eye.

'And so unnecessary,' Renzi murmured.

'It was,' Bernstorff said shortly, 'even as we were in a League of Armed Neutrality with the Russians at the time, which was a foolish action for both trade and honour.'

'And news of its dissolution and Tsar Paul's assassination came only days later?'

'Yes. Well, if you come again you will find we have not been idle – over there is Prøvesten, an artificial island whose entire nature is to make unwelcome visitors rue their arrival. With our gun-rafts and dozens of ships-of-the-line I rather fancy it will be a different tale told the next time.'

'Sir. You have been an attentive and considerate host and I would not have you misled. I will speak frankly. My presence here has only one meaning. It is to obey my king's wish that your court understands his distress at the deplorable state of our nations' relations and earnestly to seek a way through, sovereign to sovereign, before it is too late. No more, sir, no less.'

He knew the man was reaching out, hoping for something, anything, in Renzi's gift that could show a path clear of the gathering storm. And he had denied that hope. At any point the armada would reach Denmark and then this honourable man would be placed in an intolerable situation.

Count Bernstorff looked away for a space, then spoke softly: 'Then I grieve for us both, for we Danes are in hostage to Bonaparte's legions on our borders and that is an unanswerable menace. God have mercy on us all.'

Chapter 46

King Christian VII was not at the Amalienborg Palace. It seemed he was confined to the Frederiksberg Castle, several miles beyond the city walls, and it was there that the personal emissary of King George was taken with all due ceremony. It was a broad country residence set in acres of parkland, on one side a Chinese summerhouse, on another a Greco-Egyptian temple and, tucked away beyond, a Swiss cottage, all in immaculate order.

They were met on the forecourt by a modest honour guard and a major-domo who conducted them to a small but exquisitely furnished reception room.

A petite, kindly-faced woman was waiting and advanced with a shy curtsy. 'The Hofdame Rosen, my lord,' she said. 'As is the chief nurse to His Majesty.'

'Thank you. Your command of English does you credit, madam.'

The softly lined face creased with pleasure. 'I was born in England, my lord, and am widow to a Dane.'

'Then we are doubly welcomed.' It earned another curtsy.

'Frue Rosen, how does His Majesty?' Cecilia asked politely.

'My lady, this is what we need to talk about before your audience.'

The guidance was practical and to the point. The King was much cast down by his affliction but if the day was kind could be lucid and charming. Nevertheless, it were better the audience was short and serene. She herself would be in attendance and, trusted through long service to the Crown, would intervene if she thought it necessary. The noble lord should understand that anything declared or granted by King Christian in the audience would be subject to the approbation of the Crown Prince acting as regent.

They were conducted through fine state-rooms to the audience chamber.

His grand court robes heavy and stifling, Renzi stood at one end of the polished marble floor, two thrones on a raised dais at the other. The rich gold canopy and hangings, ancestral portraits and extravagantly carved furniture were of a piece with England's royalty, but with an almost defiant Scandinavian cast.

A pair of halberdiers marched out and took position each side of the dais while members of the household and functionaries waited with Lord Farndon and his lady.

Nearly fifteen minutes later a high, querulous voice could be heard echoing in a passage and a little later a stooped, robed figure emerged through the tall doors, looking about suspiciously.

All went to their knees.

There was shuffling, muttering in an undertone, then silence.

A peremptory order was given in Danish.

'All rise,' whispered Frue Rosen.

More harsh Danish rang out.

'Announces your presence and style.'

And then: 'Do approach now, my lord.'

Renzi gathered his robes and made stately progress down the length of the chamber to stop before the King. As he had done for King George not so very long before, he knelt elegantly and lowered his head, anticipating the order to rise.

There was a small pause, then movement and a rustling – and suddenly he became aware that the King was beside him, cupping his chin and peering into his face. 'You're English, Lord. I like the English. Don't be afraid!'

King Christian VII would have been barely sixty but it was an old man's features that looked back into his, with fair hair, now white, and faded blue eyes, whose sockets sagged pitifully. Renzi tried not to notice the dressing-gown peeping from under the robes of state, but took it that he should stand.

'Come, sit with us,' the King commanded, pulling him towards the two thrones.

Hastily courtiers brought up a chair and Renzi sat awkwardly in it, the King swivelling in his throne to face him. 'We never see the English these days,' he mourned. 'Those rogues in the Council always have something to say against them.'

'Sire, I bring greetings from your brother sovereign, His Britannic Majesty King George of Great Britain. He bids me to say—'

'My mother was English. Did you know? That's why I can understand you, Lord, um, Thingummy. And so also the mother of my child who . . . who . . .'

His face crumpled and, catching the nurse's horrified look, Renzi hastened to continue: 'Who brings a gift from his heart for the love he bears you, sire.' He beckoned Cecilia forward.

Gracefully she sank to her knees holding a small japanned black case.

'A gift? For me? So kind! So kind!' He stood, transformed, and hurried with childish glee to Cecilia who proffered it.

He opened it.

Inside there was a miniature sword, perfect in every detail, the hilt of gold encrusted with jewels and with a tiny tasselled knot.

'Wonderful!' he breathed, holding it reverently.

Then, cackling, he set off in a pitiable shuffle about the room in mock swordplay, his maniacal barks falling into the heavy silence of the assembled court.

'You were so good to the poor man,' Frue Rosen said, her eyes brimming. 'So many come to sneer and be cruel. I've seen him as a young man . . . when . . . when . . .'

Cecilia held her hand, murmuring soothing words.

'It's just that . . . the English are not so liked here now, the demands they make and the dreadful time when Nelson came. I do so yearn to hear an English voice, and when I learned you were coming I . . . I . . .'

'We'll stay a little longer before we go, won't we, Nicholas?'

Later, Lord and Lady Farndon retired to their gilded four-poster bed in the Amalienborg.

Renzi lay staring up at the ceiling.

Cecilia stroked his hair. 'It's your burden, isn't it, Nicholas? I do feel for you, my love – to sway those stiff-necked Danish with so little to offer.' She leaned over and kissed him. 'Never forget, you're giving it of your best, and if you cannot persuade them, it's never your fault.'

Renzi stirred and said quietly, 'The fleet will arrive directly.

Then it will be doubly difficult. My dearest, time is pressing me mortally.'

He rolled over and faced her. 'Bernstorff's sympathetic but his hands are tied, as are those of others fearful of the French. If I can think of no course to mollify London I rather fear the consequences will be dire.'

Cecilia sighed. 'At times, Nicholas, I think this is all something of a forlorn hope, born of the King's desiring, of course . . . but who's to say? You may be meant to fail, leaving the field to the warriors.'

Chapter 47

Kiel, province of Holstein, Denmark

Renzi made his goodbyes the next morning. He had been firm with Cecilia. It was not necessary for her to accompany him on an uncomfortable journey to Kiel to meet the Crown Prince in what would amount to little more than an army encampment. Why not extend her friendship with Frue Rosen?

This was not all from concern for her: he needed time to think.

The conceit of his visit as a personal gesture from King George had opened every door – but he had first to engage with the real wielders of power in the little kingdom, then cultivate a relationship of disinterested trust. But whatever he said would have no weight, no binding significance that could be translated into a formal agreement, let alone a treaty.

He'd already settled on the approach: in his character of royal concern for Denmark he would feel it appropriate to be ready with well-meant advice, placing alternatives before them in a way that could never be contemplated by a diplomat.

If, miraculously, he could bring about a change of heart he could leave Garlike to conclude the formalities.

But, damn it, what unanswerable arguments could he use to bring about this miracle?

Cecilia's words came back to haunt him. Could it be that he was intended to fail, that the government and military wanted a tangible victory and a vanquished foe to dictate terms to rather than tamely accept a diplomatic solution?

Either way, time was running out.

Bleary-eyed he joined the other passengers on deck for the last mile to Kiel docks, no nearer to a way through to allow the Danes an honourable settlement.

There was no ceremonial guard of welcome, so near to the buffer territory facing Bernadotte's army. Instead, a small carriage and four hussars waited impatiently.

A serious-looking individual stood apart, grave and upright. 'Count Christian Bernstorff, my lord. You are expected.'

There was no conversation from the unsmiling figure as they clopped along the avenues to a point opposite the docks where a frowning Germanic red-stone château dominated. Once inside Bernstorff lost no time in taking Renzi to a mock-medieval hall, hung with faded tapestries and suits of armour. 'My lord, I've a communication from my brother concerning your visit. And it disturbs me, sir.'

'Why so, Count Bernstorff?'

'You cannot be unaware of the delicate – no, acute plight we find ourselves in. If all the skills of diplomacy cannot attain a measure of agreement, how can you think to?'

'My sovereign desires I should spare nothing to bring about a reconciliation.'

'There are some who would say that the British government is using your mission as an unfair tactic to gain ascendancy over the Crown Prince to sway his decisions in their favour.' He paused. 'I am not one of them, my lord.'

'Thank you,' Renzi said drily.

'I believe you to be sincere in your intentions, and those of your king. You will have your audience, but be assured, should you press His Royal Highness in matters outside your competence I shall have no other alternative than to intervene.'

'Sir, I understand your position.'

'Then I will allow that you are arrived and do seek an early meeting.'

Chapter 48

Renzi gave an elegant and flowing bow before Crown Prince Regent Frederik, seeing before him one of quite another spirit to his father. Not yet in his forties, with fair hair, startling blue eyes and pointed chin, his sharp face was uncompromising in its determination.

He wore a military red coat with blue facings, the heavy epaulettes grey and silver. No court shoes, simply plain hessian boots over white pantaloons. A heavy sabre in its scabbard leaned against the desk.

'Your Royal Highness is most kind to see me at such notice.'

'I cannot refuse to entertain my uncle's emissary, my lord.' The tone was wary, the English accented.

'Sire, His Britannic Majesty desires me most earnestly to discover common ground that will allow us to proceed to an understanding.'

The reply was cautious but encouraging. Renzi, however, sensed tension, defensiveness. He felt some sympathy for the man: he had all power as an autocrat, but his decisions would commit his country to war or peace, survival or ruin, with none to share his burden.

By degrees the guarded conversation became less stilted, passing over subjects of family, cultural differences, the attractions of Copenhagen. A tray of glasses was brought and toasts were offered in a fine German Rheingau for health and prosperity to the Houses of Hanover and Oldenburg. But underlying all, an indefinable barrier, a line of reserve, could not be crossed.

After more than an hour of pleasantries and elliptical inferences, Renzi had the feeling he was achieving a rapport that could well lead to more substantial discussions at another audience. Tense and weary, he conceded the day and, pleading fatigue from his journey, retired to his guest suite.

It was frustrating in the extreme: he had the ear of the one individual who could stop the cataclysm with a word – if only he could conceive of a face-saving means to proffer.

After more hopeless casting about he surrendered to sleep with the resolve to go on the offensive, along the lines of offering firm advice.

In the morning he was encouraged when Frederik came down to breakfast and sat next to him, enquiring after his night's sleep. This could only be that, after mature consideration, he felt it of value to pursue the discussion.

Once again in his state-room, Frederik mused archly, 'It would intrigue me to know what Uncle George would do in my place – just out of interest, you understand.'

It was what Renzi wanted.

The careful phrasing was for the benefit of Bernstorff, who sat at a desk on the pretence of preparing the day's papers.

Renzi warmly sympathised on the dilemma the Crown of Denmark faced. He then lightly touched on the courses open, delicately pitching the consequences as they would be perceived by the King of England.

He gave a casual glance in Bernstorff's direction: the foreign minister was sitting stock still, his pen motionless in his hand.

Was it working? With an increasing tide of despair, Renzi had to accept that he did not have a magic formula to cut through the impasse. Worse, he had a premonition that both were waiting, hoping he had, and within the hour they would know he hadn't – and it would all be over.

'Therefore, Highness, this question of a binding covenant of security—'

There was murmuring at Bernstorff's desk: a functionary had arrived and was whispering urgently to him.

Bernstorff stood up. 'Sire, if you'll excuse me . . .'

He left, and Renzi cudgelled his mind for something to take advantage of his absence, but Frederik was obviously distracted.

It wasn't long before Bernstorff returned and, with a glance at Renzi, told the Crown Prince something in a low voice that made him shoot to his feet and apparently demand details. It was all in Danish and their frequent looks in his direction made him tense with foreboding.

Frederik broke off and glared at Renzi. 'My lord, a powerful British fleet has been sighted approaching the Sound. What do you know of this?'

He froze. It had happened, and at the worst possible moment. He was in an impossible situation. If he denied all knowledge of it he would be marginalised and his 'advice' would fail. If he admitted it, his mission would be seen as a smoke-screen to delay things until the assault fleet was in position.

'Sir, I would have an answer! This is a great fleet. It must have a purpose.'

He gulped – but then was saved.

Speaking in English for Renzi's sake, Bernstorff said evenly, 'Sire, I hardly think the noble lord can be expected to answer that. Yet an explanation does suggest itself. I've reliable knowledge that, since the Treaty of Tilsit, the British Admiralty has intended to establish in the Baltic a fleet of force with which to balance a hostile Russian presence. Surely this is its nature.'

'It has transports – military, troops, guns. What of them?'

'It seems to me undoubtedly for the reinforcement of the Swedes on the north Baltic seaboard, they having lately been cast out of Stralsund and the whole south shore.'

Frederik snorted. 'Then you'd say they will pass, there is no intimidation implied?'

'I can hardly think that it is intended to assault without warning a guiltless neutral, sire. The British would never do it. My explanation is much the more likely one, I believe.'

'Very well. We shall continue – but keep me informed of its progress past us, Bernstorff.'

'Sire.'

In a stroke, matters had gone from bad to catastrophic.

The primary reason for mounting the expedition was to apply decisive pressure to the Danes to concede. Instead its presence had been misconstrued, and therefore its value in negotiation was as nothing. Canning's show of force had failed – and would bring about the very thing it was intended to avoid: an armed landing and bloodshed.

It mustn't happen.

Renzi's mind raced. He was losing in his king-to-king accord and now he was the only agency that could halt the inevitable. If he did nothing . . . 'Your Royal Highness. To say I know nothing of this armada would be untrue.'

He avoided the man's eye but sensed his sudden rigid attention.

'While about to leave England I heard rumours of a fleet to be sent into the Sound at the government's direction.'

'You knew!'

'But as a king's envoy there could be no question that I be given details, or even that it would sail. Sire, I must tell you that its very presence here reveals to me something of the anxiety of the administration to conclude a form of mutual security touching the Baltic. That they dispatched it is an earnest to their intentions, I'm sorry to say.'

'You're part of this!'

'Sire, I do swear to you I am not. This is an initiative by the political heads of government.' That much was perfectly true.

'My mission is directly from His Majesty to you, sir, in trust that an understanding beyond that of politics might be achieved.'

Frederik was pacing about the room like a bear.

He stopped and stared angrily at Renzi. 'My only conclusion can be that this intrusion of a battle-fleet into our waters is to be interpreted as a form of menace, of threat to the sovereign rights of neutral Denmark.'

'Sire, as I have stated to you, I am detached from this affair and can offer only my most sincere advice, which I pray you will accept.'

'What advice can you possibly give me, sir?'

It was the last throw.

'Sire, this whole business is in train for one thing, and one only. That the British government may be assured of the security of its Baltic trade.'

'Ha!'

'In a manner that is unequivocal and committed.'

'If you're talking of an alliance or alignment of interests at diplomatic level, you're insane. The French would never—'

'No, sir, I am not. I'm speaking of a move that at one stroke would send the British armada back to England and at the same time render Denmark of no value to Bonaparte and therefore of no military interest.'

'Do tell me then, my noble lord, what will be your marvellous remedy?'

'My most sincere advice to you, sire, is to release the Danish fleet into the custody of the British admiral, to be returned in its entirety after this unpleasantness is over.'

At first he thought he'd not been heard, then saw Bernstorff's look of horror, and the Crown Prince standing rigid with anger, his eyes blazing.

'This – this is monstrous! It's barbaric and unworthy of a great nation!'

'Yet if it achieves its object—'

'It strikes at the heart of Danish honour to yield up our fleet in the teeth of a superior hostile threat.'

'Sire, if it's seen that Denmark is powerless to block the Sound neither Britain nor France may derive any further advantage from interfering with the neutrality of your nation.'

'Never! On my honour, I shall never do it.'

'Sire, I beg you. It's without question that the admiral will launch his fleet else, and with diplomacy at a stand—'

'I said no!' shrieked the Crown Prince, slamming both his fists on the desk in a crash. 'The Danes will not be dictated to! Honour demands we resist – and we shall, God help us!'

'Sire, if—'

'No more,' Frederik said huskily. 'This audience is at an end.'

'Your Highness, my duty urges me—'

'Go. Now.' He faced Renzi, his chest heaving. 'You've performed your duty, sir, now leave us to ours.'

Chapter 49

Footmen and soldiers regarded Lord Farndon stonily as he sat moodily in the waiting room. The Crown Prince and Bernstorff remained closeted together, their voices rising and falling behind closed doors. Eventually he returned to his apartment and slumped in a chair: in the face of the inexorable grind of events his mission had probably been doomed before it had begun yet he had to play it out to the last.

One advantage only remained. There would be no unleashing of the dogs of war until the fleet had his categorical assertion that further negotiations were futile, and that was far from the case. He was certain he'd at least preserved the character of a plain-speaking impartial observer, and there was still a chance that Frederik would grasp that his best interests lay in being seen by all to have yielded to insuperable force.

Renzi would then have suggestions to offer: that the fleet proudly depart in line ahead, each ship manned by its Danish crew and commanded by a Dane, with all appropriate banners and ensigns amain, nothing abroad to imply craven surrender. It could be handled smoothly and with all the honours of war.

The day ended inconclusively. He was neither summoned nor dismissed.

Bernstorff kept at a distance and Renzi dined alone. He retired, knowing that the clock was ticking towards an unknown future.

At breakfast the next morning he had hopes that the Crown Prince might have had a change of heart and come down to greet him but, lingering over his coffee, Renzi saw no sign of him.

Somewhat at a loss, he rose to return to his suite but the door was flung wide and Bernstorff entered, giving a short bow and a click of the heels. 'My lord, I would be much obliged should you grant me an interview at the earliest,' he demanded. Nothing could be read in his expression.

'Gladly, Count Bernstorff. Shall we . . .?'

This time it was an inner office and the door was firmly closed.

The foreign minister sat heavily in a chair by his desk and looked away as if reaching for words.

'My lord. This is to say . . . that His Royal Highness the Crown Prince Frederik has . . . decided on a course of action.'

'I'm happy to hear it, sir.'

'Which in confidence to you I cannot recommend and I fear will lead to ruin for my country.'

'May I know what it is?'

'Sir. He . . . he is not to be moved, no matter the arguments brought forward, and is irrevocably set in his intentions.'

'I see.'

'It is . . . to resist with all the powers at his command any assault on the integrity of Denmark's neutrality. He is determined to be seen as standing staunch and true for the honour of Crown and nation. He's to defy the worst that your armada is threatening and will not capitulate. Sir, I must tell you that during the night hours he left for Copenhagen to order it set in an immediate state of defence – this I have just heard. I do not have to tell you that any motion of your fleet will now be an act of war, and that to all the world against a helpless neutral.'

Renzi went cold. All was changed: by his action Frederik had called the bluff. The fleet must act or slink away defeated. But he knew there would be no withdrawal by the British and the end was therefore inevitable.

Bernstorff gave a thin smile. 'Sir, do not think I'm unaware of what must follow, but ministers are helpless when princes decree. My lord, I'm before you to beseech your understanding.'

'If there's anything . . .'

'Thank you. Then I beg of you, follow Prince Frederik to Copenhagen and, from your royal connection, do plead with him to disavow his action. My lord – you are our last hope.'

Chapter 50

Nyholm naval dockyard, Copenhagen

From where he stood Kommandørkaptajn Johan Krieger could see nearly every ship in the Danish battle-fleet stretching away in long rows – a sturdy, martial vision that made him swell with pride.

However, the Danish naval officer was a realist. He'd seen service fighting the English as a youngster in the Caribbean and during the hard days leading up to Nelson's ferocious action against Copenhagen six years earlier. These veterans were no match against the might and experience of the greatest sea-power in the world but, by God, if called upon again, they would sail out and do battle to the finish, like true-hearted Danes.

But it wouldn't come to that. The British fleet that had been sighted off the Sound had politely anchored and exchanged salutes with Kronborg Fortress, hardly the act of a force determined to fall on a neutral country. Besides, the English weren't like the French who, under a ruthless Napoleon Bonaparte, had few scruples about sovereignty.

Krieger had been made first lieutenant of *Prinsesse Louisa*

Augusta, an elderly ship-of-the-line, but she'd been delayed in returning from Kristiansand on the Norway station. Left between appointments, he was now strolling restlessly past the rows of ships. In deference to the frayed political situation, and to avoid provocation, they'd been prepared for winter early, topmasts sent down, de-stored and tidily moored fore and aft. But all gear had been carefully laid along in the adjacent Nyholm storehouses and it wouldn't take long to rig them for war.

There was the 90-gun *Christian VII*, blessed with remarkable sea-handling and beautiful stern-works, and beyond, *Valdemar* and *Norge*, both 80s, either of which could stand against any English 74-gun battleship. A dozen and a half of those beauties, many more frigates and others put the Danish Navy easily in the top four or five in the world. Not bad for such a tiny nation!

The officers' mess was noisy and more than usually crowded, all ranks loudly giving opinions on latest developments. Krieger nodded pleasantly to his friends and sipped his chilled akvavit.

The happy chatter died away as urgent voices were heard outside. A breathless army major burst in and announced, 'His Royal Highness has this hour returned from Kiel!'

It caused consternation. The Crown Prince was sworn to defend the Schleswig border far to the south against the menace of the massed French divisions: anything that could have torn him from that duty must be serious indeed.

Another soldier marched in and demanded, 'His Royal Highness bids all senior officers attend on him immediately.'

Krieger glanced across to Steen Bille, a thick-set, crusty commodore, who stood up quickly, looking about the officers.

His finger stabbed out at this one and that, including Krieger, then beckoned them imperiously.

The room was full, juniors like Krieger standing at the back. An unnatural quiet settled. Then the door opened and Crown Prince Frederik appeared, to massed scraping of chairs. 'Sit – there's not much time,' he snapped, striding over to the head of the table and taking the carved, gilded seat. 'This assembly is now a council of war.'

'War, sire? The English have not yet—'

'War, Generalløjtnant Bielefeldt. I have it from an impeccable source that their fleet is here in the nature of a threat, to secure a preferential pledge of security to the British nation in violation of our neutrality. I intend to resist that demand with all the force at my disposal.'

'Sir, are we sure that the fleet is not intended for the Baltic as we are expecting?'

'No. Why do you think it lies idle at anchor in the Sound when it should be pressing on to face the Russians? It is at us that it's intended, be certain of that, sir.'

'Er . . .'

'Generalløjtnant?'

'There are military transports attached. There are those who believe that the English are picking a quarrel that will allow them to capture Sjælland for use as a base in a Baltic war.'

'That's as may be, sir. Do attend to what I say. The urgent business of this convening is to mount a defence of the city of Copenhagen should they assault it. To resist strongly has three most valued objectives. The first, that our sacred honour is sustained in the face of intolerable provocation, the highest cause of all. The second: Bonaparte will see we defend our neutrality strictly, with no fear or favour to any, and therefore can have no reason to intervene. The third, and most immediate, is that the English will see we mean to repel any assault and thus any descent will be contested hotly, causing them many casualties.'

'Your Royal Highness knows that his loyal army will do its duty, but these are grave odds, sir.'

'I know that, damn it! Have you not the wit to see that if we hold out for a little longer we'll have the autumn gales as will scatter their armada, and then the ice will come? Time is not on their side.'

'Sire.'

'Then to business. General Pike being indisposed, I hereby appoint Generalmajor Peymann to supreme command of the defence of Copenhagen.'

There was a stir around the table. An engineer officer in his seventies who, as far as anyone knew, had never heard a shot fired in anger.

'Can't even ride a horse!' muttered the young major next to Krieger.

'Enough!' snapped the Crown Prince. 'The general is chosen because he has closest knowledge of the defensive works, having constructed many of them himself.' He turned to the old man. 'Well, do take your place, Generalmajor.'

Peymann lifted himself heavily from his seat and went to the other end of the table, his face lined with anxiety.

'And under him shall be Generalløjtnant Bielefeldt in command of all land forces – and Kommandør Steen Bille, the sea defences. I leave subordinate appointments to these officers.'

Bille's eyes glowed in anticipation and Krieger grinned. He was a masterly seaman with a fine record. If the English wanted a fight they'd get one.

'I shall be back in one hour to hear your dispositions.'

All heads turned to Peymann, who hesitated. Then, with a nervous twitch of his collar, he said, 'You heard His Royal Highness. It's to be expected the English will make a sally in force at the harbour entrance as will gain them entry to the city. I'll give half an hour to the commanders of the land and sea forces to confer and plan separately against this event, after which we will come together to give outline to our strategy of defence, which will be submitted to our commander-in-chief, the Crown Prince.'

Bille found a room and sat down with the naval officers.

'So! If the English think to force the *havnen* they'll get a bloody nose,' he growled, tracing out the defensive lines around the harbours on his campaign map.

Things had changed much since Nelson had closed with the city and cannonaded its defences to a standstill. The harbour itself was formed by the Strait of Kallebo narrows between the mainland of Sjælland and the outer island of Amager. Stout bastioned city walls enclosed Copenhagen and its harbour, and on the Sjælland side at its entrance the massive Citadel was armed with heavy mortars and guns. Opposite were the Sextus and Quintus batteries. Working together they could lay down a merciless rain of fire on any who dared make to enter.

Further out to sea was the fearsome seventy-gun Trekroner battery, sited to dominate the deep-water approaches, and firmly on the two-fathom line further south another, the Prøvesten fort with ninety cannon, defied any attempt to fire into the city from down the coast. Two blockships were in place athwart the entry channel, while up and down the wall and ramparts countless guns bristled outward.

Bille straightened. 'I dare to say we're impregnable. But I was here when we last faced them and it's not a good idea to underestimate the English. Krieger, I want you to set up a defence in depth with cutters, rafts and, of course, gunboats.'

The Swedish wars in the Baltic had left all players respectful of the gunboat design evolved for the conditions of that sea – sudden calms, short seas, multitudes of islands for concealment. The boats were pulled by up to eighty oarsmen and with a gun of size mounted fore and aft, which would normally be found in a ship-of-the-line, and fully manoeuvrable, they were a formidable threat in any kind of numbers.

'I'll do that, sir. I'll take Lynetten as my base.' This was a smaller sea fort handily placed by the mouth of the harbour. On a sandbank, it would provide good shelter for a swarm of craft.

'A pity our fleet is laid up – we'd never get them to sea in time. Damned uncivilised of the English not to give us warning of their call. Still, I'm sanguine we've done enough to make 'em think twice.'

They reconvened, and Peymann summoned the military to make first presentation.

Bielefeldt didn't waste words. 'Sir, this is our disposition. Almost our entire army is in Holstein, too far to arrive here in time. Within the city we have five and a half thousand regular troops and can count on a further two and a half thousand others. Should we call on volunteers for a Copenhagen burgher militia we could probably muster another four thousand, including eight hundred students from the university, a total of some twelve thousand.'

He wiped his brow. 'However, we have in the country nineteen battalions of *landeværn* to call upon if necessary and with this force I'm sanguine we can hold the city until our brothers from Holstein arrive.'

'Very good, Generalløjtnant. Kommandør Bille?'

With hard, thrusting flourishes, the sea officer outlined the situation and his intentions. So forceful was his delivery that several grim smiles surfaced around the table and Peymann's lines of worry eased. 'Thank you. I can tell you all here that I've established we have sufficient provisions in the Citadel storehouses to withstand a siege of a month or more. Our water supply is secured by pipes from the country and the municipal authorities have been most co-operative in the article of regulation.' He sat back. 'Then it seems we have something of value for His Royal Highness's consideration. I shall send word.'

It was not for some hours that the Crown Prince appeared, pale-faced and clearly distracted. 'What is it, Peymann? Have you anything for me?' he said curtly.

Humbly, the elderly officer laid before him plans and preparations, but was cut off in the details.

'That's good, Generalmajor. I can see I chose well. Then it seems I can safely leave the defence of Copenhagen in your trustworthy hands, sir.'

'L-leave?' stammered Peymann.

'Why, yes. I'm preparing my departure from Copenhagen in order to rejoin my troops in Kiel. You are left as paramount leader, and if the English make motions towards the city your duty is to defend it and its loyal inhabitants at all costs. Are my commands understood?'

'They are, Highness, but—'

'I have no time to discuss this further. Carry on with your preparations and God be with you.'

Chapter 51

As soon as the dispatch cutter from Kiel threw lines ashore, Renzi stepped on to the quay, aware of the changed atmosphere of the capital. Everywhere was noise and commotion. In place of stolid placidity, people hurried purposefully, some hailing each other excitedly.

The Amalienborg was close and he quickly found his apartment. 'Lady Farndon, how is she?' he demanded of Jago.

'Well, m' lord,' he replied imperturbably, 'she's stayin' with Frow Rosen at the Frederiksberg Castle.'

It was a relief. Away from it all in the country, with king's guards and friends, she was in no danger.

'I'll need to bathe and shave this very instant. And set out my court undress.'

As he lay back in the ornate marble tub Renzi reviewed his options.

There was no royal pennon atop the Christian VII palace so he was not in residence there, but where?

He decided to have Jago send out one of the Danish staff to hear the street gossip. If he did not learn anything in that

196

way, he would go to Joachim Bernstorff, who, no doubt, had received word from his brother by the same dispatch cutter that had brought himself. It reminded him of his late mission to Constantinople with another fleet menacing offshore, but the resemblance stopped there. In Turkey he had had no control over events and had been swept along in a spiral of horror. Here it was another matter: unbeknown to the Danish, the armada would not stir from its anchors unless it received specific word from himself.

He had time to persuade Frederik to another course, but the fleet could not wait indefinitely. The proud regent might by now have had second thoughts about the price of defiance and if he could make a compromise palatable there was a chance. He must be found.

But Jago came back with word that on the streets there were contradictions and rumours that were useless.

Chapter 52

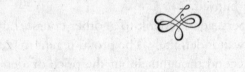

Bernstorff gave Renzi a polite bow. 'My lord, your visit to Kiel was . . . not to your advantage, as I understand from my brother.'

Renzi gave a small smile. 'I'm sanguine, sir, he will have preferred you to phrase it rather that it was not to *our* advantage.'

'This has to be accepted, my lord. Then what is to be done?'

'I desire you seek an audience for me, sir. There's still time.'

'Time? Do you know the mind of the English admiral, his orders, his objectives?'

'While he remains at anchor there is always time, Count Bernstorff. Will you now—'

'I note your petition for an audience, and from my brother, I know something of its importance.' He gave a sad smile. 'Yet I can do nothing – I have no idea where His Royal Highness is, you see.'

'Sir! I find it—'

'The Crown Prince is exercised by considerations of urgency and conceives it his duty to be everywhere there are preparations to be made. He does not see fit to inform me of his hourly movements.'

'Then I must seek him out for myself.'

'As you like. Although . . . you may wish to ponder another development.'

'Sir?'

'I happen to know, as it is my business to be so informed, that the French have received a substantial communication from their commander-in-chief.'

'Bonaparte?'

Bernstorff gave a wordless bow.

'In response to the British presence? Then it would oblige me much, sir, should you be so good as to inform me of its import.'

'Ah, would that I could, my lord. It is more than our neutral status might stand should we trespass upon diplomatic territory . . .'

It was perplexing. For what reason had this broad hint been thrown out?

'Why do you tell me of this, Count Bernstorff?'

'We are neutrals, Lord Farndon. Should we not treat evenly with both sides? It is only right you should know matters as bear upon you.'

That wasn't the reason but he had a good idea what was.

'I thank you for your civility, Count. I'm obliged.'

Chapter 53

Back at the Amalienborg Palace Renzi took stock. This was an unpleasant turn of events.

Bonaparte was notorious for his personal interventions that could in a stroke extinguish an empire or place a brother on a throne. It would not be coincidence that he'd think to take swift action in response to a British military threat, and it was critical its nature be known. Bernstorff himself was not about to risk his precious neutrality in underhanded prying, but had cast about for one who would have little to lose by it.

An act of espionage? It was out of the question. He didn't have any contact with agents here and, in any case, setting aside the personal danger, the risk of long-term compromise of his cover ruled it out completely.

Yet if it threatened the fleet – if it was even now sailing into the jaws of a trap – it didn't bear thinking about.

There was no alternative. He had to act.

His mind raced ahead. Bernstorff's information almost certainly came from a low-level clerk or plain backstairs curiosity at the fuss the receipt of such a message must have provoked. The missive itself would now be somewhere in Gobineau's office – or more probably, given its significance, his inner sanctum. To get to it, read it, was a rank impossibility.

Or was it?

French diplomatic staff were famously corrupt. Talleyrand's demands of a private bribe of tens of thousands before he would even talk to American negotiators had infuriated them to the extent that it had resulted in war. Surely the sight of a letter could be bought.

But he didn't know Gobineau or others in the French legation well enough to be confident in making such an approach, and it would leave him exposed as an agent.

At the very least he could conduct a species of reconnaissance of the premises, if only to confirm for himself the impossibility of any clandestine undertaking.

But he was known. It had to be someone else, someone he trusted utterly, and there was very little time left.

He rang the silver bell and Jago noiselessly appeared. 'M' lord?'

Renzi paused, taking in the man's close-shaven blue-black chin, his watchful dark eyes and panther-like movements. 'We need to talk, Jago.'

'M' lord.'

'A little matter of the Danish staff wages and your allowance for footmen, cooks and kitchen maids. I see we are short three persons. Will your accounts reflect their absence on the wages tally?'

Jago's eyes flickered, but only once. 'There's been expenses, m' lord. Rather than trouble you, I made bold to—'

'Quite so. And the overplus of claret is disposed of equitably?' It was an old ruse but it did no harm to reveal that it was known to him.

'And with no horse fair in Copenhagen there would seem little scope for your . . . dealings, shall we say?'

The man remained silent, his features giving nothing away.

'I think it time we extended our relationship, sir.'

Again, not a word.

'You see, we both have aspects of our lives that were better left discreet, not meat for public misunderstanding.'

Jago stood still, as unblinking as a bird of prey.

'Which it were folly to mention.'

'M' lord.'

Renzi gave a half-smile. 'I'll have you know I'm well satisfied with your service to me, Jago. And I can see how valuable your qualities must have been to my father for his own purposes.'

That this centred on procuring, horse-races, questionable market dealings and political skulduggery was neither here nor there. The man was no stranger to discreet arranging and this was precisely what Renzi needed. 'I believe we have an understanding. Should your affairs be conducted prudently, with discretion, and are not injurious to the estate, I see no reason why you should be troubled.'

'M' lord.' There was a slight bow but no change in expression.

'In return, there are from time to time small matters in my affairs of a confidential nature that it would oblige me exceedingly should you feel able to assist. Your consideration with respect to my privacy will be understood and, naturally, an honorarium will be involved.'

Renzi had no concerns that Jago would take advantage: there had been every opportunity from blackmail to extortion in his dealings with his father but none had even been hinted at.

So now they knew where they stood.

'I understands, m' lord. There's a service you desire at all?'

With a gratifying lack of curiosity, Jago heard Renzi specify that a knowledge of the French mission was needed, a feel for its internal layout, staff numbers and where Gobineau, Comte de Mirabeau, might be expected to have his being.

It was an outrageous request but Renzi was relying on Jago's base cunning and gift of cajolery.

Before nightfall he was back and handed Renzi a rough sketched floor plan.

The legation lay not far away in the Bredgade, a small but grandiose mansion in the usual diplomatic style of discreet seclusion. Three storeys, Gobineau's little sanctum at the end of a passageway on the middle floor with other working offices on each side. Guards, but bored and lazy. Most offices closed at four and Gobineau's was no exception – saving that on occasion he might be entertaining a lady and was not to be disturbed.

It was not impossible but was crazily fraught. Renzi could turn his back on the whole thing but . . . 'I want to be left inside Gobineau's office for twenty minutes. Suggestions?'

Jago didn't turn a hair. 'M' lord, I advise as you goes delivering. Can get you in b' the servants' hall. After that . . .'

'Key of his office?'

'Gen'rally can get a lend of one from a cleaning gent for a rub o' silver.'

'Do it. There's no time to lose. I'll be going in tonight.'

'M' lord?'

'Yes?'

'If you pardons m' boldness, m' lord, but you ain't a knowing cove in these matters. Y' needs a partner, like, who looks out f'r you while you does the . . . gets on with it. If'n you needs one, why, m' lord, I done it before, knows the lay.'

'That's handsome in you, Jago.'

Renzi wondered whether he should let him know something of what was at stake but discarded the idea. Whether he was willing to do it for loyalty or personal gain, additional motivation would not be needed.

Chapter 54

As darkness set in and the streets changed their aspect, they prepared. Jago had returned with a key and two threadbare sets of bearer livery, which they now put on.

There was little point in delay – any deliveries in the small hours would be suspect. As soon as Jago was able to report that the light in Gobineau's window had died they slipped out, Renzi with a cloth over a small hamper and Jago with three bottles in a basket.

Down a dark passage beside the mansion they found the back door. A lounging servant looked up and simply held out a hand. Jago found the necessary and they were in. Through a clattering scullery with the kitchen hands giving not a bit of notice to yet another delivery for the master, they found the gloomy servants' back stairs.

It was going brilliantly – too well?

Puffing at the unaccustomed exercise, they mounted the stairs, and there was the second-floor door. Hefting their burdens they passed into a long passageway, at the end of which was their goal. It was dim, only every fourth sconce alight, but sufficient to show a guard sauntering along and another, closer, sitting sprawled on a cane chair in an alcove, his hat over his eyes.

Renzi stepped forward confidently, Jago behind. As he went to pass the dozing guard a foot suddenly shot across his path.

'*Qui va là?*' the man snarled, tipping back his hat.

Lifting the key and letting it dangle significantly, Renzi gave a supercilious smile and waited with heavy patience.

The foot was reluctantly withdrawn and the hat slid back. They moved past the other who held aside to let them by.

And they were at the door.

Making play of stationing his lesser assistant outside, Renzi fumbled the key into the lock and let himself in, heart thumping.

An Argand lamp in one corner was still burning, the wick at its lowest. He turned it up, grateful for the golden light but aware that the occupant must be intending to return at some point.

He had unknown minutes to find the message.

The room was tidy, with an elaborate desk against the window. Four neat sets of papers were on the blotter ready for work. One wall was lined from floor to ceiling with books and against another was a languorous chaise-longue, next to it a beautifully carved mahogany side table with a foot-high marble statue of a weeping Virgin Mary.

Renzi worked fast, riffling through the paper piles. Next were the pigeon-holes at the rear – so many of them – and he had to be careful to replace everything.

Nothing.

The dispatch case? Or look for a place of concealment?

Near despair, he began feeling down the back of the desk, but it was awkward and—

'Stand up and turn around slowly!' a voice rapped in French.

Renzi froze. The door hadn't opened and someone was in the room with him.

Carefully he rose and turned. It was Gobineau, in a dressing-gown, carrying a heavy pistol. Behind him there was a void in the bookcase where a concealed doorway had swung open.

The count's eyes widened in recognition. '*Mon Dieu!* Lord Farndon? And in the character of a common thief? It passes belief!'

The pistol never wavered, and Renzi knew he would not leave the legation alive.

'Before I have you taken up, it would gratify me immensely to know what it is you seek, my lord. No – don't tell me, I rather think I know.'

He edged along to the desk, a cruel smile playing on his lips. Slowly bending, his eyes never leaving Renzi's, he reached for a lower drawer, drew it open and fumbled for a paper with a broken seal.

'It's this, isn't it, my lord, from our illustrious emperor with instructions that quite undo your mighty fleet's plot against the nation of Denmark? A pity you will never know its genius. Do believe, it sorrows me to have—'

The door swung open. Jago entered and stopped, stunned. In the same moment the startled Gobineau wheeled around to confront him.

Renzi reacted in a fury of despair. Snatching up the statue of the Virgin, he brought it down in a brutal, skull-crushing blow.

Gobineau dropped without a sound, flopping limply, blood and brains spilling.

Jago stared in horror.

'Shut the door – quickly!' Renzi hissed, and snatched the

paper from the corpse. Seeing Jago make for the body, he added savagely, 'Leave him! Turn the place over, get hold of every valuable you can find and make it look good!'

He crossed to the lamp and feverishly scanned the letter.

It was a copy of one sent to Marshal Bernadotte at the head of his army on the southern border and it was from Bonaparte. Short and to the point, it turned everything on its head. If Denmark did not declare war on Great Britain, Bernadotte was to cross the border, then take the country and its fleet for France.

Renzi stood transfixed.

'We has to go, m' lord,' Jago whispered urgently, a jangling cloth bundle in his hands.

Renzi took a last look at the letter, burning its details on his mind then returned it to the drawer. Without a word the pair slipped through the bookcase opening and down steps into a palatial bedroom. It had no occupant but reeked of perfume and, with desperate relief, Renzi saw it had an alternative access – a small door.

It led down a dank, cramped staircase and, after an interminable descent, to another door.

Renzi eased the bolt back, cracked it open, then threw it wide. Ahead an alleyway led to the busy street. Gobineau's route of secret assignation had been the means of their escape.

Safely back, and fortified with a stiff whisky, Renzi forced his mind to an icy composure.

If Bernadotte crossed to Sjælland and flooded it with troops, it would be all over in days. With the Baltic sealed against Britain, and Denmark's fleet in other hands, the worst nightmare would have come true.

There was only one course left: abandon his mission – and the Danes.

On his report, as a matter of the utmost urgency, the armada would be unleashed to secure the prime objective: the Danish fleet. Only this could save something of the situation, putting the closing of the Baltic beyond the power of Bonaparte.

How ironic. Sent on a mission of peace, his would be the word to launch the expedition against the blameless Danish.

He tossed back the last of the whisky and began cyphering. It was done.

His presence in Denmark no longer held any value. The sooner he was away from Copenhagen the better – not only to be gone before the final act started but to escape the bleak sense of guilt that bore down on him.

There was little time left: Gambier would act the instant he received word.

Early the next day, Renzi set Jago to preparing staff and baggage for a hasty departure. Now he had only to fetch Cecilia and they would be gone from this unhappy place.

The major-domo insisted on speaking to him personally. 'So sorry, my lord, all the carriages are not available. It is the English fleet – they are scared, my people.'

Renzi bit back a retort and, with rising anxiety, ordered Jago to find an alternative. Rumours and fright had set the population to a frenzy of aimless movement, and it wasn't until well into the morning that a run-down four-wheeler was located. There was now a pressing need to get away before the mood turned ugly. Renzi remembered how rapidly in Naples things came to a murderous crescendo when the crowd took it into their heads to go against a foreigner.

Chapter 55

Frederiksberg Castle, Sjælland

'Oh, Nicholas! I'm so relieved to see you,' Cecilia whispered. 'Everyone's in such a tizz at the English fleet.'
Behind her, Hetty stood mute, her hands at her mouth.

The guards were still at their posts and inside the palace there was a wary quiet.

Frue Rosen greeted Renzi with a fleeting smile but her hands worked together. 'Sir, I know it in my bones – no good will come of this.'

'Calm yourself, my dear. If it sets your mind at rest I do offer you a place in my party, which is soon to be quit of Copenhagen.'

'Oh, my lord, this is generous of you but, sir, my country, my memories . . . are here in Denmark. I shall stay.'

'I understand. We shall be gone directly, and do wish you—'

Outside there was the sudden clatter of horses and equipment. Hoarse, barked commands rang out and forceful voices could be heard from the hall beneath them.

'It's the Crown Prince!' gasped Frue Rosen.

More shouts came, then an order, repeated.

She started in dismay. 'I'm called. They've come to take His Majesty away.' Turning abruptly she hurried down the stairs.

Renzi ran after her.

The hall was full of men – courtiers, soldiers, footmen. He searched about feverishly for the Crown Prince but couldn't see him for the crowd. Was there now a final chance – if he could get to him?

He was jostled by men streaming out from the interior of the palace with chests and baggage and, through the windows, Renzi saw coaches draw up.

Cecilia caught up with him, clutching his arm at the pandemonium.

Then without warning the Crown Prince was in front of them. 'You! My lord Farndon! Why are you here, sir?' he cried. 'I demand to know!'

'Your Royal Highness, I'm here to collect the countess who's been staying with—'

There was a muffled scream – a tearing, unhinged wail. The bustle and noise died away at the sight of the King of Denmark, Christian VII, being dragged out between two guards in an extremity of terror.

Frederik pushed forward and snapped at the wild-eyed monarch, gesturing angrily.

'*Nej, nej, nej!*' gurgled the King, in his nightclothes a pitiable figure. His ashen-faced guards struggled to hold him.

The Crown Prince barked at his father mercilessly, bringing on a fresh paroxysm of weeping and shrieking.

Frue Rosen tried to interpose herself between them, shielding the King and weeping with frustration.

Everyone froze and a breathless stillness lay on the air.

Cecilia, wrung with pity, choked, 'The poor man! The poor, poor man!'

She ran to him, knelt down and restrained a flailing arm, stroking and murmuring endearments in English, as his mother must have done. He quietened, looking up desperately from her to Frue Rosen, and Cecilia continued her soothing words until, unexpectedly, he smiled and stuttered, 'The English! The English have come at last! I . . . I must prepare for them. Where shall I go?'

Between them Cecilia and Frue Rosen helped him to his feet. Grinning inanely, he allowed himself to be put aboard a coach, never taking his eyes off them. It ground away, the King leaning from a window and waving gaily, as if for all the world he was on holiday.

Crown Prince Frederik stalked over to Renzi. 'I should thank you, my lord,' he said, breathing heavily. 'My father is deranged as you have seen. And yet I'll have you know it was caused by you English.'

'Sir, I'm sorry to hear it, but caused by we?'

'You've not heard? This morning at ten your armada landed troops and guns on the soil of Denmark and even now advance on Copenhagen. For the safety of His Majesty I'm conveying him out of here.' He flushed. 'This is an act of war, my lord. For this I should have you taken. Your mission is finished – it is over. However, for the respect I bear my uncle I grant you your liberty but I can do nothing more for you. My protection is withdrawn.'

Turning on his heel he strode to the royal coach and it sped off with a thunderous cracking of whips.

Cecilia clutched Renzi's arm, looking around fearfully at the commotion. 'Quickly!' he said. 'Follow me.' They ran outside to the outer quadrangle to board the old coach.

It was no longer there.

Chapter 56

Helsingør, at the entrance to the Sound

In his cabin Kydd reached for an apple and tried to concentrate. There'd been such excitement and anticipation when the expedition had sailed, and every day more warships and transports joined to swell their already impressive numbers. It was a far bigger concentration of naval power than he'd seen at the conquest of the Cape, Buenos Aires – even at Trafalgar.

In this great British fleet thousands of men – troops and sailors – were confined within their ships in the late summer heat. For two weeks they'd been lying to anchor here, waiting for the issue to be decided that would see them either sail away or move to another level of threat to induce the Danish to give up their fleet.

But every hour they remained idle, word could be going out that would see the Danes establish defences and bring up troops. Or, worse, call in the French to protect them.

The odd thing was that the Danes seemed completely unconcerned, as if the great force assembled was nothing to do with them.

The beef boats and water hoys put off from the harbour of Elsinore to supply the fleet without any hindrance and in return Admiral Gambier fell in with the sunrise and sunset gun fired from Kronborg Fortress as applying to his fleet as well. Officers were strolling ashore, honours scrupulously paid and returned. A picture of peacetime serenity.

Lying further inshore was the only representative of the Danish navy, the frigate and guardship *Frederiksværn*, at single anchor and silent witness to the drama.

Still no movement. There would soon be a time when—

Through the open stern windows Kydd heard animated voices above. What was going on? They stilled. A short time later there was a burst of excitement. It was too much. He reached for as much dignity as he could muster and wandered on deck.

'All's well?' he enquired of the mate-of-the-deck, who hastily lowered his telescope.

'Sir! We sees this Dansker packet comes out o' nowhere as if he has the hounds o' Hell after him. Heads straight for Flag and in a trice commotion breaks loose aboard. Wouldn't be surprised if—'

'Signal, preparative, "all captains", sir.'

Kydd gave a tight smile.

Gambier was brief and to the point. 'I have this hour been notified that negotiations with the kingdom of Denmark in the article of a pledge of security have failed.' He waited for the murmurs to die down. 'And, further, that unless we act with the utmost dispatch the French will be enabled to intervene. Gentlemen, it is time.'

A landing on the sovereign territory of neutral Denmark was now a reality.

'Operational plans are complete and shall be issued to be put in train immediately. Nonetheless, for your general understanding I would have you know the essence of the whole.

'Failing any diplomatic solution, our objective now is to secure and convey the Danish fleet to a friendly port, if necessary by force of arms. Copenhagen is too well defended to seaward, therefore we needs must make a landing and invest the city from the inner, landward side. All siege impedimenta will be landed, to be on open view to the inhabitants, and an ultimatum issued concerning the release of their fleet. I've no doubt when this happens common sense will prevail.

'Yet, as you must realise, there are dangers to our enterprise that present themselves. The first is that Copenhagen is relieved by reinforcements falling upon our rear while we are engaged in siege. This will result in catastrophe and must be avoided at all costs. The city, however, lies on an island. Commodore Keats will lead a squadron that will encircle the island of Sjælland to prevent a crossing on to it by troops of any description, a vital – or should I say crucial? – task.

'The second is that should the Danish fleet sally from their harbour as we conduct our landing we will be sorely inconvenienced. To that end Rear Admiral Essington will lead a force to stand towards the city while the landing takes place.

'And, finally, that the Crown Prince sees fit to defy us makes me fear that he's amassed strength unknown to us to descend on our forces as we go ashore. If this be the case there are provisions in your orders for a general withdrawal.'

If it came to that, the expedition would have failed, Kydd knew. And such were the stakes that that order would be given only after much bloodshed and destruction.

'It leaves me only with the solemn duty to call upon the Lord to bless us in our just endeavours. Let us pray.'

Kydd returned to his ship with his orders. *Tyger* was to be attached to Commodore Keats. In a way it was a disappointment – they wouldn't be present for the assault, but what could be more important than the throwing of a cordon around the battlefield to prevent interference from the outside?

They were to sail immediately. Keats had been adamant that they were to be under weigh before nightfall that day. There would be time for detailed planning of deployment after they had rounded the northern coast.

Kydd beckoned his first lieutenant. 'Mr Bray, secure for sea. We're on our way!'

Chapter 57

Vedbæk, ten miles north of Copenhagen

In the armed transport *Rathlin*, the news was received with a joy born of desperation. After weeks of idleness and being packed into every conceivable space in the old merchant ship, tempers were ragged. The 52nd Regiment of Foot was a fighting force with service all over the world. Recently re-formed as part of the Light Division they were eager to prove themselves anew in the field.

Ensign Francis Maynard performed the morning inspection of his section – but this time it was in deadly earnest. At dawn the next morning the battalion would be facing the enemy. He walked along slowly, the hard-faced Sergeant Heyer close behind. The expressions varied from boredom through blank-faced inscrutability to blithe resignation. Many were sun-darkened by India service; others had the pale faces and thin bodies of recent recruits. They were not noble warriors – but they were his men. He knew all their names now, their habits and mannerisms, and had a fair notion of how far he could trust them as individuals. He was aware that he himself was being weighed up and, if found wanting, could lose their loyalty.

Maynard made a point of thoroughly checking muskets and accoutrements for this was the whole being of a light infantryman. The sergeants and corporals could be relied on to ensure their knapsacks and traps were up to scratch.

The company briefing earlier had set out the operation in detail. At dawn, under the guns of the fleet, boats of the first wave would head inshore with light infantry, who would establish a beachhead, repelling enemy counter-attacks while the line regiments poured ashore. Once there, the 52nd would move forward to extend the defended line to such a point that guns and horses could be landed.

Simple and straightforward. But if the Danes brought up even horse artillery to the fringing dunes there would be a bloodbath, with an onslaught of canister and round shot into the unprotected boats. Or ashore, as they were assembling, even a small force of cavalry could slash them to pieces.

That night Maynard slept badly. Not that he must doubt his own courage but that when the hour of trial came he would fail the regiment. His was a post of the greatest honour – and the highest danger. As ensign he would be the one to take the regimental colours ashore and plant them on enemy soil as a rallying point. He would be among the first to set foot on land, in the teeth of the worst that the enemy could bring against them.

Even before dawn the troops were assembling after a cold breakfast, detailed off in accordance with the embarkation plan. From now on it was the endurance of waiting.

As first light stole over the anchorage, a silent procession of big warships weighed and detached, the squadron about to close with Copenhagen to face any sudden emergence of the Danish fleet contesting the landing. Maynard watched in the dim light as the men-o'-war purposefully headed south, sailors distantly mounting masts to set sail, gun-ports open in grim challenge, a grand and fearful sight.

Suddenly their companion of the last weeks, the Danish guardship frigate, slipped her cable to make a break for the open sea to the north. Signals went up at the rush in Gambier's flagship and a battleship, with a frigate, dropped sail and went after it.

Now it was their turn. Maynard knew from the map that the beach selected, Vedbæk, was a dozen miles south, halfway along the coast to the capital. The assault ships had been held back until the last minute so as to give no indication of where the soldiers would go in. Now there was general movement on each ship as they prepared for the final run.

Chased off the deck by busy sailors, there was nothing for it but to go below to the creaking, malodorous dimness and endure until the rumble and shake of the anchor cable running out announced their arrival off the beaches.

Heart in his mouth, Maynard took the deck and stood by the company captain as the troops were mustered by boat, trying not to stare at the low, wood-mantled shore almost a mile away. There was no gunfire yet, and no movements that he could see of defenders assembling for the confrontation.

Spars and tackles lifted the heavy boats from their stowage and one by one they were lowered to the water. Seamen tumbled down to take their places at the oars and it was time to board.

Maynard descended steps to the little platform and stepped into the boat. Behind him, Sergeant Heyer carried the colours in their leather case and the pike. Sailors' eyes followed his progress as he went unsteadily over the thwarts to the front of the boat. The colours were passed along to him. It seemed incredible that scores of fully equipped troops with muskets and packs could fit into the confines of the awkward craft and still leave room for the patient seamen to row.

They made shift, however, grunting and cursing, squatting and wedging as they were encouraged by the sailors.

It did not head for the shore: like the others, it fell into line abreast and made ready. Three long lines of boats, lifting gently to the waves, waiting for the order.

Still there was no gunfire or troop movement ashore. It looked so peaceful and ordinary, a rustic cottage to the right and, inland, a spiral of smoke.

It could all change in an instant. The light woods came almost to the water's edge and might conceal anything up to an entire army. Horse artillery might even now be sighting to enfilade the beach and—

A sullen thud sounded from the flagship and a huge Union flag soared up the mainmast – it was the signal.

'Uncase colours!' the lieutenant commanded.

Maynard fumbled nervously in the awkward confines of the bow. Taller than a man, the colours were secured to the pike, which was ten feet long. Then the regimental colours of the 52nd floated out in all their splendour, a Union flag in the canton and the blaze of '52' prominent in laurels against a buff background, the whole with crimson and gold tassels trailing down from the peak.

Exhilarated now, Maynard stood braced in the bows, proud and erect. The colours tugged and pulled mercilessly but the winds were light and he was spared ignominy. The whole line was now in motion, scores of boats abreast of his, and more in the next wave close behind – they were going in.

It was an eerie quiet. No one spoke, all eyes on the long, pale beach, waiting for . . .

They drew nearer. Details of the shoreline became clear: a landing hard for fishermen, a straggle of grey rocks to the left, a small track going up the rise to the right.

They were halfway. Nothing, just the creak and thump of oars, the pretty gurgle of water under their forefoot. It was unreal.

'There they is!' The voice cracked with tension and the sharp-eyed Corporal Jakes flung out an arm to point.

One by one horses were topping the rise, their riders in green and black, unmistakably Danish cavalry videttes. The enemy. Carried by a strange euphoria, Maynard ignored them, standing bold, his eyes fixed on the water's edge, where that day he would do his duty whatever the cost.

The sailors pulled harder, the coxswain driving them on with low urging as the boat swayed with their efforts.

Two hundred yards now. They were well within range of a six-pounder, let alone a nine. Why were they being allowed so close in?

A hundred yards – soon they would be storming the beach.

Skin crawling with anticipation, Maynard clutched the colours staff and when the boat lurched to a stop in the shallows he was over the side, stumbling up the sand, the colours triumphantly streaming above.

Nothing.

Panting with effort, he reached the level ground below the edge of the woods. He struck the butt of the pike into the soil of Denmark, then stood noble and erect. Emotion threatened to overcome him as soldiers rallied beside him, sergeants hoarsely taking charge and drawing them up into familiar battle formations.

And no storm of fire and destruction.

The stillness was broken only by shouts of command, the

occasional baying of a bugle-horn and the cawing of argumentative rooks in the woods.

Then the spell was broken. Details were told to push out into the country to establish a perimeter as the second wave came in, splashing ashore and assembling.

Hundreds, then thousands of troops flooded in unopposed. Some marched off; others prepared to land stores and horses. A disciplined bedlam filled the beachhead.

Maynard had done his duty and now set off to join his men.

He marched up the track to find his company captain. From the glory of the colour party he must now revert to a common ensign of foot. For some reason the enemy had not been waiting – but how could this be when they'd been sighted by the videttes? It was a mystery but no one else seemed to be questioning their good fortune.

The captain briefed him on the terrain. Strong ground to the left and right occupied, the landing beach now safe. The woods thinning to open pasturage inland and a now deserted farmhouse to the right. Five parties out on an armed reconnaissance with no sighting of the enemy, the periphery of the defensive line moving out fast. Maynard was to regroup and set out on a line of bearing to consolidate a strongpoint that would form part of the perimeter.

There were still no enemy formations. In a field a farmer, their first Dane, stared at them in astonishment. They passed him with friendly shouts, many themselves no stranger to a plough.

Reaching their goal they set up a defence position then rested. Yet so rapid was the advance that within an hour they were on the move again, headed for a distinguished building set in parkland at the skyline.

'Maynard,' the captain advised, 'yonder is Charlottenlund. This is the summer palace of the Crown Prince of Denmark. I've orders from General Wellesley that if there's no resistance no one is to enter its doors, under the direst penalty.'

'Aye, an' Nosey's a hangin' general,' Sergeant Heyer offered gloomily. 'Why, after Seringapatam there was good men a-dangling—'

'That's enough,' snapped Maynard. 'Warn off the men, is all.'

They closed with it in good order in the warm afternoon sunshine, through manicured parkland, past fishponds and extensive gardens. Ahead, the neat but frowning palace was deserted.

It was uncanny. They were now several miles inland with no sign of resistance. Was it because the Danes were waiting to spring a trap, an encirclement that would see their advance cut off and destroyed? Maynard clamped a hold on his fears.

Wary and prepared, they came up to the silent palace, but there was no movement. At the back were stables, recently used and in some disorder, but nothing to suggest preparations for a stand.

Men were posted around the sombre building and evening began to draw in.

Orders were given to prepare a bivouac. Not under fire, this was clear-cut enough, but Maynard had never heard of the manoeuvre done when contact with the enemy had not yet been established. By now there were thousands ashore, headquarters staff and even artillery beginning to form up in a comforting army routine of order and discipline.

After a welcome evening meal Maynard lay down with his men, under arms by ranks, with knapsacks for pillows. They had found an arena of soft sand where the regal horses were exercised with only clouds of midges intruding. He stared up at the stars of the night and wondered what the next day might bring.

Chapter 58

The Citadel: Danish headquarters in Copenhagen

'Silence! I will have silence!' Generalmajor Peymann hissed, his face working.

With tight looks and rigid bearing, his senior commanders complied.

'We are here to regularise the defences of Copenhagen, not quarrel like cockerels in a farmyard!' He glared about. 'The English have landed, I grant you that – but what does this mean? If—'

'It means, Herre Generalmajor, that the entire expedition is ashore with all their impedimenta!' barked Generalløjtnant Bielefeldt, commander of the land forces. 'And it'll be a damned near impossible task to dislodge 'em.'

'Quite,' Peymann said. 'Yet there is a reason.'

'A reason, sir?' spluttered Bielefeldt. 'When every military rule ever made says we must destroy an assault before it can fix itself ashore? Is this why I've orders to retire my forces to avoid a confrontation with the enemy?'

'Your choice of words betrays you, sir. The English are not the enemy, as you term them, we are neutrals still. At the moment they are guilty of no more than a species of trespass. That is all.'

'Are you blind? They're—'

'Have a care, General!' Peymann said dangerously. 'These are not my words.'

His eyes flicked once to the figure of Joachim Bernstorff sitting quietly to one side.

'His Royal Highness has specifically desired me to ensure that if this is to be a matter of war, then it is to be left to the British to fire the first shot and thereby earn the opprobrium of the world. That first shot has yet to be fired.'

Bielefeldt shook his head as if to clear it. 'Let me make it plain. At the moment there are some fifteen thousand English soldiers on our soil. To oppose them I have at most five, seven thousand. They are landing artillery, we have—'

'Enough! As yet we do not know their intentions. Until now, the British have treated us fairly. They pay the Sound dues without complaint and have respected our neutrality. Why should they hazard their character in pursuit of some security pledge that is not in our power to give?'

Krieger leaned forward to offer a grubby sheet of paper. 'I think you should read this, Generalmajor. Printed by the invaders and clandestinely circulated in the city.'

Peymann took it and pursed his lips. 'It says they come in peace, to defend us against the disturbers of peace, the French. Repeats that nonsense about releasing our fleet into their custody and they'd sail away in friendship.'

'The last paragraph, sir.'

'Oh. "If these offers are rejected then innocent blood will be shed and the horrors of a besieged and bombarded capital must fall on your heads." Why, this stands with all the rest, a frightener.'

'I rather think not.' Bernstorff's words brought an immediate hush to the room. 'Consider – this paper constitutes a declaration, a public statement of intent before the world. Should we ignore it they will not skulk away, their bluff called. No, they are in deadly earnest and this you must take under the most serious concern in your deliberations, sir.'

'They will not dare to make open assault against Copenhagen.'

'I say they come prepared to do so.'

'*Disse elendige englændere!*' spat Kommandør Bille, glaring at Peymann. 'The real reason they're here is to take Sjælland and make it their sure base for their Baltic operations. All else is a mockery!'

'Sir, you will note they're very specific. They want our fleet and nothing further.'

'Our fleet? *Fandeme mig nej*, and they'll not get it while I'm still alive and in charge!'

Krieger stirred restlessly. 'Sir, it galls me that the English transports are at the beaches and I've gunboats enough to set about 'em, like a wolf among sheep,' he growled. 'Their fleet of battleships can't go inshore, they'd be helpless before our guns, and—'

Peymann regarded him coolly. 'That first shot, sir?'

'We must do something!' blurted Bielefeldt. 'Anything!'

'Calm yourself, sir. I grant that they may go so far as to encircle the city and even lay siege, but as chief engineer of the fortifications and walls I'm sanguine they'll never prevail. The Citadel and ramparts, the many bastions and miles of fosse before them will prove impossible. No, sir, if we stay within the city walls we'll be quite safe.'

'And if—'

'We remain quietly in our city while His Royal Highness

recalls his relief army from Holstein. And, as you sailors know, the season is drawing in, so they and their fleet must leave. It's only a matter of patience.'

'Then, sir, you've determined to do nothing.' Bernstorff's eyes were unreadable.

'The Crown Prince has seen fit to place the protection of his people and their city under my command. I intend to do my sacred duty by His Highness.'

Bernstorff rose with dignity and bowed. 'Very well. My further attendance at this council would seem irrelevant. Good day to you, Herre Generalmajor.'

Peymann followed him out with his eyes, then resumed the meeting. 'Points have arisen that I believe deserve a further examination, gentlemen. General Bielefeldt, what is your understanding of the readiness of the militia to take up arms?'

'Hmmph. They'll obey orders, if that is your meaning.'

'I was thinking more of—'

The door opened and Bernstorff stood there wordlessly, holding a paper.

'Yes, Herre Bernstorff?'

With a set face the minister approached and handed him the paper. 'Sir, it is war. The Crown Prince has declared war on Great Britain. Sir, you are commanded to seize all British citizens, to confiscate their property and take all measures commensurate with an opening of hostilities.'

Peymann held it in hands that trembled.

Krieger jumped to his feet, knocking his chair askew. 'War! Be damned, but we're off the leash at last.'

'And further,' added Bernstorff, 'he commands that you defend his capital and people to the last, for the honour of Denmark and the Crown. He bestows all powers on you, the supreme commander. Sir, I'm aware that this has not turned out in the way you thought it would, but time presses. I'm to leave Copenhagen this hour to attend on His Royal Highness with news of your dispositions,' he finished meaningfully.

Peymann sat with a stricken look as the paper drifted to the floor. 'Er, I . . .'

'An immediate evacuation of the capital by the civil population?' prompted Bernstorff.

Peymann seemed not to have heard, then replied unsteadily, 'The Crown Prince has placed the protection of his people in my trust. This is my first and highest duty. How can I do this if they're wandering at large in a countryside swarming with British redcoats?' His tone strengthened. 'No, sir. My orders are that at sunset today the gates to the city will be closed, before which all Danish citizens will be taken inside for their safety. We defy the English as of this moment.'

Krieger leaned across the table and glowered at Peymann. 'Then, sir, do you now say to me this is a shooting war?'

'Kommandørkaptajn Krieger – it is.'

Chapter 59

The Great Belt seaway between Sjælland and Jutland

Keats's squadron had left Elsinore and cracked on sail along the north coast to the entry point of the Great Belt, where a long finger of land ending in a grassy bluff pointed out to five miles of treacherous sub-sea reef.

They were anchored in its lee, four 74-gun ships-of-the-line with five frigates and smaller vessels, an unanswerable potency should the Danes dare to oppose them.

This was one of three entrances to the Baltic, all commanded by the Danes, but foreign vessels were restricted to just one, the direct passage past Kronborg and through the Sound. This was where the toll was collected, a substantial part of the state's revenue. The two others – the Great Belt and the Little Belt – were kept from outsiders by the simple expedient of jealously guarding the secrets of their navigation.

The reputation of this narrow, reef-strewn passage was enough to deter all but the foolhardy and few ventured this way. But for the squadron there was no alternative.

* * *

Kydd was summoned to a bracing 'all-captains' meeting with Keats, who left no doubt about the conduct of their mission, the isolating of the Danish in Copenhagen on their island of Sjælland.

'Carry on,' he told his transparently curious first lieutenant, as soon as he returned aboard *Tyger*. 'And all officers to attend in my great cabin in an hour, if you please.'

'Be seated, gentlemen,' Kydd said, as his officers entered. 'We shall dispense with formalities. Refreshments?'

The table was laid out with charts and the chairs left deliberately casual. They settled self-consciously, Bray's heavy presence at one end dominating, Bowden and Brice on either side. The master wore a deep frown and seemed unsure where to sit.

Kydd addressed him first. 'Now, Mr Joyce, I've had a good steer from the commodore as we can work to. Be that as it may, I'll not hide it from you all. This is going to be a fraught exercise by any man's reckoning.' He found the Denmark chart and smoothed it out. 'You'll know that this country consists of the mainland – that's the peninsula of Jutland – and its islands to the east. That's Fyn, then our Sjælland. Our duty is to completely surround and isolate this last to prevent any reinforcement or interference.'

Joyce hovered over the chart, muttering.

Kydd continued, 'The hard part is getting through the Great Belt, for afterwards it's an open sea swing around the southern islands to end up at the opposite end of the Sound to where we started. Clear?'

Bray caught his eye. 'Then the squadron sails back an' forth in this Great Belt while Admiral Gambier pastes the Danes on his side.'

'No, sir. The commodore's plan is to sail through and leave off a sail-o'-the-line here, a frigate there, at the most likely crossing points, while the rest sail on. Those left take station at Møn at the other end of the Sound, keeping a weather eye open for any who want to join the sport from the south'ard – remembering the whole coastline belongs to Boney now.'

'Ye said it'd be a hard beat for us, Cap'n. I'm thinkin' it's going to be even worse'n ye fear, sir,' Joyce worried. 'There's sailin' masters gone mad, conning a ship o' size through the Great Belt in light winds.'

'Steady yourself, Mr Joyce. We've a sovereign remedy for your gripes – I've a complete sailing directions, thoughtfully made up by your colleagues in Nelson's fleet the last time we were here. He gave out orders they were to take the opportunity to return by the Great Belt and survey a route as they went. It's all there for you.'

Joyce found the pack and laid it out, then looked up accusingly. 'This is no chart, sir! It's a rutter o' sorts. Safe bearin's, transits an' such – but this is proceedin' to the north, an' we're southbound. So everything is back-bearings, breasting a current instead o' going with it and—'

'The squadron will be preceded by *Mosquito* brig-sloop. She'll be going ahead with boats, laying dan-buoys as she goes.'

'Hmmph.'

'And we'll be attending her as protector, should any interfere.'

Bowden wanted to know their position should they fall in with a Danish ship.

'Well taken, Mr Bowden. As the commodore hasn't had word yet of a higher level of who should say war, then the Danes are still neutrals. No firing, no battle. If they're carrying troops or guns they're politely told to take 'em back where they came from.'

'But if they're not so obliging?'

'If they're stubborn, we lay ourselves athwart their bows and if there's gun-smoke, why, was it not they who started it?'

The delicacies dealt with, the best chart they had was consulted, a copy of a Lübecker some fifty years old and dense with pencilled comments in English.

'So what are we facing? This chart and our notes tell us it's one thing: currents. Fierce and unpredictable. Up to three, four knots, which means we have to find fair winds of at least that strength just to stay still. If the breeze dies, it's a dismal fate awaits a ship caught in their grip. We might have our fairway buoyed for us but if we can't stay with the course because of these currents . . .'

Chapter 60

The next day the squadron readied for the passage. *Mosquito* led off in the light north-westerly with four boats in tow, heading for the first hazards with *Tyger* a safe mile astern of her.

It was a seascape Kydd had never before seen: the numerous islands were flat and monotonous, dark green and iron grey-brown, so flat they could be seen from the deck only when close. And so many lay sprawled across their path.

The first barrier was between two larger islands acting as gatekeeper to the Great Belt. Using the notes from Nelson's fleet, *Mosquito*'s boats made straight for the eastern-most and, some hundred yards from its gently sloping end, began casting their lead. In twenty minutes they had a bottom profile established and the first two buoys were slipped.

With sails backed, *Tyger* lay hove to, lookouts primed.

The boats were recovered, and *Mosquito* moved into the more open waters beyond. Well astern of them, the squadron got under weigh. They were committed. There was no going back now: the north-westerly was foul for a return in these restricted waters.

A long spit stretched out from the coast, which hid a change of direction from south-west to south-east. The sloop stood off and her boats got to work again.

Kydd knew what they were after: the notes told of a deep-water channel the Danes called the *dybe rende*, a hollow depression that gave sure depths for any ship. The trouble was that the other function of a lead-line – to give notice of the kind of seabed at that point, sea-shells or mud perhaps to indicate location – did not come into play, for the scouring current kept the bottom a hard clay that could give no clue.

They found it: again, less than a mile out, and it was buoyed accordingly. Things were going well and they shaped course south-eastward past the island of Fyn to starboard and the main one of Sjælland to larboard. From *Tyger*, Kydd watched astern as the topsails of the first ship-of-the-line appeared over the spit. It was *Vanguard* cautiously rounding. It would be a much more difficult matter for a ship so large and slow to respond and Kydd felt a surge of sympathy for her master. She came into full view but then, to his utter astonishment, she altered course, heading direct for the shore.

It was madness and had no meaning. The massive ship continued on her suicidal direction until her anchors roared out and she slewed to a stop, her sail hastily doused. Like a ponderous top, she began to rotate on her anchor cables until she steadied, facing the way she'd come.

A sure sign of one thing – unlike *Tyger*, which had been experiencing a mild current heading her, *Vanguard*'s deep draught had encountered a counter-current at her keel in the opposite direction. This had embedded the battleship in a mass of water going the same way as she was, and her rudder had lost all effect. It was a chilling demonstration of what they were dealing with. It took an agonising three hours for boats to haul the great ship-of-the-line out to the point where careful sounding had shown the sub-sea current to have diminished and she could set sail for the south.

They passed another tongue of scrubby land but just beyond, as it deepened again, Kydd picked up on a flaw in the water. Years before in his first command he had been stationed in the Channel Islands, probably the most treacherous sea in the world, with its myriad reefs and islets, and he knew instantly what it was: an overfall. Somewhere in the depths not far below there was a jagged shelf of rock or reef edge over which the water was crowding, and it was directly in their path.

'Bear up!' Kydd roared at the helm. 'Lay off two points to starb'd.' That was another thing he'd learned in Guernsey: the fuss and bother in the water was not the real location of the rock's teeth – it was upstream, in the deceptive smooth water before it.

It was not a place for strangers, still less great ships-of-the-line, but they sailed on.

The passage widened and they made good progress, the squadron in a loose line ahead as they approached the most important point in the entire Great Belt – the closest the coast of Sjælland would come to the island of Fyn where the highway from the mainland to Copenhagen led across the water to Korsør on the Sjælland side and, therefore, where any reinforcements could be expected to mass.

This was now the most crucial point and Kydd doubled lookouts watching over *Mosquito* as she patiently neared the six-mile constriction, a large island neatly at the halfway mark, with a low foreland extending from the left and hiding what lay beyond; their chart told them it was the small harbour of Korsør.

There was no sign of military transports or any kind of shipping. The formidable sight of the line of men-o'-war must have driven them off.

Vanguard turned ponderously and her anchor plunged down. She was going no further: her station was to lie at this crossing point, a floating fortress to challenge anything that moved. Their notes and chart were unanimous that this side of the channel was to be preferred and *Mosquito* disappeared behind the foreland with her boats.

Tyger hove to and waited, but when sails reappeared it was not what anyone was expecting: a sizeable packet boat burst into view under a press of sail with *Mosquito* in hot pursuit. Too late, it saw *Tyger* and slowly rounded to in defeat.

Kydd looked at Bray. 'A guilty conscience. This rascal's up to no good or I'm a Dutchman!'

He looked around for Bowden. 'We've no time for a full rummaging. Board him. Any sign that makes you suspicious, throw out a signal. Clear?'

'Aye aye, sir.'

Kydd waited impatiently, watching the young officer board and disappear below. It wasn't long, however, before he took boat back to *Tyger*.

'Anything?'

'Naught as would interest you, sir. An ailing Swedish baron of sorts on his way to take the waters in Baden, a quantity of his household and all the comforts is all.'

There was no point in detaining the packet and Kydd let it go: the squadron could not be delayed in its vital task.

Eight miles further on, as monotonous flat islands began

increasing to the left, they sighted the long, low tip of Langeland. From now on, the narrow length of the island would stay to their starboard for the thirty-odd miles to the end of the Belt and the open sea. It would act as a funnel through which all shipping must pass. *Nassau* 64 and the frigate *Sibylle* took position there.

It was the last part of the transit and it would be a relief to win through to the unbounded expanse of ocean, but before they were quit of this place of sea perils it had one more surprise.

Mosquito had found that the *dybe rende* had narrowed to little more than a cable wide – two hundred yards only – and through its undersea ramparts the water of the Great Belt whirled along at an astonishing speed. With the north-westerly veering to a brisk northerly the two remaining battle-ships, *Orion* and *Ganges*, found their eight knots by the wind increased to twelve and thirteen by the current – a speed over the ground of which a flying frigate would be well proud.

Their emergence from the Great Belt was something of an anti-climax. Without fuss, on both sides the low coast fell away until they were left in a calm grey sea with nothing to disturb the placid horizon.

The passage was complete. Ahead some thirty miles was Kiel but the squadron put over the helm and bore away eastward, to pass the three big islands marking the southern bounds of Denmark: Lolland, Falster and Møn.

At one point the low dark of land to starboard became visible. Kydd stared at it with his memories. This was Prussia where, only months ago, he'd been caught up in Bonaparte's unstoppable rolling conquests that now included the entire south shore of the Baltic, save the territory of his new ally, Russia. Over there, just hours' sail away, were the ancient Hansa cities of Rostock, Lübeck and Wismar, all in thrall to the conqueror.

Now, for *Tyger*, it was a broad reach to the north until the rumpled white cliffs of Møn were in sight.

Keats had carried out his orders to the letter. This would be their station while the drama of the landing and what followed took place, clamping an iron hold on Sjælland while it played out. Kydd felt a wash of pride. This was the reality of command of the seas: ships at sea far out of sight of armies but directly affecting the strategics of their battle and its eventual outcome.

Chapter 61

At sea, southern Baltic between Denmark and Pomerania

It was not long before *Tyger* and *Lapwing* sloop received orders for further duty.

Just weeks ago, the last piece of the old Swedish empire had fallen, the island of Rügen sheltering the medieval town of Stralsund in Pomerania. The Swedes had put up a desperate resistance but had now pulled out, leaving the large port in the hands of the French.

This was now a direct threat. Less than fifty miles from Denmark, Marshal Bernadotte with his vast army was in a position to menace the landing and Kydd's duty was plain: to discourage any adventuring or, if necessary, to bring Keats's squadron down on them.

Kydd studied his charts, which for once were recent and well produced, obviously of Swedish origin. The task would not be difficult: Stralsund was tucked away in the channel between the large island of Rügen and the mainland, well protected from the outside world. It was approached only by either of two entrances through shoals and wicked reefs, which, of course, meant that any ships leaving must necessarily emerge from them.

Kydd sent *Lapwing* to patrol the northern entrance while *Tyger* would take the south or, more accurately, the south-east, between the craggy tip of Rügen and the bleak marshes of Peenemünde. Given the seaways threading for those miles through shallows and mud-banks, there would be no fear of a night sailing so they could take their ease lying off during the hours of darkness.

Tyger took up her station and began patrolling under small sail along the five-fathom line, which curved across the six-mile entrance. Sailing around Rügen, there had been a prospect of cliffs and rumpled coastline with not a sign of humanity. No fortifications or vessels disputed their presence.

At dusk they put out to sea and settled for the night. After supper Dillon brought in the backgammon board while the faint strains of the practising foremast choir lay on the air as they set to. Kydd told Tysoe to open a promising brandy he'd been recommended and had the stern windows set ajar to allow in the gentle airs of the evening.

There were worse fates for a man, he had to acknowledge, and the time passed agreeably until he retired to his cot and fell asleep immediately.

'Sir! Captain, sir!'

He levered himself up muzzily. 'Yes?'

'Sir, two o' the clock and Mr Brice would be happy t' see you on deck.'

The messenger held a lanthorn and waited. The time-honoured wording indicated that a situation was developing that the officer-of-the-watch felt was getting beyond his powers. Kydd came quickly to full alert – Brice was an experienced officer and would not have called him on deck without a good reason.

It was a pitch-black night and it was difficult to make out the little group about the helm in the dim light from the binnacle.

'Mr Brice?'

'Sir. A light was sighted and I conceived it my duty to investigate. Sir, it's a boat and there's one who desires most urgently to come aboard.'

Chapter 62

Frederiksberg Castle, Copenhagen

With no sign of their carriage Renzi looked about in great concern. Cecilia clung to his arm, pale-faced at the pandemonium around them – wild-eyed servants and functionaries, red-faced courtiers bellowing orders.

Fear for Cecilia tore at him. At any moment a cry could go up that would turn this frightened rabble into an angry and vengeful mob, bent on taking out their fears on the English in their midst. Memories of Constantinople slammed in – common folk turned in minutes to murderous butchery.

'Inside – get out of sight!' he rapped.

Hurriedly they pressed to one side of the entrance hall by the marble columns and diamond-patterned windows. Renzi put his arms protectively around his wife and tried to think. God knew what was happening out there now. Gambier must have acted instantly, sending troops ashore in a martial flood, no doubt with guns and cavalry. If the Danes were resisting it was war, and for themselves the worst possible situation, caught in the front line between two armies.

However, there was safety inside the city walls and ramparts of Copenhagen. Surely the whole thing would be resolved one way or another in days. Then they and their entourage at the Amalienborg could be diplomatically extracted by sea. That was, if they could make it the few miles from here to there, through a panicking mob that—

'Frue Rosen!' shrieked Cecilia, across the bedlam.

The nurse hurried over, horror-stricken. 'M' lord, lady!' she blurted. 'I thought you'd gone! It's not safe, sir, you must leave!'

'Our coach went without us,' Cecilia told her. 'We have to get to Copenhagen. What can we do?'

Frue Rosen hesitated, then whispered, 'Come with me – do be quick, I beg!'

They followed her outside and hastened along a garden path to a small cottage set among others in a light grove of trees.

'My lord, this is my home. If you and the countess would . . .' She left them inside and hurried away.

They sat together in the little front room, charmingly set about with roses and a mix of quaint English ornaments of another age and others with a Scandinavian touch. On one wall was a prettily framed picture of a Dane with stern features.

The muffled sounds of disturbance and confusion were increasing. If they could not get away . . .

Frue Rosen came back, kneading her hands. 'I've found a coach as will take us to Copenhagen but . . .'

'Did you say "us"?' Cecilia asked softly.

'I will go with you, m' lady. Your English tongue will betray you.'

'We cannot ask this of you, dear Frue Rosen. If—'

'The coach belongs to Second Chamberlain Pedersen. He

flees to Copenhagen too and I asked him to take me. He agrees, and I tell him I have two friends who must come with me.'

'That is well done, Frue Rosen,' Renzi said gratefully. 'You are—'

'M' lord, I must ask you to . . . to . . .'

'What do you wish me to do?'

She flushed. 'Begging your pardon, sir, but it would never do to be seen like that. If you were to wear more as your Danish gentleman is . . .'

Cecilia managed a smile. 'She wishes you to go in the character of a Dane, my dear.'

'And you, m' lady, if you'd be so good as to . . .'

In a short time Renzi had on a plain dusky red cloak and a well-worn beaver, while Cecilia had put on one of Frue Rosen's nurse's capes.

A small coach and pair drew up outside with an impatient shout from the passenger leaning out of the window. An older man with fierce eyes, he beckoned urgently.

Renzi pulled the hat down as far as he could and walked out, Cecilia and Hetty behind him.

Pederson glared at him, then started in surprise. He gestured angrily and berated Frue Rosen, his meaning all too clear.

'He says he knows you for an Englishman and will not have you in the same carriage,' she said, then shouted back in a venomous stream of Danish.

Pedersen recoiled, sulkily spitting out a reply, but retreated inside.

'I told him that if he didn't take us, the Crown Prince will be informed that he has cravenly abandoned his post to leave the palace to be ransacked by the British,' she said tightly. 'Do please go on board.'

Renzi and Cecilia sat together opposite the glowering Pedersen who pointedly looked away. Thumps sounded above as baggage was loaded, then the others hastily scrambled in and the coach lurched off.

The road to Copenhagen was thick with vehicles of every description, all headed in the same direction, as well as increasing numbers on foot with bundles and crying children, some shouting and shaking their fists at them, others doggedly tramping in an endless stream of ragged humanity.

At last, across a wide fosse waterway the massive earthen ramparts and bastioned city walls loomed. Frue Rosen leaned out of the window, then withdrew. 'They're checking everyone at the gate,' she said nervously, then turned to Pedersen and spoke sharply to him. He snarled a reply but responded by fumbling in his coat and bringing out an official pass.

'My lady, your gentleman is sick, do comfort him.'

Cecilia pulled at the cloak until it nearly hid Renzi's face as he hunched forward as though in pain.

'Pedersen understands that if you are discovered he will be implicated. We'll have no trouble from him.'

Outside there was bedlam as the crowd converged on the gate. The coach driver cursed and shouted as he tried to make his way through.

The coach jerked to a stop. A soldier's face appeared at the window, suspicious and impatient. He snapped something at Pedersen, who irritably flourished his pass, and when he demanded the same of the others Pedersen gave out an impassioned harangue. The soldier sullenly gestured them on.

Within the city the maze of medieval streets was less crowded as the fleeing citizens dispersed and they made good progress until they spotted trouble ahead.

Pedersen leaned from the window and growled at the driver to stop. At a street corner a knot of figures was arguing with a troop of militia. After listening for a space he drew back in, clearly frightened.

'They are searching for the English,' Frue Rosen said fearfully. 'There is an order that all are to be arrested and thrown in prison, their property confiscated.'

Pedersen growled.

'He says it's too dangerous. You must get out now.' She bit her lip, then spoke again to him. He nodded, troubled, but gave an order to the driver. It swung around and the horses trotted off down a side-street to join a more fashionable avenue.

'We go to the Svane Reden, a residence of Princess Caroline, who is absent. We will be safe there. I can let you in.'

It was a townhouse, discreet and with a single entrance. Nearby there was an imposing church with a spire.

'Wait, please.'

She ran to the door and swung the knocker sharply. There was no response. She fumbled with a bundle of keys and tried the door – it opened and she went inside, quickly emerging again and beckoning.

Renzi and Cecilia scurried after her, Hetty following.

'There's no one here – they've gone to their families,' Frue Rosen told them. 'We're alone!'

The dark interior was musty and full of shapes under dust-sheets. Their voices echoed in the stillness.

There was a flurry of movement. Renzi peered out of the door and saw the coach disappearing around the corner. 'He's gone off with our luggage!' he swore.

Cecilia pulled him back in. 'Darling – we're safe!' she cried. 'Nothing else matters!'

'For now, my love,' he answered, with feeling.

'You are out of harm's way in this place, my lord. No one will trouble us here,' Frue Rosen said, firmly shutting and bolting the door. 'Shall we see what we can find?'

Chapter 63

Svanemøllen, north of Copenhagen

The brigade major took Ensign Maynard's report with a grunt. In the cold damp grey of pre-dawn the lines of soldiers waited patiently, but as the young officer made his way back he was filled with a mixture of elation and apprehension. The army was on the march: they were to advance on Copenhagen and invest the capital – to surround it and formally demand its capitulation.

The sudden braying of a bugle-horn nearby startled him, part of the vast confusion of three army divisions manoeuvring in the misty dawn before being assembled into column of march, accoutred and paraded for inspection, firelocks checked, knapsacks completed.

In the distance the bagpipes of some Highland regiment summoning the clan burst into a martial squealing, clashing with their fifes and drums. In the rear a mule-train of ammunition and stores was being assembled, and further off there was activity with horse-drawn guns. But Maynard, on his first deployment in the face of the enemy, had eyes only for his own company.

They were in line, standing loose and staring blankly to their front. He watched Sergeant Heyer go down the ranks once again checking the men's kit.

He himself was second under Lieutenant Adams, who waited with affected boredom for his return. It was a new experience for him as well.

At last all seemed to settle. There was a sudden flurry of bugle calls and the volleying of drums – the column was forming up. His station was near the head with the light infantry company, and as he went to his place he proudly saluted the lieutenant colonel and the major, trying to assume the correct expression of an officer going to war.

Theirs was the third battalion of the column to march out, with a preparatory rattle of drums, silence, then a roar of command. It was taken up by the captain of the light infantry company and, with a flourish on the drums and screamed orders from the sergeants, they stepped off smartly, hearing the next company behind them brought to readiness and leave, one by one until the whole battalion was afoot.

On the flanks of the column the band rattled and thumped.

With the heady sound of the massed tramp of the host ringing in his ears, Maynard felt the exhilaration of marching to war.

But somewhere not far ahead there had to be a confrontation. He gulped at the realisation that in an hour or less he could be fighting for his life, his men relying on him.

They swung on past unkempt fields and a farmhouse. The inhabitants stared at them but in the pastures the cows grazed without lifting their heads. Immaculate dressing of the ranks was kept and the men chivvied into a soldierly bearing. The next ahead were the Coldstream Guards and it would never do for the 52nd to be found wanting in the article of smartness.

After a mile or so the order to march at ease was given and shouldered muskets were shifted to the support position in the crook of the elbow. The ranks opened, and an easy, economical swing ate up the distance. Maynard had glimpsed the captain's map and knew they didn't have far to march. The army was advancing in three columns, one on a broad sweep around the rear of the city to the other side, another to establish a strong centre and theirs was to come up with the left of the line, where the city walls met the sea.

A rise in the ground gave them their first sight of Copenhagen. Less than eight miles ahead, innocent and enchanting in the sunshine, it was all spires and a mass of buildings amid a shimmer of water here and there.

They marched on.

Out to sea on their left were uncountable anchored ships, filling the near horizon from end to end. To the front and rear a column of soldiers a mile or more long was marching irresistibly on and on – surely the Danes must take this seriously. Guiltily Maynard suppressed disappointment: it was likely that even before they'd completed their encirclement they would be treating for terms.

They passed more cottages and other houses, continuing through a pretty village with pale faces at the windows and dogs barking. Every so often they saw Danish outriders following their progress from higher ground on their right, though they gave no indication of hostile intent. Perhaps they were in communication with an army issuing out of the city gates at that very moment, set on taking the field for the clash that would decide the issue.

Maynard felt a lurch of apprehension and cursed his imagination.

A halt was called at a place they were told was Swan Mill, a placid hamlet where the road touched the sea. There, the other two columns struck out inland on their encircling, leaving Maynard's to establish their position. Here, some two miles from the city and safely out of range of its heavy guns, their part in the investment of the capital was to be made.

It was just like Shorncliffe: picquets out in front to probe the enemy, companies deployed to left and right in line, others in depth behind while the colonel and adjutant made appraisal of the terrain.

'Nice enough, should the Danskers behave themselves,' Adams ventured, as they waited for orders. 'We've a chance at a billet, I'd believe and—' He broke off and looked up sharply.

'What is it?'

Adams held up his hand for silence. Maynard heard a far-off faint popping, much like a child's toy. 'We've made contact with 'em at last, I'd say.'

Maynard's pulse quickened. It was only the picquets, but it might develop into an assault by the enemy before they could throw up defensive works. Either way, it was a turning point in his life: he was now indisputably on a battlefield.

Nobody else seemed much concerned and went about their business. It was up to the lieutenant with the picquets to advise of a breaking attack but when the horse messenger cantered past he was clearly in no hurry.

Orders for encampment had arrived. Pioneers got to work, preparing the defensive lines, while the camp took shape and the familiar features emerged of an army in the field.

Word came through that General Cathcart, general-officer-commanding the army, was establishing his headquarters at Hellerup, the village they'd passed a mile back, and later that elements of the 23rd Regiment of Foot, from Lieutenant General Baird in the centre, had linked up with their right. The King's German Legion, with its brigades of dragoons, was covering the landing of guns and stores and had the additional task of watching the road from the north in case of a breakout from Kronborg Fortress.

By the afternoon the encirclement was complete. With Major General Wellesley taking up a roving position at the rear to guard against counter-attacks from the countryside, and with scouts on the move inland, it had to be accepted: against all expectations the investment of Copenhagen at a distance of a mile and a half was a fact and it had taken little more than a day.

Chapter 64

'So now we wait?' Maynard asked Adams, over a delayed noon meal.

'Oh, perhaps we shall,' he replied airily. 'Though I can't see how the Danskers can expect to continue. Surrounded completely, no reinforcements getting through past our Jack Tars – I heard their numbers are less'n half ours.'

'We haven't got back anything from the scouts. Could be there's that out there . . .?'

'Yours not to ask questions, younker. Eat up – we're out on picquet duty next.'

It seemed absurd to think about war as they walked along the road in the sunshine, past daisy meadows and fishponds, and into woodland towards a slight rise. Yet Maynard was aware of the gorget at his throat and the sword at his side – and the file of relieving picquets tramping behind.

Nevertheless, there had been firing here before – they were moving up to a forward position where he might be in sight of some enemy sniper. With tautened nerves, he pressed on until they reached the edge of the woodland looking out over a ploughed field to where the trees resumed.

By a gnarled oak, Adams took out his whistle and gave two blasts. With a rustle of undergrowth a lieutenant appeared, bored and immaculate. 'Your relief, old fellow. Anything?'

'Quiet as Aunt Maud's grave. This morning's fracas I'd think was only a parcel o' loobies lost their way.' He sniffed and lost no time in detailing the disposition of the picquets and lines of sight of landscape features, then left abruptly.

'You take the left by the windmill, I'll do the right,' Adams said, after a careful survey of the ground.

With a corporal and another soldier following, Maynard made off down the woodland path. He felt a touch of unreality as they crunched on through the leaf litter to a fence at the left boundary of the trees. A grey windmill loomed by the road.

'A fine observation point, I believe,' he said to the off-going watcher, who touched his hat and waited warily. 'Have you taken a view yet?'

'No, I hasn't, sah.'

'I think you should. It's a—'

'Sah. Too obvious, like, an' it's rotten inside. Can't. Shall I go now?'

'Carry on, please,' Maynard said, his face burning.

'Over yonder, sir?' the corporal suggested.

He agreed, only too happy to let experience prevail over training. He'd set up a post in the woods, for the brush would allow concealed observation up to the open field. Estimating a halfway point back to the picquet rendezvous he set the man and his number two in position, then considered what to do next.

In his breast pocket, he carried Dundas, *Principles of Military Movement*, as he had ever since leaving training. He didn't dare bring it out now but his mind was a blank about what it said of picquet duty. He headed slowly towards the gnarled tree rendezvous point.

He remembered Dundas. Shouldn't he be discovering the dispositions of the adjacent postings, Adams's people? Yes. He quickened his stride.

At the tree he fumbled for his whistle but something made him look out over the field.

He could have sworn there had been movement on the far side, at the margin of the woodland. He strained to see and almost missed two figures darting away to the left. Pulse racing, he knew it was the enemy.

Had anyone else spotted them? There were no alarms and he scanned the area. Was that twitch and sway in the undergrowth—

On his left a shot rang out – one of the picquets posted near the windmill! Another somewhere on the right.

Several figures scuttled to the left. And more to the right. Skirmishers – but were they merely probing, testing the lines? Or in advance of a main force?

Swallowing hard, Maynard ran back down the path to his men. They were in a prone position behind a fallen tree, calmly waiting. 'What did you see?' he demanded breathlessly.

'This'n? Trying us out, I wouldn't wonder. Sah.'

Maynard hesitated. His was the decision: to raise an alarm or deal with it himself?

From further to the left there was more movement – and two soldiers scrambled into view. They rushed across to a small bramble copse and disappeared behind it. It was well in advance of the woodland edge and, with a dawning realisation, he understood. 'Hold your fire! On no account open fire without my express permission.'

They looked at him curiously but rested their arms.

'Corporal – go to the others and tell 'em the same.'

The man loped away.

If he was wrong there was no harm in it but if he was right . . .

A single pop sounded faintly well to the right. Adams. But it was not followed up.

Another quick scurry – this time to a depression in the middle of the field.

He gulped. Another two raced to join them. He was right, then: they were probing for the position of the British picquets, tempting fire. Like him, Adams had ordered his men not to reply.

The next few minutes would reveal whether it was in earnest or a passing brush.

Suddenly a mass of soldiery burst into view and quickly formed up in line, three ranks deep, drums behind maintaining an urgent rattle. Alien uniforms of red on blue with grey breeches. The enemy!

Blind panic threatened. What could anybody do against this?

Maynard forced himself to a coolness. The enemy clearly didn't know what forces confronted them and was assembled in defensive line for a general advance. It was a formidable front of two, three hundred yards – the strength of a whole battalion at the very least.

Training came to his rescue. Word had to be sent back, and he should deploy his men in parties along a skirmish line to distract the advance until reinforcements could arrive.

This was the long-feared counter-attack and it was his duty to face it.

'Alert our advanced posts!' he snapped at one man, who loped off. 'Corporal – all men over to the enemy left, we harry him on the flank.'

Was it the right thing to do? Hopefully Adams would do the same on the other flank, putting them under fire from both sides.

By the time Maynard had reached the edge of the wood to the left, the Danes had begun to advance, stumbling across the ploughed field in an unsteady line.

The 'light bobs' were trained for just this situation. They paired off and, under his general direction to fall back with the rate of advance, moved out quickly.

Maynard heard the first heartening crack of musketry, a tell-tale gout of smoke arising from a thicket further along. He strained to see the effect on the stolid wall of infantry and, with a leap of satisfaction, saw a marching soldier near the colour party stagger and fall, quickly disappearing under the feet of the oncoming line.

Then, in a wash of horror, he caught himself. He was glorying in the death of a human being. For that man, living and breathing just moments ago, life had ended: everything had finished. How could he—

Maynard pulled himself together. He was an officer. He held the King's commission and had a duty to lead men. 'Corporal. That windmill. Go up and get an observation. I need to know if there's other formations in the field.'

'But, sir—'

'I know it's falling down. Climb up the outside if you have to. Have a man on the ground and shout down if you spy anything.'

The corporal hesitated, then left at the run.

That left only two with him. And the enemy marched on, now within a few hundred yards.

It had been a lucky shot, he recognised. Theirs was not a rifle regiment and muskets were useless in aimed fire much beyond eighty yards – but that was not the point. The distraction of being under fire was what counted. And his men, working in pairs, were getting off three, even five rounds a minute. Ten balls a minute into that mass of men and he had four pairs out. With Adams on the other flank it surely must be having an effect.

He set his remaining two men to work. Fire, reload behind a tree while the other presented and fired. Then back down for another shot – except that instead, there was a sickening smack and a spray of blood and brain burst upward. The man slumped instantly.

Maynard's mind froze with shock, trying to cope with what he'd seen.

The other soldier knelt down, gently eased the dead man's musket from him and looked up at his officer questioningly.

Maynard flogged his thoughts under control against the ever-louder noises of the advancing line. And one above all roared to an immediate focus. He had failed as an officer and overlooked the wider scene. While he'd been concentrating on delaying the gathering counter-attack, with individual fire from his free-moving light infantry, he'd forgotten the men they'd seen first – the opposite number to themselves. They would now be ordered to neutralise the harassing fire against their main force, who themselves would never waste their massed volley against them.

Then again, wasn't galling fire on the attacking force their prime duty, and be damned to personal hazard?

He dropped to all fours, conscious of the target he made in his officer's uniform, and reached for the proffered musket. 'Mark where the bugger is,' he muttered, took off his cocked hat and used his sword to inch it above the leaves. There was a vicious *whaap* as a ball whipped through the brush not inches from it. This was a rifle pair or they were very close with muskets.

'That bush, sir.' The soldier indicated a low, straggling shrub not forty yards away, well out in front.

'I see him, Bailey,' Maynard acknowledged.

He used his elbows to lever forward next to the corpse and brought the firelock up to aim, holding the sight picture, the trigger to first pressure and waited. To the left side there was movement, a glimpse of colour and a flash of metal. Without waiting for more, he squeezed off the shot.

The effect was instant, a uniformed figure thrown into view twisting and writhing until at last it lay still, twitching occasionally.

'Good shot, sir – winged 'im only, but he's a dead 'un.'

Maynard yielded his place to him, shocked – not because he'd taken a life but because he was unaffected by it.

The marching line was nearing – they should be retiring.

The ploughed field would soon be crossed and the line would be into the woods where nothing could be done. Maynard remembered that further back there was another open field before more woodland. They should retreat and take a like position there – if the enemy front was not extended by further formations.

The windmill! He rose to a crouch and, motioning Bailey to follow, went back to the path and sprinted along to the end and the windmill. Two blasts with his whistle, taking care to remain in cover. The ground man did not answer. Annoyed, he was about to whistle again when he felt a tap on his arm and saw where the finger pointed. An untidy and very still form lay by the base of the mill.

But at the same time a nervous hail came from the crazy top structure at the sails. It was the corporal. 'Sah – there's another line same size further on. All I c'n see, sah.'

'Right. Get down here, now! You've done your—'

A burst of musketry sent splinters flying around the man, who ducked inside.

Then a ball – and another whipped past Maynard from another direction. They were under direct fire from the enemy skirmish line, which must be very near – it was past time to retreat.

'Tell 'em all to fall back through the wood, re-form across the field,' he ordered.

He hesitated. With a stab of pity he knew he had to abandon the corporal – and the other man would know it. He'd have realised that his hail down would have drawn lethal attention but he'd chosen to do his duty by Maynard and his regiment.

And the information was vital. Another line meant at least another battalion formation. And further to the right, so the centre of the assault was there too. If this wasn't a counterattack he didn't know what was.

He glimpsed a pair of his men at a crouched run retiring through the woods. It was time to go. Then he became conscious of a change in drumbeat of the oncoming line. It had reached the woods but there it dissolved and the enemy troops began crashing through the brush, no doubt to form line again in the open field.

With a pounding in his ears he ran for dear life – and, with a growing horror, he realised he and his men were now doomed. When they reached the field they would be in the open, unmissable targets as they fled across to the trees on the other side.

He'd left it too late.

Dull with resentment he slowed his pace. The edge of the woods was just ahead and . . . Facing him was the most incredible, wonderful sight: a hastily assembling line of the 52nd and what looked like the 23rd in an ever-lengthening array. Even as he watched, the deeper-toned British drums spoke and the line began advancing.

Emerging from the trees the Danish milled in confusion until horns bayed and they fell into line, three ranks with colours in the centre. Sharp commands, and the front rank knelt and presented.

The 52nd came on splendidly, in perfect step and dressed right and left by their colour, a thrilling sight as they covered the ground.

The front rank of the enemy volleyed out, nearly hidden in the swirling smoke.

It was much too early but several men fell in the steadily advancing British line. Did the Danish commander feel it necessary to hearten his men by the firing, to deter them from running away?

The second rank came forward and knelt.

The 52nd drew nearer, a hundred yards, eighty – the enemy fired, more fell – and still they came on, in their bright red coats an unstoppable tide.

Fifty yards – the third rank opened fire but with little effect as their aim was wild.

At thirty yards' range the 52nd halted and in deadly deliberation raised their weapons. Smoke billowed and roiled and through it with a full-throated roar stormed the implacable redcoats in a bayonet charge.

It was too much. The enemy line broke and ran, making for the safety of the woods. It was all over.

Chapter 65

*D*ear David . . . A wistful memory of his brother, so hard and tall in his stern naval uniform, floated into Ensign Maynard's mind. He'd never written to him before: at home there hadn't seemed to be anything to talk about that could stand next to the sea adventures his brother must be having. But now he desperately needed to share the titanic events of the day with someone who understood.

His young fellow officers were not the sort to explore feelings or reflect on deep affairs. They laughed off even the worst with some offhand understatement and treated the whole thing like schoolboys on a prank.

Most certainly his mother and father must never know what he'd seen that day.

I do hope you are well and . . . Just what did you write to someone who might recently have been in a great sea-fight, valiantly defending the expedition?

This is to tell you the news. We landed successfully at Vedbæk against no opposition, a great show in which I played my part in taking the colours to— But would David want to know how it had felt to be the one charged with such an honour, to be looked on by the whole regiment from the colonel down? Probably not. The navy's flags were much vaster in size and were flown by the ship, not an individual.

I spent the night at the Crown Prince's winter palace! Not as you might say an entertainment. The bed was very indifferent, it smelt of horse dung. That is, as we made bivouac in the sand of the riding *stables*, he added hastily, to explain to one who knew only a hammock. He scratched his head in irritation. This was not going right. It was sounding like one of the subalterns at mess. Better to get on to the real matter.

Next day we marched through a pretty enough country until we found our place in the line, where we set up camp, the Danes still shy of a mill. It was only hours ago but the time that separated the Ensign Maynard of then and now was a chasm. So ardent, proud and unsure, to now . . . *In the afternoon, however, I went forward on picquet duty. All was quiet, but then . . .* His first hearing of a shot fired in anger. The heart-freezing sight of an enemy whose sworn duty was to kill him. . . . *we took fire from Danish light forces on the loose.* When he'd had to find within himself the stature of an officer and beat down his anxieties to take life-and-death decisions that affected all around him.

As it turned out, they were scouts for the main force coming up on us. That lurching moment of dread when half a thousand men burst into view to form line of advance, and what were his orders? Thank God he'd given the right ones. *We had a pretty time of it peppering their flanks.* The sight of a human body with the life torn out of it, the questioning of his own humanity when he had gone on to kill a man, a stranger, a living being.

I fancy it would have gone hard for us if our regiment had not turned out to see off the Danes in fine style. Never would he forget the stab of stark terror as realisation dawned that they would be trapped in full view against an open field because he'd failed in his duty to establish a firm line of retreat when deploying. Or the intoxicating relief at the vision of his comrades-in-arms in warlike array joining battle – such a magnificent sight!

Then to camp and a welcome for a hero! There. Finished. It was so much more grateful to the feelings to let it all out, and now David would know how it had been for him in the fires of combat.

Perhaps the last bit was not quite as it had been. To be truthful, no one had seemed interested in where he'd been or what he'd endured. And far from a massive counter-attack to drive them back to the sea, the regimental diary would describe it as an armed reconnaissance in some numbers that had driven in the picquets, but which had then been beaten off by reinforcements for trifling loss.

Crestfallen, he had ambled about camp until Sergeant Heyer had seen him and gruffly suggested that, as the field kitchens and officers' conveniences had not yet been set up, he was welcome to join them at the light company's stirabout.

And there he entered into the fellowship of the soldier on campaign, ladling out the pieces of boiled beef, thickened by peas and lentils, crushed army biscuits and greasy flour dumplings, and in the comradely darkness by the fire hearing tales of other times and places where British soldiers had fought and endured for the honour of their king and country and a shilling a day – less deductions.

As he took his leave Ensign Maynard knew that there was nowhere else in this earthly existence he would rather be.

Chapter 66

The Citadel, Danish headquarters

The aide bowed and retired. General Peymann held the sealed document he'd just been given as though it might burst into flames. The others in the room sat in tense silence.

The Citadel had guarded the city for centuries. The man now charged with defending it against its greatest threat slit the seal. He read the contents once, then again, before laying it down slowly.

'Gentlemen. By this the commander of the British expedition against us does call on me to deliver up the city of Copenhagen and all its works, and most particularly its fleet.' He looked mournfully from one to another. 'Know that we have done what we can. At the moment we are now completely surrounded by a dozen regiments of redcoats with cavalry and guns. There's a great fleet anchored off our shores and—'

'Sir, you cannot—'

'—and the island of Sjælland is cut off from the outside world. We may expect no reinforcements or rescue.'

'Then unhappily, sir, it appears—'

'Choose what you say carefully, General.'

Generalløjtnant Bielefeldt blinked, confused. 'Sir, your words imply a fatal situation. Should we not consider our position?'

'Why?'

'Er, for the sake of our people, sir. A siege long protracted will be—'

'Sir, I have reminded this meeting only of what faces us. There is no question of capitulation.'

'If we cannot go on—'

'Enough!' Peymann spluttered. 'My last orders from His Royal Highness are to defend Copenhagen and its people, and that is what we are in duty bound to do, and, by God, we shall, sir.'

'Then there can be no surrender,' Bielefeldt hastened to agree.

'Quite. Therefore I shall reject this note with contempt.'

Krieger looked significantly at Bille, who stood up briskly. 'Sir. Permission to withdraw – to open hostilities on the enemy!'

'Do so with all means, Kommandør. Our land forces have had a first brush with the English on a reconnaissance in force and have discovered them a formidable foe. It would be gratifying should the navy take the war to the enemy by any means you see fit, sir.'

As if by unspoken agreement the two officers went to the ramparts, the great earthworks fifty feet thick, laid out in a star shape nearly half a mile across, secure and impregnable. Within them were the parade ground, storehouses and barracks.

It was only when they clambered to the top that the true

situation became clear. To the north an uncountable number of enemy ships lay offshore. From them were pouring guns and boots, horses and ammunition, victuals and tents. All with perfect impunity. And from there they would circle inland to strengthen the clamping hold of the siege while this immense sea-facing fortress lay helpless to prevent it.

Krieger studied the scene with a grim smile. 'We have our mark, then. Stop all that.'

'If we can.' Bille snorted. 'I see a full score sail-of-the-line who won't take kindly should we press our attentions.'

It was a sight to make the stoutest heart quail – an immensity of ships so dense that no part of the open horizon could be seen through them.

'I can!'

'Johannes?'

'You've not seen as much of the damned *Engelsk* as I have. They're blue-water seamen – there's nowhere they go that's not deep-sea sailing. Those out there,' he waved dismissively, 'all of 'em are fine hulls for an Atlantic blow but in waters a touch shoal, they're like to be a porker tip-toeing through a barnyard.'

'Then?'

'We've learned a lot in our Swedish wars, especially how to build gunboats as can take Baltic conditions. Flat-bottomed, we can crowd right inshore where their frigates can't get at us and we'll outgun any petty craft they send against us. I want to make sally up this corridor and fall on their store-ships and transports. Give me a dozen – a score of these – and we'll start making ourselves felt.'

'You've got them – all we have.'

'I want Lynetten as a base, with a second luff to take it in charge.'

'But—'

'I'll be in the boats. If we're going against this horde I'm not having your common *sømænd* seeing me sit on my arse while there's work to be done.'

'Anything else?'

'A working party to start this instant on rigging some trots between Lynetten and Quintus Battery. I'm having all the gunboats moored there, not in the harbour. They'll be safe under the guns of Trekroner and Prøvesten and perfectly placed for sorties.'

'It'll be done, Johannes.'

'And while we're getting the boats out I want to choose their captains myself. We've a quantity of fine officers at leisure from the fleet. Do send 'em out as who will volunteer, and I'll give them leave to pick their own crews.'

Chapter 67

Lynetten, island base for gunboats

In his lair a mile offshore, Krieger eased himself to a small desk in a musty casemate, the salt air on stone and the bronze twenty-four-pounder a peculiar tang in his nostrils. Word had quickly spread in Holmen that the navy was going to strike back at the invaders and boats had brought a stream of officers, who now waited outside.

He had before him their records but this was not needed – he knew most of them from the camaraderie of Nyholm.

It was going to be difficult: the time-honoured practices of a fleet square-rigger were not what was wanted now. A gunboat captain had to be quick-thinking, a strong leader and, above all, possess nerves of steel. To be sent against a ship fifty times the size under fire from great guns that could transform their command with a single hit into splintered wreckage and torn corpses took a different kind of courage.

And skill. With small size and agility their only advantage, to close successfully required first-class reading of the wind from the point of view of the enemy captain, and to know precisely when to douse sail and revert to oars against the same wind took a particular talent. Above all they needed to know how to act as an integral part of a team, working with others to tear down a mightier beast, like a pack in full cry, some to distract, others to go in at vulnerable points, the rest to lie off and pound.

'Løjtnant Wulff, sir.'

Christian Wulff. Third of *Skjold*, a 70-gun ship-of-the-line, now like all its kind in ordinary in the naval dockyard within Copenhagen. Girl in Falster, a fine hand with a sketching pencil.

The young man entered, his manner tense.

'You want to be a gunboat chief. Why?'

'To sit idle while the kingdom is invaded? How could—'

'That's not what I asked, Løjtnant.'

'This war against the English is going to get worse. We're crazily outnumbered in our fleet – the only way we're going to give 'em a bloody nose is with a cloud of hornets. I want to be in it!'

'You're out of a ship-of-the-line, therefore a *stort skib fyr*, a big ship sort. What makes you think a gunboat crew would follow you?'

'Kommandør Steen Bille. He throws open the Admiralty College to any sea officer in idleness who would learn another thing. We could be taking on the Swedes again, who knows? I made myself useful by hoisting in the gunboat trade.'

Active and enterprising – he would do. 'I believe I'll give you *Nakskov*, a *kanonchalup*. How does that serve?'

A wide grin was his answer.

Krieger knew it would not be easy. The listing of available hulls he'd been given included every kind of gunboat there was, some with a full-size cannon mounted, others with mortars and howitzers, even flat pontoon barges with field pieces lashed to the deck that had to be towed into action. All had been designed for a very different conflict, against equals in the Scandinavian wars of the past, not the great battle fleet that faced them now.

There were small gun-brigs but they mounted carronades only and would be massacred if they stood up even to a sloop. And a half-dozen or so other minor craft – it was madness, really.

'Løjtnant Zeuthen.'

'Julius – you?'

The older, red-haired man looked offended. 'And why not? I've smelt powder-smoke in gunboats, more'n most.'

He was well known in Nyholm for his buffoonery at mess dinners and a thirst for *brændevin* that, some said, should be measured in gallons. But he was right. He'd been in Algiers against the Berber princes and in the action at Tripoli. Even if his handling of men was abrupt he'd be relentless in leading and as stubborn as a bulldog.

'Are you up to taking a *kanonjolle* at all?' Caution suggested the smaller.

'What about a *kanonchalup*?'

'I've a notion you're a close-action man, Julius. This'll suit you better.'

'Done!'

Before the morning was over Krieger had his little fleet. Counting every tiny craft Bille could send, he had twenty-six in hand, even now fitting out for combat. Suddenly restless, he got to his feet and went out to see how things were progressing. If he had to flog them to it through the night he was determined to have each ready to strike at dawn.

The view from the crenellated walls of Lynetten was commanding and formidable. Further out to sea was the massive Trekroner Fortress but beyond from horizon to horizon was the dense pack of English ships. Facing shore-wards he could see the entrance to the harbour with the naval dockyard on the left, and on the right the Citadel. The charming woodlands of Classen's parkland garden were next, affecting in their innocence at a time of war. Not much further on were the red-topped houses and windmill of Svanemøllen, the Swan Mill, where the British lines began. He peered out: was that the red flash of an enemy soldier?

Knowing he was under eye, Krieger refused to let his dismay show. He turned on his heel and stalked over to the leeward side to see how the work was proceeding. Clustered about the landing place, eight gunboats were swarming with men, working as if the devil was at their tail. He made his way down to see into the closest, a *kanonchalup, Svendborg.*

The men stood respectfully. 'Don't let me get in the way, the *pokkers snejegaster,*' he threw at them. They grinned and resumed their work.

This was the largest class of gunboat, with a twenty-four-pounder low-mounted both on the fore-deck and stern-quarters, cunningly designed to operate on stout slides. With a gun bigger than any frigate, while admittedly having a fixed bearing, under oars the boat itself could be aimed. Broad and flat-bottomed, some sixty feet long, it was equipped with two masts that could be lowered to sit on crutches much as in his Viking ancestors' longships. Setting a lugsail on fore and main it could make good speed in light winds, helped if necessary by a jib on a bowsprit and additional balancing trysail aft. A hornet indeed!

There was a price to pay. To achieve its greatest advantage – manoeuvrability in calms and ability to go against the wind – the heavy boat pulled thirty oars double-banked, which, with gun crews, required seventy or more men. When not deployed the seamen could be accommodated in a laid-up frigate or even in barracks in Lynetten, but if in battle readiness they had to live aboard in conditions of squalor and hardship. To be a naval officer in a gunboat was a unique calling, but Krieger knew he had the best.

Beyond the *kanonchalup* was a smaller vessel mounting a single gun facing out over the stern. This *kanonjolle* was rigged in the same way but called for only twenty-five men to take the single-banked oars. It also had to be manoeuvred to fire the gun. It was considerably more agile, however, and he knew he was right to put Zeuthen in this one.

Crowding in were several *morterchalup*s, with the squat menace of a hundred-pound bronze mortar bedded deep into a flat hull, with four smaller howitzers spaced about it and supreme at hurling explosive shells into a hostile harbour. And beyond still was the *kanonbåd Aalborg*, a gunboat completely outfitted with carronades and a pair of howitzers, smaller but with finer lines and able to reach the thickest part of the battle quickly.

These were his blades of war and he was damned well going to use them against the foe to his utmost ability.

Apart from the gunboats there were gun-brigs, more conventionally rigged sailing craft, but they had all the disadvantages of sail that the rest of his command were designed to overcome.

Not so clear was what he should do with those he was left with: several *stykpram*s, glorified pontoons with field pieces lashed to their decks and needing to be towed into position; a schooner, no less than four yachts, galleys, a miniature mortar punt. Hardly calculated to strike terror into the enemy.

Chapter 68

Krieger kept his assured expression until he was back in his casemate, then sat at his desk and held his head in his hands.

'Why, Johannes, so low?'

Jerking up, he saw Bille. 'Oh, naught to speak on. Just tired, is all.'

'I came to see how you're progressing.'

'Fine. You must have seen the *matroserne* working like heroes. We'll be ready.'

'Then we'd better talk tactics. What do you say to—' He stopped and cocked his head, listening.

'What did you hear?'

'Nothing.'

Krieger frowned, confused. 'That's just it – no sound. They've all stopped working for some reason.'

'I'll get those *sløve kanaljer* bastards going!' he swore, and got to his feet but paused at the sight of a breathless lieutenant in the doorway.

'Sir, I think you'd like to come top-side,' he said, his face grim.

The British fleet was on the move. Sails were being loosed and sheeted home all along the broad front of the armada. They were headed directly towards the harbour entrance.

'Be damned to it!' Krieger burst out. 'They've got our refusal and are giving answer to it!'

They were coming on in numbers. Very shortly there would be a climactic battle for possession or destruction of the Danish fleet.

'We throw in everything we've got,' Krieger said hotly.

'I think not, Johannes.'

'What?'

Bille smiled thinly. 'We're being paid a handsome compliment, can't you see? Their main fleet is closing to stopper up our own, thinking it in shape to hazard theirs.' Seeing disbelief, he added, 'You'll see I'm right – they'll moor in the last of the four-fathom water.'

As though in obedience to his words the ships rounded to at just that point, only a few miles north of the harbour.

A detached group continued as if in insolent challenge, spreading out as they came. 'And those?' Krieger said drily.

'If I was the English admiral I'd have some sort of shallow-draught inshore squadron to protect their transports, wouldn't you?'

'As we'll have to fight through to get at them.' His face tightened in determination.

Bille called for a telescope, and as the ships took their positions he counted them off. 'Gun-brigs, a small frigate or is that a ship-sloop? There's a quantity of bomb-ketches and what looks like a cloud of their light *morterchalups*, a bit of a mixed bag, I'd think.'

Krieger lifted an eyebrow. 'So, most with deeper draught – they won't be able to get close in to stop us. And their mortars will never stand against our long twenty-fours. If we move fast we'll have a chance.'

'It's my bet that . . .'

'The redcoats will have artillery on their flank as they'll turn on us,' Krieger finished. 'I've thought of that. To clear the way to the transports I'm going to entertain 'em with some fireworks. They'll be behind earthworks so I'll have the *morterchalups* throw a storm of hundred-pound shells over the top, the *kanonchalups* slamming in some round shot to keep their heads down.'

'And you'll—'

'And there'll be *kanonbåds* lying to seaward taking on that inshore squadron, helped by other *kanonchalups* as will keep 'em at a respectful distance.'

'There's something else we can do, Johannes.'

'Oh?'

'I'm going to get our stout General Bielefeldt to make a sally of sorts first, let us get into position. Who knows? They might drive in their lines handsomely,' he finished doubtfully.

Chapter 69

⚜

There was little ceremony: it wasn't his way. Krieger stood aft in the *kanonchalup Stubbekøbing*, keeping out of the way of Peder Bruun, her captain, as the gunboats up and down the trots were manned.

It wasn't much of a battle plan because things could change so quickly. If the British found shallow-draught reinforcements, if they themselves came under fire from long range – but all the gunboat chiefs were professionals and would read the situation as it unfolded.

There was nothing to do now but wait for the signal.

The faint sound of musketry and small field pieces came across the mile or so of water. A cloud of powder-smoke rose around Swan Mill – the attack had begun.

'Go!' Krieger bellowed, through cupped hands.

A cheer arose, rolling over the water, echoing back from the old stones of Lynetten. Half a thousand backs bent to the oars and the flotilla put out on the grey-green waters to go to war.

The British had nothing to prepare them for the onslaught, no experience of the deadly effectiveness of a gunboat swarm.

He wasn't going to forewarn them: his divisions were deliberately cloaked as part of a mass of boats, all apparently sent to the aid of their army comrades.

It was an exhilarating charge stretching out powerfully for the fighting. With pride Krieger saw the Orlogsflag in each boat, the swallow-tailed war ensign of the navy, its brilliant red with a pure white cross streaming out defiantly as it had done for centuries of sea warfare.

There was *Nakskov* with Wulff standing nobly, like a Nordic warrior, his gaze fixed sternly on the enemy. And over there was Julius Zeuthen in his *kanonjolle* urging on his men like a maniac, determined to reach the battlefield first. Every man of one heart, doing what they could against near hopeless odds. It brought a catch to his throat that it had taken English perfidy to bring out the finest in his men.

Their objective was clear, marked out for them by the smoke and dust of battle in the low shore. It wasn't hard to reason that the English artillery would be removed back from the infantry clashes and there it was – the raw earth of their defensive works. It was time to go to work.

The Orlogsflag dipped and rose once.

One by one the divisions separated. The *kanonchalup*s swung their bows shoreward, the mortar craft in line abreast of them, the *kanonbåd* wheeling to face out.

Captain Bruun looked at Krieger, who nodded curtly.

A touch on one side of oars, and then his whistle pierced the air. Instantly all oars lifted clear of the water and the rowers tensed. In the next split second the twenty-four-pounder in the bows crashed out, the livid flash in a billow of gunsmoke, a heavy round shot sent into the English lines. Almost immediately it was followed by the others in an avalanche of noise and destruction.

Krieger saw the *morterchalup*s get under way, with a flurry of white as the oars bit deep, disappearing into the powder-smoke slowly drifting away in the light breeze. There was now a tapping of musketry from the shoreline and the thin crack of a field piece here and there – the English had woken up to what was happening but there was nothing they could do to fend away the approaching catastrophe.

Off the beach they came to a stop and with the same nudging at the oars the first *morterchalup* aimed the boat care-fully. A blinding flash, a deep report, and a hundred-pound shell arced through the sky, leaving a thin trail of smoke. It disappeared behind the earthworks, followed by a muffled crump. First blood!

The gunboat captains knew their business. Firing consec-utively gave time to select a fresh target and allowed each to track the fall of shot and make corrections.

The British fought bravely. They brought horse artillery to the water's edge but this meant they were within range of the gunboat howitzers, which threw case shot in their shells. Bodies of men and horses were strewn along the shoreline.

Krieger's blood was up – it seemed an age before their long gun was reloaded but the space for the ten-man gun-crew to wield rammer and stave on the cramped fore-deck was very small. At last the whistle blew, the oars went up and the big gun smashed out its fury, the entire boat recoiling eight feet backwards.

Firing was now general and the smaller mortar vessels were continuously wreathed in smoke as they hurled their bombs in a carpet of destruction into the English camp. Nothing could live in that. For the next phase, against the transports, they would be able to sail by, unmauled.

'Sir.' Bruun pointed seaward. The British inshore squadron was in full sail towards them, colours flying.

'Yes. Time to greet 'em, I believe.'

Krieger was in no mood to have his operation interrupted. 'You know what to do.'

Crisp orders had the rowers give way larboard and backwater starboard, bringing the big gunboat around until it faced the oncoming squadron. Their gun smashed out and a massive plume arose close to the leading sloop. Other gouts shot up among them as all twelve *kanonchalup*s opened up.

Krieger felt a stab of sympathy – theirs were forward-firing guns able to range in any direction; the squadron heading towards them had broadsides only and could not reply, helplessly suffering the onslaught of the heavy guns until they were close enough to wheel about and bring their guns to bear. And with relative pop-guns this would never be a decider.

They were taking hits. First one, then another fell away; one more lost its foremast. They came on, theirs the only defence in the corridor that led to the store-ships.

The pity of it was that it was all in vain. Off Svanemøllen there was not depth of water for deep-keeled sailing ships and they were going to have to yield it to the Danes, who knew the waters intimately. While they hovered impotently offshore the *kanonchalup*s could take their pick of the targets they made.

Their twenty-four slammed out again and the guns of the *kanonbåd*s joined in, heavy-calibre but inaccurate pieces that could be relied on to intimidate by the storm of shot they threw out.

As the water shoaled, the squadron eased sail, knowing their fate if they went aground, finally slewing about to open fire on their tormentors. Their six-pounders cracked out but with no hits that Krieger could see and the forest of splashes around them whipped up by the furious Danish cannonade only increased.

It could have but one result. The squadron turned and retreated to lick its wounds, unable to sustain the unequal encounter.

With leaping elation, Krieger whirled his hat in the air, acknowledging the bursts of cheering from his little fleet. Against all the odds, they were making a difference.

Deeper thuds sounded – the distant anchored British ships-of-the-line were firing at them in what must be despair and frustration, a measure of what they were achieving, but the much smaller gunboats were a near impossible target at range, Krieger knew.

'Back to work!' he snapped, and attention turned to the shore again.

The *morterchalup*s had been hurling their shells for an hour and more, the arcing trails ending in sullen thumps and flying debris from within the British encampment, which must now be a scene of havoc and slaughter. There could be no easing of it out of humanity: the next stage would be even crueller when, with their great guns, the Danes went against helpless store-ships.

'Look!'

Krieger turned quickly and saw not the inshore squadron but a dozen or more boats in a line emerging from the English fleet, stroking fast in their direction. Baffled, he watched them advance. Then he understood. These were the very ships' boats of warships sent on the cutting-out expeditions and daring raids that had brought the Royal Navy fame and respect over their hard years of war. Now they were being sent into open battle because they had the same shallow draught as themselves and therefore could close with them and bring about a hand-to-hand fight. A courageous and intelligent move.

He couldn't let it happen. His sailors were not in the same class and would quickly be bested by these seasoned veterans.

'Reduced charges!' he bellowed at the gunboats with long guns. Some grasped it immediately, others, puzzled, hung back.

When the first shots crashed out, it quickly became clear to them. Aimed directly in line with the oncoming boats the heavy shot hit the sea short but ricocheted on in a series of deadly skips until it reached the boats at their own level, smashing oars, taking lives, sinking them.

Krieger knew that those vessels mounted carronades, the short, stubby weapons ideal for boatwork but futile against Danish gunboats, with long guns, able to stand off and punish them at will. There could be only one outcome, however brave the attempt.

He felt a savage satisfaction in knowing the Danes had gone on the offensive at last – who knew, when they came back to deal with the store-ships sustaining the besieging army, might not the whole situation be turned around? The British trapped ashore for all their great fleet, starved of victuals and ammunition, themselves ending up as the besieged?

Their return in the setting sun was sweet indeed, the shore-line alive with wildly waving onlookers, who'd witnessed the whole spectacle. He'd left three of the mortar vessels to keep up an intermittent fire during the night to discourage any work of repair, and at daybreak, when they went after the store-ships, it should prove an open highway.

Chapter 70

It was a grey dawn when the flotilla put to sea in full strength, all twenty-six of their several kinds with pennons and Orlogsflag streaming out bravely – but Krieger could not join in the warrior talk around him. During the night he'd been seized with foreboding, a conviction that the invincible Royal Navy would not let rest the reversal they'd suffered. It would be a very different foe they faced this day.

'Get back in line,' he bawled at Zeuthen, in his *kanonjolle* stretching out well ahead of the others.

It was hard not to feel for the man, so determined to be first into the fight. He'd nailed an improvised flag at the fore, probably sewn by his wife during the night. On it was picked out in bold words *Gud og den retfærdige sag*, 'God and the just cause'. If there was going to be any kind of a stern encounter, Julius could be counted on to be at the front.

Krieger was today in the *kanonchalup Roeskilde* whose captain was the plain-speaking Swenson. Bruun's *Stubbekøbing* was over to the right, like them cannonading shorewards, while the other division took care of the inshore squadron.

The battle plan was brutally simple. Get into the soft store-ships and create carnage. Nothing else mattered.

Only an hour or so before dawn the Danish mortars had returned to replenish, reporting that all was quiet on shore. Out to sea the inshore squadron lay at a respectful distance – after the previous day's rough handling there would be no trouble from them.

Ahead was Classen's garden and beyond it the torn-up desolation of the English lines. Further on, less than three miles along the coastline, was their prey, ships at anchor close in, others with ramps on their sides, boats busy between them, crowded lines of men ashore taking casks and sacks. Bread and beef for twenty thousand men weighed in at tons every day, let alone the dead weight of shot and shell in the quantities that were needed.

Now they were passing the scenes of yesterday's triumph and it wouldn't be long until—

The morning stillness was shattered. From groves of maple and larch, gardens and roadways a furious chaos of firing began. Artillery, mortars, musketry – the whole shoreline seemed to rise up and blast out hate. It was a storm of shot and exploding mortar shells.

Numb, Krieger realised what had happened. Overnight, in anticipation of an attack on the victuallers, the rest of the British positions had been stripped of guns and dashed here to line the shore.

Shrieks and cries added to the din and, following an eruption of impact splashes, several boats veered off as they fought for control when oarsmen had been struck.

A terrible decision had to be made: to press on or turn back, away from the hell and fury?

On their own initiative several gunboats had turned to

face the tempest and that decided him. There was no point in staying to duel with the shore guns. If sacrifice was demanded, it would take place as they threw themselves at their objective.

He stood tall and looked about. Thrusting his sword in the direction of the store-ships, he roared, 'Go, *ro væk I elendige karle!*'

As a concentrated host, they turned their bows north, towards their goal, bending heroically to their oars. As they clawed along the shoreline there was no let-up in the thunderous barrage. At one point Krieger glimpsed artillery, limber and gun bucketing along the coast road behind six furiously whipped horses. The line of guns was being sustained in relays and they would have to endure.

It was taking its toll. One, then another gunboat fell away.

'Take us out,' he ordered harshly. It would be mean heading into deeper water, losing their advantage, and into range of the British sloops. 'Half the *kanonchalup*s to keep the inshore squadron away.'

That left eight for the store-ships, and perhaps after the squadron had been beaten off at long range they could join in the slaughter.

'They're coming in,' Swenson grunted.

It was happening again: emerging from between the ships of the squadron dozens of boats were heading directly towards them. It was madness – their fate would be the same but still they came on. Krieger shook his head in admiration, but brute courage would make no difference.

And then everything changed.

While still far out of accurate carronade range first one, then another of the squadron's boats opened fire with the gun in their bows. The balls slammed towards them in a series of skips and ricochets – they were using the same technique with reduced charges that he had used previously, only possible with a long gun of size. Damn it, but the English had overnight improvised gunboats of their own, in some way mounting at least eighteen-pounders on them.

'Long bowls, the bastards!'

This was a much more serious situation. No longer could they keep the offshore fleet at bay by standing it off with heavy long guns: the enemy had found a way of evening up the contest. They had changed it into a war of the bludgeoning of equals and in this the English had the eventual advantage.

He would not retreat! As far as he could tell in the thick of the mêlée, only five of them had the big guns and therefore he still had the numbers. For honour's sake, he could not abandon their mission.

The *kanonchalup*s would surely keep them at bay . . . But, as if sensing what they were after, more than a dozen boats detached and laid themselves in a loose line before the storeships. They could not be armed with long guns, so what was their purpose?

In the heat of the action he couldn't think, driven only by the desperate need to get up to them.

There were now only four *kanonchalup*s available for the strike and the oarsmen were tiring. From somewhere the British Army had found heavy mortars to position on a slight foreland and were firing shells that burst in the air, blasting down a lethal hail of fragments.

Another fell behind, leaving only themselves, *Nakskov* and *Stubbekøbing* to press home the attack.

They were in range! But they had to make sure – they had fought their way so far that to fail because they were not close enough to their target would be unbearable.

It seemed nothing could live in the vicious slam and whip of unseen shot, the waters lashed white with deadly fury.

Now! In a burst of nervous energy Krieger told Swenson to open up on the second nearest ship, a little further but appreciably bigger.

He took his time, getting way on the boat so the finer aiming of the rudder could be used. His whistle blasted out.

To Krieger's ears the crash of the gun seemed louder, more decisive. The ball took the store-ship squarely amidships, directly into the hold. A burst of black fragments shot up and men could be seen running for the boats at the stern.

Stubbekøbing was not far behind and her shot smashed in not far from their own. Incredibly a lick of flame showed briefly and without warning an explosion erupted that showered splinters all around the vessel, leaving a raging fire.

Strangely he felt only a numb sense of inevitability, detachment.

The line of boats positioned earlier now made sense. They were advancing together – armed with mortars, carronades, it made no difference. They would be forced to choose between defending themselves or firing into the store-ships. If they used their vital rounds in protecting themselves what was the use of fighting through this far? And if they ignored the boats and—

So close it was like a clap of thunder followed by a wave of heat. His head jerked around – to see *Stubbekøbing* a shattered and sinking wreck, blackened and smoking timbers where her powder had been detonated.

'Go to her,' he barked hoarsely.

Swenson gave the order and they swiftly closed with the sad wreck. Blasted corpses lay in the water, some still staggered at the after end, others with flayed bodies lay shrieking.

'Peder!' Krieger croaked, seeing Bruun and holding out his hand to help him aboard.

'Mortar,' he said thickly, 'Damned shell from the sky, set off our charges.' He coughed harshly, hiding his pain.

Krieger saw that little could be done now with just two vessels. With a slow rate of fire they would be overcome before they could reach much further.

'Sir.' Swenson touched his arm, then pointed.

Way ahead, Julius Zeuthen in his *kanonjolle* was in a mad charge towards the foreland where the mortars blazed. He had one shot in his twenty-four-pounder and he was going to place it deep in the nearest enemy.

'*Den Kæmpe idiot* – but I honour him for it,' Krieger breathed. It was too shoal for a *kanonchalup* to follow and all he could do was watch the scene play out.

He came to a decision. They'd done their best but had been overborne by the odds. It was time for an honourable withdrawal.

But disaster struck again. A *kanonjolle* had a fatal disadvantage. Like a wasp, its sting was in its tail – the great gun was mounted in the after end, and when it was called on to fire, the entire gunboat had to be rotated to face the stern towards the enemy. As this was being done it offered its broadside unavoidably to the enemy and they didn't waste the opportunity. They broke cover and opened up with everything they had – horse artillery, musketry, howitzers. The figure of Zeuthen, which could be seen in a maniac urging, spun and crumpled. Another fell.

The midshipman aboard found the tiller and took the craft away from the hell of shot. It passed close, and Krieger hailed, 'Løjtnant Zeuthen?'

'Dead.'

Julius – gone from this world. His jolly wife a widow as of this hour. His heart wrung with pity.

They began turning to withdraw but *Nakskov*'s length was her undoing and it touched ground, slowing, then stopping entirely, in full view of the enemy. There was an immediate burst of firing, as the troops ashore saw their chance.

Oarsmen fought desperately at their twenty-five-foot oars but the gunboat didn't move. Men took hits and the oars fell out of time into a fatal disorder.

Krieger felt a mounting desperation. Aboard *Nakskov* the impossibility of their situation became clear to them and they threw themselves into the water and stroked frantically for *Roeskilde* where they were hauled in.

The gunboat had been fully evacuated yet it was still there to be captured after they'd left, and would be the first of the Danish fleet the English had come here to take.

Something snapped. 'Get the dinghy into the water,' Krieger ordered. It was insane but he had to do something. 'Throw in a line,' he added, to the astonished Swenson.

It was only a tiny skiff tucked away under the transom but Krieger didn't hesitate. He scrambled in and took the oars. 'Secure your end,' he demanded. Swenson understood and, with deft turns, had a bowline about two thwarts.

Krieger pulled savagely for the stranded gunboat, the line paying out behind him.

He reached *Nakskov*, made for the bow and hauled himself in, the rope around his waist. The dinghy drifted away but he didn't care; the foremast partners made a fine samson post and he secured the line tightly to it.

He waved energetically and *Roeskilde* took up the strain. Affixing the line so far forward offered an enormous leverage, and with oarsmen giving it their utmost at a right-angle, it was enough. *Nakskov*'s bow came around and she was free.

Joyfully they pulled her out and Wulff's crew tumbled back aboard.

Krieger's attention was diverted to the English boats coming on – their bow carronades were opening up now and in their length the Danish gunboats were vulnerable. It would be madness to allow them to close for a hand-to-hand fight and he'd made his decision to withdraw.

The turn-back completed, tired crews pulled for their lives, running the gauntlet once more of the shore artillery pieces to face yet another blow.

The canny English had sent their boats out in two groups, one to protect the store-ships, and one curving around behind them while they were engaged. This now stood four-square across their path.

Trapped between the two there was nothing for it but to fight their way through – but, glory be, *Mercurius* and *Sarpen*, gun-brigs, and the *kanonbåd*s were coming up to join the fight from the other side: the shore artillery had ceased firing for fear they hit their own vessels.

A towering smoke plume arose over the confined area, stabbed by gun-flash. The sky was criss-crossed with crazy patterns of smoke trails as the fighting grew to a deadly climax.

In *Roeskilde* the big gun spoke once, then the twin four-pound howitzers fore and aft with a vicious crack, flinging case-shell generally about the British boats – crude, but it was all they had.

And then they were through!

In the open water past Swan Mill the *kanonchalup*s regrouped and turned to face the English once more but under the menace of their long guns they thought better of it and broke off the fight to withdraw.

It was over.

Krieger fought to control his feelings. It had been a rough and bloody contest, but had he ever thought it would not be, up against the rulers of the sea?

The corridor they'd relied on to get at the store-ships was now firmly closed. The massed artillery on shore could only get thicker and the battery they had bombarded would be reinforced against challenge from the sea, in effect forcing them out to where the heavier units of the inshore squadron would be waiting.

And if the store-ships were denied him, what purpose had they left?

No matter. Tomorrow he'd be out again, and again, until the invaders had been thrown back into the sea or . . .

Chapter 71

Svanemøllen, two miles north of Copenhagen

Francis Maynard picked up his pen and began: *Dear David* . . . He certainly had something to write about today. *Just when we thought the Danskers were tamely giving up the match, we got a bit of a surprise* . . .

That was an understatement. The 52nd had stood to arms when it became clear that trouble was brewing. The earthworks they were manning, however, were intended for an artillery battery and were incomplete, with supplies and equipment lying in the open among their encampment.

In the afternoon, out of the blue, the Danes had sortied in force. It had been a hard-fought engagement but the British engineers had pushed up the fronting glacis before the rest of the works and the attack had petered out on the fifty-yard open slope.

What happened next was a complete surprise. From nowhere a ship-sized round shot had thumped into the earthwork with shocking force, tearing a gap before finishing in splintered wreckage in the camp. Another soon followed, killing two sentries and rampaging on into their lines beyond.

Still more – and then a heavy mortar shell had hurtled in over the rampart and detonated in their unprotected camp with appalling results.

Another exploded some distance away and, as it was very clear there was going to be no defence against this sea-borne rain of destruction, the 52nd was pulled back. Was this a prelude to a sea landing to take this strategic objective? He recollected going to the little woodland rise and lying down to peer over at the powder-smoke-hidden inshore waters, trying to make sense of the violence and chaos. Where was the navy? It seemed they were being attacked only by boats. Surely that great fleet all across the horizon could deal with this.

He'd been taken up to provide men from the horse artillery, summoned to make some sort of reply, but they'd been punished badly as soon as they'd shown themselves on the shoreline. Beaten back, there'd been little they could do against the Viking marauders.

The day had ended with a wasteland of ruin and devastation where once had been the left flank of General Baird's second division.

A response was needed, and quickly. During the night the roads and trackways came alive with the urgent jingling of harness and rumble of wheels as every field piece capable of movement was brought around the rear to line the shore by Swan Mill.

In the morning the Danes were fought to a standstill, then forced to retire. *Damme, they're game fellows but we're emplacing some twenty-fours of our own as will be the medicine to be rid of 'em!*

The candle guttered as the night breeze wafted in from the tent opening. It was Adams. 'Care for a snifter, Francis?'

Before he could reply a grubby bottle was upended over

his chipped cup. A pale golden liquor splashed into it. 'Snaps, the locals call it. Rather a tasty drop, I think.'

'Um, yes.' Maynard was unsure about its foreign-tasting wormwood bitterness.

'May as well make the most of it while we're here.'

'What do you mean, Stephen?'

'Our bluff's called, old chap. We're to go home.'

'*Whaaat?*'

'By resisting they're forcing a siege. They could be well stocked, watered and so forth. All they've got to do is sit down behind their bloody great walls and wait for us to give up and fade away. There's no way we can sustain a siege of months – and who's to say in the meantime Boney won't get irritated and send in an army or two?'

'Not while the navy's here,' Maynard said stoutly. 'Got the whole place surrounded and sealed off.'

'Ha! You don't know this part o' the world. In weeks it starts getting mortal chilly, ice and snow around the corner. Your wooden walls have to get out while they can and leave us here or . . .'

'We can't give up! We'd be a laughing stock!'

More snaps was forthcoming before Adams gave a half-smile. 'Some say we take the whole of this island, Sjælland, and hand it over to the Swedes. That way we – that is to say, they – would control both sides of the Sound and no more threat to the Baltic trade, which is what all this pother is about.'

'Weren't they thrown out of Pomerania? Doesn't sound as if they can hang on long enough to defend it.'

'Sound? Sound! Ha-ha, good one, Francis,' Adams chortled.

'A good drop, then, this snaps,' Maynard murmured drily.

'Aye. No, as I was saying, those blundering great bastions

an' ramparts, we'll never get through 'em without we have a clinking great siege train in depth an' that we don't have.'

'Storm the city? Escalade? But that's always a bloody affair.'

'I'll agree. Our betters have a right puzzler they must solve. For me, I'd—'

'You pair!' the adjutant barked from behind. They started in consternation, twisting round to face him. 'Why are you still here? All officers attend at Headquarters, this hour!'

'N-now?'

'Take horse, be at Hellerup within twenty minutes or you'll rue your indolence for a week, I promise you, gentlemen!'

Chapter 72

General Cathcart's headquarters, Hellerup

The spacious farmstead was seething with activity and no one could spare the time to explain. A harassed aide eventually told them, 'We've word from our scouts inland. The Danes have landed an army to the south. It's to join another advancing from the north-west with the object of falling on our rear and raising the siege.'

'An army? Where did this come from, for God's sake?'

'No time. Stand ready to be redeployed, anything. Good luck!'

Behind the closed doors all military commanders were in conclave.

First to emerge was Wellesley, cool and patrician. He strode out without a sideways glance, quickly followed by the two divisional commanders.

Maynard and Adams stood back respectfully as brigadiers and colonels followed.

'The 52nd Regiment of Foot. All officers of the 52nd this way, if you please, gentlemen.'

The room was crowded but the major was brief to the point of curtness. 'With immediate effect, four companies of the 52nd are detached and assigned to the Reserve Division. These are . . .'

He rattled them off from a list and Maynard heard his own included.

'All others revert to their line assignments and may leave now.'

As the room began to empty of half its number, the major waited with heavy patience.

Maynard was confused. Reserve Division? What were they to do? Skulk in the background until called on to join the struggle? Then, with a stab of realisation, he understood. This division was the one set back from the others to act as a roving force against threats to the besiegers from inland. And therefore in the forefront of the first serious challenge to the invaders.

The major cleared his throat. 'You probably know by now that there are two armies of unknown force on the march against us. You will also know that—'

'Sir – where did they come from?' Maynard found himself blurting. The appearance without warning of such a hostile force in their rear . . . He couldn't believe that the navy had let them down to this extent.

'Questions after, damn it, Ensign!' he barked. 'You will know that it will be the chief object of the divisional commander to prevent a conjunction of the two forces. Our intelligence is limited, our videttes even now under attack, and all I can tell you is that you will shortly be very busy indeed.

'You will return to your men, have them in full marching order to step off at dawn, baggage to follow. You are to join with the Reserve Division at Vanløse, placing yourself under the orders of Brigadier Stewart of the 43rd Monmouths who will dispose of you as he sees fit. Understand?'

'Sir, you were going to tell us why—'

'No time! I've others to deal with. Any other questions? No? Good. On your way out, tell the 79th to come in, will you.'

The camp was in uproar but discipline took hold and the detachment was on the march as soon as it was light enough to move.

Only three miles. For light infantry swinging along through the gently rolling Danish countryside in the tentative morning light, it was far from onerous.

At Vanløse they halted and waited while Brigadier Stewart's pleasure was known. This rear encampment was in a lively state, with the battalions of several regiments to be moulded into one fighting formation with their equipage. Elements of the famous 95th Rifles, Highlanders of the 92nd and their sister regiment, the 43rd, joined by dragoons of the King's German Legion. A mixed body and none too sizeable but its character was plain: fast-moving, seasoned and professional. It had to be to face two armies in succession.

'No artillery,' Adams said moodily, surveying the drawn-up soldiery. 'I suppose His Nibs knows what he's doing.'

'You mean Sir Arthur?'

'In course, old boy. He's personal command of the Reserve Division.'

The unmistakable figure of Wellesley emerged from Headquarters, another farmhouse. He strode briskly and a gaggle of staff officers hurried to follow. He spoke briefly to Brigadier Stewart, who saluted and marched away, then called to his aide-de-camp and disappeared back inside. Maynard watched with awe: with this fighting general they would be taking the field very soon.

To his surprise, they did not. The men were stood at ease, then rest on their arms. And still the interminable waiting.

At a little before eleven Wellesley again left his headquarters with a colonel Maynard didn't recognise, who was arguing with the general.

'Damn! I'm going to see what's happening,' Maynard muttered. He found a piece of paper to flourish, walked past them, then stopped to pore over it while he listened.

'Sir! I must protest. It's – it's not to be countenanced! Common sense dictates we deal with one before they can conjoin. We must—'

'Colonel, you will obey my orders or I shall have you cashiered, sir,' Wellesley interrupted distantly, and continued on, leaving the colonel red-faced.

Maynard noticed a thin-faced staff captain nearby and sidled up to him. 'I'd be much obliged, sir, to know what the devil is going on.'

The officer swung around in irritation, but answered, 'As we've been waiting for the scouts to report. Now they have. Two forces – the north-west under one General Castenschiold, seven battalions, artillery. The other, Oxholm with four battalions, landed in Køge, the other side of the city.'

'How did they get past the navy, do you think?'

He lifted an eyebrow. 'They didn't. These are militia, raised from the countryside and islands.'

'Ah. Eleven battalions – we're outnumbered, then.'

'Is why our worthy colonel is choking on General Wellesley's orders.'

'Not to move on them now?'

'His Nibs believes our soldierly qualities are superior and desires that the joining is allowed to take place, the better to defeat them as one whole.'

'Then we'll—'

'Castenschiold is marching south to join Oxholm in Køge, which takes him across our front. We shall wheel around him by making a feint at Roskilde, but the devil is in the deployment – the King's German Legion are even now sweeping about to take them in the rear, ready for when we bring 'em to battle. Easy, really.'

Only if the haughty and patrician Wellesley really did know his men, Maynard reflected. 'And when . . .?'

'Tomorrow morning, I should think.'

Chapter 73

The first columns moved out at a brisk clip for Roskilde. The 43rd with Maynard then took to the road and, with the remainder of the British forces, they were on the way to meet the enemy.

After some miles, scouts brought news that Castenschiold had noted their advance but had interpreted it as a thrust at him. He'd taken the bait and increased his pace to effect the joining at Køge, passing across well ahead.

The columns halted and, after an hour, resumed their march, leaving the road and striking out directly south, moving quickly over pleasant meadowland and pasturage. By late afternoon they were in sight of the little seaside town, and on the gentle slope that led down to it, General Wellesley made his dispositions.

The Danes were in view across their vision, some five to seven thousand now in an arc extending out from the township into the open countryside, at a distance their uniforms unfamiliar. As well their irregular dispositions were distinctly puzzling.

Cooking fires were sending spirals of blue smoke into the evening air, birds trilled in the horse-chestnuts and birches while sheep grazed unconcerned in the river meadows – the whole a picture of late-summer contentment, as unlike a battlefield as it was possible to get.

In disciplined movements the British deployed in line and prepared, making camp in bivouac.

It was now clear that the morrow would bring a deciding clash, and the soldiers did what they could to prepare themselves in the age-old ways.

After dark and a frugal dinner, the officers were called together and Major General Wellesley made plain his expectations for conduct on the following day. In dry, forceful terms he spoke of his detestation of plunder, that any man violating the civil decencies could expect instant justice at the end of a rope. That, though outnumbered, they were going up against the Danish *landeværnet* who, while expected to resist the invaders, were no more than militia and could not stand against a disciplined turn-out of British regulars, whatever they'd heard to the contrary.

And finally, if they did not prevail the next day, the entire expedition would be put to hazard and that he was not prepared to suffer.

The night passed without incident, and when it was light enough to see, the picture was disquieting. The Danish had manoeuvred to face the British and brought up cavalry and several artillery pieces. There were pennons aloft, horn calls, every indication of giving battle. Worse still, there had been no word that the King's German Legion with its own cavalry was in place or had even finished its wide sweep.

A thin rattle of drumming started up in the Danish camp. They were forming up by battalions in fighting order.

Orders came quickly: they were to do the same.

The 52nd, augmenting the ranks of the 43rd, found Maynard on the left of the line with the light infantry. In the centre the colonel took position on his horse, flanked by the colour party, with the elite grenadier company on the right. The morning sun touched the scarlet coats and brought a martial glitter to an unbroken line of bayonets.

The band broke into a lively fife-and-drum regimental air and they were ready.

From the right came a small group of officers on horse-back. In full view of the enemy Wellesley was showing himself to the men who were going to fight for him. He made a striking figure, tall in the saddle with black-plumed hat, severe dark tunic and white breeches, progressing slowly and with grim disdain down the ranks, courteously doffing his hat to senior officers, with a gruff question here and there.

It was an impressive display, thought Maynard, the men straightening and stiffening as the general passed.

Then the Danes made their move. Three battalions of infantry in column marched to the front and extended into line, a ragged show, he thought nervously, as they spread out in numbers beyond their own.

So now was the time of decision: the King's German Legion had failed to reach them in time. If Wellesley was going to do anything, it must be with the forces he had with him, and that meant giving up their position of advantage up-slope and meeting the enemy in the level ground between, a wheatfield whose grain stalks hung ready for harvest.

The two sides faced each other in a hostile silence a quarter-mile apart, the lowing of a far-off ox clear on the morning air. Then the quiet was banished in a series of harsh commands in the British centre, instantly followed by a massed drumming – prepare to advance! Wellesley was not going to wait and battle was to be joined.

A baying of horn-bugles, the bellowing of sergeants – then the final order. March!

Stepping off immaculately, dressing in faultless line on the colours, the redcoats marched towards the enemy, ready to take the first merciless volley.

Something was happening in the Danish ranks.

A ripple of movement, gaps – faint shouting, gesturing – and the left battalion tore apart, disintegrated. Men ran for their lives, desperate for the safety of the town, stumbling, fleeing in mindless panic. It spread to the next, and in minutes the whole Danish front had dissolved into hundreds of running figures.

The drums gave the staccato double-thump of a halt, and without cavalry to pursue, the British line waited for the situation to clear, a murmur of amazement at the spectacle going up from the ranks.

The Danish commander responded with fresh battalions, brought forward and placed with Køge at their backs, a pointed manoeuvre to his wavering troops.

Wellesley wasted no time. The British battalions were manoeuvred for a general advance – but in echelon, the fierce Highlanders of the 92nd leading. Before the enemy could consolidate, the entire line stepped off, a fearsome concentration of violence and grandeur closing in on the Danes.

As Scottish bayonets lowered for business it was too much

for them. They broke and ran. Frantic to escape they threw down weapons, leaving guns, horses and equipment. Some brave souls stood their ground but were easily routed.

The battlefield was Wellesley's.

Chapter 74

Light infantry companies were detached and moved forward quickly in extended order. The logic of war dictated that, as the prime objective of the engagement was the destruction of any threat that lay in the British rear, it was necessary to pursue and annihilate the broken horde.

They pushed forward to the road. It was chaos – corpses, abandoned guns, prisoners wandering dazed and helpless taken by the score.

Shocked, Maynard saw who he and his fellows had been fighting. Not soldiers, they were rustic country folk taken up by the militia, long-haired farmhands and pig-herders in odd pieces of uniform over fustian and woollen breeches. Others wore red-and-green-striped jackets with wide hats not seen in England since the last Charles.

This was no glorious victory. These citizens had been defending their homeland and were wildly ill-matched against the veteran redcoats, who were now mercilessly hunting them down.

Maynard kept his men pressing forward towards the town.

On the road there were pitiful relics of the encounter discarded by the fleeing militia: improvised weapons, a scythe tied to a pole, broken muskets, a rusty lance. Knapsacks, bundles and, most poignant of all, many wooden clogs that had been cast off for the owners to run faster. Even their 'cavalry' had been riding plough-horses that now grazed contentedly in the fields.

They approached a hamlet, the warm yellow and red of Danish houses attractive in the sunshine. A severe church tower dominated a rise to the south behind some trees over a churchyard, and to the right was a small square.

The tap of a musket sounded ahead and a tell-tale puff of smoke rose over a ditch. Without waiting for orders Sergeant Heyer motioned for two to double away and take the sniper from the side but there were more shots. One of his men was dropped by a hit and in the general firing a bullet closely missed Maynard with a savage *whaap*. He gulped: as an officer he was a prime target.

They pushed forward to a low wall and looked over warily as a message came from Adams: he was advancing on the right and would be obliged if Maynard would move up on the left.

Before a safe passage had been identified there was the sound of distant horns blending into one – a harsher tone than that of their own. It was from the opposite end of the town and into view burst a squadron of the King's German Legion cavalry.

Their appearance caused all firing to cease, and in the distance the fleeing militiamen stopped in their tracks, mesmerised by the thundering mass. It was fatal – the Hanoverians brutally sabred those they could reach and drove the rest screaming into side-streets and houses, where some tried to retrieve their honour by firing from an upper floor.

Wellesley's main force arrived, and enraged Highlanders were sent to batter their way in to finish this nonsense. In a short time the streets were cleared.

They regrouped in the little square, and word was brought that the last resistance could prove harder to crush. The churchyard, whose perimeter walls were old and massively thick, held the last fighting remnants of the Danish force and, it was rumoured, their general.

It was a hopeless defiance. In rapid, decisive moves, the churchyard was isolated. The British troops did not press an attack: they kept under cover until a pair of six-pounder guns of the horse artillery arrived and efficiently set up opposite.

A demand of capitulation was sent in.

Before long a white flag was waved and Generalmajor Oxholm emerged at the head of his men. To all intents and purposes all resistance on the island of Sjælland had ceased. Only the city of Copenhagen and its garrison were left and all hope of relief for it was now summarily extinguished.

Chapter 75

British headquarters, Hellerup, five miles north of Copenhagen

Commander-in-chief of British land forces Lieutenant General Cathcart opened the meeting without mincing his words. 'I have to acquaint you, gentlemen, with the fact that General Peymann has seen fit to reject my repeated call for a cessation of arms and treat for a peace.'

'Good God,' muttered Major General Finch of the Guards. 'He's beaten and doesn't know it. After Køge they've not a hope in Hell of—'

'They fight for the honour of their country,' Wellesley said stiffly. 'Do you expect any less?'

Cathcart eyed the recent victor warily. He'd need to tread carefully for this was no mere subordinate. The well-born Wellesley had returned from triumphs in India to become a Tory Member of Parliament. In a very short while he had been elevated to government as the chief secretary for Ireland and privy counsellor with the ear of the highest in the land, which placed him in the peculiar position of being a member of the administration that was giving him his orders.

'This is very true, Sir Arthur. Nonetheless it places us at some difficulty in knowing how to proceed in achieving the purposes of this expedition.' If the expedition failed, the siege lifted with an inglorious return, his would be the humiliation and disrepute, not Wellesley's. 'I'd consequently be interested to hear your several views, gentlemen,' Cathcart invited.

The commander of the inshore squadron spoke crisply and with conviction: 'A direct seaborne assault on the fleet, my lord.'

'Captain Paget?'

'Our object is the neutralising of the Danish fleet. If this is achieved, we can raise the siege and return home in the fullest satisfaction.'

'Sir, the harbour is closed to us. The Citadel and other defences are too strong to contemplate a frontal assault, not to mention your pestiferous gunboats all of a swarm.'

'I'm persuaded we can do it in one stroke.'

'Oh?'

'A grand seaborne assault on the Trekroner Fortress in overwhelming strength. We take that and we turn its heavy guns on the Danish fleet in Nyholm. As well, it allows us to bring up our bomb-ketches and mortars for a very complete destruction. As to the gunboats, it will be my particular pleasure to first blast their lair at Lynetten to kingdom come.'

'All of which leaves the navy hero of the hour,' murmured Finch.

'Sir, that is an unworthy remark,' Paget burst out hotly. 'I demand you retract it.'

'Gentlemen, it is in any case irrelevant to this discussion,' Cathcart intervened smoothly. 'It was never in contemplation that the fleet be destroyed except as a last resort. I beg you will think again.'

'It does strike me that we may have overlooked one possibility,' Stewart of the 43rd offered.

'Yes, General?'

'Copenhagen is strongly invested to one side of the Strait of Kallebo only, namely the north. The south is untouched, being upon the island of Amager. A landing on that island to take the Danish on both sides will halve the forces facing either, and at the very least increase our pressing upon the enemy.'

'A capital notion, Richard,' Wellesley said, with enthusiasm. 'As you have the Reserve Division still in place across the water.'

'I cannot in any wight advise it,' Paget said, with some feeling. 'The same channel that separates the two halves of the city is a sovereign highway for the gunboats, which I'm sanguine can be relied on to go through untroubled to dispute any landing. This is a place infested with shallows. No ship with weight of metal can be expected to work up into the bight to defend the descent.'

An icy glare from Wellesley was his only reply.

'The siege, it seems, is fated to continue,' Cathcart said heavily, fiddling with his pencil. 'Unless we can conjure some stroke as will have Peymann reconsider his position. In the circumstances I think that unlikely.'

'Not even with—'

'I may have omitted to tell you that we lately captured dispatches from the Crown Prince. In them he's ordered to defend Copenhagen to the last and then destroy the fleet. It can be assumed that he received a duplicate by other means and therefore we can take it this is what he will do.'

In the glum silence that followed, there was no mistaking the sentiment. If they held out, the British had won the battles but the Danes had won the war, for the Great Belt blockade must be abandoned in weeks with the onset of ice.

He glanced across to a quiet, precise officer. 'General Bloomfield, for the lateness of the season we cannot possibly contemplate a customary siege with all your parallels, trenches and so forth. You are our artillerist. What are the prospects for a concentration of fire to procure a quick breach in order to storm the city by main force?'

'None.'

'Sir?'

'I have been well provided with guns, my lord, but no formal siege pieces of a weight that could reduce the walls and ramparts we see here. I can offer you no hope of a quick end to the business.'

'Then?'

Stewart raised an eyebrow. 'It does cross my mind that we may be playing it too much the strategicals. Our motions are purely military, intended to remind the commanding general of defences of his parlous situation. We're at a mile and a half distant of the walls of Copenhagen, out of range of their batteries but as well out of sight of the common people.'

'What the devil are you saying, Richard?' Wellesley snapped. 'I don't follow.'

'Should we close well in with the walls, show ourselves in force and numbers, not to say with our host of guns, then would not this dread presence give cause to the populace to beseech General Peymann to treat for terms?'

'Seeing us clamping a hold on 'em, meaning business, what?' Finch put in quickly. 'We'd be under fire but what the devil? We must do something. I'm for it.'

Chapter 76

Egilsgade, one mile south of Copenhagen city ramparts

Rain teemed down and squally gusts rattled window panes in a fit of autumnal spite. Still in his soiled uniform, Ensign Maynard stretched out luxuriously on the big bed. It was no officer-like indulgence, his men were similarly cosseted, and the aroma of bacon cooking was promising a welcome end to the day.

He stood up, went to the little side table with its twin lamps and retrieved his unfinished letter to his brother. At that moment the poor fellow was no doubt in a good deal less comfort, bobbing about on the sea in this weather. *And consequent on Headquarters deciding on a close siege we moved on the Danish outposts, we being a mile or more distant from the city.*

It had been a close-fought, vicious action, driving them back within the ramparts, for the open countryside had given way to houses, a spill of the Copenhagen suburbs beyond the wall. The house-to-house fighting had caused losses but the 52nd had past experience of urban warfare that brought it short. Rapid penetration deep within, and parallel squads sent to make their presence felt, brought confusion and fear to the defenders. Afraid they'd been passed by and cut off, they fell back. *A smart fight, but with results you'll appreciate when I tell you we're safely tucked in under their walls and my situation is most agreeable, courtesy the owner of this house, who, being unaccountably absent, I'm unable to thank personally.*

The Danes had made a grave error in not levelling the suburbs: everything the British did was now hidden to watchers in the bastions and ramparts and they could think only the worst of what must be happening.

And it was not altogether true that they were at the walls themselves: except in their particular position in the rear of the city, and another directly opposite the Citadel, Copenhagen was surrounded by a fosse, a broad moat that was impassable under fire from the frowning fortifications. But these had been constructed in another age and modern guns drawn up even outside it could easily range to the walls and city.

It seems they're out of sorts at our temerity and seek to annoy us at any opportunity. A sullen thump somewhere along the ramparts would be a Danish heavy-calibre gun opening up on some real or imagined target. A reply from a British battery could be relied on and firing would then be general up and down the line of fortifications until it tailed off, with nothing to show for it.

What was more worrying were the sharpshooters, daring skirmishers skulking among ruins and upper floors picking off whoever they could, then making off rapidly. There was no defence except vigilant picquets, who were very often in clashes of their own with enemy picquets opposite and now so close.

I shouldn't criticise my betters but this is looking much like a stale-

mate, brother. We can't stay for much longer and . . . It was not what he should be saying. He put down his pen and looked moodily out of the window at the grey evening. Why couldn't the Danes see sense?

Chapter 77

In the morning the rain had stopped. Following the Køge success, the officers and soldiers of the 52nd and other detachments were ordered to return to their unit. For Maynard and his men it would now be back to bivouac or tents at best, their billeting in comfort a fond memory.

The line of march to the Swan Mill encampment circled around Copenhagen at a respectable distance, but the mutter and grumble of artillery exchanges could be heard, and in the heavy air a pall of dirty smoke hung over the besieged city, like a portent of doom.

Nearer, a distant swell of noise grew and intensified. Somewhere out there on their right the Danes were making a sortie, by the sound of it in numbers and determined.

They marched on but it didn't die away, and Maynard realised uneasily that it was coming from more or less the direction of their camp. Imagination supplied the rest: the only other traverse across the fosse was at the Citadel – which directly faced them. Almost certainly this was a sudden thrust into the British lines, and if they used a substantial force, it was a real threat.

A tell-tale haze of powder-smoke hung over their positions – or did it? It seemed to be well short of their breastwork.

In the last mile the sound of the affray slackened and stopped.

They halted while scouts were sent ahead, then marched on into a battlefield. The camp was untouched. There were no signs of an assault but under guard a group of prisoners sat on the ground, each with the exhausted, vacant features of the defeated.

'So, you missed our little entertainment,' said the adjutant, looking pleased with himself.

'What happened?'

'Danskers made a sally from the Citadel. Odd thing, they didn't go for our lines. Instead set to chopping down trees.'

'Trees?'

'Well, we have it from the prisoners they wanted to level 'em to get a clear field of fire on the only place over the fosse. Didn't get very far before our chaps disputed with them. Want to have a look?'

Ironically, a pretty grove of woodland and park had been the scene of so much bloodshed.

'A garden belonging to a chap called Classens. I doubt he'd recognise it now.'

The ornamental parades, shady nooks and flowerbeds were torn and ravaged, trees hacked and gouged by shot.

Maynard's gaze was drawn to the pitiable sight of the dead in rows next to a pond. They lay face up with the glassy stare of death but what wrenched at him was their youth. With fair hair in fashionable ringlets, some could have been no more than sixteen.

'Students.'

'Of the . . .?'

'Not military. These are university students who banded together and called themselves Lifeguards of the King. Wouldn't retreat.'

Their death wound in almost every case was a bayonet thrust to the front. They'd not run when the 52nd had come on and stood no chance against professionals trained in the savage parry and thrust of close-quarter combat.

A lump rose in Maynard's throat and he turned away, eyes pricking. That it had come to this! What had Denmark done that she'd paid with these young lives?

Chapter 78

'Something's afoot,' Adams said, taking off his cloak and shaking the rain from it as he entered the tent.

'What do you mean?' Maynard asked, looking up.

'All officers to Headquarters.'

'Ah. Knew they'd have us out in this, the villains.'

'Not us.'

'Why not, pray?'

'All officers of colonel and above only. And they've mounted a guard at sixty paces to enforce it.'

This was unprecedented – not to say disturbing.

'And I saw our own beloved colonel take horse. He was wearing his do-or-die face.'

'Any orders?'

'None.'

'I wonder . . . We're about to throw it in and sail away?' Maynard said hopefully.

Adams frowned. 'I'd be careful what you wish for, youngster. We do that and the 52nd will be known for ever as the regiment bested by a mess of peasant soldiers.'

'Then we sit and wait. 'Twas ever thus.'

The commander-in-chief of His Majesty's land forces met each officer when they arrived, ushering them personally into another room from the usual. There was not a map or great table in sight for this was a drawing room, well supplied with armchairs and ornaments but far from a military staff room.

His field commanders took a place warily and Lord Cathcart closed the doors.

'Gentlemen, I've asked you here for a singular purpose. I'll not have you in any doubt – this is not a planning meeting, neither is it a council-of-war. It is by way of a . . . a discussion.'

Wellesley stiffened. 'Am I to understand, my lord, that we have been brought together at this time for no other reason than to talk?'

'If you'll bear with me, Sir Arthur,' Cathcart said carefully, 'there is good and proper explanation for this course.'

He glanced once at an officer who sat nearby, a satchel at his side.

'You don't need me to tell you that we are at a stand in the matter of persuading the Danes to deliver their fleet to our safe custody during the present war, being the objective of this expedition as ordered by His Majesty's government. Even a close siege of their capital has not moved them to comply.

'As well, you'll know that time is running out for us. Unless a resolution is found very soon we are left with only two courses: to raise the siege and withdraw in defeat, or the taking of Copenhagen by storm, by no means a certainty, and necessarily attended by much bloodshed.'

Several of the officers shifted uncomfortably.

'It is while in this quandary that I was approached by Lieutenant Colonel Murray, our deputy quartermaster-general. He laid before me a plan that seeks to cut through our difficulties and bring this business to a swift end. Gentlemen, I'd be obliged by your views.'

Murray stood up, gave a slight bow and drew out his papers. A slim figure, he was dressed faultlessly and spoke in dry and precise tones. 'My lord, I go from the assumption that all alternatives such as a reduction of Trekroner and a landing on Amager have been dismissed.'

'Yes, quite.'

'Then our objective might be simply stated. It is to apply such pressure on the Danish authorities as they are compelled to seek terms.'

'And?'

'Just that. Given our capability in troops and guns, we cannot normally hope to effect a conclusion, yet with the same military resources there is left a way open to us.'

The room held quiet.

'To oblige the inhabitants to suffer a general bombardment such as will lead them to beseech their commander to sue for peace.'

For a moment a shocked silence held, then a babble of protest burst out.

'Sir, this is monstrous! To rain fire and destruction on an innocent people – this is not an act of war, this is barbarism.'

'It will damn the character of an Englishman for ever.'

Cathcart waited and responded mildly, 'Your feelings do you honour, gentlemen, but are of little value to me at this time. This plan has the merit of being within our power and

323

has the prospect of being effective in the larger difficulty. I'm minded to consider it.'

Wellesley asked quietly, 'What assurance is there that a bombardment, however offensive to our honour, will be successful in its object? Do we continue until all Copenhagen, so lately a neutral, has been laid in ruins? It were better we consider most carefully before embarking on such a course.'

Major General Finch rubbed his chin. 'My lord, for myself I have the gravest reservations concerning the legality of such an act. To fire upon the common people not in arms against us is surely in breach of the laws of war.'

Cathcart glanced to Murray for an answer.

'My lord, the Danish commander had the opportunity to evacuate the city before we invested it and chose not to do so. That the citizens are thereby caught up in a military action is unfortunate but by no means without precedent.'

'Sir! This has been a neutral country and should—'

'The Crown Prince of Denmark has since seen fit to declare war on us and has thereby relinquished any rights of neutrality.'

'Sir, we've seen how they're possessed of the merest peasant army, who cannot possibly stand against our potency. Has every avenue of diplomacy and persuasion been exhausted? Can the Danish not see that . . .' Finch tailed off at Cathcart's stony expression.

'General, this Peymann is obdurate and inflexible to a degree that astonishes,' Cathcart responded. 'I conceive that only the strongest measures will oblige him to see reason as will save his people much distress. The plan before me is such a one.'

'Sir, I must nevertheless protest at this abominable act, so unbecoming a civilised power.'

Cathcart held up his hands for silence. 'Gentlemen, I've heard your several objections and do openly confess that I'm deeply troubled in myself. While the decision is mine alone, I do wish for your views before I determine on a course.'

Some of his officers looked away. Others sat rigid with set faces.

'Therefore I will ask you now a simple question. I only ask that you deliberate in your mind long and hard before answering. It is that at this very hour the fate of England herself no less rests in our hands. If we cannot contrive a proceeding whereby the Danish fleet is withdrawn from the equations of war we are lost. Should we abandon the attempt, Bonaparte will be enabled to seize the fleet to add to his own. With the Dutch and his new friend Russia, it forms an invasion force that can overcome anything we can bring against it. At the very least we must sue for peace, and at ruinous terms. At worst is the spectacle of Emperor Napoleon in triumphal procession down Whitehall. We are quite alone, gentlemen. All our allies are kneeling before the tyrant. If we do not act to save ourselves, there are no others to do it for us.

'My question is this: do we place the niceties of conduct, the unfortunate fate of Denmark caught between two unstoppable forces, before our very survival? Our fear of what the world will think of us before resolute action? I do not think we can.'

After a long and uncomfortable silence, Wellesley spoke: 'If we accept our hand is forced, do we have the guns to effect a bombardment of significance? A weak or paltry showing will produce the opposite effect – General Bloomfield?'

'Ah. I have twenty, no, thirty twenty-four-pounder pieces, but these are of no account in your customary bombardment, being reckoned levellers of the ramparts only. More to be valued are the forty mortars and ten heavy howitzers that, brought forward, may bear directly on the city centre. Besides these we can land a quantity of Congreve war rockets – and, indeed, Colonel Congreve himself who ardently desires to see his weapons in use. I'm sanguine such will be adequate to produce a satisfactory degree of ruination.'

'Good God! We're talking about the destruction of the ordinary folk, an ancient city of charm and—'

'Do control yourself, General Finch. We abhor this as much as you do but are nevertheless seized by its necessity. I must further tell you that I've arrived at my decision. It grieves me beyond the telling but it is that we make preparation for a bombardment of Copenhagen. When all is complete, General Peymann will be offered terms of a generous nature, providing only that the fleet is delivered up. He will be led to understand that, failing an agreement in this wise, a bombardment will take place within twenty-four hours.'

Chapter 79

An entire city under their guns in cold blood? It was inconceivable – but Maynard couldn't deny the reasoning. Even the stubborn Danes must see that they'd done enough to secure their honour, and this new compelling reality made nonsense of any attempt to hold out until winter drove the British away. They would finally have reason to yield.

It was essential to make all warlike preparation in earnest so there would be no mistaking their intentions, for if it were once suspected that there was no determination to go through with it, all bargaining power would vanish.

Ensign Maynard and Lieutenant Adams of the 52nd Regiment of Foot soon found their professional education extended – in the military preparations for a formal bombardment.

First, gun emplacements. Ringing the city, batteries were thrown up at speed. Horse and field artillery were expected to move about a battlefield but siege guns were dug in for protection against the defender's return fire and needed a hard base to allow continual firing from the same spot. Their placing was a science: engineers had three or four proven designs to match terrain but all had in common sturdy wooden platforms for the guns, inclined in reverse to damp the recoil, embrasures and flanking parapets with concealed magazines.

Then, guns. The massive twenty-four-pounders were retired to their park, howitzers put in their place. These were stubby guns, not designed to fire iron round shot into the massed ranks of an enemy. Instead, out of sight and angled up, they could hurl an explosive shell over a ridge or the walls of a fortification to reach deep within. Mounted on a broad, massive-wheeled carriage with a bore near double that of the standard six-pounder, their ugliness added to their menace.

More dreaded even than those were the mortars. Not the light, rapidly deployed battlefield pieces but tons of bronze ordnance, only a few feet long with gaping maws eight or ten inches across. They were not mounted on a carriage but on a low, flat cast-iron bed that could take the colossal recoil to the ground. There was no pretence at any kind of aiming, for their purpose was simple: the descent of every kind of destruction into the midst of the enemy.

With horrified fascination, Maynard and Adams watched the bombardiers make ready.

It was skilled work, traversing lugs and capsquares, barrel gyns and limbers, linstocks and portfires in a bewildering manipulation to turn the inert bronze and iron into deadly weapons of war. Before long there were dozens, then scores of the gleaming beasts turned hungrily towards the city.

In the rear a supply train was set up. Not bread and beer but munitions – stocks to feed each battery with its fill of flame and death.

An obliging artilleryman showed them the common round shot for plunging fire. Then a shell: black and spherical, packed with explosive and with a fuse hole, the whole protected by a wooden sabot. He passed across the fuse: a tapered piece of beechwood with a thin hole drilled lengthways through it and filled with strands of quickmatch soaked in a composition. The side was marked with half-second lines, and the art of the bombardier was to cut its length to ensure it detonated at the precise point of the trajectory desired. It was hammered into the iron shell with a mallet and the act of firing would be sufficient to start it on its destiny.

And the carcass. Resembling the shell, it had quite another purpose. Packed within was not gunpowder but a complex compound of resin and saltpetre. Fired into a general area, the interior ignited and fierce jets of flame were ejected from several vents, which would set alight everything combustible nearby. Impossible to extinguish, they would flare away for up to twelve minutes.

Finally – the war rockets. Colonel Congreve was in great good humour, unmistakable in white coat and hat, conspicuous and everywhere at once, his animation and vitality infectious. 'So you wish to know of my splendid invention? Do step up, gentlemen!' Like a showman at the fair he presented his wares. 'Here we see an eight-pounder of the breed,' he said proudly, standing over a long wooden chest. In it were six blunt-headed projectiles, dull black and lethal. 'For the delivering of explosive force where its medicine will do the most good.'

Gingerly Maynard touched one. Its cold iron casing lay dormant but he sensed a pent-up ferocity that unnerved him.

'And this.' Congreve crossed rapidly to another chest and threw out his arms. 'This is my pride and joy, gentlemen.'

Inside were four much larger missiles, which had needle-sharp nose cones, in the same iron-black.

'A thirty-two-pounder carcass-armed rocket,' he breathed, 'that may pierce into any building from a stupendous height. With a patent composition that spreads itself like lava after impact and whose blazing essence can never be put out. As well, in each one, a smoke-ball of noxious quality is included that will suffocate even the bravest attempting to douse the conflagration.'

'Er, what is their range, if I may ask it, sir?' Adams asked, clearly trying hard not to be impressed.

'I would be disappointed at less than one or two miles, far beyond your common mortar, however large.'

'And how does it . . . That is to say, how is it fired?'

'With a gun? No, sir! I like to say that this is ammunition without ordnance. It requires nothing but a frame of the kind you may see yonder.'

Propped up against the earthwork were several flimsy tripod devices.

'And when ready for flight, we fasten on a stabilising pole – for the thirty-two-pounder, of about ten feet in length. The entire procedure is effortless and capable of a rate of fire that would make you stare. I wish I could tell you more, gentlemen, but time presses. Let me leave you with this one thought. The cost to the Treasury of one mortar carcass, with its powder charge, is two pounds, three shillings and elevenpence. For a thirty-two-pounder rocket of superior destructive vehemence, it amounts to little more than twenty shillings. There – what do you think of that?'

Maynard and Adams trudged back together in silence, each with his thoughts.

'Sah!'

Adams acknowledged Sergeant Heyer with a salute.

'Took the liberty, sir, got a message in fr'm the Guards as would welcome a party to help 'em, like. Sent Corporal Reid and ten.'

'Doing what, pray?'

'They's scouting in the country, finds the pipes from the reservoir at Emdrup as supplies the city. Wants to stopper it off, quick, like.'

It had to be the final straw.

Besieged and outnumbered, a terrible array of fire and ruin waiting at their gates and now their drinking water denied them. It was the end for the Danes: there was no alternative but to concede defeat and yield.

Chapter 80

British headquarters, Hellerup

'R ead it again. By it, I want General Peymann to be in no doubt about what it means to his situation. No doubt whatsoever.'

Cathcart leaned back while his secretary smoothed out the paper and read.

Summons to the Governor of Copenhagen

Sir. We, the Commanders-in-chief of his Majesty's sea and land forces now before Copenhagen, judge it expedient to summon you to surrender the place, for the purpose of avoiding the further effusion of blood. The King our gracious master used every endeavour to settle the matter now in dispute, in the most conciliating manner. To convince his Danish Majesty, and all the world, of the reluctance his Majesty finds himself compelled to have recourse to arms, we, the undersigned do renew to you the offer of the same advantageous and conciliatory terms which are proposed through his Majesty's ministers to your court.

If you will consent to deliver up the Danish fleet it shall be held in deposit for his Danish Majesty, and shall be restored as soon as the provisions of a general peace shall remove the necessity which has occasioned this demand.

Sir, should you reject this summons it will not be renewed, rather your fleet will belong to its captors and the city, when taken, must share the fate of conquered places.

A response is expected before four pm this same day.

J. Gambier

Commander-in-chief of his Majesty's Ships and Vessels in the Baltic

W. Cathcart

Commander-in-chief British land forces

'Hmmph. If that's not clear to the meanest intelligence then I can do no more. What do you think, James?'

Grave and troubled, Gambier seemed reluctant to reply. Eventually he said, 'My lord, man proposes and God disposes. I pray most humbly that the Danish see fit to acquiesce else we must say that all things are then in God's hands.'

Chapter 81

The southern Baltic, off Rügen

The autumnal wind cut into him like a knife and Kydd shivered, pulling his grego tighter. Still muzzy from being summoned on deck in the early hours of the morning he peered over the side to where Brice was indicating.

'The boat, sir,' he said. 'We were hailed out of the night, sounded urgent. Not, as you might say, a cry of distress at all.'

It was an ordinary inshore fishing vessel with three occupants, their faces pale in the lanthorn's gleam. What was this little craft doing so far out to sea at this hour?

One of the figures cupped his hands and shouted up hoarsely. The words meant nothing to Kydd but he told Brice to allow one aboard.

The man heaved himself over the bulwark. He looked around warily.

'I'm Captain Kydd, of His Majesty's frigate *Tyger*. What is your business, sir?'

'*Kapten, ja?*'

'Yes.'

'I Sven Halvorsen. From Rügen. I haf much to discuss.'

There was something about the look of intensity on his face that jerked Kydd to full alert.

'Come below, then.' He leaned over to Brice. 'Send for my coxswain,' he said quietly. 'He's to go to my cabin and, without saying anything, hear this fellow and tell me afterwards what he thinks.'

Tysoe lit the oil lamp and left.

Halgren entered soon after, intelligently with a pistol in his belt as though on guard.

'Now then, Mr Halvorsen. Pray tell me what this is all about,' Kydd said.

'I ha' been sent by Överste Taksa, colonel of the Swedish Patriots of Stralsund. When our brave army was overcome by Bonaparte, Stralsund taken into his empire. We only on Rügen island are left to fight on.'

Kydd nodded sympathetically. 'I honour you for it, sir.' He'd heard how the Swedes had put up a fierce resistance but had been overwhelmed so the last portion of the Swedish empire on the southern Baltic was lost to them, and only recently. No wonder there were still forlorn bands on the larger, inaccessible island with hopes of one day restoring their lands.

'He know you English do not wish to involve, that he unnerstands.'

'It is because we are extensively engaged at this time, unfortunately,' Kydd replied. The Swedes were friends, the only ones left, and it would not do to show unwilling. On the other hand becoming involved in a desperate patriotic struggle on a foreign shore, whatever the cause, was out of the question.

'So he offer you something you want in return you give him muskets, guns, pay.'

This conversation must have been played out so many times along the edge of Bonaparte's empire where his rapacity and ambition had driven the conquered to desperate measures. At least he could listen politely, Kydd decided. 'Go on.'

'He say, first he can give you information, good information, for he has spies in Stralsund, Rostock, Lübeck. When ships sail, what they carry, where they go. Second, he has plan. He want you British to join with him – he make secret place on Rügen, you bring trade ship there, unload, he can take it inside Europe, not bother you. Much profit!'

This was something else entirely. Intelligence of the kind Nelson had set the greatest store by. And a gateway into the continent for British manufactures, utterly confounding Bonaparte's Continental System of economic blockade, and worth almost any effort in securing.

It was very good. Too good?

'You have some form of authority to speak of this, of course?'

Halvorsen fumbled inside his waistcoat and brought out a paper, folded many times.

Kydd opened and scanned it.

To the kapten of the British ship which cruize our shore . . . In essence it confirmed Halvorsen as an emissary of the Swedish Patriots of Stralsund, and accredited to discuss any matter. It was signed with a huge flourish and bore a red stamp.

If the man had been caught by the French with this, it would have been his death sentence. It must be genuine – and what was being proposed was too vital to be discussed and relayed at second hand. He had to see the principal.

'It would be better I discussed this important matter directly with Mr Taksa, I believe.'

'Överste Taksa.'

'Yes, of course. Do you think it possible I could meet him?'

Halvorsen hesitated for a moment. 'Very well. I take you to him – but only a few peoples come with us.'

'When do you think . . .?'

'He at north-east Rügen, at Lohme, not so far. We go now in the dark, stay one day, return in the next dark.'

Tyger was in a slow and uneventful cruise about the island and wouldn't miss his absence for twenty-four hours, and in that time a great deal might be accomplished. 'A good idea. I'll ask the gunroom to find you some refreshment while I prepare. Till then, Mr Halvorsen.'

He waited until the man had left, then asked Halgren, 'What do you think? Is he a Swede?'

'He's Swedish,' his unsmiling coxswain replied.

'Do you know anything of his organisation?'

'No, sir. I've not been to Stralsund since Swedish Pomerania falls.'

'Of course. You know Rügen at all?'

'Sir.'

'Well, this Lohme, for instance.'

'Very wild. Not people or animals – forest, cliff, small harbour. Very far from Stralsund, nobody likes this.'

'So a good place to hide.'

'Sir.'

It would be away from any French, who would not have consolidated their hold that far in this unpromising island. A quick dash in under cover of darkness . . . It was all very possible and, in any case, he had no reason to commit to anything if he was not convinced.

'Halgren, I think I'd like you to come with me. Keep a weather eye on the beggars.'

'Sir.'

Dillon was happy to record proceedings and Kydd had his little team.

Leaving *Tyger* to a doubtful Bray, they set off in the fishing boat into the outer darkness on a compass bearing.

When the blacker shadow of Rügen formed, Halvorsen quickly had their position and put down the helm to westward. In a short while, he doused sail, and while the boat drifted offshore he muttered something at the two hands, who produced a lanthorn and set it alight.

He brought it up clear of the gunwale and then down; up, then down, three times. They all stared ashore intently. The procedure was repeated – and a pinprick of light answered.

'Good,' Halvorsen grunted. 'All is clear.'

The small harbour was still and quiet, not a light to be seen. The little party hurried along the stone quay and through the silent town. A steep path led up the cliff, through woodland that reeked of resinous Baltic fir. At the top they found a clearing and a decrepit building, some kind of summer house. Two figures stepped from the shadows and Halvorsen lifted a hand in greeting, bringing his party to the front door, which opened for them.

Words were exchanged and they were taken into a musty parlour. The curtains were tightly drawn and a single candle lit on the table.

'Wait in here. I get the Överste,' Halvorsen said. 'On no account you leave this room!'

He left quickly, voices fading into the heavy stillness.

Minutes later, Kydd heard the clop of horses coming up the inland road, then snorting and snuffling as riders dismounted, the jingle of equipment clear on the night air.

At the sound of approaching footsteps, Kydd stood to greet the colonel.

The door opened and three soldiers strode in, wearing uniforms in green and buff with large boots and ornate curved and plumed helmets, their epaulettes and metalwork gleaming in the candlelight.

One bowed briefly to him and snapped in French, 'Capitaine Jominie. Twelfth Dragoons of the Stralsund Garrison. Captain Sir Kydd, an escort awaits. You must now consider yourself a prisoner of the French Empire. Your sword, if you please.'

Kydd fell back in shock.

The French! How had this happened? He'd been betrayed, but by whom?

In a red flush of shame he unbuckled his sword-belt and handed it over. The officer nodded and the two others took position behind them with drawn swords.

'March!'

A plain closed carriage was drawn up outside, escorted by a squadron of well-armed dragoons, a disciplined force well able to discourage any attempts at rescue by the Patriot band.

Keeping a fierce rein on his emotions, Kydd climbed inside and sat opposite the French officer, who smirked. Burning with anger at himself, Kydd looked away. Dillon sat next to him, his expression wooden; Halgren was told harshly to ride outside. They jerked away down the road.

Kydd forced his thoughts to an icy logic. Betrayal. He'd been addressed by name and therefore he was expected. Thus it had to have been an elaborate plot by the French to take him.

It had been so easy. A well-crafted and credible bait, a worthy performance from Halvorsen, and his own gullibility had done the rest. It stung that he'd been so readily taken in. It would echo about the world – the Royal Navy relieved of one of its celebrated frigate captains. Whatever else, his career was finished.

It was galling and his fault – but at least *Tyger* was safe. Bray would hesitate to leave while Kydd's important 'negotiations' were dragging on but would eventually report to Keats off Møn.

As dawn softened the landscape, it brought no relief from his raging thoughts and he sullenly watched the monotonous prospect of endless woods and copses go past until they arrived at a ferry crossing. The city of Stralsund was clearly visible across the water.

At last the carriage clattered into a fortress courtyard and Kydd was invited to descend by a grinning trooper. Conscious of his dress uniform in ribbon and star, he stood for a moment, adjusted his cocked hat and strode forward through the curious spectators, not giving them the satisfaction of displaying any emotion.

He was led up broad stone steps, then a spiral staircase to the highest level of the building. Passing guards at every corner, his heart sank. His captors were taking no chances on escape.

They were pushed into a cell, small and awkwardly shaped, a truncated L, at a corner of the fortress. The door clashed shut, a peephole flashed with an eyeball and the three were left alone.

'I – I'm sorry for what has happened,' Kydd began. 'It was—'

'Sir Thomas,' Dillon said quietly. 'If you'll allow me to make a personal observation?'

'Yes?'

'I would think it no less than a dereliction of duty were an officer to abandon an opportunity such as you were presented with. You had no choice – and it turned out this way. I believe we must accept it.'

'Thank you, Edward,' Kydd said.

He went to the single barred opening and peered through. 'Damn them. It looks out over this villainous city and never a sight of the sea.'

The cell was sparsely furnished and gloomy. Two low beds occupied opposite walls – one of them would have to doss down on the stone floor. A single rickety table and two wooden chairs completed the furniture.

'I rather fancy escape from here will be a vexing concern. Even if—'

The lock rattled and the door opened wide.

'Sir Thomas.' An officer in a flamboyant uniform gave a cynical smile. 'If you are at leisure, Commandant Moreau desires he should meet you.'

'Ah, the famed Kydd of *Tyger*,' the florid, corpulent fortress commandant declared, regarding him with interest. 'An honour to meet such a one.'

'Sir, I protest at the scandalous conditions that I and my staff have been subjected to,' he said hotly. 'This is neither honourable nor acceptable to my station.'

Moreau spread his hands widely. 'I'm desolated, please believe, Sir Thomas, but I have my orders for your strict confinement. You see, you are now a prisoner of note with a destiny that cannot be denied.'

'I do not understand you, sir.'

'You have not heard? I do apologise. It is the direction of

the Emperor that you be put on trial in Paris before the world for crimes unspeakable among civilised nations.'

Kydd reeled in disbelief. 'Crimes? This is preposterous! What am I accused of, pray?'

'For complicity in the violation of the sacred soil of neutral Denmark, of course.'

It didn't register at first. Then he realised what was going on. It was not the first time that a naval officer had been held responsible for an action in general. Sir Sidney Smith himself had been captured and taken to Paris for a show trial as an incendiary, having been active in Admiral Hood's firing of the French fleet in Toulon four years earlier. He'd escaped with the aid of royalists before the trial could take place.

Now Kydd was being made a public spectacle and focus of confected indignation as Bonaparte trumpeted the guilt of the British nation to the world. He'd be found guilty, naturally, and his execution would be managed theatre.

'I see. May I ask—'

'Soon. The authorities have their preparations, you will appreciate.'

Kydd was led back to his cell in a daze of horror.

'Sir?' Dillon said, in great concern.

'I'm to be put on trial in Paris before all the world as a violator of neutrality. This whole has been a plot to seize me for that purpose.'

Dillon gasped in dismay. 'The duc d'Enghien!' he blurted.

In a move that had shocked and dismayed all Europe, troops sent by Bonaparte had crossed the border and kidnapped the duke, taking him to Paris where, after a quick trial, he had been summarily executed. There was little that Napoleon would not do to serve his purposes and Kydd's fate could now be considered certain.

Halgren gave a hoarse cry and battered on the door in hopeless fury. It suddenly opened, a guard thrusting out savagely with the butt of his musket, sending the big Swede groaning to the floor.

'We have to get out, whatever it takes,' Dillon said in a low voice, kneeling by the hunched figure.

Chapter 82

They tapped and explored every stone slab and recess with no result. The barred window was no exit: it was four storeys up and the door was massive and impregnable. There were no implements: their soup and porridge were eaten with wooden dippers, and even Dillon's penknife had been taken.

Kydd looked through the peephole carefully. A single guard directly outside, standing. No other in sight . . . but on the extreme right he saw something that gave him a stab of hope.

'They've put us as high up as they can. Even if we got out there's not a prayer we can get past the sentries on every floor. But . . .' He paused. 'The spiral staircase we came up. It goes on a bit further and stops at a small door. It's my guess that it opens out on the roof. Once we're up there . . .'

There was the tiniest chance they could turn it into an escape. But then to scale down the walls and . . .

It was an agonising wait for the midday meal but when it came they were ready.

The guard opened the door and a grinning kitchen hand entered with a soup kettle and half a loaf. Kydd leaped at the man, knocking him unconscious, and Halgren wrenched the guard inside, chopping down on his neck to let him drop soundlessly.

'Go!'

They hurtled up – the iron door was not locked – and out. A blast of cold, damp air gloriously embraced them, the meagre brightness of the daylight intoxicating. Squeezing through they saw an anonymous humping of lead-covered roof stretching away. It glistened and danced with water for it was raining in solid sheets but Kydd didn't care. They were free!

Halgren yanked the door closed behind them and Kydd lunged forward but slid to an immediate stop. They were on a projecting battlement with a splendid view of the city but separating them from the main expanse of roof was a yawning chasm five feet wide, a vertiginous sheer drop to the ground.

As a young topman, Kydd had thought nothing of leaping out into space to snatch a backstay for a quick descent to the deck. He steadied himself and launched – a brief flash of distant ground and he was across.

It was Dillon next. 'I – I can't!' he gasped, freezing.

'Try!' Kydd urged.

Halgren moved swiftly. He stood behind Dillon, grasped him by his collar and trousers, then hurled him mightily across. With a strangled cry, Dillon fell on top of Kydd in a tangle of bodies. They quickly moved back so Halgren could join them.

The trio slithered across the grey wetness. Kydd saw through the driving rain that battlements like theirs were at every corner: almost certainly prisoners were kept on the outer, which meant that the centre would be administration, and hopefully a route for them to escape.

They dodged through the humps and slopes to the middle, and a flat, sheltered area with a large skylight. It had a small, raised windowed door, very like a ship's companionway.

Plunging towards it, Kydd grabbed at the brass handle and swung it open but he stopped in his tracks. A French officer was slowly mounting the steps with a party of guards.

He swung around but soldiers were spilling out on to the roof from several other points.

Kydd looked back – and the officer beckoned him with a cruel smile.

Chapter 83

The manacles were the least of their punishment. Their cell was now shared by two guards whose orders were to prevent any conversation and whose sharp gaze followed every movement.

Halgren sat cross-legged, his head on his hands. Kydd recognised the posture – it was often adopted by those confined to bilboes aboard ship and he allowed a tiny smile as he wondered what in the past the Swede had done to deserve such.

What hurt unbearably was the sight of his knightly star and sash brought to such a dishonourable baseness by his own foolish credulity.

Time hung in a succession of empty moments. Without distraction, his mind retreated into a wandering, self-pitying maze of memories and emotions that sapped the spirit.

The night brought no relief and he woke blearily.

Even before the light had strengthened, there were foot-steps outside and Moreau stood in the doorway with a piece of paper in his hands and a polite smile in place. 'Sir Thomas,

I'm happy to tell you that very soon you will be released from your confinement here.'

An insane leap of hope surged – an exchange? A change of heart for Bonaparte?

'Yes. Your carriage is being prepared. At noon you will leave for Paris.'

Kydd's heart turned to stone. This was the final chapter: at his 'eminence', and after their forlorn attempt at escape, he would now be guarded more closely than the Crown Jewels.

'Very well. I shall endeavour to be ready,' he said loftily, clinking his manacles meaningfully.

It was ignored and Moreau left with a bow.

There was not even the solace of words from his comrades and the morning stretched interminably.

At some time mid-morning there were faint sounds from the outside – shouted orders, a body of men: no doubt his guard and escort arriving for the long trip to Bonaparte's Paris.

But a few minutes later Moreau arrived again, this time somewhat flustered. 'Come!' he demanded of Kydd, without explanation. Four guards, it seemed, were necessary to convey him to Moreau's office but, oddly, they passed it by and entered private apartments.

'You will bathe and be shaved before you meet . . . the escort commander.'

It was extraordinary. Surely it would suit their purposes to have him arrive in the capital ragged and dirty, a thief-like object?

Only when he'd been set to rights and made presentable did he discover the reason.

Moreau appeared, splendid in a magnificent uniform,

gleaming boots and ostrich-feathered helmet. 'You are to be presented to the Prince de Pontecorvo, who desires he should see you before beginning the journey.'

Kydd blinked. A prince to be his escort? This was absurd.

They paused before a pair of double doors. They were flung wide and Moreau stepped forward hesitantly. 'Your Highness, the state criminal Sir Thomas Kydd.'

A figure standing at the window turned abruptly. Tall, handsome and with a dark intensity, he was arrayed in a black velvet uniform with intricately worked gold adornments and a broad sash, also in gold.

'Sir Thomas, this is His Highness the Prince de Pontecorvo, His Excellency Jean-Baptiste Bernadotte, Maréchal de France.'

The ingratiating voice held real fear. This was none other than Marshal Bernadotte, commander of the army corps that lay to the south of Denmark and in the French Empire ranking only a little down from Napoleon Bonaparte himself.

Stiffly he bowed, unsure of what the situation meant.

The gesture was returned courteously and the man regarded him for long moments with unsettling severity. 'Leave us,' he ordered Moreau, who hesitated. 'Get out, man! And you pair. Do you think I need guarding against an unarmed man?'

The voice was hard, accustomed to command, and they scuttled out.

'Do sit, Sir Thomas,' he said evenly, indicating a carved chair, taking another opposite.

Kydd did so elegantly, holding to himself that not so very long before he had been entertained by the King of England.

Bernadotte looked at him thoughtfully, stroking his chin. 'There are certain tides of events that make mockery of man's striving, don't you agree?'

'In my situation I do have my views you'll believe, sir.'

Bernadotte smiled thinly. 'Quite. Do understand that your trial and execution is abhorrent to me, a fervent admirer of la République in all its humanity.'

Kydd allowed a twisted smile.

'Which is why I am here, in all my glory as Marshal of France, pondering a course of action that requires the understanding of a Briton, a sworn enemy of my country.' A glimmer of humour showed in his eyes but there was wariness as well, coiled tension.

'An understanding?'

'Of my position. Why I must do as I must.' The expression was now speculative, considering.

'Sir, I'm at a loss—'

'Things will be made clear in due course. For now, allow that our conversation is private and unrecorded, deniable by both.'

'As you say.'

'Then you shall know my dilemma.' He hesitated as though weighing distasteful alternatives. 'It is that . . . the Emperor Napoleon is sometimes given to hasty and ill-considered acts of a nature that can only redound upon the honour and virtue of France.'

Was he hearing right? What did this near-treasonous admission mean, coming from one so high-placed? Was it simply an apology for Kydd's eventual fate?

'It places me in a painful situation indeed when I know the consequences to be both avoidable and undesirable.'

Unsure and wary, Kydd kept his silence.

'The kidnapping and conveying to Paris for trial is repugnant in itself, but when it involves one noted and respected by the world, the effect is disastrous and the opposite to that intended.'

'Just so,' Kydd said, with feeling.

'Oh, I didn't mean to refer to your own good self,' Bernadotte said, with embarrassment. 'One in far higher station.'

'Please do tell,' Kydd said woodenly, suddenly tired of the game.

'Sir Thomas, I've been made aware of an intention by the Emperor that causes me much unease, not to say alarm. You're aware that, following our success in east Prussia, an accord with Tsar Alexander was reached at Tilsit.'

'I am.'

'Then it's with sorrow I have to tell you that plans are in train to seize the person of no less than Louis Xavier, Count of Provence, now residing in Courland. That is to say, in Russian Latvia beyond the Neman. The assumption is that the Tsar, at this delicate stage of negotiation with the Emperor, will not dispute it.'

'Sir,' Kydd said heavily, 'I cannot possibly see how this can bear upon my situation.'

'Do forgive me. It will have more meaning for you when I say that the count in exile is the brother of the late King Louis the Sixteenth of France, put to the guillotine by the will of the people. Should Napoleon Bonaparte suffer catastrophic reverses – which God forbid – then the Bourbons will be restored and the Count of Provence will be placed on the throne as Louis the Eighteenth, King of France.'

Kydd fought off a sense of creeping unreality. What did this talk of kings and emperors have to do with him?

'Any attempt on the person of a notional future king is madness. All the royal houses of Europe would turn against us. That an emperor would stoop to such underhanded scheming in the cause of personal insecurity would as well rock the foundations of the Republic. It cannot be allowed to happen.'

'A problem indeed,' Kydd said caustically, 'which you will solve, no doubt.'

'I'm too late. I find a party has already left to accomplish this, which in this season of rains would be very difficult to overtake.'

At Kydd's ironic smile, he smacked the arm of his chair and shot to his feet. 'A lost cause, you say? True enough – but there is yet one person who may prevent it happening.'

'Oh?'

'Why, you, sir!'

Kydd recoiled in shock.

'I am powerless to move on the matter, however many divisions I command. First, it would be seen as an open defiance of the Emperor, and second, as I've mentioned, the many hundreds of miles to Courland would take weeks and would see the count spirited away before we arrive. A fast passage by ship would answer but, sadly, your navy objects to our presence on their sea. This is why, when I heard of the success of the plot to lure you ashore, it seemed too good to be true – here is a way my object may be achieved with discretion and dispatch.

'Sir Thomas, I have an offer to make. It is within my power to throw off your chains and set you on the deck of your ship once more. In return I ask only that you swear you will instantly set sail for Riga to secure the Count of Provence and convey him to a place of safety. If you do this now in your fine ship you will undoubtedly overtake the party and be in time. Will you do it?'

Would he rescue the King of France? Kydd looked directly at Bernadotte; the man's face gave no indication of deceit.

He drew himself up. 'On reflection I think it possible, yes, sir.'

'Not overlooking the other laudable end that the people in Paris may be spared yet another gaudy trial. Then, sir, we may proceed with the details. Moreau is put out that I have assumed personal command, but it is my decision, given your importance. Your escort will be my men whom I trust completely, as they do myself. They will be told that your "escape" – to be blamed on the Stralsund Patriots – is for a secret purpose, such as the purveying of false information at a high level to the British. In the nature of things your capture has not been announced. The sudden triumphant production of your person in the capital for all to see is the usual form. Therefore your disappearance will be quietly forgotten. On the larger issue I will not be implicated, and matters will be handled with a pleasing discretion.

'Sir Thomas, it will be expected that you travel with me in my coach, the others to follow in due course. The rest you may leave to me.'

Kydd tried to find words.

Bernadotte gave a dry smile. 'At this point I should ask you to so swear, but that would be a trifle pointless, wouldn't you agree? Once out of sight you will be free to do as you desire. In our short acquaintance, however, I fancy my trust is not misplaced. Shall we go now, sir?'

Chapter 84

All the panoply and magnificence of a marshal of France was on display in the courtyard. Plumes, frogging, bearskins; sword hilts, halberds, gleaming muskets; officers haughty with pomp; troopers rigid with pride. Bernadotte led the way to a plain but deeply polished carriage, chatting amiably with Kydd. Inside, the lavish appointments were of tasselled red silk and pearl satin, the seats of enfolding softness. The entourage moved off with fanfare and circumstance, through the gates and into the town. Gaping onlookers were held back as the cavalcade swept by and out into the countryside, on the road west to Paris.

As the sun sank lower it became necessary to seek encampment for the night and the village of Löbnitz found itself host to a squadron of the imperial guard. In the ferment and disorder of such an arrival no one noticed a small group make its way in the gathering dusk the mile and a half northward to the water's edge where a fishing boat was drawn up.

'One of your ships was sighted off this coast only this morning and I've no doubt if you floated about a trifle you would soon be spotted,' Bernadotte murmured. In a brisker tone he ordered, 'Bring the other two here.'

A stunned Dillon and Halgren were bundled aboard the boat.

'I fear I must make my farewell here, Sir Thomas. That I owe the honour of France to the actions of an Englishman is something we shall both remember.'

'You have my word upon it, sir,' Kydd said.

Bernadotte gave a tiny smile and turned to his aide-de-camp who on cue gave him an object wrapped in a cloth. 'Then if we wish to part on terms of amity it were better I returned to you your property.'

It was Kydd's precious sword, and he took it with a short bow. 'I will never forget your nobility of character, sir.'

Bernadotte contemplated him intently for a space, then nodded, turned back for his coach – and they were left to their freedom.

The sea was calm, the winds light, and under a single lugsail they stole out into the gunmetal expanse of the Baltic, seeing the ruler-flat coast diminish into insignificance. At the tiller was a hoary old fisherman who saw everything and noticed nothing, his rheumy gaze unwavering on the open sea.

Halgren seemed lost in a world of his own and Dillon's eyes were fixed on a pair of seagulls swooping and soaring in their wake. It didn't seem to be the time to talk about what had happened, how they had been spared and why.

After an hour the horizon dissolved into pale grey, which hardened: a rain curtain. Yet another in this essentially inland sea. It advanced, then enveloped them in light, insistent rain. Kydd didn't care – after a prison cell, its cold purity was almost a sensual experience.

It brought problems, though, the first of which was that they could not see beyond thirty yards and any cruising British ship would miss them entirely. The other was that the wind had dropped almost to nothing and their progress with it. They were at the mercy of offshore currents, and if those trended inshore they would find themselves taken back whence they'd come.

As far as Kydd could see there were no oars, only a scull. The fisherman seemed unconcerned, keeping way on with the bows to seaward but if—

'There!' Halgren's hoarse shout made them all start. Over to the right – a thickening shadow slowly moving. It could be anything and Kydd prayed it to be that which his soul had cried for these past two days . . .

A chance wind flaw and the veil was momentarily drawn back to reveal His Majesty's frigate *Tyger*.

In an instant Halgren was on his feet. The boat swayed alarmingly as he delivered a mighty bellow through cupped hands: '*Tyger!*' The age-old hail indicated that the boat contained the august person of the captain himself.

Kydd motioned for quiet – and faintly in the stillness they heard the bull roar of Bray, rousing the watch-on-deck to throw off lines and heave to. Then more bellowing to muster a side-party.

Chapter 85

Bray was visibly disturbed when they came aboard. 'Sir, it's been two days and more! We were right fretful, which is to say knowing you're ashore in these heathen parts, and no orders left.'

'Hmm. We were but detained a mite longer than planned,' Kydd said, flashing a warning glance at Dillon. 'But we came away with an intelligence of the utmost importance.'

'Sir.'

Kydd thought quickly. They were going to fulfil their mission, nothing was more certain, but that would mean leaving his allotted station off Rügen with *Lapwing*, a serious disobedience of Keats's orders: the commodore would assume he was still there when it came to calling for reinforcements in some important engagement.

His judgement was that, in this case, his move was justified, but should he first find *Lapwing* and tell her? There was no knowing how long that would take and time was running out.

No. It had to be now.

'Mr Bray. Shake out all sail – take us out to seaward and catch a wind, then course nor'-east. I'll tell you more later.'

'Aye aye, sir.'

'Oh, and stand down Halgren. He's to get an immediate double tot and off all duties for twenty-four hours.'

What his shipmates would make of his story, if ever they could get it out of the taciturn Scandinavian, would be put down to a fine sailor's yarn.

Kydd insisted Dillon come below for a restorative, and while Tysoe fussed at the state of his uniform, over a hastily conjured meal of pork pie and pickles, they shared a fine claret and let the tensions of the last days ease.

As he reached for a second glass he was taken with a breaking wave of tiredness that threatened to fell him. He looked up, saw Dillon's red-eyed exhaustion, too, and grinned. 'In this wise we're neither any use to His Majesty. Shall we get our heads down?'

The last thing he was conscious of as he slipped into a deep sleep was the gracious sway to starboard as *Tyger* took up to a strengthening north-westerly.

He'd let the world take care of itself until he'd claimed his rest.

Chapter 86

'A fine nor'-westerly, Mr Brice,' Kydd said briskly, sniffing appreciatively, as the ship ploughed steadily up the Baltic.

'Pleased to see you on deck, sir.'

'Thank you. Do pass the word for all officers in my cabin in twenty minutes, will you?'

They assembled promptly and Kydd didn't waste time. 'You'll want to know why I've taken us off station.' He fought to hold off a boyish grin at the thought of the effect of his next words. 'So I'll tell you. We're off to rescue the King of France.'

There were sideways glances and troubled frowns.

After a stunned silence, one ventured, 'Did you say, "King of France", sir?'

'I did.'

'B-but—'

'*Sa majesté le roi Louis le dix-huitième.*'

Bray looked away in embarrassment and Brice blinked in bewilderment, both unsure of what was going on.

Bowden caught on first. 'Ah. Your meaning is the Bourbon pretender to the—'

'Never the pretender, sir!' Kydd said severely. 'Should Bonaparte lay down his arms and throw up his hands in surrender, France will be restored to the man styled King of France, he who is now in exile in the Duchy of Courland.'

'I've never heard o' this gentleman,' Bray managed.

'Well, now you have.'

'Sir, you mentioned a rescue?'

'I did,' Kydd said, more seriously. 'Boney has sent a parcel of footpads to seize him and take him back to France. This we cannot allow to happen.'

'And we . . .?'

'They're coming by land, we by sea. We arrive first and convey him to safe haven. A simple enough task, I'd have thought.'

'Courland. I don't recollect I knows where this is, sir.'

'Lay the Duchy of Lithuania to starboard thirty leagues, Mr Joyce.'

'Oh.'

'If I said Riga, would it signify more?'

'Ah. An old trading port of our'n. Past where we was wi' the Prussians. An' I'm grieved to say, sir, I've nary a chart nor directions for such far.'

'Have you been there? Anyone?'

There was a doleful shaking of heads. Kydd frowned. Not only was the further Baltic known for its hazards but when they arrived he had to find the palace. Other than what he'd learned from Bernadotte, that it was at Mitau in Courland, he had no idea where it was and time was not on their side.

'Sir.'

'Mr Brice?'

'Why don't we stop one of our merchant jacks and ask the way?'

Kydd answered wryly, 'A good idea, but haven't you heard? The Danish Sound is in uproar. There'll be nothing getting past.'

The lieutenant smiled indulgently. 'Sir, if I know your merchant captain at all in these parts, he'll be main pleased to be through without he pays the toll, for just a trifle in the way of shot about his ears.'

In the main shipping lane to the north they soon had a stout Baltic trader hove to in their lee.

Kydd made the boarding himself, pacifying an irate master who thought it a scurvy trick to press men in these perilous waters. Further mollifying had him produce his charts and passage notes, which Joyce snatched up with glee.

'So where are you bound then, Captain?' the ship's master asked, eyeing Joyce at the charts.

'To Riga.'

'I won't ask what a king's ship is about there, but if you're in anything like a dash, I wouldn't advise it.'

'Why so?'

'As the Gulf o' Riga is found well in off the Baltic some hundred mile, but it's set about with wicked shoals at the entrance, as can make anything of a westerly foul for leaving. You get in, you'll never get out while the wind's like it is now.'

'Thank you for the advice, which I'll take. So how . . .?'

'In the main we anchors in Libau Roads, a tidy bit closer and clear o' the gulf. Has a highway direct to Riga.'

'And have you heard tell of a palace, Mitau Palace, at all?'

'Palace? The likes o' we don't have dealings with such, Captain.'

Chapter 87

Libau Roads, Duchy of Courland, Latvia

Kydd anchored at a discreet distance on the pretence of taking aboard stores to continue his cruise. Like all good captains, he'd naturally feel the need to go ashore to hear the latest news and trade gossip.

Libau, a prosperous ancient town, had done well out of the many nations that had traded there over the centuries, and the war was still at a comfortable distance. Kydd learned there were agents and factors from a score of countries, and communications from this ice-free port into the interior were excellent. He needed only to locate the palace and the grateful king could be rapidly whisked away to safety.

Back on board he had second thoughts. A Russian official had come out to satisfy himself that the presence of an English frigate had no military significance, a timely reminder that this was a Russian protectorate. Anything of the importance of what Kydd was contemplating would need at the least permission and in all probability a reference to the Tsar. That was out of the question, so the whole thing would have to be clandestine. King Louis would understand once the danger was explained, and some kind of disguise would get him here. Then it was simply a quick boat trip out to *Tyger*. All could be managed discreetly.

It was left only to locate the palace and proceed . . . Was it all to be so easy?

There was no question but that he himself should appear to inform the King. Who else should go?

Then there were details. If he went in the full panoply of a knight of the realm, in keeping with attendance at a royal court, not only would he stand out as curiously exotic but it would bring every spy worth his salt on his tail. So he'd go in his best plain clothes, those which he'd had Tysoe stow for discreet occasions – even if they were hardly of the quality to be expected at a French court.

Just how did he go about getting an audience? He could hardly tap on the palace gates and demand to see the King.

It was all rather murky and he longed for Renzi to give him a steer about such matters but, of course, he was now far away.

But there was Dillon. He'd been in Renzi's employ and must have learned something of the ropes . . .

'In course, Sir Thomas, you should send ahead. A letter of introduction, your trusted man to see you shall be received with all due compliments, delicate discussion as to your status – are you to be an official guest, victualled in to the King's account? There are pecuniary implications, you'll understand.'

'Ah, yes. But who—'

'It were better I started immediately. There's much to do.'

'Edward, after what happened I can't ask you to—'

'Can you think of one else?'

Kydd gave a small smile. 'Very well, I accept your kind

offer. Now, we don't even know where this palace of exile is. I've a notion it's not going to be easy to locate.'

'Leave it to me. I've yet to meet a merchant factor of delicacies without he knows his market. Now, sir, I humbly suggest you make travel in the character of, say, a British projector of manufactories seeking opportunities.'

'Alone?'

'With a manservant, of course.'

Kydd grinned at the image of Halgren in an exiled Versailles, but Dillon seemed to read his mind. 'Not your coxswain but Tysoe, whose appearance of colour will be singular and much admired in these parts, testifying to your undoubted standing.'

'I'd feel safer with Halgren.'

'Sir, I fancy this will be an occasion of delicacy and diplomacy rather than peril and adventure.'

'You're right in course, Edward.'

'I shall shortly land to make my way there. The harbour-master's office will hold my note of direction for you to take carriage yourself and details of where we shall meet at Mitau.'

'I'm obliged to you, dear fellow. Until we meet at the court of King Louis?'

Chapter 88

D illon's hastily scribbled note informed Kydd that Mitau
was a twenty-mile detour off the Riga road to the south
and that he should stay at the Lielā inn and await him. Tysoe
had taken his instructions with vexing composure, clearly of
the opinion that an appearance before a mere French king
was nothing exceptional for someone at his master's eminence.

The road to Riga was smooth and the carriage well-sprung.
As he gazed out of the window Kydd couldn't help pondering
the workings of Fate for a young wig-maker of Guildford
who had heard with his family the horrifying news of the
Revolution and execution of the King of France – and was
now on his way to save his brother and successor. A tale to
regale Renzi with indeed.

After an agreeable journey through a medieval landscape,
Kydd and Tysoe transferred to another coach for the last
miles to Mitau. It was evening when they arrived at the town.
The coachman stopped outside a charming inn of the old
style, set beside a river. He mimed a deep bow and the placing
of a crown on his head, then proudly pointed to a long

island in the river where the end of a grand building peeped above the trees. The Mitau Palace?

The rooms at the inn were small, but quaint and snug. Tysoe ignored the looks of curiosity and nobly set about his duties while Kydd accepted a glass of wine from a wide-eyed serving maid.

There was not long to wait. A quiet knock on the door and Dillon entered in severe but smart black attire that Kydd hadn't seen before. 'I trust you travelled well, Sir Thomas?'

'Indeed. And you?'

'Sir, the situation is not necessarily in our favour.'

'Oh?'

'The British representative is insistent that he is unable to assist in the matter of obtaining an audience.'

'What?'

'He will tell you himself – he's coming here shortly and knows only that you wish to see the King privily.'

The envoy of the court of St James to the court of King Louis arrived quietly in the anonymity of darkness, regarding Kydd keenly before accepting a chair. A ruddy-faced, portly gentleman of years, with silver-tipped cane and old-fashioned breeches, he looked like a country squire.

'Sir Benjamin Tucker, sir. And I've heard a strange tale from your man that you wish audience with our Louis.'

'Of some urgency, Sir Benjamin.'

'You'll never get one.'

'Pray why not?'

'You're a stout son o' the sea, can't be expected to know.' His shrewd blue eyes held a hint of humour in them. 'This is a court of exile. It's run-down, threadbare and lives on past glories and future impossible dreams. It's also the first place royalists go with their wild plots, mad schemes and petitions for funds, and you may believe there are well-tried defences. You've a letter of accreditation, a form of diplomatic introduction, perhaps. No? Then regrettably there's nothing that can be done.'

'Then why are you here listening to me?' Kydd asked.

'I'm sanguine there's a very good reason why a distinguished sea captain desires the ear of the French King and, frankly, I'd wish to know it. Not that I can do anything about it, of course . . .'

Kydd hesitated for a moment. 'Sir, for your ears only.'

'Of course.'

'I have intelligence that very shortly a party of Frenchmen will reach here whose task it is to seize the person of the King and carry him to Paris.'

'Oh dear.' A sorrowful smile spread. 'I do hope you didn't pay too much for this bauble. You've no idea how many of these rumours are about these days.'

'I have it from an unimpeachable authority,' Kydd said stiffly. 'You may accept it as trustworthy.'

'Might I enquire—'

'No, sir, but I give you my solemn word upon it.'

Tucker paused, looking at him speculatively. 'I'm minded to believe you. You will not profit by this knowledge, and it seems beyond belief that any lesser concern would see a child of Neptune so far from his natural element. Do tell me more.'

'I have little to add other than that they'll be here in a matter of days at most and that it is my sworn duty to convey His Majesty to a place of safety beyond the seas.'

'Ah. Then you will face more than a few difficulties. Let me be frank. My rank and position is anomalous and low, for King Louis the Eighteenth of France is an embarrassment to the British government, who are reluctant to acknowledge him as an equal or yet more a supplicant. In short, my duty here is that of friendly ear and from time to time disburser of the generosity of King George's private purse, no more.

'This implies you will not be thanked for any gallantry that involves a king's ship, for that does morally bind the principal into offering sanctuary, an alternative place of exile. At ruinous expense, you may accept. For that reason it would be trespassing beyond my powers should I assist in this way.'

Kydd bristled. 'Sir Benjamin, I'm astonished at your attitude. Do you not have a duty to your masters?'

'The Parliament of Great Britain and Ireland. Which requires I do not fluster them with distractions.'

'Then, sir, out of your own mouth you are condemned. Our own King George thinks him of value, else why does he find it in his heart to fund the poor wight out of his own pocket? It would not go well with you, Sir Benjamin, should King Louis be taken by Boney's assassins.'

'Calm yourself, please. I cannot assist, but I can most certainly be free with my advice, which if followed might achieve the object you desire.'

'Which is?'

'Let me set the scene for you. The Mitau Palace is in the gift of the Tsar of Russia who now, being under Bonaparte's spell, would be miffed indeed if its chief guest decides to depart, he no doubt seeing the King of France as a valuable bargaining piece. Therefore all Russians are your enemies. Now, in the palace our sainted king is at the pinnacle of a vast and complex establishment, all of which ceases to exist should its principal be removed, resulting in the throwing into penury of a legion of nobles and followers beyond counting. And so we must accept that all royalist Frenchmen are your enemies.

'The country you are in does not even have a name. The Duchy of Courland, the Livonians, the Polish-Lithuanians, others, even the Teutonic Knights have all ruled territories but none paramount. The natives speak a heathen tongue, Latvian, and cling to the distinction. But, mark me well, all are proud that the King of France has chosen their land for exile and revere him. Therefore you must count the local peoples as your enemy.'

'What of his family here? If they heard that—'

'His queen, Marie Joséphine, is his unforgiving foe for having been deprived of her female lover and would like nothing better than to see him to perdition. The Comte d'Artois, his brother, is a well-known thief of France's patrimony and requires the King to practise upon, while his closest confidant, the Comte d'Avaray sees everything, circling like a hawk over all, and would, without question, take it as his duty to frustrate any attempt to spirit him away. The *garde du corps*, his personal bodyguard, is half a regiment strong and are sworn to defend his body to the death. Added to which the palace heaves with spies and corruption in which nothing may pass unseen.'

Kydd smouldered. 'Sir, I believe if I may have audience with His Majesty I can—'

'As I've made abundantly clear, sir, that can never happen.'

'God rot it, sir, but you're a sad comforter,' Kydd came back.

'You'd rather I left it in your hands, an innocent to blunder about in such a moil? No, sir. I've but given you the lay. Now without doing violence to my conscience I believe I will tell you something more to your advantage. The Queen is long retired to her apartments, taken by the dropsy. In her place as chatelaine, as we may say, is this king's niece whom he dotes upon. Marie-Thérèse is married to Louis Antoine, Duc d'Angoulême, a callow youth but of known sympathy to England. Should you declare a pressing desire to be introduced to this noble lady, then of my esteem for your rank, naturally I will feel obliged to grant it. It is then for you to convince her of your case, after which, if you are successful, she will go to the King and matters may well take another course for you.'

'Sir Benjamin, I'm most obliged to you.' Like a foul wind turned fair, he was back on course.

'You should be aware that the lady is a summer short of thirty and intelligent, but has suffered most grievously. In a fortress prison with her kingly father and mother while the revolutionary mob raged, she was torn from them, first one then the other taken to the guillotine, while she remained in durance for some years. She has the melancholy honour of being the only royal prisoner to survive the Terror, and has reason to fear the regicides. I conceive, Sir Thomas, that you will find a ready ear.'

Chapter 89

The Mitau Palace, Duchy of Courland

'Sir Thomas Kydd,' blared a bored functionary. Kydd advanced, executed an elegant leg and raised his eyes.

'Dear sir, be welcomed to us.'

The curiosity in her voice was undisguised – how many Englishmen of note would reach this far into the continent of their own desiring? And Tucker had been right: she was a handsome woman of character, her direct and strong features reminding him of Cecilia.

'Oh, old chap, well met, what?'

Astonished, Kydd acknowledged the slight figure to one side, presumably her husband, the Duc d'Angoulême.

'Sir, your English does you credit,' he replied.

'As I was guest in your splendid country for too few years, Sir Thomas.'

'Yes,' the duchess said cuttingly, in French. 'Captain, Sir Benjamin did allow that you have something of mutual interest to discuss.'

The duke fiddled nervously with a tassel.

'Of the most urgent and compelling nature, Your Royal

Highness.' Kydd looked about him meaningfully. 'As must be communicated privily.'

She contemplated him with interest. 'I really cannot conceive of what an English sea captain might consider a French duchess must know in so importunate a manner. However, I shall indulge you, sir, for a brief space.' An imperious wave of the hand and the drawing room was vacated by all save the duke, who stood up uncertainly, then sat again. 'Now, Sir Thomas, pray what is your business?'

'Madame, I'm captain of a frigate lately cruising off Stralsund.' He spoke in low, urgent tones and with as much conviction as he could muster. 'And lately in possession of intelligence of an unpleasant nature concerning your king.'

'Go on, sir,' she said steadily.

'There is at this very moment, a party of assassins sent by Bonaparte to seize King Louis and take him to Paris. I'm here to provide a means of conveying him to a place of safety.'

The duke spluttered, 'Even the Corsican would not stoop to—'

'Be quiet, *cher cœur*. Captain, we've rumours enough in this place. Why should I believe this?'

'The information came from one who is in a position to know the truth of the matter and can gain nothing by its falsity.'

'Sir, this is hardly grounds for requesting the King of France to flee with you. I'm mindful that a distinguished gentleman such as yourself would not be here unless convinced, but to satisfy me you must disclose your source and why you do believe the same.'

'Madame, it is . . . Marshal Bernadotte of France.'

There was a frozen silence.

'From his lips?'

'Just so. He deplores the tyrant's dishonouring of the name of France for reasons of personal insecurity, and—'

'He is known to me. You will tell me his appearance, his style and bearing that I may be assured it is he.'

'Ah, he is tall and slender, with dark curled hair. He dresses richly but plainly and, er, women might well account him handsome. He commands men as if born to it and—'

'Thank you. Even if he serves Bonaparte he is a man of honour.' She bit her lip, concentrating, then came to a decision. 'Very well. I will accept that you have trustworthy information. Because of the need for haste I shall go to the King immediately. Do hold yourself ready to see him, if you will, Captain.'

She left in a swirl of brocade.

Kydd tried to make conversation with the agitated duke and was glad when Marie-Thérèse swept back in.

Wringing her hands, she told Kydd, 'He refuses to leave, saying they wouldn't dare to move against him in his own palace, this is only another foolish rumour, and there is no proof they exist.'

'Madame, I must press you. In a very short while they will be here. If there are traitors and such who will aid them there's every—'

'Sir, I know more than you do that this may well be so, but you must understand. My uncle is stubborn and, as a king, set in his ways. I cannot so easily move him.'

'You must, Madame! Time presses and this band—'

'You ask too much! He's the King of France and not to be commanded.'

Kydd saw there was no more to do. He'd done all he could

and had been spurned. Already guilty of being off-station he was not in a position to wait indefinitely. 'Then, with much sorrow, I fear I must take my leave, Your Royal Highness. There are duties my ship must perform that require her presence in distant waters. I shall depart in the morning.'

'Is there nothing I can do to persuade you to remain a little longer? The King may—'

'It is a time of war, Madame. My ship's movements are out of my hands. I'm desolated to refuse you but I must.'

Chapter 90

Kydd knew the charade could play out over weeks or months if Bonaparte's agents didn't end it first. He'd kept his word to Bernadotte but his attempt to save the King of France had been disdained, so he could depart with a clear conscience. When Dillon heard what had happened, he agreed there was nothing else to do but prepare to leave.

The morning was grey and dull, suiting Kydd's mood. The coachman chatted to Dillon in German, letting it be known that a return to Libau instead of the crowded squalor of Riga had much to commend it.

As the quaint-coloured houses gave way to fields they lurched to a stop and the coachman shouted down.

'He says someone follows,' Dillon said darkly.

The sound of a galloping horse closing with the carriage grew louder and Kydd leaned out of the window to see a single rider, who was up with them in a crash of hoofs. A sealed note was thrust at him, the horse gyrating in impatience as Kydd tore it open.

It was from Marie-Thérèse: 'Return, I beg you. Everything

has changed. We have desperate need of you.'

Did this mean . . .?

'Take us to the palace!' Kydd ordered.

Outwardly all was calm as a blank-faced major-domo escorted him to the quarters of the Duc d'Angoulême.

She was waiting for him. After a warning look to remain silent until they were alone, she said flatly, 'You were right. They are here, now. A spy has reported seeing Lecoq – one of Fouché's assassins – in a nearby village. There's a coach-and-six with him.'

The fastest mode of transport, impossible to catch in pursuit.

'The King?'

'He's prostrated in dread – his memories. He desires nothing more than to be taken from here by any means.'

The whites of her eyes were showing – this woman of any would know what it was to live in terror.

'My frigate lies at Libau. On board he'll be perfectly safe, I do assure you.'

Marie-Thérèse paced nervously about the room. 'To get him out of the palace will be hard. If he's seen to be fleeing it will cause chaos, panic. And it will tell Lecoq all he needs to know. We must think.'

Her husband entered, distraught and unsure.

Glancing at him, she came to a decision. 'Yes. We will move immediately. Captain, if by some means we bring the King to you in hiding as it were, would you take him with you to your ship?'

Kydd bowed. 'Yes, Madame.'

She considered for a moment, then went to an ornate desk and wrote something on a slip of paper. 'Give this to your coachman and tell him to wait in the courtyard of this house.'

'Your Royal Highness, I—'

'Leave now, and you will not be suspected. We will meet again in happier times, you may be sure.'

Chapter 91

Kydd, Dillon and Tysoe waited in the spacious courtyard of a country manor as inquisitive servants were driven inside by an agitated owner. Their coachman remained on his seat, keeping the restless horses still.

Suddenly, in a burst of noise, a white-plumed carriage crashed on to the cobblestones and swept into the yard. Footmen and guards dropped to the ground, the cipher-emblazoned door was opened and a nervous Duc d'Angoulême was handed down.

'Th – the King,' he gulped, turning aside to hold a deep bow.

From the dark inside of the curtained carriage there was movement and Kydd dropped to an elegant courtly bow, hearing a strangled gasp from the coachman, who hastily got to the ground.

King Louis XVIII of France emerged – wig askew, eyes wild. He was heavily overweight and puffed like a whale as he pushed past Kydd into the other coach, hastily followed by the duke. 'Let us go, Captain!' he called urgently.

The coachman thrust himself in front of Kydd, jabbering angrily.

'He swears he won't be a part of this, Sir Thomas,' Dillon interpreted.

A chinking purse was thrown from the vehicle and landed at the man's feet. He picked it up, weighed it appreciatively and, without a word, returned to his seat.

'Dillon, you and Tysoe ride on top.'

Kydd entered the carriage. The King took up most of one side, the duke was opposite. With muttered apologies, Kydd sat beside him and gave an awkward nod to the King.

The coach swayed and they were off, leaving behind the royal carriage with its attendants.

It was absurd, bizarre. In the coach with him a king was pulling a lap rug over his head and doing his best to slide down low while a duke in plain garb had on a too-large floppy gardener's hat.

'Your Grace was successful in leaving the palace without difficulties?' Kydd asked the duke, at a loss as to the demands of etiquette.

'Oh, yes. My wife is very clever and advised I take His Majesty for his morning ride in my carriage with picked men, then to draw the curtains and quit the palace as if going to see . . .' he giggled foolishly '. . . my mistress.'

'So no one knows the King has departed?'

'No. The duchess will say that he desires not to be disturbed and later will allow that he left with me for Riga.'

'She's a fine woman, sir.'

'Yes,' the duke said distantly, and stared obstinately out of the window.

Kydd wondered what would happen when the King was found to be absent.

In the midst of the consternation Lecoq would move fast to discover his escape route. The Riga deception would last only so long – with a coach-and-six at his disposal, he could make the distance in an hour or so and, not having overtaken the fleeing king, would reason that he must be on the only other major road out of Mitau, the highway to Libau.

They had very limited time in which to reach the sea. As the endless plains passed by in dull succession, Kydd tried not to think of the fate of witnesses if Lecoq caught up with them.

Changing horses was the only relief in the tedium, and eventually, without incident, the outskirts of Libau came into view.

'He wants to know where to go!' Dillon shouted through the coach window.

Kydd told him to make for the waterfront. There, it would be simply a matter of hiring a boat to take them out to *Tyger*, lying offshore. It really did seem that they were going to succeed.

The King cowered lower as they trotted through the streets. When they reached the harbour Kydd saw at once that they were in trouble. Between the approach roads and the wharf there was a spacious open area thronged with stevedores and porters, Customs officials and beggars. The instant the King emerged from the carriage he would be mobbed. Should he take a chance that they could fight their way through? Too risky.

'Drive on!' Kydd ordered.

There had to be—

For a heartbeat in a chance alignment of side-streets he saw a vision: a low, sleek coach pulled by six horses.

Time had suddenly run out.

By now Lecoq would have extracted full information on which coach had been taken. If they were seen it would all be over. There was only one course left.

'Dillon!' he snapped. 'Ask the coachman if there's a quiet cove or sandy beach along the coast as will take a boat.'

A few moments later he had an answer. 'Then you're to hire a fishing boat and take it there.'

It was little more than a windswept passage through to a small sandy inlet, deserted and exposed, but hidden on all sides by dunes. The coach came to a stop on the flat hard at the head of the beach. Kydd hadn't the heart to tell the frightened passengers what he'd seen, for they were already in a state – but who was he to judge, given the horrors they'd experienced during the Revolution?

Something else caught his eye on the skyline along the top of the dunes. Small figures, excited, pointing.

Children. Nothing to worry about – unless they told someone of the remarkable sight of a coach and pair for no apparent reason sitting squarely at rest on the beach.

They disappeared after a while but returned with older children, who stared down at them. More arrived until there was a small crowd.

Where was Dillon's fishing boat, damn him?

If this excitement brought Lecoq they were trapped: there was only one track to the beach. They would stand no chance against armed professionals and—

A fishing boat suddenly appeared around the point, dousing sail and loosing an anchor. A dinghy was soon in the water and two figures got into it, one taking the oars.

It *was* Dillon!

The dinghy came in and grounded in the sand. Dillon leaped out and the fisherman boated oars and stood edgy and resentful. Without waiting, the King burst open the coach door and tottered down to the water's edge. Dillon held out his hand to steady him amid a swelling roar of amazement from the dunes.

The fisherman gobbled in fright. He tried to work the boat out again but Dillon held on to it, the man's increasing panic threatening to upset it.

'Give! Give!'

At this, the King struggled to remove an emerald ring from his fat finger. He thrust it at Dillon, who passed it with a bow to the pop-eyed fisherman, probably more wealth than the man had seen in his life.

The tiny boat put off, rocking alarmingly, but the King of France was on his way to sanctuary.

On the dune the crowd was growing and becoming noisier.

The dinghy eventually returned and Dillon with the pale-faced duke set off next.

After an age the last run was made. Kydd and a perfectly unruffled Tysoe found their places and the boat put off.

A sudden swell of noise from the gathering made Kydd look back.

To the satisfaction of the enthusiastic watchers the show had concluded in a finale that saw a full coach-and-six race down the sandy track and come to a flying stop at the water's edge. Half a dozen angry figures spilled out to watch helplessly as the dinghy made its way out to the fishing boat.

King Louis of France was safe and had escaped Bonaparte's clutches.

'Hmmph.' Commodore Keats was not to be persuaded so easily. 'What if the French had decided on a sortie to the

382

east, hey? No one there to see 'em go, follow the beggars. Your orders were plain, sir. No gadding about on a whim to suit yourself.'

'Sir, I conceived it my duty to preserve the government of the day the embarrassment of explaining—'

'Yes, yes, any fool can see that. I suppose I should now send you to Admiral Gambier to tell him you've left the King of France on his own in Sweden – where was it? Karlskrona?'

'Sir.'

'Very well.' A reluctant smile surfaced. 'My occasional dispatches will go to Copenhagen with you. Tarry a while – over dinner you can tell me all about your little adventure.'

Chapter 92

Svane Reden, Copenhagen

R enzi listened politely; the nurse was taking great risk in concealing them.

'And then the gunboats returned in victory, after sinking nearly half the English fleet!' Frue Rosen finished, not quite smothering a burst of pride.

'Are you sure? Half?' he teased.

'That's what they're saying in the market, m' lord.'

They were in the billiards room where lights could not be seen from the outside. By now they were used to moving about in the dimness of the deserted mansion.

Renzi gave a half-smile. It was past the point where he could logically deduce the truth. Since the news that Copenhagen had been completely surrounded he'd tried to reason out the course of events but nothing made sense. He'd accepted the landing as necessary if the Danes had not been impressed by the armada brought against them. But since then not only had they been cut off from all succour but he'd heard guns and sharp musketry exchanges, a full-scale war that could have only one ending. Why weren't the Danish treating for some kind of honourable armistice?

'I beg you'll excuse our dining tonight, my lord,' Frue Rosen said humbly. 'There's only this bacon with your cabbage, all I could get.' Crestfallen, she held up a sorry-looking piece of meat.

'Why, that's wonderful!' Hetty said, with forced enthusiasm. 'Our thyme will go so nicely with it. I'll fetch some for you when it's dark.' There was a herb garden on the roof that had gone far in making their increasingly bleak rations palatable, all that Frue Rosen could find in her daily expedition.

Days had turned into weeks. Rumours flew and Renzi realised that the situation was worsening. This was a siege and everyone knew what happened when a city fell.

He kept his fears from the ladies. It was conceivable that the Danish command could eventually see reason and come to an arrangement but all the time they dragged it out the tensions and frustrations would build until the British, with time not on their side, would be forced to resort to drastic measures.

Two days later reports came of a dreadful clash-at-arms near the Citadel when many university students had apparently gone gladly to their deaths at the hands of the English. In the same desperate engagement General Peymann, governor and gallant leader of resistance, had been wounded at the head of his troops and carried back.

The mood had changed.

Frue Rosen returned with tales of hunger and want: families scavenging and dogs killed for meat, bands of roaming vigilantes and militia turned out against looters. She came back with less and less, bread and fresh vegetables near unobtainable, meat at ruinous prices, milk an impossible luxury.

Surely the people had suffered enough in upholding the honour of the Danish nation and could now reluctantly capitulate. A depressing mood of hopelessness hung over the city but it was shot through with defiance. Several times a day columns of volunteers passed with a jaunty, stubborn air, armed only with poles tied with sickles or hay-forks.

Then the water failed. The steady gush from street-corner pumps and stand-pipes slackened and turned to a sad trickle, which despairing citizens queued to catch in any utensil to hand.

That siege-breaking move by the beleaguerers should have brought a final conclusion but it did not. A proclamation of defiance was issued by the Citadel that left no room for weakness.

Renzi knew then that the end game would be brutal, bloody and sudden. The Danes had resisted heroically to unreasonable lengths. The British could not abandon the contest so would be forced into the last sanction: a terrible storming by force of the city against the ramparts and fortifications, a savage slaughter that would end with soldiery flooding in to sack Copenhagen with vengeful barbarity.

Something of his mood communicated itself to the others. Cecilia clung to him with an unspoken devotion while Hetty retreated into herself. Frue Rosen wore a haunted, stricken look.

Chapter 93

Egilsgade, one mile south of Copenhagen city ramparts

Adams and Maynard stood together. It was a strange, eerie sensation. The ever-present rumble of gunfire had petered out and a heavy stillness hung over the city that allowed the chirp of birds and occasional farmyard lowing to be heard for the first time in days.

Adams hailed a passing fellow officer and crossed over to him. 'When did the summons go in to the Danskers?' He returned to Maynard with his answer. 'Says they're to have all the time they want to think about it, save we get a reply this day.'

The 52nd had the simple task of holding the line of guns should the Danish make a desperate sally, and had little to do but watch proceedings.

Along the emplacements howitzers and mortars stood ready, their crews lazing at their posts, deadly projectiles stacked neatly in their protected earthwork magazines. A line of supply was in place for each, all the dread paraphernalia of siege warfare complete, primed and waiting.

'You have to admire the rascals,' Adams murmured.

'Leaving it to the last moment possible before conceding.'

'So we'll be cheated of our bombardment,' Maynard said lightly, hoping his feelings didn't show.

'One entertainment I'd be happy to miss, m' friend,' Adams said, in a low voice.

The morning passed but with the noon rations came news.

A reply had been received but it was not what was expected. General Peymann had acknowledged the peril Copenhagen stood in but wished to refer any final decision to the King of Denmark. The response from British Headquarters had been immediate: a rejection of the delay and a repeat of the original ultimatum.

'Damme, but they're sailing close to the wind,' Adams muttered.

The sensation of unreality heightened, time dragged into the afternoon and then the evening.

'How will we know if . . .?'

'You'll know it.'

Everyone agreed the Danes had to give way and they were not helping their situation by holding out for some alternative outcome. They were risking the whole thing turning bad and damage being done to their fair capital.

Night drew in. A moonless Stygian dark. Lights were going on in Copenhagen but the walls and ramparts in the foreground were in utter blackness.

The gunners were still stood to, as they had been all day, but now it was night with no aiming points. They would shortly be obliged to secure their weapons for the morning, when—

At seven thirty precisely a signal rocket hissed low across the sky, its red trail vivid in the blackness of the heavens. At its height it exploded with a thud in a pretty twinkling light.

'Let's be 'avin' you, lads!' came a bellow from the gun emplacement, and in a general stirring men closed up at their guns.

Battle lanterns were brought up and, with portfires and linstocks glowing, it dawned on Maynard what was going on. Incredibly, the bombardment of Copenhagen was really about to happen.

Two mortars opened up nearly simultaneously, the livid flash and hoarse bellow catching him off-balance. Others quickly joined in, gun-flash leaping up and down the line in a continuous roar.

In perfect parabolas red lines traced across the sky, the smouldering fuses of mortar shells, to descend somewhere in the interior of the quiet city with their lethal detonations. Other lines criss-crossed them: howitzers firing carcass shells to set buildings ablaze and still more with explosives to bring ruin and devastation.

Grouped together, stands of war rockets burst into action – an immense bright flare and roar, then a release to vanish instantly into the heavens in a vast arc up and away, trailing flame, then descending like a vengeful bolt from the gods. Another, and another, still more, stunning the senses.

Maynard stood rigid as the pungent stink of burned powder wafted by him. He tried to control his thoughts. What must this be doing to a city full of people?

Chapter 94

Svane Reden, Copenhagen

All day the guns had remained silent in a fretful peace that lay ominously over the city. Frue Rosen came back to tell them excitedly that an important message had been sent to British Headquarters. Renzi's heart lifted. Were the Danes going to bow at last to the inevitable?

The quiet lasted into the evening, and as the night drew in, he allowed himself a flicker of hope that reason had at last asserted itself.

As soon as it was fully dark he and Cecilia accompanied Hetty to the roof garden where they could take the open air without fear of discovery. All of Copenhagen was spread out before them.

Moonless, with cloud obscuring the stars, it was suitably sepulchral for any apocalypse that threatened, Renzi reflected.

Cecilia held his arm tightly, in thrall to the same baleful mood. Only the *snip-snip* of Hetty's scissors and the whisper of night zephyrs disturbed them on their rooftop eyrie.

'Nicholas – fireworks!' Cecilia pointed to a rocket that had soared up and across, to explode with a dull thud in full view of where they stood. 'Does this mean celebrations are starting?'

Renzi felt a lurch of premonition. It had been a signal rocket and it had come from the outer darkness of the British lines. In the next minutes the dogs of war would be unleashed – there was going to be—

As one, the guns opened up. Livid flashes played all along the lines, the menacing rumble and thunder of massed artillery unmistakable in its angry spite. From beyond the ramparts scores of guns joined in, until the entire periphery was alive with gun-flash.

It was a bombardment, but on a scale he'd never conceived. The air was filled with criss-crossing dull red lines tracing through the sky. He knew what it meant for he'd been present at Granville those years ago when mortars had been used against invasion barges. But that had been only two from bomb vessels. Here there were uncountable numbers hurling in an avalanche of death and destruction.

The first shells fell with a leaping flash and visceral crump among the streets and buildings below them, some in a flaring of unquenchable fire – carcasses, filled with a mixture that could not be extinguished. Here and there he could see the steady blaze of a house or shop afire – and sharp against the flames figures were in disciplined activity, firemen in heroic battle with the flames while all the time death came out of the sky.

But a new phenomenon thrust itself on his senses: a whining hiss that became rapidly louder – a missile with flame in its wake that streaked over and nosed down to vanish into a house. Seconds later from deep inside, the red glow of a fire grew while people spilled out of the door in panic, falling to the ground in their desperate flight from the nightmare.

From the bastions and ramparts Danish guns opened up, hitting back at the merciless barrage without the slightest chance of countering it, only adding to the insane sound and fury.

Nearby came a louder crash, followed by the smash of falling glass and screams. A mortar round had visited a house close by – and Renzi realised they themselves were exposed and vulnerable.

'Down – get off the roof!' he shouted, and pushed the dazed women to the stairway.

They hurried to the ground floor and huddled together in the drawing room. Renzi drew open the curtains a few inches. The darkness outside was shot through with flashes and the diabolical flickering red of fire.

Occasionally they felt the tremor of an explosion through the floor, and once there was the hideous flash and detonation of a shell outside a house opposite. Its entire front slowly collapsed in an appalling roar and up-welling of dust. Whitened victims emerged, staggering and falling.

A riderless horse raced by in stark panic, a child's terror-stricken cries carrying clear above the madness. A dog barked witlessly, on and on.

The nightmare had only just begun.

Chapter 95

Danish Headquarters, the Citadel

Peymann was propped up in a Bath chair, the wound in his thigh bound tightly but clearly causing him pain. Several of his staff stood about him.

The bombardment was now only a faint background grumbling of guns but a dozen or more fires were still alight in the old city.

An aide arrived but did not meet Peymann's eyes as he laid the paper in front of him. 'Your report of damage, Generalmajor.'

'Nørregade, Gammeltorv – the Helligaands. This is a dreadful price, Knud,' he whispered, more to himself than the others.

'Sir, the people are frantic, knowing not where to go to escape the terror,' Bielefeldt ventured. 'How can I tell them—'

'They must endure – as must we all,' Peymann said, lifting his head and glaring at him with blood-shot eyes. 'His Royal Highness has not seen fit to vary his instructions. I'm bound to obey him in this, to hold and protect Copenhagen with my honour and life.'

There could be no answer to that, but a major in crumpled and stained uniform said flatly, 'The firemen have not rested. I cannot answer to their effectiveness should the bombardment continue. If it does, all Copenhagen will be left ablaze and—'

'Sir! Your cares are noted. Allow that I have the higher concern. The decision is mine. And that is to fight on.'

'But—'

'Enough!' Peymann blared. 'How are we to know what the Crown Prince intends? At this moment an army of thousands may be on the march to relieve us. Should we cravenly surrender before it's had chance to reach us, I shall answer for it with my head.'

'Then—'

'Then you shall do your duty, sir, as I will do mine.'

Chapter 96

British Headquarters, Hellerup

'It's insufferable!' spluttered Cathcart, holding the paper at arm's length. 'Worse than that – it's rank madness! Peymann has an offer of terms such as no besieged ever had – yield up custody of his damned fleet and we go. Quit! Leave! What more can he ask of us? It bears heavily on me that we're obliged to visit ruination on his capital but we've no other recourse, given his intransigence. This he sends as answer on the day following. Listen to it:

"*My Lords*

"*Our fleet, our own indisputable property, we are convinced is as safe in his Danish Majesty's hands as ever it can be in those of the King of England, as our master never intended hostilities against yours.*

"*If you are cruel enough to endeavour to destroy a city that has not given any the least cause to such a treatment at your hands, it must submit to its fate; but honour requires—*"

'He gives not an inch, damn it! We're no further forward than the day we landed and time is sorely lacking. How can we proceed in the face of this? Hey? Hey?'

Ludlow, of the Guards, smiled sadly. 'My cousin Joan is married to a Dane. Says they're incurably stubborn and declares it's of their Lutheran persuasion. We'll never move them by ordinary means, I fear.'

Gambier shook his head gloomily. 'Lord Nelson accounted them his fiercest foes at our first encounter in the year one. They do not lack the spirit and courage to defy us and for myself I have the gravest reservations of the outcome.'

The cool voice of Wellesley intervened: 'There is little to discuss, I believe. We have embarked on a course of coercion, which we cannot retract or abandon, else we render the whole business a nullity.'

'Your opinion is then—'

'My opinion is neither here nor there. Logic requires us to go on – to resume the bombarding until a satisfactory conclusion is reached.'

'This is bitter medicine, sir!' Finch ground out. 'Can you not conceive of the terror in the breasts of the inhabitants, the innocents caught in—'

'In war there can be no allowance for feelings of a delicate nature, sir. The dictates of one's strategics are the only consideration and here they are plain. Do you propose to deny them?'

Cathcart shifted irritably. 'Gentlemen, gentlemen. Sir Arthur has clarified the situation that faces us beyond disputing. We have no alternative – the bombardment will resume tonight with the utmost rigour, the quicker to bring an end to it all.'

Chapter 97

Svane Reden

The terror returned. Once darkness had fallen the air became alive again with the evil whine and drone of high projectiles, the lethal swash and hiss of lower trajectory missiles and always the crump and tremble of explosions in a never-ending dread that the next would seek them out and end their lives in a blinding instant.

A street away, a market took fire, its towering flames impossible to control. And as medieval houses were hit with exploding shells they crumbled to gaunt ruin. There were so many now, stark and desolate. The rockets hissed unseen from the sky, their sharp iron points enabling them to pierce deep within a building where the flare of their patent composition would leap from the floors to the walls and bring inferno to yet another ancient habitation.

Through the drawing-room window they were confronted with a hellish picture. The fire and destruction were reaching into the sky, the clouds now tinged an ominous blood-red, flashes playing on their undersides in a devil's tattoo.

They shrank from the scene and sat together by the dead

fireplace but could not speak. What could be said in the circumstances?

As midnight passed, Frue Rosen collapsed, inconsolable and broken, weeping softly.

Hetty and Cecilia held her by turns, comforting and quieting her.

Renzi waited until Frue Rosen was settled, then took Cecilia aside and held both her hands. 'My darling love.' He struggled with the lump that was forming in his throat. 'My very dearest. You cannot conceive how it beats on my spirit that I've brought you to this place of ruin and death. If it were only myself . . .'

Cecilia gripped his hands so tightly it hurt and, looking deep into his eyes, whispered, 'Dear Nicholas – believe me, my love, when I tell you that I'd a thousand times be here by your side than safe and without you.'

They clung to each other for a long moment.

Dabbing his eyes, Renzi pulled himself together. 'I do believe we must seek shelter lower down. The cellar, perhaps.'

'Then that's where we must set up our home!' Hetty said, with brittle gaiety. 'Do go down and I'll bring our things to you.' She hesitated, then said in an off-handed way, 'Dear Frue Rosen was not able to go out today, the people being all of a moil. We can do without our foodstuffs but we're in sore want of water. The pump is at the end of the street – I'll see if I can squeeze out a dish or so.'

'No!' Cecilia said in consternation. 'They'll see you're English and – and hang you!'

'There's not so many out there and they'll have other things to worry on. I'll be quick, don't bother about me.'

She shooed them down the stairs to the cellar and found a pan.

Chapter 98

Hetty cringed in fear. In the open air every explosion and rending smash was clear and immediate as though she were part of it. Fires leaped and crackled on all sides, and drifting fragments of ash came down in a constant soft rain.

The flash and detonation of an exploding shell nearby made her jump. Moments later shards of stone and iron skittered down around her while the raw stench of burning and ruination hung heavily in the air.

The pump was only a hundred yards away and seemed to have been abandoned. She hurried towards it, heart pounding. There, she was confronted with an appalling sight. A cross street led to the dignified Vor Frue Kirke and its lofty fine spire. The church that had seen the weddings of the kings of Denmark and their coronations was now ablaze, a giant torch, engulfed to the very steeple tip. Against the merciless flames the black outlines of dancing figures were trying vainly to save what they could.

Mesmerised by the awful sight, Hetty couldn't move – and

then, in a stupendous flare of heat and flame, the steeple gave way and the church collapsed, swallowing the people below in a surge of victorious conflagration.

Stricken with horror she dropped her pan and turned to flee back, whimpering, desperate to reach their sanctuary.

But at that precise instant a mortar shell detonated in a blinding flash nearby, closely followed by another further along. The blast reached her and tore at her flimsy dress, and when her sight cleared, she saw that the entire front façade of their town-house refuge was now a smoking pile of rubble along the road, the dark voids of rooms on the upper floor grotesquely exposed.

Heart in her mouth she was about to run forward when the remaining structure teetered, masonry crumbling, then fell, with a heavy and prolonged crash and swirling dust.

Where before there had been a princess's mansion there was now only a collapsed ruin – and lying crushed and dying within were Lord Farndon and his countess.

Choking with emotion, Hetty ran towards the devastation, a vast pile of brick and shattered stone. She fell on it, tearing at the rubble with bleeding fingers, blinded by tears of frustration.

She felt a hand on her shoulder, patting, comforting. A deep male voice uttered soft words in Danish and instinctively she flung herself at him, weeping and howling. The man held her, gently saying something over and over and lifting her face to see if she understood.

But she had no idea what he was saying.

She pulled herself together and tried a weak smile.

Awkwardly, the man spoke again, then turned and left.

As he disappeared into the distance Hetty surrendered to a tidal wave of inconsolable grief.

Chapter 99

Hetty woke. In a wash of terror it all came back – but in the dull daylight the situation had changed. The leaping flames of the night had given way to a drab bleakness, a desolation of ruins and scattered debris almost unrecognisable as the street she knew. From all directions sullen columns of discoloured smoke rose over the dull red of fires still alight, and the street was full of shuffling figures, some with pathetic bundles and trailing children.

There had been light rain during the night, which had laid the dust somewhat but had left her dress wet and clinging, grimed and spattered with blood from her fingers. She shivered and pulled it tighter as reality hammered in: under this sprawling mass of rubble were the dear Lady Cecilia and her husband, Lord Farndon.

It rocked her sanity and brought on an empty, dry sobbing at her sheer helplessness in the face of what had happened so quickly. All that was mortal of the ones she cared about most was there and only she could do something about it.

She looked up at the passers-by, dully plodding on to who

knew where – but they were Danish. Why should they help their enemy?

She gulped and looked about. Was there no one she could turn to?

Yes. Mr Jago was in their Amalienborg quarters. Imperturbable and impassive, he would know what to do. She had to get to him.

She and Cecilia had left for Frederiksberg Castle through the West Gate. Therefore she would walk east into the morning sun until she reached somewhere she recognised, her goal the big square of the Amalienborg complex.

'Don't just stand there – give me a hand!' Jago grunted to Golding, one of the servants, as he peered out of the window. 'That's Miss Hetty out there.'

The door had been well barricaded with a sofa and chairs and took some time to open.

He hauled her in. 'Miss Hetty, what've you been up to, walkin' the streets like that?'

'Oh, Mr Jago! It's terrible, terrible.' A wave of emotion seized her, leaving her weeping and trembling and clinging tight to him.

'Why, here's a to-do,' muttered Jago, clearly embarrassed. He led her to a chair and sat her down. 'Now you tells me all about it.'

She took a deep breath, held it for a long moment, then recounted what had happened.

'We've got to rescue them, Mr Jago! Get them out of there!'

'After what you said, if'n they're still alive,' he reflected darkly.

She cried in anguish. 'Please help, I beg you. *Pleeeease!*'

'There's a war on. I don't rightly know . . .'

'But we have to do *something* – anything!'

'Don't take on so, Miss Hetty,' he snapped. 'He's my master as well, an' it doesn't help, you pipin' your eye like that.' He began pacing around the room. 'Could be there's a way. Look, I know you's had a time of it, but can y' see your way clear to takin' us to 'em?'

'Of course!' she replied instantly.

'First things first. We finds a few tools to carry, then I've got a job for that kitchen boy as has the English.'

A furtive search around the lower floor produced only some gardening implements but Jago seemed happy with the haul.

The kitchen boy agreed to be their translator, for a ready sum.

'Now you be on y'r best behaviour, young lad, 'cos we's on a special mission, and if you promises not to tell a living soul, I'll let you in on it.'

Outside it was quiet and no one seemed inclined to question a group of men, a ragged woman and a boy as they trudged along.

'There's no guns, Mr Jago,' Hetty said.

'Course not. They gets going at night.'

'No, it's not that – there's not even the others.'

The irregular thumps and rumble of artillery exchanges at the ramparts had stopped completely. Not even distant bursts of musketry.

'They've given in, surrendered.'

'Never. See? All the flags are still up.'

As they reached the corner Jago bent down as if to tie a bootlace and glanced back. To his satisfaction he noted a sudden scurrying of figures diving out of sight. 'Well, let's be on our way.'

When they reached the scene Jago paused, as if considering what to do.

'Mr Jago, there's only the few of us. Where are the others to help?' Hetty pleaded.

He gave a tight smile. 'They'll come – magic it'll be, you'll see.'

He strode forward and pointed at the rubble, then set to with his mattock.

It was a signal: from their hiding places scores of men raced out and, roughly shouldering him aside, went at it with a will, heaving off slabs of brick, tossing aside fragments and reducing the pile.

Passing men joined in the mad scrabble.

Hetty stared open-mouthed. 'M-Mr Jago, how did you . . .?'

She turned to Golding, standing back and leaning on his rake. 'Do you know how he did it?'

The young man tipped his hat in admiration. 'Ha! Cautioned young Andreas not to tell a soul, but he'd heard the mansion where the Crown Jewels was hidden just fell down an' we were on our way to help ourselves. They has to keep out o' sight until we shows 'em which place it is, then they goes at it for 'emselves, like good 'uns. Mr Jago knew he'd snitch, the scamp.'

The rubble was fast disappearing revealing a once splendid ground floor in a shattered state, bowed down under the tons of debris, but now rapidly clearing. A shout brought Jago and Hetty running – a section of the floor had given way, exposing a dark void.

Jago used his fists to work his way to the front and peered in.

There was movement. A glint of something. He eased down to lie prone at the edge of the pit. As his eyes grew accustomed to the darkness, he saw Nicholas Laughton, sixth Earl of Farndon in a wine cellar, sitting beside the countess and swigging extravagantly from a bottle of excellent white wine.

'So early, m' lord?'

'As it has served us for water these past days, Jago. Do be a good fellow and help us out, will you?'

Chapter 100

Danish Headquarters, the Citadel

Every eye in the room was on Peymann as the recitation went on. Then it was the turn of the Danish land forces commander, General Bielefeldt.

'Sir, it's with the greatest reluctance I have to tell you that many of the burgher militia have abandoned their posts on the defences in the face of the bombardment. They're on the front line. It leaves the ramparts undefended. Should the British choose to storm us, there can be no hope.'

'I see.' Peymann rubbed his bloodshot eyes. 'It had to happen, I suppose, poor fellows.'

Significant glances were exchanged around the table. Did this mean . . .?

'Sir, I really think that—'

'Gentlemen,' Peymann said, and sighed, placing his hands on the table in a gesture of finality. 'This you may take to be a council-of-war, with the object of establishing the most advantageous terms of capitulation. Note that down, will you, Knud?'

'No!' blurted Bille. 'There's still the—'

'Kommandør,' Peymann said, in tones of the utmost weariness, 'we have resisted valiantly and can do no more. I shall ask for a cease-fire as of this hour and will expect to be discussing terms with the English commander shortly. Shall we begin?'

It had to be faced. They were defeated. Even the Crown Prince's exhortations couldn't change that.

'We ask for the honours of war, of course. Due ceremony, the exchange of prisoners, that sort of thing, yes. But one question stands above all. This war was brought to us by the British, who wanted one thing – our fleet. This question therefore is, do we yield it up lightly or do we destroy it before they can lay their hands on it?'

'No question! I shall set a torch to it in person,' Bille ground out. 'The honour of Denmark is not to be preserved by tamely surrendering our glorious fleet, undefeated and unbowed.'

Peymann winced. 'I really cannot support you in that, Kommandør. The dockyard is in the centre of Copenhagen and will lay ablaze any of our city still left to us.'

'And it will antagonise the British beyond their enduring. Our terms will be so much the sterner, and I fear—'

'Antagonise? Damn it, if they—'

'There's one outcome of denying them the fleet that disturbs me greatly.'

'General?'

'That they may decide instead to remain in Sjælland, take Elsinore and turn it into a second Gibraltar to safeguard their Baltic trade. They'd then be very hard to cast out.'

'True enough. Gentlemen, we can do no other than comply with the demand.'

Murmurs of agreement came reluctantly but Bille sat red-faced and tight-lipped.

'In consequence of which I desire you will accordingly sign your agreement to our resolve.'

'I will not!' Bille spluttered. 'On my soul, I will not do it. Arm every true Dane, I say, to follow me as, with gunboats and all that floats, in a last glorious charge we throw ourselves at the English invaders of our motherland.'

Chapter *101*

British Headquarters, Hellerup

'Well, now, and they've finally come to their senses,' breathed Cathcart. 'An armistice to discuss terms. Thank God that carnage is over. It sickened me to think of those poor wretches . . . We'd better get to work and settle what we want of the beggars. I shall give 'em a cease-fire until four, in which they are to state to me what they'll consider acceptable as terms. If by then they're still footling about, we will resume our bombardment.'

'The fleet.' Admiral Gambier had no doubt about the first item.

'You think they'll give it to you without an argument? Or worse?'

'They must. We'll not be moved until we have it – they must know that.'

'Umm.'

'And surplus stores, sailing gear, that sort of thing.'

'Very well. We get the fleet. What else?'

'To take Sjælland itself?' Brigadier Stewart came in brightly. 'With our Swedish friends across the Sound, 'twould make a capital base to control the Baltic trade for ever!'

'I rather fear our men-o'-war will soon be iced out to the Skaggerak in the north,' Gambier said gloomily, 'as will leave your military unprotected.'

'And I'd think in any case that thirty thousand not too many for the garrison, a number I fear would not be countenanced by the government at this time.'

'A pity. Well, we'll settle for the fleet and no conquests. It's what we came for, was it not?'

Unexpectedly it was Wellesley who spoke for the Danes. 'I rather think it would be contrary of us not to accept that the Danish fought nobly with what little they had against our superior forces. Can we not show it by a leniency in our terms?'

'That's nobly said, Sir Arthur,' rumbled General Bloomfield.

'Besides which,' Wellesley continued smoothly, 'should the conceit be that, having secured the fleet, we are satisfied with no territorial gains, then it is no longer terms of surrender under discussion, for we will have left immediately and with no conquests.'

'Quite!' said Cathcart, with satisfaction. 'By that we are spared the expense of an occupation.'

'So no need for military parades, hauling down of flags, so wounding to the feelings. They cannot object to that.'

Chapter 102

At the gates of the Citadel, close to the scene of the hardest-fought encounters, instruments of ratification for an armistice were exchanged by a small group of officers. Then, without ceremony, the Danish guard marched away. The rest of the garrison left the Citadel, an empty fortification, for the British to take possession.

It was agreed that the Citadel and dockyard alone were to be occupied and only for the period needed to fit out the Danish fleet for sea, after which the British would leave for ever. The commanders took up their temporary residence and the last details could be put into train.

'Maynard!'

Jolted by the adjutant's irritable shout he presented himself.

'A task for yourself, a sergeant and six. Here's a list of the last-known addresses of British citizens, merchants and such in Copenhagen. Visit each and see if they're about, then offer them escort back. Clear?'

A tight-faced interpreter consulted the list and suggested a route. They set off into the city.

At first there were no signs that war had visited; they passed grand squares and avenues, statues and churches. People watched them with differing emotions: from cautious and respectful to naked hatred. Many more were shattered, blank-faced and staring.

After a mile or so the first damage appeared – a house with one half of it in a fallen ruin. As they reached deeper into the suburbs it was a different matter. Ruins and desolation became common, the stink of fire-gutted old buildings drifted about with wisps of dust and smoke.

The landscape was now a hideous travesty of what it had been, the interpreter often finding himself disoriented and having to ask one of the shuffling passers-by where he was.

It beat in on Maynard. Here were homes and lives of ordinary folk, those near the same as might be found in Bath or Oxford. Events far away, over which they hadn't the slightest control, had put in train a sequence that had climaxed with a ferocious hail of death. There was a catch in his throat at the injustice of it – was it hundreds or thousands that had paid with their lives for the failings of their leaders?

War had come to Copenhagen and he himself was one of its agents.

An ugly fire still smouldered in a collapsed apartment building. In front of it were corpses in a neat line and several kneeling figures, some weeping.

As they passed, he broke away and went to the bodies – they'd been burned alive and their last agonised expressions were still in place in seared flesh, eyes staring up through unendurable pain, a final accusing of the world that had condemned them to such a death.

A torrent of emotion flooded him, sweeping away his pretence of manly indifference. In that moment he knew that he'd failed. He couldn't go on. As a soldier and officer, he was not fit to lead men. He'd joined for glory and honour and had found that he couldn't face the reality of war.

He fell to a broken weeping.

''Ere, sir, don't take on so.' Sergeant Heyer took him by the arm and spoke in urgent, embarrassed tones. 'Please, sir – it's unsettlin' the men.'

With a heroic effort Maynard forced himself to a brittle calm. 'S-sorry, Sar'nt,' he said, in a small voice, keeping his face averted. 'I – I forgot myself.'

One thing was certain: when they returned to England he would hand in his commission.

'Not in front o' the enemy as was,' Sergeant Heyer added.

Enemy? This nearly brought on another bout – these piti-able creatures, the enemy?

Then a picture of his brother came into his mind. What would David think of him? He'd been in worse battles and had never once spoken of the other side of his war. By some means, he'd found a way to overcome his feelings and continue to do his duty. The image of his grave and upright older brother steadied him, and as they marched away, Francis felt the beginnings of an understanding.

Was not this part of the profession of arms? Not the central purpose but the regrettable outcome of a higher duty. Just as a physician must find ways to shut out the sounds of pain and sight of sawn limbs so he must strengthen his resolve and determination.

The sights he had seen that day were piteous and brutal, but if he was to be numbered as a king's officer, charged with the urgent task of defending the realm against the tyrant emperor now towering above Europe, it was his duty to rise above his natural feelings.

A flood of release entered him and he straightened as he marched. Yes, this was how it was and had to be.

And one guilty but gratifying thought came to him: he had been blooded in battle, he'd seen the worst – just like his brother, whom at last he could stand next to.

Chapter 103

The Citadel, now British Headquarters

It was a deep shock for Kydd. The Danish capital had surrendered – but at what cost? Its inhabitants must have held on to the end with their dogged courage, much as they'd done against Nelson, but what a price to pay for their honour.

Gambier was apparently ashore in offices in the Citadel and in a sombre mood Kydd took boat for the fortress. An all-pervading reek of burned decay hung over the city and the effect of the ordeal was on every face he saw.

'Thank you, Sir Thomas,' the admiral said, distracted, as Kydd handed him Keats's dispatches. Nothing significant had happened in the Great Belt command to stand with events here except one thing.

'Ah, Sir James. I have to acquaint you that, for his safety, I've lately conveyed the King of France to Sweden. King Louis the Eighteenth that is,' he added, when Gambier showed little interest.

'Did you indeed.'

'He's alone, but with a duke of sorts. Sir, do you think we should allow him passage or some such at all?'

'I wouldn't have thought so. He's safe with the Swedes, isn't he? We've got enough work here to concern us at the moment. Oh, do make your number with our captain-of-the-fleet, will you? He's much pressed, I've heard.'

Kydd paused outside the door. It had been only a year or so but much had happened since those dog days off Cape Town when he and Popham had faced a future rotting in a backwater together and joined in a desperate enterprise to break out of the situation. Then there'd been Popham's court-martial at which Kydd's evidence had not gone to his aid.

As soon as he entered, Popham was on his feet in a warm welcome. If he bore Kydd any grudge there was no evidence of it. 'Well, now, and how is the gallant Sir Thomas taking to his laurels?' he teased.

'As were dearly won, Dasher,' Kydd said, calling him by his nickname as he'd done in the past, and easing into a chair.

'I've no doubt, old fellow. I heard of your splendid rencontre.'

'Not the enemy, is my meaning. The ship was in a state of mutiny, which sorely distracted me, I'm bound to say.'

'Then we'll dine together on the strength of it, just as soon as I can get out from under this raffle.' He gestured grandly at a startling overflow of papers and folios.

'Can I help at all, Dasher?'

'The very man. We've got the fleet, glory be. Now we've the task of getting it to England. It means stripping our ships of skilled hands and putting 'em to work in their dock-yard fitting out for sea. I'd take it kindly if you'd accept the post of regulating captain there, see all goes smoothly, that sort of thing. Will you, old bean?'

'Very well.'

'Splendid! You'll have an office there – Nyholm, I think they call it. Now I want you to be especially vigilant. See they render up their ships in good order, holding none back, no vandalism or such-like mischief.'

'Do we have a list of what we're taking?'

Popham gave a satisfied smile. 'Ah, as to that, I can say to you plainly that we most strictly only take that which is specified in the Articles of Capitulation.'

'Being?'

'Which were drawn up by a parcel of landlubbers. They conceive the Danish fleet to be their sail-of-the-line, the battle fleet. To any right-thinking sailor a fleet is all ships that fly the naval ensign.'

'You mean . . .?'

'Yes! Everything that floats is ours by right. Battleships to gunboats, frigates to dispatch cutters. We take the lot.'

'This is hard medicine, Dasher. After we're gone, they're going to have to defend themselves in the usual way – but without any kind of navy at all? Can we not at least leave them a ship-of-the-line, a couple of frigates?'

'No. Everything goes.'

Kydd felt resentment flare. These were a brave people who had resisted with what they had. Did they not deserve a little to be retrieved from the wreckage of surrender?

'And I'll have their stores.'

'You can't—'

'I can and I will. Those same lubberly articles specify we might take any surplus stores. Now, if they haven't any ships how can they need sea supplies? All sea stores, timber, rope and so forth are therefore surplus. Get it all, old fellow!'

'I'll have you know, sir, that I mislike topping it the plunderer. This is nothing but bare-faced thievery.'

Popham's smile slipped. 'Call it what you will but you'll do it. They turned down a perfectly good arrangement when we first arrived and put us to much bother and expense, not to say blood, to come to the same end. All their fault, therefore.'

Chapter 104

Nyholm

Kydd sat in his office, depressed and moody. As well as the cloying fetor of smouldering debris desolation and bleakness lay over the city, impossible to ignore. The sooner they were quit of the place the better.

He turned to his lists. There was no option but to fall in with Popham's demands. He was the designated naval representative under the Articles.

Was the man still a friend? He rather doubted it.

There was a knock at the door.

'Come in,' he called heavily.

Dillon entered with a lopsided grin. 'Um, I've two persons desiring passage to England, should you be kind enough.'

'No, by God!' Kydd blazed. 'Not even if they're the King and Queen of Lilliput! Tell 'em to go to the army transports or other – *Tyger*'s not a convenience for fallen travellers.'

'Sir, if you'd be good enough to tell them yourself.' He stood aside.

'What – who the devil . . .?' Kydd spluttered, as two apparitions came in, stopping before his desk. Ragged, caked in pale dust and with eyes bright but red-rimmed, they waited respectfully.

'Nicholas? Cecilia?' Kydd gasped, unable to believe what he was seeing.

'The same,' croaked Renzi. 'Lately delivered from durance vile.'

'And . . . and Cecilia?'

'Your sister, Thomas,' she managed quietly.

It was too much and she threw herself on him, sobbing with a deep, wrenching relief.

It took some time for order and naval discipline to be restored before Kydd could indicate that, as of that moment, HMS *Tyger* should be entirely at their service, the great cabin of her captain their especial residence.

'You're too kind, dear fellow, but we do not wish to inconvenience. For now we'd be satisfied with our present quarters until you're ready to sail and—'

'Nonsense! I won't have it – Cecilia might feel need to make use of my copper hip-bath and you could—'

'Thank you, brother, your kindness is much appreciated. I believe, however, that we must be content with our present situation while you're engaged with your current duties. Please don't concern yourself on our account – the Amalienborg Palace is renowned for its civilities.'

'But perhaps dinner tonight? At which all shall be revealed, I promise.'

He grinned. 'Of course, Nicholas, you may count upon it.'

They left and Kydd sat down, bemused and curious by turns as to why his closest friend and his sister should be in the very place in the world he wouldn't wish any to be.

'Sir?'

He looked up. The duty master's mate had poked his head around the door. 'I've a kindness to ask of you, sir.'

'What is it?'

'Sir, I've a care for my younger brother, who went ashore with the 52nd and . . . and I'd be beholden to you should you allow me to step ashore and see if he . . . is in health, as it were.'

'Mr Maynard, go as of this minute!'

Chapter 105

The day was grey, in keeping with what was about to take place; the only points of bright colour the ensigns and pennants of the great fleet that Britain had sent to exact its will.

It was so vast that it stretched in an unbroken forest of spars well up the Sound. In the van was the majestic *Prince of Wales*, flagship of Admiral Sir James Gambier, at the head of a concourse of ships-of-the-line such as had not been seen since Trafalgar.

In the centre were even more – eighty ships, the transports for the army divisions that had compelled the Danes to bow to their fate, and the dread weapons they had employed to such effect.

And in the rear, *Superb* and other sail-of-the-line of Commodore Keats, with his three frigates lying off the Trekroner Fortress.

'Preparative,' *Tyger's* signals midshipman reported importantly, his telescope on the flagship.

The English were about to leave Copenhagen to its inhabitants and sail away for ever.

Standing on the quarterdeck, Renzi murmured to Cecilia, 'A memory that will never leave us.' She squeezed his arm tightly, gazing back at the stricken city.

'Execute!' came the next signal.

From the yards of the van and centre, sail appeared and slowly, ponderously, the grand fleet got under way for the open sea.

The rear remained where it was, theirs a solemn duty.

'Give me that glass, younker,' Kydd rapped, taking the telescope and training it on the shore. He'd spotted unusual movement along the waterfront, like the stealthy advance of an army. He held his breath and stared – was this going to be a last frenzied falling upon the forces that had so grievously hurt their city?

Yet there were no trumpets or drums, wild shouts or gunfire. In an unearthly hush, a ghost-like mass of people flooded forward until the foreshore was black with silent figures, standing, watching. From Swan Mill to far along into the harbour, hundreds, thousands of Danes had come to witness the last act.

The first of the Danish fleet emerged from its refuge.

Christian VII, flagship, powerful enough on her own to take on any one of the British 74s that waited for her outside. No white ensign was flaunted aloft, for this was not a man-o'-war taken in battle.

She was closely followed by *Waldemaar, Prindsesse Sophia Friderica*, more. One after another, the proudest vessels of the Royal Danish Navy passed through the harbour entrance by the Citadel seeming, to the still figures along the waterfront, almost close enough to touch.

In an endless stream, battleships, frigates, others emerged to join the British fleet. Still more – even the gallant *Nakskov kanonchalup* going now to serve a different master.

And in all the time it took to assemble there was not a murmur from the crowded foreshore.

'Hands to the braces,' Kydd ordered quietly.

Superb's signal to get under way soared up.

Tyger's post was in the rear, the last ship to quit the scene and therefore granted the final view of Copenhagen harbour.

Where a first-rank navy had rested in the bosom of its nation's capital, now there was nothing but bare wharves, deserted storehouses and an expanse of empty harbour. A bleak and unforgettable sight.

As the last ship took up on its northward course, *Tyger* braced about and followed.

Guessing Renzi's thoughts, Kydd went over to him. He gave a twisted smile. 'Nicholas, m' friend. Do know we've scuppered Boney, that's true enough . . .'

Without taking his eyes from Copenhagen and its army of silent watchers slipping astern, Renzi whispered, 'Yes, dear fellow, but how will history judge us?'

Author's Note

John Lethbridge of Newton Abbot is an almost unknown figure – and a surprising hero. 'Wrackman', as he was known locally, was a modest wool merchant who in mature years, and with a large family to support, took it upon himself in that inland Devonshire town to think about wreck-diving in a special contrivance of his own devising, after he had spent half an hour in a barrel at the bottom of his pond. At a time when Blackbeard and Teach were ravaging the Spanish Main, he was quietly at work in places like Cape Town and Madeira, where he brought up three tons of silver in his 'diving engine', retiring years later a wealthy man.

When I came across an item in a local paper, reporting that in the 1840s a full working set of his gear had been found on a Dorset farm, my creative juices began to flow. Readers interested in the device can today view a faithful replica in Cherbourg's Cité de la Mer. Incidentally, the legendary Tobermory Galleon has not yet been found – the latest attempt, by Sir Torquhil Ian Campbell, 13th Duke of Argyll, was begun in 2014.

As for the main thrust of this book, it's astonishing to me that this episode in Napoleonic history is not more widely known. It was undoubtedly of global significance and at a time of the Emperor's highest pinnacle of conquest. Given the odds against her, Britain was arguably at greater peril even than on the eve of Trafalgar. She chose to make a bold and desperate stroke that some have termed a war crime – but it worked, at the cost of abhorrence at home and abroad. There was questionable intelligence, true; there was politicking and ambition; but there is proof that Bonaparte intended to invade Denmark and seize its fleet. This was at a time when he was overheard boasting to Fouché, his chief of secret police, 'Europe is a rotten whore who I will use as I please with my eight hundred thousand men.'

The Royal Navy's part in this largely army-mounted bombardment was crucial. The Great Belt sailing isolated the island of Sjælland and sealed the fate of the Danes before even a shot was fired. It was a feat of great seamanship and deserving of recognition, the irony being that today, instead of the direct route through the Sound, modern ships of deep draught prefer this passage, tracking the *dybe rende*, as Keats and his squadron did.

The future King Louis XVIII did flee from his Mitau exile, leaving his family, but it was actually a Swedish frigate that ferried him to safety in England. He was a distinct embarrassment to the British government who were anything but grateful to those who brought him. Far from a triumphant landing, he was kept cooped up in his ship for a fortnight off Yarmouth while the cabinet debated what to do with him. Customs and Revenue were given the awkward task of coming up with a stream of pretexts to delay his touching English soil. In the event he was granted residency and allowances from the Prince Regent. He set up a court in exile at a modest mansion in Buckinghamshire until, after Waterloo, he became the restored Bourbon King of France.

Bernadotte became increasingly disenchanted with his ever-rapacious master and later turned on him, eventually facing and defeating his compatriot marshals Oudinot and Ney in battle. Such was his charm and appeal that he was beseeched to accept the throne of Sweden, and the House of Bernadotte still reigns in Sweden today.

One can only sympathise with the hapless Danes. Struggling to maintain their strict neutrality, trapped between giants locked in mortal combat, they had no chance. It did not help that the Crown Prince abandoned Copenhagen to the plodding Peymann, who took his orders so literally, among other things failing to evacuate the city of civilians when invited to by the British, and playing it out so hopelessly to the bitter end. On his return to the city, after everything was over a furious Crown Prince Frederik put the old soldier on trial for his life but then relented.

At bay in an impossible situation the Danes grimly fought back – one's heart can only wring with pity at the thought of country-folk with pitchforks sent against the future victor of Waterloo or men in tiny gunboats going in against a mighty battle-fleet. Of the previous time of Danes against English, Nelson had declared, 'The French fought bravely, but they could not have stood for one hour the fight which the Danes had supported for four!'

For the British, while they eventually employed four of the captured fleet, the main objective was achieved – the Danish fleet could not close the Sound, and its warships were denied to Bonaparte either as battleships or as invasion troop transports. Above all, the vital Baltic trade was saved.

Canning and others, however, endured much vilification in Parliament and the press for a barbarous act, and debate about its morality continues to this day.

In Copenhagen there is little left to show of the devastation wreaked over those four days except some atmospheric displays at several fine museums and the sight of an iron ball still embedded in the wall of the Rosenborg barracks on the Nørrevold side. Congreve's rockets are still talked about; they would go on to achieve immortality with their red glare in Baltimore.

As an aside, the Crown Prince, fleeing with frail King Christian, was stopped by one of Keats's patrols but in a cunning disguise they made it through, an incident I ascribe to Bowden in Chapter 60. Even more improbably, the ancient Crown Jewels of Denmark could not be evacuated in time and were successfully hidden in a coffin in the crypt of a church, preserved to this day for visitors to admire in the undercroft of Rosenborg Castle.

One could be forgiven for thinking that the inhabitants of this charming city, which endured twice at the hands of the British, might set their face against an Englishman, but my experiences when researching this book and in quite another role as a naval liaison officer during the Cold War have been nothing but warm and friendly.

I especially think of Kaptajn Poul Grooss, who very kindly undertook a battlefield tour for me, and Jakob Seerup and Søren Nørby who pointed me in the right directions academically. There was also Marcus Bjørn, who went out of his way to make my path smooth, and Henrik Hey of the superbly preserved Skibsklarerergården, with its archives where ships' masters cleared for the Sound, and Peter Kristiansen at the Rosenborg Castle with his insights into court life at the time.

And never forgetting the larger-than-life retired Danish submarine captain Johan Knudsen, whose reflections sailing under the Orlogsflaget were essential to this tale.

As usual, my sincere appreciation of their efforts must go to my editor at Hodder & Stoughton Oliver Johnson and his team, my agent Carole Blake, and my wife and literary partner Kathy – never forgetting Chi and Ling, our pair of Siamese author cats who run a very tight ship indeed!

Glossary

barky	affectionate term for ship
beckets	small lengths of rope used to tidy or secure
between wind and water	close to the waterline
block sheaves	the grooved moving part at the interior of a block
breeks	trousers
canvas-backing	sleeping in one's hammock
chinks, a hill of	an impressive pile of coin
claw dog	two-armed hinged hooking device
cobbs	generic term for coin, unknown Spanish
cully	colloquial neutral form of address
curlicue	flourish of adornment in older forms of calligraphy
dan-buoy	small buoy used temporarily to mark a position at sea
dimber	exceptionally fine, admirable
Exchange	London Stock Exchange
fanfaronade	swaggering ostentation
firkling	Scottish; rummaging about as in a pocket
flamming	fooling
geggy	Scottish; mouth
hard a-weather	put the helm down to come perilously close to the wind
havering	talking to no purpose
hookum snivey	tricks with hook and line that a burglar uses to lift articles from a house

jorum	the amount of liquor a large vessel, like a bowl, contains
juggins	thick-headed low-life
kiddleywink	Cornish; tavern
killick	anchor
knaggy	behaving objectionably
long bowls	firing at a range where a hit is uncertain; after lawn bowls where jack is at a distance
lubbardly	acting like a novice
Manzanilla Pasada	fino sherry
Ministry of all the Talents	the administration put together following Pitt's untimely death
mort	a lot
Mr Vice	vice president of the wardroom; traditionally the most junior officer present
mucker	close friend on a potentially dirty job
neats-leather	cowhide treated to make it pliable
oragious	superlative
pawky	diminutive
pennon	long, narrow banner, normally atop a lance
poxy shicer	diseased and worthless
puckle-headed loon	fool with vacant expression, like a fish
put a reef in y'r jawin' tackle	cease talking
Receiver of Wreck	appointed to ensure the Crown's interest in a salvage
refulgence	bright quality of light emitted from an object
rhino	hard coin
runnel	a thread of water sufficient to flow
rutter	old style book of sailing directions
scroat	useless and of no ambition
shant o' gatter	a quart of good dark ale
shicer	worthless person
shoal	water shallow enough to hazard a ship
skerries	dangerous half-submerged rocks lying just offshore
small repair	where a ship has no need to enter a dry dock
stayed traveller	a block free to move along a stay, sifting the point of lift
strake	one of the lengths of side-planking of a boat or ship
strop	a spliced circle of rope
syebuck	common sixpence
taphouse	common tavern
threepenny ordinary	cheap meal

to clap t' your tally	to add to your reputation
train oil	whale oil; Dutch *traan*
trots	piles driven into the river or sea bed to enable vessels to moor
Ward's drops	patent medicine of doubtful efficacy
younker	young person

Timeline

1773	Thomas Paine Kydd is born 20 June, in Guildford, Surrey, son of Walter and Fanny Kydd.
1789	The Storming of the Bastille, 14 July.
1793–1794	Louis XVI executed, 21 January 1793.

1793–1794 Louis XVI executed, 21 January 1793.
France declares war on England; Kydd, a
wig-maker by trade, is press-ganged
into the 98-gun ship-of-the-line *Duke
William*. **KYDD**

The Reign of Terror begins, 5 September
1793–28 July 1794. **ARTEMIS**

Transferred aboard the crack frigate *Artemis,*
Kydd is now a true Jack Tar who comes
to love the sea-going life.

1795 The Netherlands is invaded by France, **SEAFLOWER**
19 January, and becomes the Batavian
Republic.

In the Caribbean, Kydd continues to grow as
a prime seaman.

1797 Battle of Cape St Vincent, 14 February.
Mutiny at the Nore, 17 April.

	Kydd is promoted to acting lieutenant at Battle of Camperdown, 11 October.	*MUTINY*
1798–1799	Kydd passes exam for lieutenancy; now he must become a gentleman.	*QUARTERDECK*
	From the Halifax station, Kydd and his ship are summoned to join Nelson on an urgent mission.	
	The Battle of the Nile, 1 August 1798. Britain takes Minorca as a naval base from Spain, 16 November 1798. Siege of Acre, March–May 1799.	*TENACIOUS*
1801–1802	Prime Minister Pitt resigns February 1801. Battle of Copenhagen, 2 April 1801. Kydd is made commander of brig-sloop *Teazer* but his jubilation is cut short when peace is declared and he finds himself unemployed.	
	Peace at Treaty of Amiens, 25 March 1802.	*COMMAND*
1803	War resumes 18 May, with Britain declaring war on the French.	
	Unexpectedly, Kydd finds himself back in command of his beloved *Teazer*.	*THE ADMIRAL'S DAUGHTER*
	Kydd is dismissed his ship in the Channel Islands station.	*TREACHERY*
1804	Napoleon's invasion plans are to the fore.	
	May, Pitt becomes Prime Minister again. Napoleon is crowned Emperor, 2 December 1804.	*INVASION*
1805	Kydd is made post-captain of *L'Aurore*.	
	The Battle of Trafalgar, 21 October 1805.	*VICTORY*
1806	The race to empire begins in South Africa. British forces take Cape Town, 12 January.	*CONQUEST*
	A bold attack on Buenos Aires is successful, 2 July 1806.	*BETRAYAL*

Effective end of The Fourth Coalition,
14 October 1806.

In the Caribbean, the French threat takes a new *CARIBBEE*
and menacing form.

1807 Napoleon tightens his Continental Blockade *PASHA*
and moves on the Levant to break out
of Europe.

Balked of empire by Trafalgar, Bonaparte *TYGER*
strikes east and crushes proud Prussia.

Crowning his vanquishing of all Europe with
treaties at Tilsit, Bonaparte is free to strike
at England but is thwarted by a desperate
British assault on neutral Denmark.

Now read an extract from Julian Stockwin's thrilling novel

TYGER

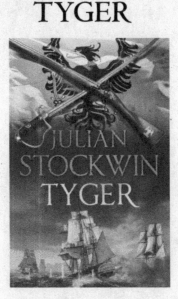

Captain Sir Thomas Kydd's part in Britain's doomed occupation of Buenos Aires has put him on the wrong side of some powerful men at the Admiralty. He is given a poisoned commission that some hope will destroy his career: a recently mutinied ship.

But enemies aboard and on the high seas are just the start of the problem. Soon he will have to take his untested and untrustworthy crew into the Baltic where they will get entangled with Napoleon's invasion of Prussia. With the stakes desperate, the task seemingly impossible and the French implacable, Kydd could return home once more a hero – or find himself facing a court martial.

Chapter 1

L'Aurore was new-moored off the legendary Plymouth Hoe. After so long at sea, and the strangeness and allure of foreign shores, it was gratifying to take in the deep green softness of England.

'Do excuse my not seeing you ashore, Renzi old fellow,' Captain Sir Thomas Kydd said, taking his friend's hand warmly. 'You know I'm bound to sail back to Cádiz to rejoin the fleet and—'

'Dear chap, allow that I've a modicum of experience in the sea service and do respect your bounden duty. To be borne back to England in your inestimable bark has been more than my deserving.'

Kydd's commander-in-chief, Admiral Collingwood, had been generous in allowing the frigate that had rescued this peer of the realm from a Turkish prison to continue on to England. Now they must part – Renzi to his seat in Wiltshire and Kydd to restore HMS *L'Aurore* to the blockading fleet as soon as possible.

'You'll give my respects to Cec— that is, your noble wife,

won't you?' That his young sister had married an earl and was now a countess was still a thing of wonder to Kydd.

'I will. Providing I have your promise that you'll honour us with a visit just as soon as you're able?'

'You may count on it, Nicholas.'

He watched his closest friend swing over the bulwarks and, with a last wave, descend into the boat hooked on alongside. He heard his coxswain Poulden's gruff 'Bear off – give way together,' and saw it stroke smartly off.

It had been this way before: a boat bearing Renzi shorewards after far voyaging, once after the near-mortal illness that had ended his naval career, and again after his highminded but doomed attempt to start a new life in New South Wales, Kydd himself, as a lowly sloop commander, heading ashore to social ruin after spurning an admiral's daughter for a country girl. But now he and Renzi were immeasurably different creatures.

The first lieutenant broke in on his thoughts with a discreet cough.

'Yes, Mr Curzon?'

'The carpenter asks if he might have a word.'

The mild and obliging Legge came forward with a worry frown fixed in place and touched his hat. 'Sir Thomas, m' duty, an' I begs to know how long we'm here at all.'

'Why do you need to know that, Mr Legge?'

'Me an' m' mates had another look at that garb'd an' I has m' strong doubts about 'un.'

'Go on.'

'It's druxy timbers, I'd swear on it.'

Kydd's expression tightened. This was not good news: the carpenter suspected rot, and in the worst part of the ship – the garboard strake was the range of planks that met the keel, all but impossible to get to from inboard. It was, as well, the natural resting place for bilge water. In those dark and secretive spaces, ill-ventilated and never to be kissed by sunlight, it would be the first to yield to the insidious miasma that would turn to rank decay.

It was said to have been the cause of the loss of *Royal George* at anchor in Spithead, with the deaths of her admiral and nine hundred souls – the bottom had dropped out of her. And so many other ships had put to sea to disappear for ever, meeting a lonely fate far out on the ocean when rotten timber deep within their bowels had given way under stress of storm.

'Very well, Mr Legge. I'll send for a dockyard survey.'

They arrived promptly and disappeared below with their augers and probes but came back up with dismaying haste. The extracted sample told it all: instead of tough, dark timber, this was spongy, white-veined – and spurted foul water when squeezed.

Kydd went cold.

'We recommends you comes in f'r a better look, like,' the shipwright surveyor said impassively.

L'Aurore went to the trots in the Hamoaze opposite the dockyard, joining the long line of pensioned-off vessels and others for repair to await her fate.

A frigate, however, was worth every effort to retain for service and no time was lost in bringing out the master shipwright and his team. *L'Aurore* was heeled and investigated and the contents of her hold discharged into lighters alongside. Then her footwaling, the inside planking, was taken up to expose her innards.

There was no doubt. An area on the starboard side,

extending from midships right to her forefoot, was condemned.

'Middling repair, great repair – either way it's a dry docking as will take a lot o' months,' the master shipwright pronounced.

Kydd slumped back in despair. It was almost too much to bear – he knew the navy would not allow them to spend the period in idleness. The expense of maintaining a ship and officers all this time was out of the question – and, besides, the country needed every man jack it could find in its desperate grappling with Bonaparte. *L'Aurore* would be taken out of commission and her ship's company scattered throughout the fleet.

He had to face it, however much it hurt. The beautifully forged weapon that was his crack frigate was now no more. The trust and interdependence that had grown between captain, officers, men and ship, the precious bond stemming from shared danger, adventure and achievements, was broken for ever.

All in a day.

Lieutenant Bowden's features were troubled as he entered the great cabin. 'Sir, you've had word?'

'Yes. *L'Aurore* is for repair. Docking. Months. I rather fear this will mean the end of the commission.'

Bowden stepped back as though he had been slapped. 'I – I . . . Shall you tell . . .?'

Kydd nodded gravely. There were formalities: the Admiralty to be informed, and by return, orders for *L'Aurore*'s decommissioning and paying off would arrive. The master attendant would have to consult his docking schedule but soon it would be all over. 'Yes, the people have a right to know.'

The young lieutenant turned to go.

'Mr Bowden – Charles! Please stay.'

It came out before he could stop it. Years ago, as a lieutenant, Kydd had taken him under his wing as a raw midshipman and had seen the lad develop into a man. Bowden had witnessed Kydd's reading in of his commission to his first command and their destinies in the service had interwoven ever since.

'Sir?'

'I'd take it kindly should you tarry to raise a glass to *L'Aurore*.'

'That I'll do right gladly, sir, should we drink as well to the Billy Roarers.'

A pall hung in the air as the news spread. *L'Aurore* had been a happy ship and lucky with prizes under the legendary captain they called 'Tom Cutlass'. She was a barky to boast of in sailors' haunts and wherever seamen gathered to spin yarns about daring and enterprise on the seven seas. From the shores of Africa to South America to the turquoise waters of the Caribbean. The monster guns of the Turks. Trafalgar to empire. Glory and prize money.

Kydd was determined he would see them right: they would be paid off and no guardo tricks with the pay tickets. It was the least he could do. The men would have one glorious spree and, after it was all spent, return to sea, necessarily to give their allegiance to another ship.

Nevertheless, there were duties that had to be performed before they could be discharged ashore. The first was de-storing: the landing of all the provisions and war impedimenta a frigate needed to sustain herself at sea. All to be noted up in due form – a painstaking task to enable Kydd to clear his accounts with the Admiralty.

Even with the assistance of the ship's clerk and the purser it was going to be a long and arduous job, and the day wore on while all the time unaccustomed jarring and strange thuds told of the dismantling of the life-essence of his lovely frigate.

There were tasks of special poignancy: his duty at the end of a commission was to render to the Admiralty his 'Observations of the Qualities of His Majesty's Ship *L'Aurore*', which detailed her sailing capability. Form questions had to be answered: how many knots does she run under a topsail gale? What is her behaviour in lying to or a-try? In a stiff gale and a head sea?

How much more revealing it would have been to tell of her heroic clawing from the path of a Caribbean hurricane, her exquisite delicacy in light airs so close to the breeze that none could stay with her – that endearing twist and heave in a following wind . . .

A subdued Dillon, his confidential secretary, brought the completed copy of the captain's journal for forwarding to the Navy Office.

This was not the ship's log, maintained by the sailing master and replete with plain and practical observations of course and speed, weather and incidents, it was an account of what her captain had done with *L'Aurore*. In it were such details as the various gun salutes fired and with what justification; reasons for condemning three barrels of salt pork, and why he had authorised the purser to purchase petty victuals, viz, five quintals of green bananas, from a port on the African coast.

The most explicit of all were accounts of the actions *L'Aurore* had fought. In carefully measured tones the whole course of each engagement was laid down – the signals passed, the exact time of opening fire, the dispositions of the enemy. Its dry recounting would never stir the reader's blood but Kydd would remember every detail to the day he died.

It was all so sudden, and before the shock of the situation had ebbed he found himself sitting down in the gun-room with his officers for the last time. Tried in the fires of tempest and combat, now, through no fault of their own, they were unemployed and on half-pay.

There were more officers in the navy than appointments available and their fate would assuredly be a dreary waiting on the Admiralty for notice and a ship. Even if they were successful, the chances of a frigate berth were scant; more to be expected was to be one of eight lieutenants walking the quarterdeck of a battleship on endless blockade duty.

'Well, at least I'll be able to see through a whole season in Town.' Curzon's attempt at breeziness was met with stony looks. With his blue-blooded family he would not want for an easy life, but money could not buy preferment in the sea service.

'And you, Mr Brice?' Kydd prompted his taciturn third lieutenant.

The man flashed him a dark look. 'Should I not get a berth quickly I'll sign on with the Baltic trade as a merchant jack out of Hull.' He'd joined *L'Aurore* in somewhat mysterious circumstances and was close-mouthed, but with his experience in the North Sea his seamanship was excellent and he was a calm and fearless warrior.

Bowden was next. 'And I shall hold myself blessed that I saw service in the sauciest frigate there ever was,' he said, adding, with a forced gaiety, 'and so will be content with anything after that swims.'

THE ADVENTURES CONTINUE ONLINE

Visit julianstockwin.com

Find Julian on Facebook
f /julian.stockwin

Follow Julian on Twitter
🐦 @julianstockwin